Patry Francis is a three-time nominee for the Pushcart Prize and her work has appeared in a number of publications in America. *The Liar's Diary* is her first novel and was a huge word-of-mouth success in the US.

THE LIAR'S DIARY

School secretary Jeanne Cross is an ordinary wife and mother with a seemingly perfect life when Ali Mather, the new music teacher, arrives on the scene. Ali is everything Jeanne isn't: flamboyant, reckless and sexy, with a habit of breaking rules and hearts wherever she goes. Despite their differences, the women are drawn to each other and an unlikely friendship develops. But beneath the surface, both of them are troubled. For Ali, it is the suspicion that someone has been breaking into her house — not to steal, but to terrify her. For Jeanne, there are secrets too dark and too brutal to face alone; secrets that will be dragged into the light with devastating results for her family and her friend.

PATRY FRANCIS

THE LIAR'S DIARY

Complete and Unabridged

CHARNWOOD
Leicester

First published in Great Britain in 2009 by
Old Street Publishing Ltd., London

First Charnwood Edition
published 2009
by arrangement with
Old Street Publishing Ltd., London

The moral right of the author has been asserted

British Library CIP Data

Francis, Patry.
 The liar's diary
 1. Female friendship- -Fiction.
 2. Secrecy- -Fiction. 3. Women- -Crimes against- -
 Fiction. 4. Mothers and sons- -Fiction.
 5. Diaries- -Fiction. 6. Suspense fiction.
 7. Large type books.
 I. Title
 813.6–dc22

 ISBN 978–1–84782–838–5

Published by
F. A. Thorpe (Publishing)
Anstey, Leicestershire

Set by Words & Graphics Ltd.
Anstey, Leicestershire
Printed and bound in Great Britain by
T. J. International Ltd., Padstow, Cornwall

This book is printed on acid-free paper

For my mother, Eleanor Heney Doody,
quite possibly the best person on earth.

And in memory of my father, Richard Doody,
who lived each day with zest
and always came home with a great story.

1

There was so much talk about the new music teacher before she arrived that her coming was almost anticlimactic. However, I would soon learn that Ali Mather never allowed herself to be upstaged — not even by her own advance publicity. The very first day of classes, she wrinkled her nose when a student called her Mrs Mather. 'Please,' she said. 'Call me Ali.' Well, you can bet our principal, Simon Murphy, straightened her out on that one. On the second day of school, the words MRS MATHER appeared in huge block letters across her blackboard. Smiling ironically, Ali corrected herself: the students were to call her *Mrs* Mather as *Mr* Murphy requested. By the end of her little speech, however, it was obvious that in the us-against-them atmosphere that frequently permeated the school, Ali was one of *them*. Even if they did have to call her Mrs Mather.

As the school secretary, I was the first one to see her on opening day. She had to be pushing forty, but she zipped past the front desk with such energy that I almost mistook her for a student. Maybe it was the hair that flowed over her shoulders in undulant waves, or the jeans she was sporting in defiance of the dress code. But mostly, I think it was that *zest* — a spirit that practically gave off sparks as she sailed down the hallway.

'*Wonderful* morning, isn't it?' she called out, smiling.

'Yes, lovely,' I said. I came out from behind my desk, wondering what kind of person had the audacity to name a day that was cloudy and far too humid to be trapped in school 'wonderful.'

Avery Small, the janitor who was usually too hung over to mutter more than a hello, stepped out of the supply closet and leaned on his broom. 'Sure is a *lovely* day,' he called after Ali, a smile breaking new ground on his face. 'Finest one I've seen in a while.' There was no mistaking his lascivious tone — or the gaze that was fixed distinctly on her ass.

'Don't you have some work to do?' I said acidly. 'A puddle of vomit to clean up or something?' But Ali just looked over her shoulder and flashed her most brilliant smile. The woman was nothing if not generous.

Avery grumbled as he walked away with his broom. Meanwhile, I stood in the foyer and watched the new teacher like I was hypnotized. Her violin case swayed provocatively to the rhythm of her walk. It was a battered old thing — hardly what I expected a professional musician to carry. It reminded me of the nicked cases the kids toted to school on Wednesdays when strings lessons were taught. But it wasn't those students I was thinking about as I stared at that violin case swinging like a metronome in time with Ali's personal rhythm. No, something about the sight of it had tapped into a deeper place for me. What had almost become a forbidden place.

I closed my eyes and saw my brother loping through the house, swinging his own weathered violin case. *Hey, J.J., you home?* he'd call as soon as he got in, thumping on my bedroom door. How long had it been since anyone called me J.J., my family's pet name for me?

Without warning, my eyes filled with tears. What was I doing? It was the first day of school, for goodness' sake! I straightened myself up, and wiped my face, wondering where on earth *that* had come from. My brother had been dead for twenty-four years — and I rarely thought about him anymore. Or about my parents, who had died shortly thereafter. Oh, I missed them and all, but there was nothing to be accomplished by dwelling on the past. My husband, Gavin, had taught me that.

Abruptly, Ali Mather stopped, turned around, and looked directly at me — almost as if she'd read my mind. I must have been imagining it, but her eyes seemed to reflect my own sadness and confusion. But above all, those eyes regarded me with an almost uncanny understanding. Once again, I fought the ridiculous impulse to burst into tears right there in the school building. Fortunately, the music teacher turned away and resumed her walk to the classroom before I totally humiliated myself.

Still, for some reason I couldn't explain, I felt shaken. For the rest of the day, every time I glanced down the hallway where Ali had disappeared, I saw my brother walking through the house with his violin, trailed by my mother's voice, *One hour of practice, Jimmy; that's all I ask.*

How many afternoons had she spent harping on him to practice? If only she'd known how soon he would be gone, how soon they all would be, maybe she would have left him alone. I sighed deeply.

As soon as I had finished logging the absentees from the attendance sheets onto the computer, I found an excuse to go into the file where the applications were kept. The first thing I learned about our new music teacher was that 'Ali' was really plain old Alice. Alice Christine Mather. AGE: forty-six. *Forty-six!* I admit, I had to look at her date of birth at least three times before I believed it. I even cross-checked it with the dates of her high school and college graduations. But there was no mistake. Ali was forty-six — nine years older than me.

Under MARITAL STATUS, she'd penciled in *separated* — as though that were subject to change at any moment. I knew all about her husband from the gossip that drifted through our small town with the momentum of a nasty virus. Half the women in town believed Ali had personally stolen George Mather from *them*. You'd never know it to look at him now, but when he practiced law on Main Street, Ali's husband had ignited dozens of fantasies as he coasted through the streets with his dark suits and moody blue eyes. With an air of distraction and a hawklike nose, Ali's husband was never conventionally good-looking, but he was that rarest of specimens: a truly *good* man. People

4

said his skill in the courtroom was exceeded only by a compassion that extended to victim and accused alike.

All the fantasies about our brooding home-town lawyer abruptly ended when a beautiful violinist careened into town to play a concert at Howell College, and scooped up our most eligible bachelor. After he married Ali, George underwent a dramatic change. One day in the courtroom he abruptly turned on his own client, saying he would no longer represent people who were obviously guilty. Then he niftily banked a shot that landed his briefcase in the trash can, and walked out of the courtroom, freer than any newly exonerated defendant.

When George decided to go back to school to get a graduate degree in philosophy, ducking into classrooms in the rumpled suits that had looked so dashing in the courtroom, the longing he had once excited turned to pity. Those who thought they knew George Mather were sure who was to blame for his new, erratic behavior: his artsy wife, the violinist who travelled so much she was rarely seen in town.

Under CONTACT PERSON, Ali had not listed her devoted husband but Jack Butterfield, another familiar name in Bridgeway. Handsome Jack Butterfield owned the Saab dealership and was believed to have charmed more women into buying cars they didn't want than anyone in the state. Also 'separated,' if I remembered correctly. In describing their relationship, Ali had written *Close personal friend*.

I was still contemplating those provocative

words when Simon Murphy walked in. I quickly returned the file, slamming the metal drawer shut so fast I almost snagged a recently manicured fingernail. Fortunately, Simon's not the suspicious type. The only thing on his mind was the coffee, which for the first time in eight years, I had forgotten to make. As I filled the coffee machine, I chided myself for the risk I'd taken. Really, there was no need to poke through the files — not when gossip was as cheap and plentiful as the rubbery pizza in the cafeteria.

★   ★   ★

I didn't have to wait long to satisfy my curiosity. That day in the lounge, I took my usual seat with the CDT teacher, Brian Shagaury. Our table was in a quiet corner, away from the gossips. We both hated the way students were labelled trouble-makers or slackers before they even had a chance. I was particularly uncomfortable when-ever I heard a student berated. I couldn't help wondering what they said about my son, Jamie, when I wasn't around.

'Air pollution alert,' Brian said when I slid into the chair across from him with my tray. It was our code for the slander that passed as benign chitchat in the lounge. It was soon obvious that the subject was none other than Ali Mather, who was taking her lunch on the lawn just outside the window. Beside her, Adam Belzner, one of the brightest students in the school and a gifted musician himself, lounged on the grass, listening with rapt attention. He must have said

6

something particularly amusing because Ali threw her head back and laughed, causing her reddish-gold hair to shimmer. I thought of how gray the morning had been earlier, and wondered if the sun had come out just because Ali Mather ordered it.

'Look at her in those jeans. Has she ever heard of a dress code?' Eleanor Whitfield huffed. She had been teaching algebra for longer than anyone could remember, and the students joked that she'd worn the same three knit dresses ever since she'd taught their parents. 'She might have at least put on something presentable for the first day of school.'

That's when Nora Bell appeared in the doorway in her white cafeteria uniform. Though she rarely ventured into the teachers' lounge, she seemed to possess a homing device that alerted her to the sound of gossip — particularly about the music teacher. Ali lived across the street from her, and Nora considered herself the world's leading authority on her neighbour's life.

'Look out, it's the CEO of Gossip Incorporated,' Brian announced, since my back was to the door. I laughed at our name for Nora Bell, but Brian was already up, emptying his unfinished lunch into the trash. 'I just lost my appetite. Wanna go out for a cigarette?'

'Don't tempt me,' I said. 'I'm trying to quit.' Prompted by my husband's incessant nagging, I was *always* trying to drop my noxious pack-a-day addiction. And always failing. Brian, who knew all about my doomed efforts, cast me a sceptical glance before he headed toward Ali's picnic ground. I was not about to admit that, for once, I was curious about what Nora had to say.

'Why should she care about the dress code? It's not like she needs the job,' Nora said, picking a crumb from her blouse. 'George Mather still supports her — and very well, too. Why, just last week, she told me she wasn't taking the job for money. She's doing it because she likes to work with young people.'

Nora might as well have tossed a match into the room. 'If she doesn't need the money, she can have the checks sent to my address,' the history teacher said. It was well known that Tom Boyle had recently gone through a divorce and was having trouble making his child support payments.

'She *likes* working with adolescents? We'll see how long that lasts,' Eleanor Whitfield added, to much laughter.

'Poor George Mather,' Nora said, steering the subject back to Ali's personal life. 'All those brains and he can't see what a fool he is. He still shows up at her house regularly at seven P.M. for a walk and a cup of coffee — that is, if his wife doesn't have a date.'

Well, that was enough for me. I thought about the kindness I'd seen in her eyes in the hallway — and that swinging violin case. If sides were being drawn up, the decision was easy: I was on Ali's side. The petty gossips were still clucking and giggling in the lounge as I slipped out to look for Brian.

From that day on, whenever she loped past my desk, making one of her cheery pronouncements about the splendour of the day, I smiled. And when I heard that Ali broke another rule, or heard her laughing in the hallway with a student, I cheered inwardly. *Good for her*, I thought to myself, following her down the hallway with my eyes. *Good for her.*

As for Ali, the only time she noticed my existence was when she passed the desk, calling out one of her ebullient morning greetings. She never stopped and asked me to copy handouts or research something on the computer like the other teachers did. And even when she did eat in the lounge, Ali blithely ignored the groups who clustered together around Formica tables, complaining about troublemaking students or aides who weren't doing their jobs. Ali never attempted to penetrate the well-established circles like most newcomers did. Instead, she cheerfully greeted everyone, then buried herself in one of the books from her back-pack — usually novels with unfamiliar titles. Occasionally, she took out a book covered in a rich red silk and wrote in it quietly in her corner. She'd write a bit, then chew meditatively on the end of her pen before going back to it. I envied her ability to tune out the murmurings of the lunchroom.

'What's that — her diary?' Tom Boyle asked one day, watching Ali write. 'I thought that stuff was for thirteen-year-old girls — '

'Apparently, you never heard of Anaïs Nin? Or *The Journals of Sylvia Plath*, maybe?' I said — more sharply than I intended.

'Whoa, don't get so defensive!' Tom said,

holding up his hand like a stop sign. 'She a relative or something?'

I didn't answer, but the question lingered. Why did an insult against a woman I barely knew feel so personal? Because she played the violin like Jimmy had? Because she'd smiled kindly at me on the first day of school? Was I that desperate for any sign of friendship? Suddenly I felt queasy. I took my tray and emptied my lunch into the trash uneaten. I knew Tom Boyle was watching me, but I didn't care.

★ ★ ★

Maybe Ali, too, had heard some snide comments about her diary. Or she was concerned that a curious student might read it. For whatever reason, she stopped bringing it to school. And of course, even that was fodder for the bored lunchroom crowd.

'Guess someone finally told her that X-rated literature isn't allowed in a school building,' Marnie Lovejoy said with particular glee. Marnie taught social studies, and until Ali came along to supplant her, she had been a hot topic in the teachers' lounge. Her desperate quest for a husband. The short skirts she wore despite her heavy legs. The way she was always there to 'comfort' Tom Boyle when he talked about his divorce.

People teased me that she had a thing for my husband, too. Ever since he'd set her badly fractured arm a few years earlier, she'd been raving about the handsome orthopedic surgeon who had 'saved' it. She'd never found me, a lowly secretary, worth talking to until she realized I was Dr Cross's wife. Since then, she couldn't be friendlier. She'd even been treating me to her lumpish attempts at baking. Heavy coffee cakes that sat in your stomach for days, chocolate chip cookies that were burned on the bottom.

'Tell Dr Cross, Marnie sent them,' she'd say with a wink. I always told her that Gavin loved them — though in truth, my health-conscious husband regarded coffee cake the way most of us think of rat poison.

At our quiet table, Brian Shagaury spoke to me in a low voice. 'Good thing Ali started leaving that diary at home. Imagine if one of these sharks got their hands on it? It would be headlines in the *Bridgeway Patriot*.'

As for me, I wasn't at all interested in what the music teacher wrote in her diary. It might have been something as benign as musical scores for all I knew. What fascinated me were the books she read. After she left, I scrawled down the titles in the notepad I kept in my pocketbook. I, too, was a hungry reader. I devoured over a hundred books a year, sometimes reading until the early hours of the morning. I read until I forgot whatever troubling incident had occurred in my household that day, or until the book fell from my hand — whichever came first. But the books Ali read were different. Not only were many of them set in exotic locales, they took me deeper into the landscape of the human heart than I'd ever been. Frankly, some of them, particularly

11

those that probed unhappy families, made me uncomfortable. Still, I kept reading.

On one occasion, Ali spotted one of the books she'd unknowingly 'recommended' on the table where I'd left my things.

'Who's reading this?' she asked as she slid into the chair opposite mine.

When she found it was me, she even nodded — as if she weren't surprised. 'Isn't it wonderful?' she asked.

I felt secretly pleased by the glances that were exchanged when people saw us sitting together, talking about a book we both loved. The conversation didn't last long before we each returned to our reading, but a bond that went beyond books was formed that day. When one of the teachers made a particularly disparaging remark about a student, Ali looked over her book cover and caught my eye. The anger flashing in hers was clear, and I'm sure she saw response in mine.

★ ★ ★

Ali didn't frequent the lunchroom that often, however. Perhaps she sensed that, aside from Brian and me, no one particularly welcomed her presence. On the few occasions when she attempted to join the conversation, her remarks served only to further alienate her colleagues. One afternoon when a substitute English teacher was complaining about the high cost of a repair job she'd done recently on her SUV, Ali unexpectedly looked up from her book, pulled off her reading glasses, and let her views on automobiles in general be known. She had let her license lapse more than fifteen years earlier, she said, and never missed it. 'If you ask me, cars are destroying America. It's not just the pollution and the depleting resources — they've made us fat and lazy.' After her little speech, she got up and rinsed her coffee cup at the sink before giving us a view of her well-toned butt as she flounced out of the lunchroom.

There was a moment of stunned silence before the substitute cracked, 'I don't know about the rest of you fat, lazy people, but I'm having another brownie.'

Okay, maybe Ali did sound a little self-righteous, but the woman had a point. I was about to speak up and say as much when I noticed that, seated across from me, Brian was more than annoyed. He was downright angry. When his eyes met mine, I knew right then and there that something was going on between him and Ali. Oh, it was nothing I could have proven. It was just one of those things you *know*.

As the weeks passed, I watched my friend for signs that I was wrong. But Brian began to avoid the lounge and grew increasingly evasive with me. When other teachers noticed him loitering outside Ali's room, or spotted the two of them sharing some tea on the lawn, they, too, began to nurture suspicions. But for me, all it took was one glance to know that Alice Christine Mather had garnered herself another 'close personal friend.'

* ★ ★

I felt almost personally betrayed. Brian Shagaury was the only teacher I really liked. We not only ate lunch together, but he frequently lingered at the office, telling me stories about his three small children, or about his personal passion: the metal sculptures he did in his garage on weekends. I was also grateful for the sensitive way he handled students who were CDT-phobic — like Jamie. What was worse, I had hoped that Ali and I might become friends. But since this thing had begun with Brian, she seemed to be avoiding all the school personnel — even me.

I worked hard to convince myself that both the lunchroom gossips and my own instincts were wrong. For one thing, why would Ali want him? She already had a husband and a boyfriend, for goodness' sake. And at only thirty-one, Brian was far too young for her. But then I thought of all the reasons I had been drawn to Brian: his sensitivity, the sense that he didn't quite belong in the chaotic high school building, his quiet good looks. He was almost the perfect foil for the self-dramatizing violinist.

To make matters worse, I also knew Brian's wife. Before her third child was born, Beth Shagaury had occasionally subbed at the school, and we still ran into each other all the time. The Shagaury kids were much younger than Jamie, but Beth and I frequently saw each other on the soccer field between games. We also seemed to be on the same shopping schedule. On Saturday afternoons, I often encountered her in the aisles

14

at the Shop n' Save. She looked tired and harassed as she tried to steer her two active boys through the store, while the baby, a boy of about nine months, reached for things on the shelves from his perch on her hip.

After that look from Brian in the lunchroom, I studied his wife more carefully the next time I saw her in the store, comparing her to her unknown rival. Beth wore her dark hair in a short, low-maintenance cut and her face was utterly devoid of makeup. But, then, she had the kind of natural good looks that really didn't require a lot of cosmetics. Blemish-free with good colour and well-defined eyes, she probably possessed more natural beauty than Ali ever had. But what good was lustrous hair and strong cheekbones to a woman whose forehead was creased in a perpetual frown, who lived in baggy jeans and sweatshirts and probably crawled into bed smelling like baby carrots?

Watching her innocently selecting apples in the produce section, I wondered how she would take it when she found out her husband was involved with a woman who was almost old enough to be her mother.

As if she knew I was thinking about her, Beth looked up at me. Immediately, I thought of how Brian's expression had ignited when Ali passed the two of us in the hallway. 'All done for the day?' she had asked Brian. It was the most ordinary of questions, but something in the tone of her voice made it sound flirty. Exciting even. As if the day were suddenly brimming with possibilities that hadn't existed before Ali

15

strutted down that hallway. In response, Brian followed after her like one of the besotted schoolboys who trailed her around the building. 'Talk to you later, Jeanne,' he called back to me, almost as an afterthought.

Interrupting my thoughts, Beth flicked me a quick wave and went back to her apples, obviously hoping to avoid the perfunctory conversation we usually had on Saturday mornings. *How's Jamie? Ready for soccer season? The baby sure is getting big. Yes, into everything, as you can see . . . Well, have a good weekend.*

On this particular day, however, I felt a rush of shame — as if my insight into what was going on between her husband and the music teacher made me somehow complicit. I turned abruptly into the next aisle and consulted my grocery list. At the bottom of my notepaper, Jamie had added a few items of his own, written in his cramped childish scrawl: half capitalized, half not. PotAtOe chips. HOSteSS dEviL doGS. mInT CHoclatE CHip ice Cream. Peanut buTTer Cups. Tacked on to the end was a plaintive, PLeese, MOM! Just reading the list, a familiar churning sensation entered my stomach. I wasn't sure what annoyed me most: the childish handwriting, the misspelling and irregular capitalization, or the request for more junk food when he knew he was supposed to be on a diet.

At sixteen, Jamie was at least fifty pounds overweight. And despite my best efforts to follow the pediatrician's advice, I just couldn't seem to keep him away from the sweets and fat-laden snacks he craved. Even if I resisted his demands, even if I came home with nothing but fruit and carrot sticks, I knew I would find the same mountain of candy wrappers, soda cans, and potato chip bags in the back of his closet and under his bed. But despite these signs of forbidden foods, and my curiosity about where he got the money to buy them, I never confronted Jamie with what I found. Somehow I felt his endless hunger for the things those packages contained was a shameful secret between us, as much my fault as it was his.

Defeated, I threw a package of peanut butter cups into my cart, wondering why I bothered. Why any of us did. From the next aisle, I could hear Beth Shagaury's voice, telling her oldest to grab a box of strawberry cereal bars. Thinking of all the effort she made at family life, only to have her husband stolen away by a woman who probably didn't even want him, I tossed a pack of candy bars that Jamie hadn't requested into my cart. Abandoning my list, the cautious menu plans that were careful to include the four food groups, I filled my cart haphazardly, eager to get out of the store.

By the time I got to my car, I was shaking. *What's wrong with you?* I asked myself as I loaded the plastic bags into the car. *You have no proof that anything's going on between Ali and Brian. And even if it is, what's it to you?* But deep down it wasn't the sight of poor Beth dragging her kids through the store while her husband sat around mooning over the music teacher. It was Jamie. It was my own family, my own home, a place where everything appeared to be in place, under control, but where nothing was. Not really.

2

Jamie was in the driveway, watching a couple of his friends shoot baskets, when I got home. Only a week earlier Gavin had put up a hoop in yet another attempt to interest our son in sports. 'Have you noticed how tall Jamie's getting?' Gavin said with a forced optimism that almost made me pity him. My husband was a natural athlete who had lettered in three sports in high school; and from the first time he held his son, he'd hoped Jamie would share his interest.

'Over six feet — and he's only sixteen; I was only five-nine at his age,' he went on. I didn't say a word, just turned toward the house, leaving Gavin in the driveway, Jamie watching his father pound the nails with his strong athletic arms.

Later, when we were alone, Jamie sat close to me on the couch so Gavin wouldn't hear our conversation through the walls. 'Don't say anything to Dad, but I'm too slow for basketball. I'll never be any good, no matter how tall I get.'

Don't tell Dad. More and more often, those words passed between Jamie and me. *Don't tell Dad what I got on my report card; he'll never know the difference, Mom. He doesn't even know when the marking period ends.* And when I bought Jamie a forbidden hot fudge sundae or splurged on an overpriced pair of shoes for myself, I used those words, too: *Don't tell Dad ... Your father doesn't have to know.*

19

Increasingly, my relationship with Jamie was based on secrets, on our implicit promise that we wouldn't tell. We would never tell.

At the sight of my Jeep, Jamie smiled broadly and loped toward me. 'Need some help?' he asked, opening the door for me before I had come to a full stop. At the sight of his smile, the inexplicable tension that had begun in the grocery store dissipated, replaced by the kind of helpless love that the mother of an only child feels. I turned off the ignition and flipped him the keys so he could open the back. 'Don't be so eager,' I teased. 'I didn't get anything on your little list.'

A crestfallen expression flitted across Jamie's face before he spotted a bag of tortilla chips poking from a bag. Forgetting his offer to help, he seized the package and ripped it open. After taking a paw full of chips for himself, he passed them to his friend. Toby Breen was a trim athletic boy who seemed to eat as much as Jamie did without gaining an ounce. 'I told you my mom wouldn't let us down.' Jamie smiled winningly.

'Just a few,' I warned. 'It's almost dinnertime, you know.'

'Sure, Mom,' Jamie called from the driveway, though we both knew he wouldn't be in until the bag was empty. Well, there *are* three of them, I told myself. Three growing teenage boys. Did I expect them to eat little baggies full of chips like they did when they were five?

Once I had put away the groceries, I looked at the clock. It was almost five. Gavin would be home in less than half an hour. At the thought of my husband coming home, every muscle in my body tensed. I had planned to make coq au vin, had even posted it on our newsboard in the kitchen that morning, followed by a sunny exclamation point. But in my distracted shopping trip, I had forgotten half the ingredients. Well, I decided, foraging through the fridge, it would have to be something simple and unpretentious.

I was pounding out the chicken breasts when Gavin came through the door. 'Hello there,' he called from the mudroom. *Hello there.* It was the kind of impersonal greeting he probably gave his patients at the office. When I responded in kind, Gavin didn't seem to notice. He wandered toward the window that opened on the driveway and lifted the curtain. 'Looks like Jamie's really enjoying that hoop.'

Silently, I tore romaine into pieces for a salad. It was brown around the edges, but it would have to do. Only when Gavin had gone upstairs to change did I mutter, 'If you really looked at your son, you'd notice it's Jamie's *friends* who are enjoying the hoop. Jamie hasn't touched the ball once all afternoon.' The bitterness in my voice startled me; and when I opened the oven door to check on the baked potatoes, I involuntarily slammed it shut.

A few minutes later, Gavin sauntered through the kitchen in a pair of jeans and a T-shirt, sniffing the air for a hint of what was for dinner.

'It's herbed chicken,' I said in answer to his unspoken question.

'Smells great,' Gavin said absently as he fixed himself a gin and tonic. As soon as he'd settled himself in the family room, he turned on his iPod while he read the newspaper. I knew Gavin loved his newest 'toy,' but every time he put in his earphones, I felt a little insulted. In the past, the music that flowed through our house whenever we were home, the lively discussions we once had about it, and the frequent concerts we attended had been our deepest source of connection. Music was, in fact, the thing that brought us together.

★　★　★

Everyone had been surprised when Dr Cross, the good-looking resident from orthopedics, took an interest in me: plain Jeanne, the newest hospital secretary, and so quiet that I'd been on only two dates in my whole life. Jamie would find it hard to believe, but I'd never even been to a single high school party. Never 'hung out' at a pizza joint or other gathering spot waiting for a certain boy to appear. Never sat up all night giggling and gossiping with a friend at a sleepover. At least, not after my brother's accident.

Jimmy had filled the house with life, and when he was killed just before I turned fourteen, the family never really regained its balance. We lived in a house where sorrow was so tangible you could taste it in every dish my mother served, hear it in the creaking of the floorboards when we moved through the house, see it in the furnishings that grew old and frayed and dusty but were never replaced or restored. If bad luck had been looking for a door to knock on, our dilapidated house where the shades were perpetually drawn was the perfect address. And knock it did.

My father died of a heart attack only seven months after the accident. My mother always laughed bitterly when anyone called his death *sudden*. We both knew he'd been dying since the moment we got the call about Jimmy.

For the next four years, Mom and I lived separate lives in the same house. She tried hard not to show it, but I knew she'd always felt closer to Jimmy than to me. And they were so much alike I couldn't blame her. After he died, she was inconsolable. Anything could trigger a day of crying — a snatch of the music he'd once played, an encounter with one of his friends, the blue of a favorite shirt he used to wear.

Though I had once hoped to go to college, there was no thought of that after my father's death. There was no money, for one thing; but even more significantly, I couldn't imagine leaving my mother alone. When she was diagnosed with pancreatic cancer at age fifty-one, she seemed almost relieved. Her only concern was what would happen to me when she was gone.

Gavin Cross answered those fears and worries beyond her greatest expectations. She always took credit for the match. It was Christmastime, and despite the gravity of her prognosis, Mom seemed to have regained some of her old zest and energy. In fact, she was doing so well that I surprised her with tickets to the annual Bach Christmas concert. I'd even splurged on a new black cocktail dress for myself. In happier years, my parents had often attended the concert together. Despite their modest means, Mom always looked sleek and gorgeous in a black dress and pearls when she attended a concert. Music, she often said, was the great equalizer; and she was determined that no one would look down on her as she enjoyed it.

However, on the day of the concert, Mom was hardly able to get out of bed. I wanted to stay home with her, but she insisted I go. 'The music is so joyful, Jeanne; it's exactly what you need,' she said, holding my hand. It was the first time I realized how frail she was, how soon I would be alone.

I dressed carefully, even borrowed Mom's old pearls and put on a little makeup. When I was ready, I was startled at the young woman who stared back at me from the mirror. She was almost pretty; and despite the gloom in the house, she looked surprisingly eager for life.

Later, however, sitting alone among the happy couples and families only exacerbated my loneliness. The emptiness of my mother's seat beside me felt like a vast chasm separating me from everyone in the hall. I was probably the only one there who wept during the exultant Advent cantatas. You can imagine my dismay when I looked across the aisle and saw a familiar face turned toward me. I recognized Dr Cross right away. At the hospital, he always seemed to be surrounded by a throng of buzzing girls, nakedly eager to land a doctor husband. But here at the concert, he, too, seemed to be alone.

I could hardly believe it when he abruptly got up and crossed the aisle. 'Mind if I join you,' he said, moving into my mother's empty seat. It didn't sound like a question.

Later, when the powerful music again drew on my long-suppressed emotion, Gavin startled me again by reaching for my hand. He was still holding it when it was time for intermission.

'I heard about your mother's illness, Jeanne. I'm sorry,' he said softly.

I was frankly shocked. I never thought the handsome doctor knew I was alive, much less my name — or that my mother was terminally ill.

At the end of the concert, Gavin invited me for a drink. Then apparently remembering that I was underage, he amended it to coffee. But the way I opened up that night, you would have thought I was under the influence of alcohol. There in that dark coffeehouse, encouraged by the warmth in Gavin's eyes, I spilled everything, beginning with my brother's death right through the day when we first heard Mom's diagnosis.

'How could so many bad things happen to one family?' I asked. Then, before Gavin could answer, I blurted out my true fear. 'Sometimes it feels like we're cursed.'

Once again, Gavin took my hand. 'But you're not,' he said. He spoke so firmly and confidently, I almost felt something physically lifting from me. Leaving the café that night, I felt happy for the first time in years.

My mother adored Gavin from the moment he walked in the door. Truthfully, I don't know how I would have ever gotten through the last weeks of her illness without his presence — and his help. We were married in my mother's hospital room just three months after that Bach concert. Though she had less than a week to live, and her body was racked by pain, she looked more serene than she had since my brother's death.

'You're going to have a beautiful life,' she whispered to me after the service. 'The kind of life your father and I always wanted for you.'

To Gavin, she just said, 'Thank you.'

Since we'd always rented, my only inheritance was a run-down cabin in New Hampshire, a little place that held all the ghosts of my family's happy times. I'd often wanted to go up there, to share the cabin with my husband and son, but Gavin worried about the amount of grief and loss I'd absorbed in my short life. 'You never know what it would trigger, Jeanne,' he'd say. 'Memory can be a dangerous thing.'

And I always acquiesced. Why invite a return to the dark days that had blighted my adolescence?

Now, whenever I felt myself inwardly complaining about Gavin's frequent criticisms of Jamie and me, or the isolation I sometimes felt in spite of all the social events we attended and the prestige we enjoyed in the community, I reminded myself how lucky I was. Not only had Gavin prevented those painful memories from gaining entry to our sunny home, he'd given my mother a peaceful death.

I thought of what she often said when I failed an exam or couldn't pick up an instrument and draw something magical from it like my brother did: *you just don't try hard enough, Jeanne.* Again and again, I vowed to work harder at my marriage, to be more patient and understanding, a better wife. And when Jamie complained about his father's badgering, I reminded him how hard Gavin worked, how stressful a doctor's life was. But increasingly, my words and my efforts felt hollow.

★　★　★

When we sat down to dinner, Gavin and Jamie wore their usual demeanors: Jamie, cheerful and painfully eager to engage his father in conversation; Gavin, moody and quiet. While I served the salad, Jamie prattled on about Toby's new dirt bike. 'You know how much that baby cost?' he asked, his eyes widening. 'Almost sixteen hundred bucks. But the thing cruises. It's rugged and light at the same time.'

'I hope he didn't let *you* on it,' Gavin said, glancing up from his dinner to enter the conversation.

At first, I thought Jamie hadn't registered the cruelty of his father's remark, but then I saw the gradual reddening that began in the folds of his neck and spread in slow blotches to his forehead. 'It's okay,' he said. 'Those things can handle at least three hundred pounds. Like I told you, they're rugged little suckers.'

Shaking his head in chilly dismissal, Gavin

turned his attention back to his meal. As I often did during dinner, I felt a strange combination of rage and panic fomenting inside me. The sight of the chicken congealing in its own grease suddenly filled me with nausea.

'Have you got any homework?' I said to Jamie, after discreetly spitting a mouthful of the offensive food into my napkin.

At the mention of that dreaded subject, Jamie slouched in his chair. Homework was the one source of conflict between us.

'Nothing much. Just a couple of geometry problems,' he said, attempting to escape the table. 'I can do them later.'

'Well, don't think you're going out till I see that assignment book,' I said.

'If you stopped doing his homework for him, maybe he'd learn to take a little responsibility himself,' Gavin said. Though I should have been used to it, I was still rattled by the level of hostility in his voice, the dark emotions just beneath the polite skin of our marriage.

'The school encourages parental involvement,' I said, sounding like one of the newsletters I found crumpled in Jamie's backpack.

'Parental involvement is one thing; doing the work for the kid is another matter altogether. Why do you think Jamie's failing at school?' Without even pouring himself his ritual cup of coffee, Gavin headed toward his study.

'He's *not* failing,' I called after him, as angry as I dared to be. 'The semester just started, for goodness' sake.'

'Give him time,' Gavin called cynically before

he disappeared into his sanctuary and slammed the door. Increasingly, that was where he spent his evenings. Sometimes I heard him on the phone laughing in an easy way he never did with me or Jamie, and I wondered if he might be having an affair. The worst part was, I didn't even care.

When the echo of Gavin's cutting remark dissipated, Jamie shrugged, as if to reassure me that it hadn't touched him. 'You know how fast that thing goes?' he asked eagerly.

'*Thing*? What thing?' I asked, reeling from the storm that had passed through the room.

'Toby's bike, Mom,' he said impatiently. 'What else?' As he always did, he smiled. Disarmingly. Almost shyly. And with no small amount of sadness. When I saw him reaching into the cabinet for the chocolate chip cookies, I didn't say a word.

★　★　★

I was scrubbing the sauté pan and brooding over my skirmish with Gavin when the phone rang. 'Not too long on that phone, Jamie,' I called out when I heard someone pick up in the other room. 'Remember, you have homework.' Though I knew his endless phone calls cut in on valuable study time, I was proud of my son's popularity. He may have been a bust at sports and academics, but with his outgoing personality and a deep sense of loyalty, Jamie had more friends than anyone I knew.

But to my surprise, Gavin pushed the door

open, the phone in his extended hand. 'It's for you,' he said coldly. 'Someone named Ali Mather.'

I reached for the phone, wondering what the music teacher could possibly want from me.

Ali went straight to the point. She'd injured her knee that afternoon and would be off her bike for a few weeks. Would I mind giving her a lift to work in the morning? Of course, I quickly agreed.

For the rest of the evening, I felt ridiculously excited — almost like a teenager with a date. I imagined what we would talk about in the car. Should I ask her about her music? Ali would be pretty surprised at how much I knew about the subject. Then there was the latest novel I was reading. Though I'd seen another one by the same author poking from Ali's backpack, I wasn't sure if she'd read this one. Maybe I could introduce her to something for a change.

Or maybe we could just *talk*, I thought, standing in the middle of my pristine kitchen. I didn't realize how desperate I was for a female friend until I felt the sting of tears in my eyes.

3

'I really appreciate this, Jeanne,' Ali said as she climbed into my car. But I was so busy looking at her house that I hardly heard her. Covered with vines, and surrounded by a fence that buckled under a cascade of late-season roses, it looked like it belonged on a country lane in England rather than our suburban neighbourhood. It was as unique and out of place as its occupant.

'You're only a few blocks from me,' I said. Ali settled herself in the passenger seat of my Jeep, arranging her unwieldy back-pack on her lap. This was closer to her than I'd ever been before, and in the lemony light of morning, I noticed the crow's-feet around her eyes.

I started the ignition and waited for Ali to continue the conversation. But apparently feeling no compunction to fill the silence in the car, the music teacher stared straight ahead like a passenger in a taxi, showing off her fine profile.

To tell you the truth, I was disappointed. Though I certainly didn't expect any revelations about her relationship with Brian Shagaury, I was hungry for the kind of stimulating talk she shared with the students who gathered outside her room every day after school or shared her picnic lunch on the lawn. I'd imagine us growing closer as talks of the books we loved segued into

31

more personal conversations. Confidences shared. Plans to get together and shop or go out for a drink. But apparently, Ali had something on her mind; she was resolutely silent.

We were nearly halfway to school when the quiet in the car got to me. 'So what happened to your knee? An accident on your bike?'

'My knee?' Ali repeated, lost in some deep reverie.

'Yes, when you called last night, you said you couldn't ride your bike because you hurt your knee.'

'Oh, that. Actually, it's an old injury,' Ali said, flipping her hair over her shoulder. 'A torn ligament from my college days. But every now and then, I turn my leg the wrong way, and it starts to swell.'

As if to prove she was really hurt, she rolled up her jeans and showed me the Ace bandage she had wrapped around her knee.

'How long do you have to stay off your bike?' I asked.

'Usually when this happens, I rest it for a few weeks, then go back to my normal activities,' Ali said, waving at the postman as we passed by. Apparently, she was chummy with all the men in town. 'I hope you won't mind if I ride with you — just till my leg heals. I'll help with the gas of course.' Her eyes were on the road, as if she were the one driving, not me.

'No problem,' I responded once again. 'And don't worry about the gas. You're on my way.' Privately, however, I wasn't too excited about the prospect of several weeks of uncomfortable silence on my daily ride to school. There was enough of that in my home life.

★   ★   ★

Things didn't improve much in the first week; and as the days passed, I grew increasingly uncomfortable in Ali's presence — not to mention irritated. Had I just imagined the connection between us? I blushed when I realized how I'd conjured a bond that didn't really exist. To make matters worse, Ali seemed totally at ease in the silence. When I struggled to make conversation, she gave me distracted one-word answers. Then she scanned her date book, or checked her image in the mirror. Sometimes she even sang a little snatch of a song, almost as if she'd forgotten I was there at all. I don't think I'd ever seen such perfect — or infuriating — poise in my life.

'Mind if I play a CD?' she asked the second week, startling me with the sound of her voice, a voice as snakily seductive as a saxophone. I don't know why she bothered asking. Even before I had a chance to respond, she inserted a thin disc in the player, flooding the car with raucous hard rock. The kind that jangled my nerves when Jamie played it in his room. 'God,' I blurted out. 'I thought you were a classical musician.'

Briefly, Ali treated me to the silvery laugh that had charmed half the men in town. 'It sounds so violent, doesn't it?' she said, but made no effort to remove it. She took her time in explaining, too. We'd sat through a complete song — if you

33

could call it that — before she said, 'The CD belongs to one of the kids at school; he wanted me to listen to it. You can learn a lot about a person by the music that rattles their spirit.'

'Well, that music gives my spirit a headache,' I said. 'Maybe you could listen to it at home.'

But once again, Ali seemed to have forgotten I was there. She was caught up in the music — and probably thinking of the student who had lent her the CD. A brief but clearly troubled expression flashed across her face before she abruptly pressed the eject button. I would have loved to know the name of the student who had aroused her concern, but Ali spent the rest of the drive staring out the window, lost in her own thoughts. Even more mystifying, she actually seemed angry with *me*. When we reached the school, she climbed out of the Jeep and slammed the door without a word.

'You're welcome!' I called to her retreating form, though the windows were closed and Ali couldn't hear me. I was so irate, I stayed in the car until she disappeared inside the front door, already laughing with a boy I recognized as Aidan Whittier, one of Jamie's friends. When I finally got out of the Jeep, I, too, slammed the door. *What nerve!* I said to myself as I click-clacked across the parking lot in a new pair of elegant leather boots I'd bought the previous weekend. She contaminates my car and my mind with that infernal music, and then *she's* angry with *me*.

Simon Murphy noticed right away that I wasn't in my usual sunny mood. And for once, I actually told someone what was bothering me — for all the good it did me. Simon only laughed when I described the music teacher's rudeness.

'That's Ali for you,' he said. 'But you've got to admit, the students adore her.' He was still chuckling to himself when he closed the door of his office behind him. Obviously, it wasn't only the students who were under her spell.

Alone for a minute, I put my head in my hands, still hearing the music Ali had played in the car. It was the angriest music I'd ever heard. Except in my own house, from my own son's room. For a brief moment, I wondered if Jamie might be the student who had lent Ali the CD. Then I quickly ruled it out. Lots of high school boys listened to music like that — probably even most of them. And besides, Jamie wasn't in Ali's class this year. There was no reason he would seek her out or lend her a CD. And yet, all day, I couldn't shake the uncomfortable feeling that Ali had deliberately played that music in my presence. That there was something in those violent drumbeats and hateful lyrics she wanted me to hear.

By the end of the day, I was determined to tell her she'd have to find another ride to school. I'd even prepared my excuse: I was behind in some of my paperwork, and from now on, I would be going to work a half hour early. For Ali, who had trouble getting ready on time as it was, that would be her cue to find herself another taxi service.

On the ride home, however, it was apparent she realized she had gone too far. She actually made an effort to talk to me — not much, just a few bland comments about the high school football team, and a big game that was coming up at the weekend. Then she asked if my son played — which surprised me. Most of the time, she seemed so oblivious to me I wasn't even sure she knew I had a son.

'Jamie's not much of an athlete,' I said, feeling the familiar jolt of shame. 'But he's a huge sports fan. And he has a lot of friends on the team.'

'Sounds a lot like me at his age; I was a complete washout at sports,' she said. 'In fact, I'm probably the only person I know who actually failed phys ed.'

I didn't say so, but I was a little bit shocked by this confession. Our town's most avid bicyclist had failed gym? Maybe there was hope for Jamie after all.

Ali flicked on the car radio like she had a right. 'What kind of music do you listen to when you're alone, Jeanne?' she asked. 'What rattles your spirit?'

The truth was, I now listened to old love songs when I was alone, avoiding the lofty music that Gavin and I once shared. Whether it was a moony melody from the forties or the familiar staples that blared on the golden oldie stations, I was a sucker for any song that crooned the words my husband never said to me anymore. But I wasn't about to tell Ali that.

'Classical,' I said without missing a beat. 'Why don't you put on 92.8?'

I think she was surprised by my answer — and even more surprised when I recognized Mozart's

36

Concerto No. 2. Maybe that was why I changed my mind about telling her to find another ride to work. For some reason I couldn't explain, I needed to prove that there was more to Jeanne Cross than she thought there was. A lot more.

★   ★   ★

The morning when everything changed between Ali and me was a particularly dreary one. I pulled up in front of her little cottage and found a dark blue Saab parked askew in the driveway. I didn't recognize the car, but the dealer's plate tipped me off. It belonged to Ali's 'close personal friend.' Jack Butterfield had obviously been so eager to get inside, he couldn't even take the trouble to park his car straight, I thought, feeling irrationally peeved.

It was seven forty-five, the same time I picked Ali up every morning, but there was no sign of her. I had told her from the start how important punctuality was to me. I had never been late to work once in eight years, and I intended to keep my record. I pulled away from the curb, figuring that Jack would drive Ali to school, and feeling more than a little annoyed that she hadn't called to say she didn't need a ride. But at that moment, Ali appeared in the doorway, signalling frantically.

'Wait, Jeanne!' she mouthed. And when I pulled down the window, she yelled, 'Just give me a minute.' Without even a bit of lipstick to brighten her face, it was obvious that she'd had a long night. I was about to tell her that I couldn't wait when, to my surprise, the door to the Saab popped open, and Jack Butterfield climbed out. As he strutted toward Ali, she glanced in my direction, holding up an index figure, and silently pleading with me not to leave.

I put on the brakes — not because I thought Ali needed a ride so badly, but because of the expression I saw on her face: she was afraid. In the gray morning light, Jack Butterfield looked nothing like the suave salesman I'd met at the Saab dealership when Gavin was shopping for a new car, or the handsome man with the teasing smile who looked better in a tux than anyone else at charity functions. His dark blond hair was uncombed, and he was sporting at least two days of growth on his face. Furthermore, the jeans and T-shirt he wore were so rumpled that it looked like he'd slept in them. The temperature had dipped to thirty-five that morning, leaving him extremely underdressed, but he didn't seem to notice that either. The only thing he saw was Ali.

But the amazing thing was that sleep-deprived and agitated, Jack Butterfield had never looked more attractive. He was not charming or smooth or any of the other adjectives that his many admirers around town used to describe him. He was just plain animal sexy. I watched him, transfixed. For the first time, I understood why Ali had ruined her marriage to a wonderful man like George Mather over a car dealer.

By now it was clear that Ali was afraid, but she wasn't about to back off. She twisted her long hair into a coil and wrapped it around her neck

— a gesture at once provocative and self-protective — as Jack approached the cottage. From the Jeep, I could hear his voice, but the only words that drifted through the air intelligibly were curses.

When he shoved Ali roughly against the door, I jumped out of the Jeep. Jack, however, never even turned in my direction. He remained impervious to everything except Ali. As I hurried toward them as fast as my high-heeled boots could carry me, Ali held up her hand, indicating that I should stay back. The closer I got, the more obvious it was that Jack Butterfield was more distraught than threatening. It was also clear that he didn't recognize me from our various social meetings. Nor did my presence mean much to him.

As his anger visibly weakened, Ali stroked Jack's chest, and he pressed his forehead into hers, as if trying to force his way into her mind. There was something so intimate about the scene that I felt as if I'd walked in on them in the bedroom. She appeared to be bargaining with him, probably telling him that she needed to get to work, maybe promising to see him later. Finally, Jack took a step backward and again ran a hand through his hair. Briefly, he shook his head, before he stormed back toward his ill-parked car. He backed out of the driveway so wildly that if I hadn't jumped out of the way, he would surely have run me over.

Ali appeared frozen in the doorway. Her eyes were closed, but when I ran to her and put my arms around her, she was trembling. 'Are you okay? He didn't hurt you, did he?'

Ali shook her head. 'I only wish he had,' she said sadly. 'But I'm afraid it was the other way around. Sometimes I don't know what's wrong with me.' It was the first time I'd noticed the dramatic golden colour of her eyes. Even without makeup, her skin was translucent and shining with emotion.

'Are you sure you're okay? Simon will understand if you can't make it in to school.'

But Ali only shook her head. 'No,' she said quickly. 'I need to get out of here. Out of my own life for a little while.' She looked at me deeply. 'What about you, Jeanne? Do you ever feel like that?'

I was stunned by the abrupt shift in focus, but as I would come to realize, such turnarounds were part of her nature. Just when I was convinced Ali Mather was the most self-absorbed person I'd ever met, she would startle me with a sensitivity to others that took my breath away.

Of course, I wasn't entirely caught off guard. I was ready with the usual stock lines. The lies I told everyone around me — including myself. *Not me. I was too busy for feelings like that. And besides, my life was so boring and routine . . .* But somewhere in the middle of my spiel, I found myself choking back something when I tried to speak. It was more than the clichéd lump in the throat. No, what prevented me from reciting my usual lines was nothing less than the truth. The truth that I could no longer keep back.

'Yes,' I said, staring into Ali's topaz-coloured eyes. 'I do feel like that. Almost all the time.'

★   ★   ★

On the ride home from school that day, we were both quiet, but it was a different kind of quiet from the silence that had permeated our previous trips. It was a knowing quiet. For once, I felt like I understood a little bit about Ali Mather. I understood how the charm that aroused so much envy and fascination in others frequently wearied and baffled her. What was it she had said? *Sometimes I don't know what's wrong with me.* It was a confession as potent and deep as the one I myself had made.

When we reached the house, Ali regarded me with a certain sadness — and that weariness I had felt during the ride. Impulsively, she reached out and covered my hand with hers. 'Thanks for being so understanding this morning, Jeanne,' she said. 'It meant a lot.'

She was halfway up her walkway, the pack she usually carried high on her back sagging behind her like a great weight, and I was about to pull away when she abruptly dropped the backpack and came back toward the car. 'Feel like coming in for a glass of wine?' she asked when I opened the window.

The stock answer was no. *Of course not.* In my view, coffee mornings and book clubs, not to mention afternoon cocktails, were activities for the undisciplined. People who had nothing better to do with their time than sit around and

41

gossip. As for me, I needed to get home. Jamie would be there, undoubtedly with several of his friends, and I wasn't the kind of mother who left a group of adolescents alone in the house. After they left, I planned to take a jog before starting dinner. There was mail that needed to be answered promptly (never touch a piece of mail twice was my rule), a load of whites that were ready for washing, errands to run. Keeping up was the secret of running an efficient household, something most women — including Ali Mather — knew little about.

And yet, for the second time in one day, I surprised myself by turning off the ignition. 'A glass of wine sounds great,' I said. Walking inside, I glanced briefly at my watch, promising myself I would stay only a half hour.

Ali flicked on the stereo, a gesture she performed so automatically that I assumed it was the first thing she did when she came home every day. For a split second, I was afraid that she was about to assault my ears and heart with the angry music she'd played in the car, but the sweet sound of Ella Fitzgerald's voice soon reassured me. Ali flung her coat on a chair, and dropped her backpack beside it.

Then she beckoned me into a warm, open room that served as a combination living and dining area. 'Make yourself at home,' she said before disappearing into a galley kitchen. I smiled. The kitchen was the largest room in my house, but apparently cooking wasn't much of a priority in Ali's life.

'Red or white?' she called from the kitchen.

'Whatever you're having is fine,' I said. Not knowing where to put my jacket, I folded it neatly and placed it on top of Ali's. Then I wandered into the room where she'd told me to make myself at home. It was eclectically decorated and cozy, but the first thing that caught my eye was the disorder. There were CDs out of their jackets everywhere, books spilling from overstuffed bookcases, and on the coffee table two stemmed glasses, still half full of red wine, and an empty bottle remained from the night before. But what really drew my eye was a pair of black lace panties that had been tossed beside the couch. Right beneath the spot where I was sitting with my hands folded in my lap, prim as a librarian.

'Don't go to any trouble; I can't stay long,' I said uneasily when Ali appeared in the doorway with a tray of cheese and crackers.

'It's no trouble, and I know you can't stay,' she said, as if reading my mind. Her gaze drifted toward the abandoned panties, but she made no effort to pick them up. Nor did she appear to be a bit embarrassed. Once again, she was looking at me the way she had in the morning. As if she knew me better than I knew myself. She smiled briefly as if she found my discomfort with the abandoned lingerie amusing.

Feeling embarrassed, I glanced away.

Ali took a sip of her wine and laughed. Her legs were folded under her, and she had loosened her hair and twisted it over her shoulder. 'As you can see, I had company last night.'

'Mr Butterfield,' I said, imagining a lover's

quarrel, followed by a sleepless night for both parties. Suddenly the scene I'd witnessed in the morning made sense.

'Actually, it wasn't Jack. It was — ' She hesitated, as if deciding how much she trusted me, and then simply said, 'Someone else. The problem was that *Mr Butterfield*, as you call him, decided to drop by at, um, a most inopportune moment.'

'You mean he has his own key?' I'd long suspected that Ali was sexually involved with more than one man, but I still felt shocked when she spoke of it so matter-of-factly.

Again, Ali laughed at the details I chose to focus on. 'We've been seeing each other for three years, Jeanne. Of course, he has a key — not that it mattered. The door was bolted, but the car parked in front of my house and the drawn shades were all the information he needed. *Evidence*, as he called it.' Remembering, she twisted her hair between her fingers. 'Would you believe he spent the night in his car?'

Thinking of how Jack had appeared in the morning, I certainly could believe it. 'So — was there a confrontation? I mean, when the other man left?' I don't know why, but I imagined poor Brian Shagaury being pummelled by the much taller and rangier Butterfield — then being forced to go home to Beth and explain the bruises.

Ali shook her head. 'At least we were spared that. He went out through the sunporch in the back and then crept through the neighbour's yard to his car. Jack must have been focusing on

44

the door. Or maybe he'd fallen asleep.'

'He was so angry,' I murmured, thinking of the animal energy Jack Butterfield had exuded as he crossed the lawn. 'Do you think he'll go after him?'

But again, Ali shook her head. 'All Jack's anger is directed at me. I'm the one who has betrayed him — at least by his definition.'

'But not by yours?'

Ali got up and began to pace up and down the room, the glass of wine in her hand. 'I never promised anyone fidelity. I'm not even sure I'm capable of it. But that doesn't mean — ' Ali paused in the centre of the room and placed her glass on the table so she could swipe at the tears that suddenly filled her eyes.

'It doesn't mean you're not sorry that you've hurt him?' I said, completing her thought for her.

'Exactly,' Ali said, once again taking up her wine glass. 'I love Jack. I really do — in spite of our differences.' She slumped back into her seat, and stared at me, and repeated the words she'd said in the morning. 'Sometimes I don't know what's wrong with me, Jeanne.'

I'd never seen anyone look more miserable. For the second time that day, I hugged her, inhaling the subtle perfume of her skin.

When we separated, Ali seemed calmer. She brushed her hair out of her face and, once again, assumed the pretty pose she'd taken earlier: feet tucked beneath her, her head slightly angled upward. 'God, I'm actually doing it.'

'Doing what?' I asked, feeling mystified.

'Confiding in another woman. This might be a

common occurrence for you and every other woman on the planet, but not me. I've never had a close female friend in my life. I was too involved with my music, I guess.'

And men, I thought. But all I said was, 'It's not all that common for me either.' This had to be one of the biggest understatements I'd ever made.

4

Ever since the night my brother was killed in a car accident, I've been driven to panic by the sound of a phone ringing in the middle of the night. Thus my heart leaped in my chest that early Sunday morning when the blaring ring of the portable startled me from sleep. The numbers on my digital alarm clock informed me it was 5:16. Too early for anything but a wrong number or an emergency.

Gavin generally sleeps through everything, but he was on his feet even before I was. On his feet and headed for the hallway with the phone in hand. Later, when I had gotten over the jarring associations the call triggered, I would wonder at his actions — his quickness to answer the phone, and his apparent desire to keep an obviously anticipated call from me. Maybe he was trying not to wake me, I reasoned. Still, I couldn't help wondering when he had become so considerate. And why.

A minute later, Gavin came back into the room and tossed the phone onto the bed. 'It's for you,' he said, irritably running his hand over his close-cropped hair. 'Some guy who works with you at school. At least, that's what he says.' From another husband, it might have sounded like jealousy, but in Gavin's mouth the words reflected mere annoyance. Annoyance at being disturbed. Annoyance that the caller was not

47

who Gavin was expecting.

Taking his cue, I carried the phone into the hallway, wondering why in the world anyone from work would be calling me at this hour. And a *guy* . . . I leaned against the wall in the hallway. 'Hello?'

When there was no answer, I thought it must have been a wrong number — or more likely a prank. Probably a bunch of students at an overnight party, tanked on beer and dialling the numbers of various school personnel. Still shaking from that moment of fear that brought back my childhood trauma, I spoke angrily into the phone. 'Listen, I don't know who this is, but I will find out. And I want you to know if you disturb my family again, I'll notify the police.'

I was ready to press the button on the phone, dismissing the caller from my life forever, when I heard a deep sigh. 'I'm sorry to wake you like this, Jeanne. And believe me, I wouldn't have done it, but I'm out of my mind with worry.'

I paused, unsuccessfully trying to identify the caller's voice, as my heart began to pound again. Mentally, I took inventory of the whereabouts of my loved ones, or should I say loved *one*: Jamie was downstairs asleep in his bed. 'I'm sorry, but who — '

I didn't even finish my sentence before the caller blurted out. 'It's *me*, Jeanne — Brian.'

'*Brian?*' I repeated, feeling dumbfounded. Ever since the rumours about him and Ali started, my former ally had avoided me at school. 'What's wrong?'

There was a brief silence as if Brian were

collecting himself. 'It's my wife, Jeanne. Beth took the kids and left last night.'

I wiped my sleep-encrusted eyes. 'I'm sorry to hear that, Brian,' I said, still trying to figure out why he would call me. Beth Shagaury and I were only casual acquaintances.

'I — I thought you two had been talking lately,' Brian said vaguely. 'So I figured you might know something.'

'Talking — Beth and I?' I repeated. Was he referring to our occasional banter when we were waiting in line at the deli counter? Or the time last week when we'd run into each other at the sporting goods shop and had a profound conversation about the high cost of the hockey equipment she was buying for her oldest son?

Again, there was a deep sigh on the line. 'Like I said, I'm sorry for waking you up, but I thought that you might have told her about — ' Then, without finishing his enigmatic sentence, he said, 'Listen, I'll let you get back to sleep.'

But the latent panic in his voice had struck a chord with me. It was the same panic I had felt coursing through my own blood only moments earlier when I feared someone close to me might be in danger. He was clearly about to hang up when I stopped him. 'Wait, Brian. Why don't we meet at Ryan's — you know that little donut shop on the corner of Ames? In, say, fifteen minutes? From what I understand, they're open at this ungodly hour. Maybe I *can* help.'

'Are you sure?' Brian said, sounding as tentative as the adolescents with whom he spent his days. 'I mean, it's all right with your husband?'

'Gavin doesn't own me,' I said fiercely. Just thinking of how I'd walked in the night before and caught Gavin berating Jamie mercilessly for getting a D on a history test fuelled my fire. I swear, sometimes he acted like he *hated* the kid.

Quietly, I slipped into a pair of jeans and a pullover sweater. Dressing quickly, I listened for the sound of Gavin stirring, but the house was heavy with silence. Either my husband had fallen back to sleep — or more likely, he was waiting for me to come back to bed. Waiting for an explanation as to why someone would call *me*. Particularly a man. Well, he could lie there and stew, I told myself, full of a new rebellion. For the first time since our marriage, I had my own friends, my own intrigues, my own secret life.

In the weeks since school started, I'd let my hair grow out a bit. To my surprise, it was just long enough to stay back in the clip I'd found in the bottom of my makeup bag. With my hair pulled off my face, I felt like I was getting a glimpse of some long-lost part of myself, as if a more reckless side of my personality were emerging. After applying a slash of scarlet lipstick and a little eyeliner and donning my running shoes and a jean jacket, I slipped out of the house.

From the driveway, I looked back. I was startled by the sight of Jamie peering out at me from the door, his round face etched with curiosity. In a flash, the door sprang open, and he called out. 'Mom! Where you going? Is anything wrong?'

'Just for a walk,' I said, not wanting to get into any complex explanations. 'I'll be back before breakfast.'

But Jamie only pushed the door open wider, and stepped onto the front steps in his bare feet. Wearing only boxer shorts and the Columbia University T-shirt one of Gavin's cousins had recently sent, he stood knock-kneed in the doorway. In the sharp light that emanated from the kitchen, his body looked even paler than usual, his innocent face bloated with flesh. The usual rush of pity I felt when I saw my son in a vulnerable state of semi-dress washed over me.

'A walk?' he said, squinting at me. 'It's still dark out, Mom. You want me to come — you know — for protection?' he asked.

'I'm a grown woman, Jamie. Now get back inside before you freeze to death.' My voice sounded harsher than I intended.

'You're going to meet *him*, aren't you?' Jamie said, his eyes shining with excitement. 'The CDT teacher — Mr Shagaury.'

His words confirmed an uncomfortable feeling I'd had lately when I was on the phone, the sense that someone was listening in on the other line. Wordlessly, I glared at him.

Jamie quickly stepped back inside. But even with the door separating us, I could see the hurt on his face. Still, I kept going, telling myself I would explain everything to my son later. I also intended to have a serious talk with him about eavesdropping on other people's conversations.

51

Despite the early hour, most of the tables and every stool at the counter in the narrow donut shop were taken. I looked around, wondering who besides me and a guilty husband would be driven to seek out the old-fashioned selection of jelly donuts and crullers that Ryan's offered at five A.M. The counter was lined with men of retirement age who apparently met at Ryan's regularly. In fact, this was probably the highlight of their day, I thought. Waking up early like they had when they were working and meeting 'the boys' down at Ryan's. The rest of the claustrophobically small restaurant was filled with an odd mix of truck drivers and a few boisterous young people from Howell College, who were apparently capping off a night of partying with a cup of coffee and one of Ryan's famous lemon donuts.

It took me a minute to find Brian Shagaury in the crowd. By the time I spotted him, I had begun to wonder if it really had been him on the phone. When you work with six hundred adolescents every day, the possibility of a prank is always foremost in your mind. But then I noticed him in the corner, tucked behind a noisy group of twenty-somethings who looked like they were still inebriated from the previous night's revelry.

Signalling me somewhat furtively, Brian appeared exhausted — and deeply troubled. His face was surprisingly gaunt and those clear green eyes of his were deep hollows. Though we worked in the same building, I hadn't actually seen him in weeks. Ever since he got involved with Ali, he had avoided both the teachers' lounge and my office. I'd heard rumors that he 'seemed depressed' and 'wasn't himself' at school — even that he was unlikely to be hired back in the fall — but the rumors didn't prepare me for the shock of his deterioration.

For the first few moments, as I waited for the waitress to bring me the coffee and lemon donut I had ordered, Brian and I sat in an awkward silence while he strummed the table nervously. I was beginning to wonder what had possessed me to suggest this meeting. Except for our formerly easy banter at school, what did I really know about the man sitting across from me?

After the waitress had served my coffee and left the table, Brian sighed deeply the way he had on the phone. 'I can't stay long,' he said, consulting the clock. As if I were the one who had called him, I thought, feeling even more annoyed.

'So you have no idea where she's gone?' I paused to take a sip of my coffee, staring deeply into Brian's eyes. I'd once found Brian rather attractive, but sitting across from him in the glare of the donut shop, I couldn't help wondering what my friend saw in him. While despair over his relationship with Ali had added to Jack Butterfield's unruly sexual allure, it had no such effect on Brian. He fidgeted at the tiny table with the edgy demeanor of a heroin addict in need of a fix.

Instinctively, I reached for his hand. It felt so

clammy I almost recoiled. 'Brian, you can't hope to get your family back until you pull yourself together.'

Brian jerked away and leaned back in his chair in a posture of defeat. 'I lied to you. My family's at home in their beds — at least for now.'

'You mean you got me out of bed at five in the morning for no reason?'

'I had to talk to someone, Jeanne; who was I going to call — Gossip Incorporated?' he said, but our old joke fell flat. When I got up to walk out, he seized my hand. 'Wait, Jeanne. Last night Beth told me she's planning to go back to Indiana; she said I'll never see the boys — '

'So she knows about Ali,' I said, pretending to know more about the relationship than I did. I slid back into my seat and gulped my coffee.

'Someone told her a couple of weeks ago,' Brian blurted out, obviously too tired and distraught to deny his affair. 'Someone from school.'

'And that was why you called me — you thought *I* was the one who went to Beth?'

'Well, you're the only one in the building Ali really talks to — besides me, of course,' Brian said with a cloying hint of pride. 'So naturally I thought of you. And besides, you know Beth.'

Ali had never talked to me about her relationship with Brian — whatever it might be. A friendship? A serious affair? Something that took place largely in the confines of his obviously disturbed brain? I thought of the lace panties I'd seen on Ali's living room floor and of her admission that 'someone' had been with her the

54

night before. 'Someone' I had assumed was Brian, though I couldn't have said for sure. For all I knew, it might have been poor devoted George Mather who had aroused her lover's jealousy.

'Listen, Brian, you made a mistake, but these things happen,' I said, as if I were an expert on the subject. 'You can't let it destroy your family. You could try counselling. Something.'

But Brian just stared at me. 'Beth suggested that,' he said abruptly. 'But there's no point. I've made my choice, Jeanne.'

'Your *choice*? What are you talking about?'

'I haven't been staying at the house for weeks.'

'You've left your family — over Ali?' I blurted out. 'God, Brian, don't you know — '

'I'm staying at the Oak Tree,' he said before I could add anything he didn't want to hear.

I didn't respond, but Brian must have seen my unconscious reaction. The Oak Tree was a dilapidated motel where the town alcoholics rented rooms infested with cockroaches and infused with the scent of urine.

'I don't need you feeling sorry for me either,' Brian said angrily, reading my thoughts. 'I'd rather sleep alone at the Oak Tree than spend one more night beside a woman I don't love. My family would probably be better off if they go back to Indiana and forget I was ever born.'

'Brian, I came out here practically in the middle of the night because you said — '

But the fury in Brian's eyes stopped me cold. 'I know what I said, but I was desperate, Jeanne. I've left eleven messages on Ali's machine, and she still hasn't called. Then last night, I camped outside her house all night. She never came home. I don't know what to think.'

So this wasn't about Beth and the kids at all, I thought, feeling irate on their behalf. What Brian had really gotten me out of bed to talk about was his obsession with Ali.

Around that time, the college crowd paid their check and noisily cleared out, several of the girls in ultra-short skirts in spite of the cold. I noticed most of the old men at the counter had left, too, and were gathered outside the door for a smoke, leaving the place largely deserted. Even the waitress had ducked into the back, probably for a cigarette break of her own.

Thus, except for a romantic-looking couple who were huddled in the opposite corner, oblivious to both their uneaten donuts and our presence, we had the place to ourselves. I was about to tell Brian that he'd called the wrong person; I wasn't as close to Ali as he thought. Anything to get away from him.

But then in another abrupt mood change, he again put his face in his hands and began to sob. Without thinking, I reached out and touched his arm. 'I'm sure you can convince Beth to stay and give it another try. It won't be easy, but you have three kids to think about.'

I sounded like one of those late-night psychologists you hear on the radio. And like most of them, I was spouting platitudes.

But Brian angrily threw off my hand, accidentally spilling the cold coffee that he'd left untouched. 'You don't get it, do you? I can't go

56

home. I don't want to go home. Until I met Ali, I was living a zombie life. I was a dead man at thirty-two. But now — well, I don't have to tell you. You know what she's like. Shit, I feel horrible about the kids, but I'm not giving her up.'

Suddenly feeling shaky myself, I pulled a pack of cigarettes from my jacket. Fortunately there was one left. I was trying to quit and, in fact, hadn't had a cigarette in two and a half weeks, but listening as Brian described my life to a tee, I was suddenly desperate for a smoke. *Yes, I know what she's like*, I thought, thinking of the way I myself had changed since my friendship with Ali developed. It wasn't just the way I'd pulled back my hair or stopped taking the car everywhere I went. It was something far deeper than that.

'I'm sure you know Ali's married,' I said, still believing I could talk sense to him. 'Even though she's not living with George, she's very devoted to him.'

'Is that what she tells you? That she actually *loves* the old geezer? Myself, I think it's more a matter of pity,' Brian said. But a dark expression, which painfully reminded me of the way Jamie had looked when I left the house, crossed his face.

'Whether she's in love with him or not, Ali will never divorce George,' I said flatly, giving Brian a dose of the cold truth — just as someone from school had apparently done to his wife. 'And even if she did, she's almost twenty years older than you, Brian. Do you really think you two have a future together?'

'*Fifteen* years,' Brian amended. 'It's not so much of a difference when two people feel the way Ali and I do.'

I closed my eyes, thinking of Beth Shagaury in the grocery store, the boys innocently arguing about who got to choose the breakfast cereals, while somewhere their father was off obsessing about Ali Mather. For the first time since Ali and I had become friends, I felt some of the town's censure toward her. Ali had never talked about Brian to me, but I felt reasonably certain he meant nothing to her. And from the dangerous despair in Brian's eyes, it was obvious that he was beginning to realize the same thing. And yet that hadn't stopped Ali from breezing into our school and destroying not only his life, but his family as well.

'It's not just her husband, you know,' I said, as gently as I could.

'What do you mean?'

'I hope you don't think you're the only man Ali's sleeping with. Or even the one she's most serious about.' I knew it was futile, probably even dangerous to try to press the truth on someone in Brian's state of mind, but I couldn't stop myself.

The colour seeped from his face. 'You don't mean that car dealer?' he scoffed. 'That was over when she started seeing me.'

'Ali's in love with Jack Butterfield, Brian. Has been for years,' I said. 'She told me so herself.'

If it were possible, Brian grew even paler than he'd been before. Then slowly he began to shake his head. Whether it was a gesture of disbelief, or simply stunned denial at the depth of his own folly, I didn't get the chance to find out. Because at that moment, his eyes were diverted to the counter where a woman stood watching us. I don't know how long she had been there, or what — if anything — she had heard.

Beth Shagaury looked haggard and drawn, but most of all, worried. 'Brian, please,' she said, approaching the table. 'Maybe you don't care about me, or even about yourself anymore, but you can't go on like this. For the boys' sake, you have to get some help.'

5

When I arrived back home, I was glad to find that Jamie had already left for his morning 'run.' Gavin had recently outlined an ambitious exercise program for him in the hopes that Jamie would shed some flab. But I suspected as soon as he rounded the corner of our street, Jamie had shambled over to Ryan's for a couple of lemon donuts and an extra-large hot chocolate. I probably had just missed him.

Feeling exhausted from my abridged night's sleep and the draining conversation with Brian, I would have liked nothing better than to crawl back under the covers and snooze the day away. But when I thought of Gavin's inert body, spread out across the bed in my absence, I headed for the kitchen instead. There I fixed a pot of coffee, intending to settle myself at the kitchen table and forget the troubling events of the morning.

But as soon as I sat in my usual spot, I saw the messy note my son had left before me: MrS MaTHa CaLLed!

That was all it said, but for some reason — maybe it was just the excited exclamation point at the end — I suddenly felt clammy, weak, and suffused with rage at the same time, the way Brian Shagaury had looked in the donut shop. How many people knew where Brian had gone besides Jamie and me? Trying to erase the thoughts from my mind, I ripped the note into tiny pieces.

The last thing I wanted to think about at that moment was my growing worries about Jamie: the learning disabilities that a battery of tests had failed to diagnose, a mountain of candy wrappers that accumulated in his closet each week, and the thing I tried hardest not to think about — a trove of pornographic magazines I'd found at the bottom of the drawer where he stored his off-season clothes. I had hardly looked at them before I threw them into a dark trash bag and hauled them away, but there was no way I could banish the violent images I'd seen.

Who would sell such things to a kid? I thought angrily as I carried the bag into the garage. Of course, I intended to tell Gavin. I even went to the phone and dialled his office. But as soon as his secretary put him on the line, I froze. Not just because Jamie and I had made an unspoken pact never to tell Gavin the truth about each other, but because of the way I knew Gavin would respond. If I had the temerity to suggest that Dr Cross's son had been secretly amassing a collection of violent pornography, I knew he would find a way to blame me. I was *too lenient* or *too overprotective*, depending on his mood. But whatever the case, any problems with Jamie rested on my shoulders.

Quietly, I pressed the disconnect button, wondering what had possessed me to call in the first place. It was hardly the kind of thing you discussed by phone — especially when Gavin was in the office.

After I hung up, I decided I would talk to Jamie myself about the matter. After all, we'd always had such an open relationship. There was nothing we couldn't say to one another, was there? Perhaps more disturbing than the pornography was the possibility that my relationship was coming to mirror the one I had with his father: two people divided by an ever higher wall of secrets and evasions.

But when Jamie came home from school, I found it impossible to broach the subject. As usual, he immediately dove into the cabinets, searching for snacks, while prattling on about an upcoming party at a girl named Amber's house.

'I can't believe she invited *me*, Mom,' he said, tearing into a bag of chips. 'Amber Ryan's the hottest girl in the whole school.' He seemed so happy, excited, and well, *normal* — the same bright light he'd always been. It hardly seemed like the time to bring up the stash of ugly images I'd found in his room. There was no getting around it: this was a topic a boy needed to discuss with his father.

That night when Gavin was in his study, I knocked on the door, intending to bring up the matter with him once and for all. But as soon as I saw him, I knew I couldn't do it. He lowered his glasses in that way he had, indicating I had disturbed some important work.

'Yes, what is it, Jeanne?'

I found myself stammering like an idiot — with my own husband. 'Well, I thought maybe w-we could talk a little bit . . . But, if you're busy . . . It doesn't look like a good time so — ' God, what was wrong with me?

'Actually, I'm in the middle of a research piece I'm writing for an orthopedic journal. Is this important?' He spoke softly, but his impatience bristled in the air.

'No. Well, yes. I mean I've been feeling, well, a little *edgy* lately, and I thought that maybe you might prescribe something for me.'

Gavin set his glasses carefully on the desk and regarded me thoughtfully. In the past, he had prescribed various sedatives, using the very same word, when he handed me the bottles. I was *edgy*. I needed something to take the *edge off*. Valium. Xanax. Ativan. I'd seen the same labels on the bottles Gavin kept inside the drawer of his bedside table. Usually when he brought the prescriptions home to me, I dumped the contents in the toilet. But a couple of times I'd tried one or two of the innocuous-looking tablets. Now when I thought of the floaty, emotionless state I had entered, the pills didn't seem like a bad idea.

'I'm glad you're ready to deal with it,' Gavin said, smiling and nodding like he did with his patients. 'You haven't been yourself lately, Jeanne. I've noticed and I'm sure lots of other people have, too. Think about it: you work at Jamie's school. The last thing you want to do is add to his problems.' He shook his head the way he always did when he mentioned Jamie's 'problems.' But he was already removing the prescription pad he kept in his locked drawer and scrawling the words.

I left the study shaking. Was I really acting so

strangely? *Had* other people noticed? I went to the kitchen and poured myself a glass of wine. Then I carried the portable phone onto the deck and dialled Ali's number. Though the weather had turned cold, I didn't care. I would warm myself with the wine and my friend's honey-sounding voice.

As soon as she answered, I blurted out the story of what had happened in the study. All of it. I even gave a nasally imitation of Gavin saying, 'Really, Jeanne, you should have come to me earlier.'

Ali laughed out loud before her mood abruptly turned. 'Bastard,' she said.

Immediately, I balked. What the hell was I doing, talking about Gavin to someone outside the family? Making fun of him even. 'I know he's trying to help, but — ' I said, beginning to feel queasy.

'Help? Is that what you call it?' Ali pressed. She clearly sounded like she'd had too much wine. 'Telling you that everyone from school is watching you? Then pulling the ultimate guilt trip — that you're hurting Jamie?' She seemed to take a long sip from her wine. 'None of which is true, by the way. If anyone's acting strangely, it's that husband of yours.'

'Well, he probably went too far, but he means well. I *have* been edgy lately, and it can't be easy for Gavin — '

'Whatever you want to tell yourself, Jeanne. It's your marriage,' Ali said, with a hint of the impatience I'd heard in Gavin's voice. I don't know who was more eager to get off the phone

— Ali or me. I dumped the rest of my wine on the frozen lawn and went inside.

But that night, when I went to bed, I could not exorcise her voice from my mind. Or her words: *whatever you want to tell yourself, Jeanne.*

During morning coffee break at school, I slipped out and filled my prescription. Of course, I intended to wait till I got home to take a pill, but just as I was entering the building, Ali's words returned unbidden: *whatever you want to tell yourself, Jeanne.*

I poured myself a glass of water from the tank and popped a pill into my mouth, then I wrapped the telltale bottle in a Kleenex and stuffed it to the bottom of my purse. Yet another secret I was keeping.

⋆   ⋆   ⋆

Despite my best intentions, days and weeks had passed, and I never found the right time to talk to Jamie about what I'd found. Nor did he mention his pilfered collection. And the more time passed, the less pressing the matter seemed. When I saw my son come down the stairs in the morning, wearing the same tired grin that had charmed me when he was a toddler, I wondered how I had doubted him. Obviously, some sicko had passed the collection to Jamie. Maybe he was even hiding it for a friend. In any case, it was natural for a boy to be curious, wasn't it?

But I couldn't shake the disturbing sense that Jamie was listening in on my phone calls, a suspicion that was exacerbated by his breathless three-word note. Obviously, he had 'overheard' our call this morning; he knew that the Shagaurys' marriage was in trouble. What was worse, Jamie was clearly titillated by this bit of gossip. I could picture his flushed face when he'd heard the CDT teacher's anguished voice on the phone, as adolescent embarrassment mixed with voyeuristic relish. When Jamie got home, we would definitely have a talk about the importance of staying out of other people's business. Particularly *adult* business.

In the middle of my thoughts, the phone rang; and as soon as I heard Ali's voice on the other end of the line, I forgot my other concerns.

'Have you heard from Brian?' I asked before she had time to say much more than my name.

Sounding slightly breathless, but remarkably free of curiosity, she said, 'No, but I hear you two had coffee this morning.'

For a moment, I lapsed into stunned silence. How could she know? Had Brian called her?

'Your son told me when I called earlier,' Ali explained before I could ask.

Moving on to the next topic, as if there were nothing unusual about her lovers waking me at dawn to chat, she said, 'Listen, Jeanne, I was just calling to tell you not to bother picking me up for school this week. I'm taking a few personal days.'

I paused, waiting for Ali to fill in the silence on the line with an explanation. When none was forthcoming, I said, 'I hope there's not a problem — no one sick in the family or anything.'

66

Again Ali hesitated, as if considering how much she wanted to tell me. 'No, I just need to get away for a few days, that's all,' she said at last. Apparently she had been weighing whether to confide in me or not — and had decided against it.

I was about to tell her exactly what I thought of her affair with the married CDT teacher, making sure I added a description of Brian's disturbing demeanor in the donut shop, when Ali abruptly cut me short.

'Well, listen, I won't keep you. There's a few things I need to pack. I'll give you a call when I get back, okay?' Then, without even waiting for an answer, she was gone. But just before the connection was broken, I was sure I'd heard the unmistakable rumble of a male voice in the background.

I held the phone in my hand for a few moments, staring at it as if it had the answer to my questions. When I looked up, Gavin was standing in the doorway to the kitchen in his bathrobe, his lips fixed in the straight line that said he was trying to conceal his anger. 'It's that teacher again, right? The one you've been driving to school,' he said, starting for the coffeepot. Then, before I had a chance to respond, he added, 'Tell her to get herself another taxi service.'

I stared at his rigid back. It was rare for Gavin to order me to do anything, least of all in that tone of voice. And when I asked why, he said, 'The woman's a bad influence on your son, for one thing. Jamie was up at five this morning,

67

pacing around the house like a lion, caught up in her tawdry little drama.'

Of course, my mouth was full of protest. How could a friend I never brought home be any kind of influence on our son, good or bad? And next year, Ali would be Jamie's music teacher whether Gavin liked it or not. There were a lot of things I wanted to say — perhaps I might even spit out a few words about the kind of influence Gavin himself was, with constant criticism and his rejecting silences. But before I had the chance to speak, Jamie came in from his jog, his face ruddy from running the final block.

'Hey, Mom,' he said, sounding winded when he entered the kitchen. But then spotting Gavin at the table where he was nursing a cup of coffee, Jamie cringed noticeably and fell silent.

'Pretty chilly out there this morning, huh?' Gavin said, looking up from his coffee. Then before Jamie had a chance to say another word, Gavin added, 'You better go upstairs and have a hot shower before church.'

After casting a brief miserable glance in my direction, Jamie put his head down and lumbered up the stairs.

I sighed deeply, wondering how I would get through another Sunday: smiling at my fellow parishioners while *wonderful* Dr Cross greeted everyone by name, cooking a gourmet dinner that my family would gulp down so distractedly they hardly tasted it, facing Jamie's uncompleted homework assignments at night. And meanwhile, Ali was off, taking a few *personal days* . . . listening to music, taking long walks somewhere, working on her music, and undoubtedly spending long afternoons in bed with Jack Butterfield, the best lover she'd ever had, according to her. For the first time, I felt some of the envy that flared through the lunchroom seeping into my thoughts like a poison.

6

'I know what you're thinking,' Ali said, crossing her legs in my car. We had reached the school parking lot, and after a mostly silent ride, she remained settled on the front seat. 'And the worst part is, you're right. Every nasty thing you've thought about me these last few days is true.' Students drifted past the car, waving excitedly at Ali, obviously pleased to see her back. A few even acknowledged me.

I looked at my watch. 'It's eight on the nose. We better get inside,' I said. I wondered why she waited until we got to school to bring up the subject. If she wanted to talk, why didn't she speak up when she first got in the car?

But when Ali reached out and touched my arm, looking more troubled than I'd ever seen her, I forgot my annoyance. 'Do you know how many messages he left on my machine while I was gone?' she asked quietly. 'At least a dozen. Each one more desperate than the last. And if the tape hadn't been filled, I'm sure there would have been more.'

'*He?*' I repeated, though I knew she meant Brian Shagaury. I also knew that she was lingering in the parking lot because she was afraid he would be waiting for her outside her classroom. But in the meantime, she was keeping me from my duties at the front desk.

'You know who I'm talking about,' Ali shot

70

back. In spite of her obvious trepidation and guilt, she looked particularly striking that day in a simple black skirt and a sweater, her face lit from within.

Again I consulted the timepiece on my wrist. 'All I know is that it's already past eight, and I, for one, have to get to work.' With that, I got out of the car and crossed the parking lot without once looking back.

Ali came in about fifteen minutes later, looking straight ahead as she passed the front desk, her striking profile betraying none of the disquiet I had seen in the car. And for a moment, I was stricken by conscience. Obviously she had needed to talk badly. What kind of friend would allow her need to collect attendance sheets override Ali's desperate concerns? From her aloof attitude as she passed, I wondered if she would even want to ride home with me after school.

However, Ali, who usually made me wait while she chatted with the ever-increasing pack of students who lingered outside her door — 'Ali's groupies,' the lunchroom crowd sardonically called them — was in the car even before I got there. As soon as we pulled out of the lot, she resumed our conversation from the morning as if it had never ended.

'This whole thing has been a huge mistake, Jeanne. It never should have happened,' Ali began.

But before she got the words out, I felt myself overflowing with confusion — and yes, anger. I couldn't help remembering Beth Shagaury's stricken face in the donut shop. And Brian's desperation. 'Then why did you do it?' I said. 'Ali, you have a husband who's crazy about you. Not to mention Jack Butterfield. What in the world did you need with Brian?'

Ali sighed, clinging to her book bag on her lap as she gazed out the window. 'I don't know,' she said miserably, as if someone else were directing her fate, not her. 'Oh, Jeanne, someone like you couldn't begin to understand the things I've done.'

Without commenting, I took a corner near the school at a reckless speed. A group of students who were walking home turned toward the sound of my squealing tires. Then, seeing it was me, they began to point. I could see my name on their lips. 'It's Mrs Cross!' someone yelled, obviously impressed by my wild driving.

Deciding it was probably better to be relaxed while listening to Ali's tempestuous story, I asked, 'Feel like going to Paradise Pond?' But I had already made the sharp right that led to the small wooded park before Ali had a chance to answer.

It was unseasonably warm, and as soon as I parked the car, Ali opened the window on her side and inhaled the pretty blue day. The sight of trees, even bare as they were, and the air that streamed through the window seemed to calm her. She stared outside for several moments, lost in the beauty of the spot. She had previously told me that she always came here when she was in trouble, and the place unfailingly calmed her. She was even working on a piece of music she'd entitled *Paradise Suite.*

Then she turned back to me, her face as defiant as a teenager's. 'I don't expect you to understand this,' she said. 'But I have no idea why I ever slept with Brian. Maybe I just did it to see if I could.'

Genuinely confounded, I blinked. 'I guess you're right. I *don't* understand . . . '

'If I were a man, you would,' Ali said, her chin lifted in a childishly stubborn expression. 'Men pursue younger women for sport all the time — whenever they start feeling a little insecure. But when a woman does it, it's another thing altogether.'

I think the one word that stunned me most was *sport.* Was it really possible that the woman I had come to think of as my best friend had broken up a family simply to test her well-proven powers of seduction? Not wanting to believe that, I focused on the phrase that cast Ali's actions in a more understandable light. 'So that's why you did it. Because you were feeling insecure?'

'I don't know if that's exactly the right word. Maybe *unsure* is more like it. When I first met Jack, I was so intoxicated with him I would have done anything for the man. And I did. I gave up a wonderful husband, a life that most people would consider as near to perfection as you can get. But in recent months, well, things changed. I wasn't sure if I felt the same. Or if he did.'

Hungry for the breeze that had begun to waft through the dark lacy trees, Ali opened the door. 'It's so nice out, why don't we walk?' she said.

And indeed as we made our way across the quiet park, I realized exactly how hungry I'd been for warmth, for air, for the sight of trees.

Wearing only her thin sweater and skirt, Ali, who always dressed too lightly for the weather, wrapped her arms around herself, as if to protect her fragile frame from the power of her feelings for Jack Butterfield. Just thinking of him, she once again became luminous.

'Ever since he found out about Brian, it's been like it was in the beginning,' she said. She stopped and loosened the tumble of reddish blond hair and let it flow over her shoulders. 'But then I guess you know that jealousy is the world's best aphrodisiac.' Of course, I knew nothing of the kind. Nor did I know much about the kind of passion that existed between Ali and Jack, an emotion that made her virtually shimmer as she spoke about it.

'The strange thing is, Jack isn't even my type. I mean, if anyone ever told me I would lose my mind over a car salesman, I would have had them declared legally insane. George and I have much more in common. Our passion for music, for one thing. George knows more about music than anyone I know. And more significantly, we believe the same things. Jack, on the other hand — well, really, we have nothing in common.'

'To tell you the truth, I could never picture you two together,' I said. 'I know it's a cliché about car dealers, but Jack seems so . . . so, well, *slick*. Like someone who couldn't be quite trusted.'

'Maybe that's his allure,' Ali said, taking a seat

on a bench where she looked up at me, her face looking unfairly young. 'I mean, there I was married to the kindest and most loving man I've ever met. I had everything to make me happy — and I *was* happy — don't get me wrong. But something was missing. I could feel it in my music.

'I know it sounds selfish, but before I met Jack, I felt like I was going through life with my eyes closed. I had lost the power to see bright colours, to really feel the music I played. But then I met Jack, and I started to write music with real fire in it. That's when I realized that some people need the unpredictable, the untrustworthy, the dangerous in their lives — and I'm one of them. I thrive on it.'

I sat down beside her. 'I hate to say this, Ali, I really do, but — '

Ali looked at me curiously. 'That's your problem; you never say what you think. Just go ahead.'

Flushed with the truth of her words, I plunged ahead. 'Okay, then. I *do* think it sounds selfish. And self-justifying, too. You go and break the heart of the kindest man you ever met. Then you have the nerve to say you did it for your music. And this thing with Brian, you broke up a *family*, Ali. I'm sorry, but if you could have seen Brian that morning in the donut shop. The guy is falling apart.'

I guess that after my little lecture, I expected Ali to get up and walk away. To tell me to go to hell. But instead, she turned to me, and laughed softly. 'I'm sorry, Jeanne,' she said. 'I'm not laughing at you. It's just — well, we're so unalike. Sometimes I've wondered why I would choose to confide in someone like you. Up until this moment, I never knew the answer.'

'Which is?' I said, not sure whether to feel insulted or vindicated by her words.

'You're my conscience. You're the girl I always wanted to be in some way — the one who knows where things are in her desk, who's never late with an assignment, the one who pays the gas bill on precisely the third of every month.'

'Don't make me sound so boring,' I said, staring at a dog that had gotten loose from its master's leash and was chasing squirrels around the park, with his owner in futile pursuit. 'You talk about me the way you do about George.'

'No, not boring. And certainly not like George. For one thing, George would never tell me I was selfish. That's the poor man's problem: he refuses to see anything bad in me. No, George would probably say I was adventurous, or a free spirit. You, on the other hand, you're my mother superior, Jeanne. And I — I'm your — your — well, I think you need something from me, too.' Catching the harsh look in my eyes, Ali hesitated.

'Well, go ahead. If you're going to psychoanalyze me, don't stop now,' I said. 'What do you think I need from you?'

Ali took a deep breath, and stretched out, folding her hands behind her head. 'Maybe I'm your dark side, Jeanne. Maybe you became my friend because you'd like to be a little selfish yourself. Or maybe there's more darkness in your life than you'd like to admit. What's beneath all that self-control, Jeanne? All that secretiveness? There's got to be something.'

Unaccustomed to thinking about my own inner life, I stared after a loose dog who was bounding through the park. 'I'm afraid your first assessment was the right one; I don't talk about myself much because there's not a lot to say. I'm hopelessly boring.' Then, quickly and artlessly, I directed the conversation back to a topic with which I felt more comfortable: Ali's problems. 'So that was the only reason you got involved with Brian? Because you wanted to revive your relationship with Jack?'

'I'm not saying Brian doesn't have his charms. There's something to be said for all that youthful energy, for one thing,' she said, smiling mischievously. 'And it wasn't like I planned to break up his family, for God's sake. I thought it would be a nice diversion for both of us.'

She stopped, and stared at me more closely. 'But then I found out Brian was a lot more complex than I'd thought. Come to think of it, he's a lot like you, Jeannie. Someone who keeps his dark side under lock and key. But now that it's out, and he's convinced himself I'm the great passion of his life . . . ' Her voice trailed off.

Needless to say, I wasn't too pleased with being compared to a guy who obviously had deep psychological problems. 'But now that it's out, now that you've freed him from his prison of conscience, you don't know what he'll do. Is that what you're saying?'

Again, Ali looked out over the park. The sky

was now clotted with clouds, which made the air suddenly chilly. Again, she hugged herself, emphasizing her slenderness, her hidden vulnerability.

Speaking more gently, I touched her arm. 'Ali, you looked pretty scared when you told me about those messages he left on your machine. Brian hasn't threatened you, has he?'

Ali turned to me, her face more troubled than I'd seen it. 'It wasn't the messages that scared me, Jeanne. Someone was in my house when I was away. Touching my things. Lying on my bed. Drinking juice from my glass. It's nothing I can prove, and I suppose the police would think I was crazy if I called them, but I'm sure of it. Someone was in my bedroom. Someone who wanted me to know they were there. And that they could come back whenever they wanted to.'

7

If proof was ever needed about the danger of affairs between coworkers, it could have certainly been found in the halls of Bridgeway High School in the months that followed Ali's breakup with Brian. While the music teacher moved on with her life, Brian Shagaury fell apart before the prying eyes of the staff and students alike. After Ali refused to see him in private and stopped returning his calls, he joined the group of students who waited outside her room after school, hoping for a word with her. In response, Ali began to leave school a few minutes early to avoid him. Once when he caught her alone as she was coming out of the music room, Ali had spoken sharply to him. A young flutist who had approached her to talk kept a respectful distance. But she was sure she heard the music teacher mention something about contacting the police. Whether Ali was actually threatening Brian — or what he had said to elicit such an extreme response — no one exactly knew. Not even me. After our talk in the park that day, Ali had been oddly silent about what other teachers referred to as 'the Brian problem.'

But if I thought the end of the affair was also the end of the juicy gossip that had moved through the corridors like a hurricane, reaching maximum force when it hit the teachers' lounge, I couldn't have been more wrong. With dark fascination, the staff chewed on every detail of Brian's unravelling: the way he started showing up late for work looking unshaven, with dark circles under his eyes. And of course, the students knew what was going on; they, too, had witnessed the furtive glances exchanged between the two teachers when they were lovers. Experts in the art of romantic relationships, they lingered outside the shop, peering through the door at the distracted teacher, who sat at his desk drinking deep from cold coffee and misery.

'So he's been dumped. It's not the end of the world. The dude needs to move on,' a boy with curly red hair opined one day when I passed.

'But he's in *lo-ove*,' another boy added, dragging the word out until it sounded like a disease. Everyone laughed.

'If I was the wife, I'd take his sorry ass for everything he's got. The guy's pathetic,' a tall girl said, a hand braced on her slender hip.

Even Jamie, who'd never expressed much interest in girls or dating, was fascinated by the ongoing school drama. He begged me for inside information he could pass on to his friends. 'So what's going on, Mom? Is he still calling her?'

You can imagine the giggles that erupted in the hallway when Ali lowered her head as she passed Brian waiting outside her classroom. Or once, when he grasped her arm, and she responded with three words before she wriggled away. 'Please, Brian. Please.' Just three words, but they were repeated with various inflections around the school for days. In some versions, Ali sounded frightened. In others, angry and imperious. But when she told me, her tone was simply exhausted.

As for Brian, he didn't seem to care that the entire school was laughing at him. He waited shamelessly outside that room every day, watching Ali long after she'd turned the corner, unaware of the audience that was basking in his humiliation. Apparently, he was so hungry for the sight of her, and for the faint scent of lilies she exuded when she passed, that he had become oblivious to everything else — even to the laughter of his own students.

Though I had begun to avoid the lounge, choosing to eat in my car on warm days or behind my desk, I couldn't help hearing a lot of what was said. From the school nurse, I learned that Brian was still staying at the Oak Tree. And from Simon Murphy, our principal, I heard that the CDT teacher's contract definitely would not be renewed for the following year. Though Brian had tenure, there had been so many complaints about his performance in the classroom that Simon wasn't anticipating any trouble in terminating him. And besides, Brian Shagaury hardly looked like a man ready to put up a fight.

I had scrawled down the name and number of one of Gavin's friends, who was also a first-rate psychiatrist, and planned to pass it on to Brian when I got the chance. Clearly, he needed help. But after our intimate conversation in Ryan's Donut Shop, Brian had avoided me. And when our eyes did meet in the office or the hallway, he glared at me — as if I were somehow to blame for Ali's rejection.

Another person who apparently thought I was an accomplice to the troubles in her marriage was Beth Shagaury. I'd heard she'd postponed her trip to Indiana, but I was still surprised when our carts almost collided one Saturday morning in the Shop n' Save.

I reached out to touch the youngest of the Shagaury boys, who was riding in the shopping cart. But before I could reach his downy head, Beth immediately yanked the cart out of my reach. The laserlike hatred I saw in her eyes made me immediately take a step backward.

'Beth, I — I'm sorry — ' I stammered lamely. But then I had no idea what to follow it with. I'm sorry your life is in shambles? I'm sorry your husband has come unglued over a woman who doesn't even want him? What could I possibly say?

'Save it,' Beth snapped, sparing me the effort. While she was glaring at me, her two oldest were tossing sugary cereals into the cart, but Beth didn't seem to notice. She started to push the cart away, but then abruptly turned back. 'Does your friend have any idea what she's done?'

Again, I muttered a feeble 'I'm sorry.'

'Don't be sorry for me,' Beth said fiercely. 'Be sorry for your friend. She doesn't know what she's gotten herself into.' Then she shook her head in disgust — a repulsion that seemed to extend to me as well as to the woman she referred to simply as my friend. And before I could say another word, she disappeared.

When I got home, I was so shaken I dialled Ali's number without thinking.

Ali answered the phone in her usual breathless voice. She always sounded as if she were anticipating good news — which I'd come to understand she was. I immediately realized I couldn't tell her about my encounter with Beth.

'Oh, Jeanne,' she said excitedly. 'I've been meaning to call you. What's up?' It was obvious that Ali had put 'the Brian problem' firmly behind her, and nothing was going to drag her back into that morass.

When she talked about it at all, which wasn't often, Ali admitted that she felt terrible about Brian's decline, but she was hardly responsible. Or at least not *totally*. Clearly, a man who would go to pieces over a brief affair had problems long before she came along. And if his marriage had been viable, it wouldn't have collapsed like a cheap tent at the first sign of trouble. Her one regret was that she had allowed herself to be pulled into his dark orbit in the first place.

In any case, so much was happening in Ali's life that she had little time to think about Brian Shagaury, or to wonder what the CDT teacher would do if he lost his job on top of everything else. There was her music for one thing. As we careened toward spring and the end of the school year, Ali's career, which had been stalled when she took the job as music teacher, was developing in several exciting directions. A symphony she'd written the previous summer had been performed by the Boston Symphony Orchestra in their winter program, earning rave notices; now several notable orchestras around the country had requested to see more of her music. Even though she loved her students, she had already decided that she wouldn't be returning to the constricted world of Bridgeway High in the fall.

★ ★ ★

One Friday afternoon when I stopped in for my usual glass of wine to celebrate the end of another workweek, Ali pulled out a letter she had received from an orchestra in Minneapolis, inviting her to join them as a lead violinist in their fall season. 'It's what I've always wanted,' Ali said, her eyes glistening. 'I don't know if I've told you, but my father played with the symphony when I was a little girl. I only wish he were alive so he could see this day.'

'I thought what you always wanted was Jack Butterfield. Silly girl dreams, remember?' I don't know why, but I felt betrayed; I could feel Ali being pulled away from the narrow world of Bridgeway High, of our pretty but confining New England town. She was stretching, growing, and as always, my life remained numbingly static.

'Silly girl dreams have their place,' she said, stretching out her long, silky legs before her. 'But these are serious woman dreams we're talking here. If I let Jack — or any man — stop me from taking this job, then I don't deserve to play with a first-rate orchestra.'

'You mean you'd just leave? Walk out on George? And what *about* Jack?' I couldn't help thinking how only weeks earlier Ali had said that

84

she and the car dealer were closer than ever.

Now she merely shrugged. But I noticed that at the mention of her lover's name, Ali had frowned almost imperceptibly. 'I'm sure Jack would visit from time to time,' she said coolly. 'And I've already talked it over with George. He's a hundred percent behind me. He even promised to take care of the cottage — just in case it didn't work out and I decided to come back.'

As if sensing my feelings of desertion, Ali took my two hands and held them with her own. 'Of course, you'll have to come out for weekends, Jeanne. Sit in the front row for my first performance.'

As usual, her enthusiasm was so contagious that I couldn't help smiling, imagining myself dressed in some slinky little black dress, clapping as Ali took her final bow. The prospect of getting away from Gavin and Jamie, of being alone in a strange city even for a weekend, excited me more than I cared to admit.

Still, I couldn't help feeling I had hit a nerve when I mentioned Jack's name. I poured myself a second glass of wine, though I was already feeling the first. 'All right, Ali, spill it. What's going on with Jack? He's not seeing someone else, is he?'

Ali laughed, in that wonderful loose way she had. Her long wavy hair was streaming over her shoulders, and the sun from her abundant windows made the silvery strands admixed among the reddish gold glisten. At times she looked every one of her forty-six years, but on her, each year seemed to make her more luminous.

She hesitated before she answered. 'If he were, I suppose, I'd be wild with jealousy. Probably wouldn't even consider going to Minneapolis. But no, Jack is the picture of devotion.' A vaguely troubled expression altered her smooth brow. 'Maybe that's the problem.'

I poured more wine into Ali's glass, though it was only half empty. 'Let me get this straight,' I said, settling into the nest of pillows on Ali's comfortable couch. 'Now that you've got the man of your dreams, you're not sure you want him.'

'Story of my life,' Ali said, smiling the way she did when I said something that indicated I understood her perfectly. 'I guess I'm like one of those spoiled kids who wants a toy in the window desperately. But as soon as I have it at home, as soon as I've taken it apart and seen exactly how it works, I lose interest. Pathological, isn't it?'

'You mean you actually like being with someone who acts like they couldn't care less about you? Yes, that *is* pathological,' I said. Then, undoubtedly under the influence of the wine, I added, 'Maybe I should fix you up with Gavin.'

Ali laughed. 'I always knew that husband of yours couldn't stand me. Thanks for verifying it. But yes, I do seem to be the type of woman who likes a challenge. Once a man starts following me around like a sheepdog, I'm gone.'

'And that's what Jack has been doing?' I could hardly picture the confident — some might say *arrogant* — Jack Butterfield acting like anyone's devoted pet. Even Ali's. Then I recalled how distraught he'd been that morning outside her house.

'Not exactly. And it's not that I don't still adore Jack. It's just that ever since this thing with Brian, I've become leery of overly attentive men.'

'And that's what Jack has become — overly attentive?' Starved for attention as I was, I couldn't imagine anyone complaining about her man being too devoted. 'I guess your ploy to make him jealous with Brian worked a little too well.'

'All in all, it was the dumbest thing I've ever done,' Ali agreed, suddenly looking sheepish. She glanced around the room nervously, almost as if she saw some menace in the familiar and lovely objects she had assembled there. 'You remember what I told you about all the strange things happening in my house, the objects that I've found out of place, used glasses left out on the counter. Well, Jack's gotten so protective. First, he wanted to move in with me — which, of course, is out of the question. I mean, this house is half George's. And when I reminded Jack about that, well — would you believe, he's been talking marriage, Jeanne?'

'Marriage?' I repeated excitedly, remembering how Ali had glowed when she spoke about Jack in the park. 'But if you really love him as much as you say you do — '

Ali shook her head. 'I'm already married, Jeanne — and like I told you, I have no intention of divorcing George,' she said resolutely, as though the very suggestion were shocking. 'And even if I weren't — now that I've looked at Jack more objectively, I can see there's not much between us. Nothing but our crazy passion for each other. You certainly can't build a marriage on that.'

Unexpectedly, I rose from the couch and went to the window that overlooked the garden Ali had just begun planting. Like everything she created, it was a place of solace and beauty. I particularly loved the little stone bench she had placed right in the middle of it, a corner where someone might sit out late after dark, lost in the fragrance of the night-blooming flowers and the glittering stars. It was the kind of place I never had for myself, a place where you have no choice but to confront the truth of your life. I pulled the curtain shut, blocking out the light, and turned to face my friend.

'If not passion — *love* — then what do you build a marriage on?' I said, turning to face Ali in the room that was suddenly drenched in shadows. I hoped she wouldn't see the tears glistening in my eyes.

Ali was off the couch so quickly she knocked her wineglass over in the process. What I loved about her was that she didn't even stop to clean it up as I surely would have done. Instead, she came to me, and wrapped her arms around me. 'Oh, Jeannie, I'm sorry,' she said, stroking my hair. 'I can be so selfish at times — all this talk about love and marriage, when you're so unhappy.'

At first, I was stunned by her words, the

simple statement I never made out loud, never even allowed myself to think. Then for some reason I couldn't explain — perhaps it was just her sympathetic touch, the first I could remember feeling since my parents died — I wept like a child.

'You need to talk about it, Jeanne,' Ali murmured into my hair. 'If you keep holding everything inside like this, it's going to destroy you. And your son.'

I don't know what it was — her pressing me to talk, or simply the mention of Jamie — but I immediately pulled away, suddenly feeling stone sober.

'I have to go,' I said, gathering up my belongings like I was fleeing a house fire.

All the way home and for days afterward, I felt Ali's topaz-coloured eyes on me as they had been when I left the house. Sorrowful eyes. Compassionate eyes. For some reason, they disturbed me more than if she'd slapped me.

★ ★ ★

Later, over dinner with Gavin and Jamie, I chided myself for my silly behavior, blaming it on the wine. For the first time in months, Gavin actually seemed to be in a good mood. He even complimented me on the meal I had prepared, grilled salmon with chutney relish. And after dinner, he mentioned a particularly popular action movie that was playing down at the mall, and suggested the three of us might take it in. Though I recoiled from the violence such films inevitably depicted, I took him up on the offer. And sitting in the dark theatre, wedged between my husband and my son, I felt almost happy. While lust, mayhem, and betrayal whizzed across the screen before me, I told myself that perhaps my own fears and misgivings were no more real than these celluloid dreams.

But when Gavin glanced over at me, something in me cringed.

At home, I found there was a message on my machine from Ali, inviting me to attend a concert she was playing on the Cape the following Saturday. While I was planning how I would get away from the house for an evening, I turned around and saw Gavin standing behind me. At first, I froze, expecting sharp words, the kind that the subject of Ali always elicited from him. But instead he stretched his mouth into a tight smile. 'A concert on the Cape, huh? Sounds interesting,' he said. 'I'll talk to Jamie about it. It's about time this family took in a little culture.'

'Great,' I said, but inwardly my heart sank. I had been hoping to make the trip with Ali alone. 'I'll call Ali and let her know.'

I don't know why, perhaps it was just the tightness of Gavin's smile — the falsity of it — but instead of looking forward to the concert, I went to bed that night with a heavy feeling of dread. Even though I slept well, aided by the contents of my little bottles, I woke up the following morning feeling shaky and exhausted.

8

'You mean you want me to sit there in some dumb suit and listen to classical music? For three hours? Mom, please, Toby and the guys were going to rent a couple of movies, maybe hang out at Brad Simmons's house.' Jamie was sitting at the island over a mixing bowl full of cereal, despite my exhortations that he wait until dinner to eat. His dark eyes were plaintive.

I turned back to the counter where I was preparing a marinade for chicken. 'Give it a chance. You might even enjoy it.'

Jamie snorted. 'It's not just the music; I'm almost sixteen, Mom. I don't want to spend my free time with my mom and dad, pretending like we're a family. First Dad forces me to go to the movies with you guys like I'm ten years old, and now *this?*'

Immediately something in me froze, the way it always did when someone violated the unspoken code our family lived by. This time it was one simple word: *pretending.* Above all, we could never admit that was what we did. When we sat down to dinner at night, and linked our hands in prayer. When we lined up in our pew at the Congregational Church in our elegant clothes, Jamie wedged between Gavin and me. Or when we climbed into our beds at night, each locked in our secret thoughts. Was that what we were doing? *Pretending to be a family?*

In the past, I would have let such a comment drop. That, too, was part of the code. Maybe even Rule One: if anyone speaks the truth, act as if you didn't hear it. But since I'd known Ali, I had absorbed some of her courage and honesty. I, too, was tired of living in a climate of falsity and subtle intimidation. Escaping the patterns that had developed over seventeen years, however, was no easy task.

'What do you mean?' I repeated, dropping my garlic press on the counter, where it made a clattering sound. But neither Jamie nor I noticed. We looked at each other in a startling, open way; and when Jamie opened his mouth to speak, I knew we were really going to talk to each other this time. This time there would be no pretending.

'We walk around like we're this perfect family straight out of Nickelodeon reruns,' he said, his voice lowered, the spoon he was using to eat his cereal poised in midair. 'It's *bullshit*, Mom — and you know it. Something's missing here; something's wrong.'

But before he could elaborate, the door that separated the kitchen from the family swung open, and Gavin appeared.

'Wrong? Did I hear someone say something was wrong?' he asked. He had just returned from the gym and was still wearing his nylon pants and a tank top under his jacket. Though he was smiling, there was a familiar edge in his voice.

Secretly, Jamie's eyes caught mine. I turned back to my marinade. 'Jamie was saying he really doesn't want to go to that concert on Saturday.

Maybe he could invite Toby over for a movie and a pizza or something.'

Gavin crossed the kitchen without saying a word. After he had poured himself a large glass of orange juice, he leaned against the counter and took a deep breath. 'Not much of a classical music fan, huh, pal?' he said, slapping Jamie heartily on the back. 'Well, I don't suppose I cared for the stuff much when I was your age either.'

Jamie smiled weakly, looking to me for help.

Gavin picked up the gym bag he had deposited on the floor while he drank his juice, and headed for the shower. Though he passed me silently, I could almost feel a cold wind at my back. Still, he continued to talk to Jamie in a forced, amiable voice that was almost more frightening than outright screaming. 'If you really didn't want to go to that concert on Saturday, all you had to do was tell me, buddy. Your old man's not such an unreasonable guy.'

'You mean I don't have to go? I can stay home?' Jamie said. I hated the note of pleading in his voice.

But Gavin had already left the room, and soon we heard the sound of the shower running. This time when I looked at Jamie, he was concentrating on his cereal bowl, eating rapidly, mindlessly, his eyes almost glazed. I began to dip chicken breasts into my prepared marinade. I was relieved when Jamie got up from the table, saying, 'I'm going up to my room; call me when dinner's ready.' Though he had gotten what he wanted, there was no mistaking the dejected tone in his voice. With Gavin, there was a price for every small victory. Obviously, we were both wondering what this one would cost us.

★ ★ ★

The night of the concert, I wore a short black dress. Though I'd been working out religiously for three months, it wasn't until I stood before a full-length mirror in my slinky dress that I noticed the results. My stomach would never be as flat as Ali's, no matter how many crunches I did, but for the first time since Jamie was born, I had a real definable middle. And my legs had never looked better. A new pair of stilettos with a rhinestone strap that wrapped around the ankle emphasized their taut curves. Now that my hair was growing out, I coiled it into a sleek French twist, set off by the diamond earrings that Gavin had given me on our tenth anniversary.

'Wow, check out your mom,' Gavin said, winking at Jamie when I came down the stairs. But when he kissed me perfunctorily on the cheek, his lips felt dry and cold; instinctively, I recoiled, hoping that neither father nor son noticed.

'You really do look nice, Mom,' Jamie said, the glow of unabashed admiration in his eyes.

But by then Gavin was looking in the mirror, tilting his face this way and that, as if studying his own reflection. Vanity, I thought, was a particularly unattractive quality in a man. Still, I couldn't help feeling a bit proud when I caught the look on Ali's face when I walked through the door on my husband's arm. Though she and Gavin had spoken on the phone several times, they had never actually met. From the flash in her golden eyes, I knew she was immediately impressed.

'You never told me he was so good-looking,' she whispered as soon as we were alone. 'And quite personable, too. Is he a runner or something?'

'Runner. Weight lifter. Whatever it takes to keep the body beautiful, Gavin does it,' I said.

As the night progressed, I was pleased to see the heads of several women turn in the direction of my tall, trim husband. *Dr Cross*. Though I rarely thought much about it, Ali was right. Gavin was an exceptionally good-looking man. And standing next to George Mather, his handsome profile and military bearing were even more striking.

Though I'd heard that George was almost fifteen years Ali's senior, I was still surprised when I actually met him. Oh, he was good-looking for his age, I suppose, but the contrast with Jack Butterfield was striking. Furthermore, George was so quiet and watchful that I couldn't imagine him in a courtroom, aggressively cross-examining witnesses or delivering a fiery closing statement. I bet he bored the students in his philosophy classes at Howell College to tears.

But it took only a few minutes before my opinion changed, and the quiet magic of George Mather's presence captivated me. Maybe it was the way he took my hand, enfolding it in his own, which were bearlike and warm when we were introduced. Or just the way he asked, 'And how are *you*, Jeanne?' As if he really wanted to know. Though his eyes were buried within pouchy dark circles, they were particularly bright and alive. The more time I spent talking to him, the more my first impression was altered; I felt myself being transformed by his attention. It wasn't hard to guess how Ali had fallen for a man of such obvious and rare warmth. And as the concert progressed, it was further obvious that just as Ali said, he was a connoisseur of good music. Whenever I glanced over at him, he seemed positively transported.

His obvious pride in his wife was equally touching. Several times during the concert, he reached over and touched my arm, saying, 'Isn't she wonderful?' And during the intermission, he took me aside, whispering in an excessively loud manner that made me wonder if he was hard of hearing. 'If you ask me, Ali has outgrown the quartet. Oh, they're competent musicians and all, but they're amateurs. With the talent she has, Ali needs an opportunity to stretch. Has she told you about her offer in Minneapolis?'

Of course, I felt embarrassed for George when I looked over and saw the young cellist smiling indulgently in our direction. But I quickly forgot my consternation when I gazed past him and saw Gavin and Ali, leaning toward each other deeply engrossed in conversation. Gavin's head was cocked to the side the way it was when he was particularly engaged, and he was smiling. I wondered how many years it had been since he'd smiled like that when he spoke to me.

Following my gaze, George's eyes lingered on his wife for a long moment before he turned his attention back to me. 'Come on, Jeanne,' he said, taking my arm solicitously. 'I'll buy you a glass of wine.'

As he led me to the small bar that had been set up in the back of the room, I enjoyed the warmth of his cashmere jacket pressed against me, and the deeper warmth that he himself emanated. I doubted that I had ever met a gentler man in my life.

However, as we sipped our wine, I saw that George's eyes were not only soft and kind but also penetrating. After a few moments of surprisingly comfortable silence, he spoke. 'It was difficult for me at first,' he said out of nowhere. Though I knew he was only sixty, hardly the age of senescence, I wondered if George was so confused he momentarily forgot that he hadn't said anything leading up to that strange remark. But then he turned toward the corner where Gavin and Ali were still talking, and I realized once again that George was probably the least confused person in the room. Ali was laughing, but she had wrapped her arms protectively across her chest. Though Gavin was clearly enthralled with her, she looked wary in his presence.

'She's very beautiful, isn't she?' George said fondly, intruding on my observation.

'My husband certainly seems to think so,' I said, with only a hint of irony. The truth was, Ali never looked more lovely than she did on stage.

And when she played her violin, she became so lost in her music, she glowed.

George sighed deeply, and then took a sip of his wine. 'Yes, as I say, in the beginning it was very difficult for me. You see, I'm from a traditional Lebanese family. Very protective of our women. Our honor. Years ago, I would have gone wild to see a man looking at my wife the way your husband is doing right now. But over the years, well, I've come to realize that Ali is like the sunset. It's only natural that people should be a bit dazzled by her.' He smiled sleepily, and again looked in Ali's direction. When she saw him watching her, she lifted her hand to wave, openly returning his fond gaze.

George wrapped his arm over my shoulder, and once again I allowed myself to lean into the comfortable softness of his cashmere jacket. He smelled like the old-fashioned pipe tobacco my father had smoked. 'As for your husband,' he said softly. 'I wouldn't take it seriously. He's just gazing at the sunset, that's all.'

I immediately pulled away. 'Is that what you think — that I'm jealous?'

George stared into my face, obviously studying me. 'I saw you look in their direction several times. And perhaps I was wrong, Jeanne, but I thought there was pain in your eyes.'

'You *were* wrong,' I said, taking a step backward. I had raised my voice slightly, and a couple who were near us turned to look. But at that moment, all I cared about was making George understand. 'I've never been jealous of your wife, George; I love Ali. And as for Gavin, my so-called *husband*, well, I couldn't care less how he looks at her or any other woman.' I was startled by the bitterness in my own voice, but even more startled by the words I had blurted out to a virtual stranger. Their undeniable truth made me shudder.

For a long moment, George was silent, but his eyes never left mine. Finally he whispered, 'I see.' Just that and nothing more, but the troubling part was that it was obvious that he *did* see. And more than I wanted him to. Ali's husband took me by the elbow and led me back to our seats. There, he artfully steered the conversation back to the subject of Ali's music.

'They're going to introduce the *Paradise Suite* tonight. Has Ali played it for you?' he said, smiling irrepressibly, his excitement apparent. 'I think it's the best thing she's ever written.'

'It is a wonderful piece,' I said, in answer to his question. 'I guess we both know how important this is to her.'

'This is the piece she plans to play for her audition with the symphony,' George said, relating a fact I already knew.

By then the three accompanists had taken their places and were looking over their scores. Ali was the last to be seated; and there was an air of excitement as she smiled out over the crowd. Most of the audience were friends and fellow musicians who had followed her career for decades and were aware that the new piece of music she was about to introduce was the one she regarded as her breakout piece. For a moment her eyes settled on me, and I felt the power of the unlikely friendship that had developed over the past months. I wanted to give her some sign that I was behind her, a high five like Jamie would have done with his friends, but in the present setting, I had to let the obvious pride in my eyes and face speak for itself. And by then, of course, she had transferred her attention to the man beside me. In that one moment, the strength of the bond between husband and wife couldn't have been more evident.

However, when Ali turned to the score of the *Paradise Suite*, she gasped audibly, immediately changing the mood in the room. 'My — my music — ' she said in a ragged voice as she pushed her chair noisily back from her stand.

Immediately, George was on his feet, hurrying toward the stage with the agility of a much younger man. I followed him, having no idea what had elicited such a reaction from Ali, but knowing that it was something serious. Perhaps I knew even then that it was related to the string of troubling incidents that had occurred in her house recently — the rearranged items, the used glasses that appeared on the counter overnight, the perfume that was sprayed throughout her rooms, indicating a recent presence. In any case, I found myself standing behind George on the stage while the audience stared up at us in confusion and dismay.

Of course, George's immediate concern was to help Ali regain her composure. 'Why would someone do this to me?' she said, speaking into the well of sympathy in his dark eyes. 'And why now? After all my hard work — '

As for me, I focused on the sheet music, which had so disturbed my friend. At first, it took me a moment to find the score of *Paradise Suite*, which she had immediately covered with the music from the first half of the concert. But when I did, it was instantly apparent that Ali's alarm was justified. Not only was the score defaced with blood, it had been poked and slashed in a way that indicated the perpetrator had used a knife. The title had been violently Xed out and replaced with a new one — also written in blood. As soon as I saw it, I felt something give way in myself.

Immediately, Ali's eyes fastened on mine, knowing that I alone understood how frightening this was to her, how invasive. To anyone else, it might have seemed like a silly B movie stunt. The slashed score certainly wasn't anything the police would have taken seriously. But for Ali, it was verification that she was being stalked, that someone was running his hands over her silky garments when she wasn't home, reading her mail, even penetrating the sacrosanct music room. And furthermore, the perpetrator was letting her know he meant her harm.

Feeling unsteady, I reached for George's arm. But it was too late and he was too far away, all his attention focused on Ali. In an instant, I was falling, falling deeper into the darkness inside me, and nothing could stop the descent.

I'm not sure how much later it was that I awakened to the solicitous faces of Gavin and Ali. My head ached and I had no idea where I was.

'You fainted, Jeanne,' Gavin explained, speaking more tenderly than he had in years. Only later would I realize that, as always, his tenderness was for the benefit of an audience. But in that dark moment I nodded, accepting the glass of water Ali offered. But even before I could drink it, everything came back: the words I had seen, the truth I would somehow have to make myself forget.

9

The truth is, I'm good at forgetting things. Good at erasing images from my mind. Good at *pretending*, as Jamie called it. After seventeen years of marriage to the master, how could I be otherwise? But this time I could not allow myself the easy way out. I had to talk to someone, and Gavin was the only one I had. Of course, I knew he would not want to discuss it. I had seen his face when someone had shown him the score that ended the concert and caused me to faint. It was obvious from the sudden darkening I read on his familiar features that he, too, had immediately been drawn to the top of the page. The words PARADISE SUITE had been crossed out and replaced with a new title: dEaTH SWeeT. And the name of the composer had been changed from A. C. Mather to SLaY-hER.

What scared me most was the not the words themselves, but the handwriting on the defaced score. The misspelled jumble of capitalization and small letters that was unmistakably the work of my son. Waiting for Gavin to come up to bed, I relived the shock that the sight of those words had first elicited from me.

But when my husband emerged from the shower in his T-shirt and boxers, he was obviously determined to avoid any discussion of what occurred at the concert. He glanced at me briefly as I sat there waiting for him, and then turned away. Shamefully, I was reminded of the nights when I had tried to revive his interest in me by following the advice found in silly magazines. Strolling in from my bath in a silk camisole and lace panties. Festooning the room with candles. Then, as now, he had stonily turned from me. I watched as he turned to face the dresser where he was laying out his clothes for morning.

'We have to talk, Gavin,' I said, knowing that I was violating the code.

Gavin sighed deeply. 'It's late, Jeanne; you know we have to be up early for church,' he said. He continued to concentrate on his clothes, checking to be sure the blue flecks in his tie matched his socks precisely.

'I don't care if it's three in the morning, Gavin. We can't just pretend this didn't happen.'

For an instant, I thought I heard the soft padding of footsteps in the hallway, but my concern was instantly blotted out by Gavin's icy manner when he faced me. 'Are you trying to wake your son? Perhaps even the people next door?'

'To tell you the truth, Gavin, I don't care how many people I wake up. You saw that sheet music as well as I did,' I cried. Then, instinctively lowering my voice, I added, 'And you know who did it, too.'

'I know no such thing,' Gavin said, his eyes emitting cold fury. 'I'm not a detective, Jeanne. Unlike you, apparently.'

'Gavin, you saw that handwriting. It was — ' A

note of pleading had entered my voice.

'I'll tell you what I saw. I saw a middle-aged woman with her hair down, sashaying around like a girl. A former beauty who can't get over the fact that her time is past.' Carefully refolding the T-shirt he planned to wear the next day, he turned away.

'What are you saying — that Ali did it *herself*? Gavin, that's patently ridiculous and you know it.'

'I'm not accusing anyone of anything. You're the one who wants to play Sherlock Holmes here. All I said was that the woman was obviously desperate for male attention. And she certainly got plenty of it after the little fiasco with her sheet music.' He climbed into bed and turned off the light, apparently hoping to end the conversation as he had terminated so many in the past.

'As if Ali needed to stoop to cheap tricks to get attention from men. I saw you, Gavin. You couldn't keep your eyes off her.'

'So that's what this is really about?' Gavin said, rolling onto his side away from me. His voice sounded bored. 'Your jealousy. As I said, Jeanne, I'd love to stay up and chat, but I have to get up early in the morning.'

But this time, I wasn't about to let things drop as I had so often in the past. I sat up and switched on the reading light beside my bed. 'What this is about, Gavin, is our son. There have been signs of problems for months. Maybe even years. We have to deal with it.'

Without warning, Gavin sat up in bed and

seized my wrist with a force that startled me. He glanced toward the bedroom door as if he were certain someone was outside, listening. Then he lowered his voice to a harsh whisper. 'And just how do you propose we do that, Jeanne? Call in some little psychologist with a fresh B.A. to test her schoolgirl theories on our family? Go to the police and turn in our own son? Over a piece of sheet music?' He squeezed my wrist tighter. 'What you saw was *nothing*, Jeanne. Got that? Absolutely nothing. Now turn out that light.'

And this time, my wrist aching, the dark place inside myself pulling me downward, I complied. It was obvious that I was alone with a problem I couldn't even discuss with Ali. Feeling more solitary than I had ever been, I closed my eyes and tried to sleep.

Perhaps a half hour later, I tiptoed down the short corridor that separated my room from my son's. I knocked softly on the door and when there was no response, I entered. A shaft of moonlight illuminated the room, highlighting the ordinary detritus of adolescence: jeans and T-shirts strewn around the room, the school-books he rarely opened on his desk, posters of athletes making the kind of fantastic leaps and dunks that Jamie would never make, encircling him on the walls. And in the centre of all of it was my son, the hulking boy-man. In sleep, he had never looked more innocent. I approached the bed and stroked his soft cheek as I had so many times when he was small. There was no guile in that sleeping face, nothing to indicate

106

the potential for malice. Maybe Gavin was right: I was overreacting.

And even if Jamie *had* marked up Ali's sheet music, what did that prove? It didn't mean that he was the one who had been prowling around her house. Surely, it could have been done anywhere — at school most likely. Maybe Gavin was right and it had nothing to do with what had been happening at Ali's house. Maybe it was just a prank. Probably incited by those friends of his. I could see Toby and Brad in the background urging Jamie on, taking advantage of his compliant nature so that he would take the blame if they were caught. I felt the muscles in my neck clenching, just thinking of the way some of Jamie's so-called friends used him. Disturbing nothing in my son's sleepy adolescent universe, I crept out, vowing to myself that I would have a talk with him in the morning.

But first I had to get some sleep. I slipped into the bathroom and opened the medicine chest. I reached for the Ativan and quickly popped one in my mouth, followed by another for insurance. That night I wanted to sleep like the dead.

The next morning, I woke up feeling bleary and tense at the same time. Still only half awake, I remembered there was something I had to do, something that filled me with dread as surely as my lungs filled with the air of a new day. And then I remembered: I had to talk to Jamie. I stood up feeling shaky, the familiar knot behind my sternum, and realized there was no way I was going to get through this without a little help. After slipping into my bathrobe and slippers, I walked edgily toward the bathroom. My hand was trembling as I reached toward the medicine chest. In the mirror, plain Jeanne had never looked worse. I grabbed one of my bottles randomly and stashed a couple of pills in the pocket of my bathrobe — just in case. Then, still in my pyjamas, I put on my eyeliner, banishing plain Jeanne from my sight.

However, by the time I got downstairs, Jamie had left for his so-called jog. Instead, Gavin sat at the table. Before him, a cup of coffee that looked cold and the paper that Jamie always brought in for us were both untouched. He was trying to appear nonchalant, but I could feel the tension rising from my husband's body like a dangerous magnetic field. When he got up to pour me a cup of coffee, my own increased. When was the last time *wonderful* Dr Cross had waited on me? In the early years, before Jamie was born perhaps? On our honeymoon? When we were dating? When exactly had the romantic veneer begun to peel away, slowly exposing the void that was at the heart of our marriage? I couldn't remember the last time Gavin and I had been happy, or even really relaxed together.

'Feeling better?' he asked as he placed the coffee before me. He attempted a smile. But somehow his words sounded less like a question than a command. A warning.

I nodded, then took a sip of my coffee. It was sickeningly sweet. Even this small preference Gavin couldn't get right. How much did he know about me after all these years? Or I about him? I pulled my robe closer as if to ward off a chill. When he excused himself and headed for his study, I dumped the sugary coffee, then poured myself another cup. I was hoping for a half hour of self-forgetfulness as I lost myself in the Sunday *Globe* before Jamie came home, and I was forced to confront him with what I knew. But as I was settling myself at the table, Gavin again appeared in the doorway. I was so surprised I nearly upset my fresh cup of coffee.

'I've been thinking about our problem,' he said to my amazement. But before I could ask him if he had any idea how to help Jamie, he continued, 'It's your job, Jeanne. Between working full-time at the school, and taking care of everything here, you're exhausted.'

'But I . . . I like my job,' I said, fingering one of the pills in my bathrobe pocket between my thumb and forefinger. 'And if I didn't work, what would I do all day?'

At that, the veneer once again cracked, and Gavin answered impatiently, 'If you're that bored, why don't you go back to school, get yourself a degree?'

I felt myself redden. Gavin knew how self-conscious and inadequate I felt around his friends, particularly the other doctors' wives. Most of them had attended prestigious colleges, and if they worked, they had impressive careers. As for me, I clung to the job I had taken to help out in the early years when Gavin was building his practice and we were still struggling with student loans. I no longer needed to work, but I liked the structure it gave my day, liked the respect and appreciation of the teachers at school, and most of all, I liked having my own income. The thought of asking Gavin for cash whenever I wanted to buy a new lipstick or a special treat for Jamie made me wince.

'Maybe when Jamie graduates, I'll think about taking a course or two,' I muttered, not saying what I really thought: that I had never been a great student no matter how hard I tried. Now that I'd been out of school for so long, I doubted I could even pass a college course.

'That sounds reasonable,' Gavin said. He emptied his cold coffee and poured himself a fresh cup. Once again, he was trying to appear amiable. 'And in the meantime, you could bone up on your reading a little. Prepare yourself. Once you quit your job, you'll have time for things like that.'

'Who said anything about quitting my job?' I said, surprised by the panic that leaked into my voice. 'It may not be big or important like what you do, but I like the contact with the kids; I like being able to see Jamie during the day; and I — I enjoy the work I do. I'm the one who really makes that school run efficiently. It may not seem like much to you, but I take pride in that.' I had never articulated how I felt about my work before, had never even thought about it, but now that the words were out, I was flushed with their truth.

But Gavin only scoffed. 'Please, Jeanne. You're a *secretary*, not the superintendent of schools. I'm sure Bridgeway High School will run just fine without you. And quite frankly, it's an embarrassment to me.'

110

'An *embarrassment?*' I repeated, feeling as though I'd been physically hit.

'Yes, how many doctors' wives do you see in dead-end, sub-servient jobs? People must wonder what secret vice is sucking up all our income. Really, Jeanne, let's look at this thing rationally. I'm offering to liberate you. Don't be a fool.'

Once again, I heard a hint of warning in his voice. Gavin was not suggesting I quit my job this time; he was *ordering* it. When he stood up, indicating the conversation was over, I felt menace in his bearing. I rubbed my wrist unconsciously, remembering the way he had squeezed it the night before when I brought up my concerns about Jamie. It was still sore.

Though everything in me cried out against the 'liberation' he was offering, I soon heard myself tentatively bargaining for time. 'Well, I couldn't just leave them flat in the middle of the year.'

'I'm not suggesting you leave without giving two weeks' notice. Really, Jeanne, how difficult do you think it will be to find another secretary?' Gavin said, once again flashing his cold, victorious smile. I reached stealthily into my bathrobe pocket for my little blue pill, and as soon as he turned his back, I popped it in my mouth. My personal ticket to oblivion.

An hour later while I sat at the table nursing my coffee and trying to focus on the newspaper as the tranquilizer took effect, Gavin suddenly appeared in the doorway, dressed and ready for church. Though I never missed church, he didn't seem at all surprised to find me still in my robe.

'Jamie's in the car waiting for me,' he said. 'If

anyone asks, I'll say you were a bit under the weather this morning.' Apparently, my son had slipped in the front door — perhaps hoping to avoid the confrontation I was planning.

Gavin was nearly out the door when he turned around casually, and said, 'Oh, yes, one more thing, Jeanne. Do you really think it's wise for you to continue to drive that music teacher to school?'

That music teacher. Already he had stripped Ali of her name, her identity. 'Why not?' I asked, feeling my speech slow, the effect of the medication already apparent. 'She's on my way. And besides, I enjoy the company.'

Gavin drew himself in closer, a familiar scowl tightening his face. 'I'm sure you do enjoy your little gossip sessions, Jeanne. But this isn't about you. This is about our son. I thought we agreed last night that the woman is a bad influence on Jamie.'

I tried to replay the conversation we'd had in my mind, but despite the chemically induced fuzziness I was experiencing, I was sure we had agreed on nothing of the kind. And though I had no intention of giving up my friendship with Ali, I continued to smile and nod. 'Don't worry. Now that the weather's getting warmer, Ali's going to be taking her bike again anyway.'

That Sunday, I spent most of the day sleeping, or lying on my bed, trying to follow the plots of various TV movies. When Ali called sometime late in the afternoon, I crept to the top of the stairs and listened as my husband lied into the receiver. This time when Gavin talked to Ali, his

112

voice was stripped of the flirtatiousness that I'd witnessed the night before. Instead, I heard the same tone of menace and implied threat that had so easily subdued me earlier. Fortunately, Ali didn't scare so easily. From the stairs, I listened to their terse conversation, imagining what Ali was saying on the other end of the line. When she obviously expressed concern about my fainting episode, Gavin quickly sloughed it off, reassuring her that I occasionally had such 'spells,' but that I quickly recovered. In fact, he told her that right now I was at the mall shopping.

It was there on the stairs listening to his cold, dismissing comments that I realized for the first time exactly why Gavin had insisted I quit my job. It wasn't concern for me, as he'd said, or even 'embarrassment' over my position. It was *Ali*. If Gavin could get me away from the school, he thought he could abort the growing friendship that was a threat to our entire way of life. Briefly, I felt a surge of rebellion course through my blood. No matter what I'd promised Gavin, I wouldn't give up my job. But by the time Gavin had replaced the receiver in its cradle, I was again overcome by fatigue, passionate about nothing but my desire for sleep.

However, when I jumped out of bed at the command of the alarm clock the next morning, I was strangely revved up and angry — though at whom, I wasn't quite certain. Was the anger directed at Gavin? At Jamie's friends? Or just at myself and the life I could no longer pretend was perfect? Whatever it was, I moved around the house making beds, fixing lunches, toasting bagels, and wiping up the crumbs with more than my usual efficiency.

Even Jamie, who seemed increasingly lost in his adolescent preoccupations, looked up from his breakfast. 'Is everything okay, Mom? You're zipping around this place like you're wired or something.'

Well, that did it. I threw the rag I was using to wipe down the counter into the sink, and turned to my son. 'No, actually everything's *not* okay. And you know it.' I sunk down into the chair opposite him.

My son continued to regard me with the same innocent gaze he always had. 'What's up, Mom? But you better make it kind of quick. Brad's brother's picking me up for school in eight and a half minutes. More or less.' After consulting his watch, he smiled up at me sheepishly. 'Did I do anything wrong?'

I stared at him a hard minute before I got up and began emptying dishes from the dishwasher at a furious pace, again feeling the tightness in my neck. 'Did I say you did something wrong?' I asked, my voice sounding clipped and strange. 'No, it's those friends of yours. Jamie, sometimes I don't trust those kids. There's something about that Toby, for instance — '

Jamie chuckled. 'Toby? The kid likes to goof around a little, Mom, but it's not like he gets into any major trouble or anything.'

'I know that,' I said, leaving the dishwasher still half full, as I went back to the table where I sat across from my son. 'But sometimes I worry.

114

Peer pressure can be almost overwhelming at your age. If Toby or Brad or any of those kids asked you to do something you knew was wrong, would you do it?'

'What do you mean — like drugs?' Jamie's eyes were dark. Sometimes when I looked at him these days, I had no idea what he was thinking.

'Not drugs necessarily,' I said, looking down at my hands, twirling my wedding ring around my finger. 'Just something that you knew was wrong. Something that could hurt — or even just scare — another person.'

By then Jamie was on his feet, gathering up his backpack. He hugged me, leaning the comforting softness of his oversize body against me for a moment. 'I'm not sure what you're talking about, Mom. But you know I'd never do anything to hurt anyone else. No matter who told me to.' He smiled disarmingly. 'You believe me, don't you?'

Unaccountably, my face felt damp. 'I know what you did to Mrs Mather's sheet music,' I blurted out. 'Didn't you think I'd recognize your handwriting?'

The red flush that rinsed Jamie's cheeks and neck made denial impossible. He was so transparent, I thought. How would he ever handle the police?

'I guess I had a little crush on her or something,' he muttered. 'But I'm not the only one; a lot of the kids think Mrs Mather's hot.'

'A *little crush*? So you pour blood — or something that looks like it — on her music? And you change her title to *Death Sweet*?'

115

'It was a joke, Mom,' Jamie said. 'I retitled it like it was a metal song. Death Sweet, get it? And you know the band Slayer? Well, the last part was a play on their name. You know, slay-her? What — you actually think I meant it like a threat?'

'Well, no — I mean, of course not. But someone else, someone who didn't know you . . . God, Jamie, didn't you think how it might sound?' I began, before I was interrupted by pounding at the door, and the boisterous cries of Jamie's friends.

'Hey, Cross, you ready?'

Once again, Jamie hoisted his backpack onto his shoulder. 'You're right, I shouldn't have done it. But it was just a dumb joke, Mom,' he said. 'You believe me, don't you?'

And what could I say? What besides, 'Yes, I believe you.' Followed by, 'We'll talk about this more later.' But by the time I got that last part out, Jamie was already out the door and running awkwardly down the driveway.

★ ★ ★

By the time I reached Ali's house, most of my anger had been transferred to *her*. After my discussion with Jamie, I was more confused than ever. Maybe in this case Gavin was right: she *had* overreacted. While her rapt audience looked on, she had played the little drama on stage for all it was worth. Unwittingly, I had only added to her melodrama with my embarrassing collapse. Surely, she or another member of the quartet had an extra copy of her sheet music. Couldn't she just have discreetly gone on with the concert until the end, then brought it up quietly to George and me later? Did she really have to stop everything with that terrified gasp?

Apparently, my talk with Jamie had made me a little late because Ali was already standing on the sidewalk when I arrived to pick her up. She was wearing her favorite black skirt, a tight jersey, and long earrings. The sight of the dramatic outfit I usually found so attractive on my friend only added to my irritation. Did she really think clothing like that was appropriate for a teacher standing before a class full of hormone-crazed adolescents? Did she *ever* consider how her actions impacted on others?

I was desperately curious to hear whether Ali had contacted the police about the incident at the concert, but I didn't want to bring it up. Secretly, I feared that my astute friend might begin to suspect that Jamie was involved — just as I had. And worse, that my reaction to the slashed score might be read as a confirmation.

But Ali seemed more concerned about my fainting incident than she was about the threat against her. 'How are you feeling?' she asked, touching my arm gingerly, as she slid into the Jeep. 'I've been so worried about you. Did Gavin tell you I called?'

As soon as I heard the tenderness in her voice, I felt like I was going to cry. Briefly, I took my eyes from the road and glanced into my friend's face, taking in the gold flecks in her eyes, the crevice that formed between her eyebrows when she was concerned. And for one crazy moment, I

117

was tempted to tell her everything — my concerns about Jamie, and my own increasing reliance on pills to get me through my days. I seriously considered pulling off the road and spilling it all, including the dark truth that lay at the centre of my marriage: that after many years of subtle intimidation, fear had become my natural climate, the climate in which I was raising my son.

Who cared if we were late for school? Even if we never returned at all. I would tell Ali all the secrets, all the lies I had stored up for so long, and together we would figure out what to do next. For that one crazy moment — or no, it was less than a moment — I really thought that was possible. And in that fraction of time I swerved slightly from the rigid course I had chosen years ago. But just when I felt the car veering out of control, I stopped myself, realizing it was too late for the truth. Far too late. I seized the wheel harder than ever and stared straight ahead. 'Yes, of course, he told me. You called when I was at the mall,' I said, giving Ali the false smile I reserved for my nearest and dearest. Then, when she still didn't look convinced, I added, 'Really. Everything's fine.'

10

For me, a phone call at work is almost as rare as a call in the middle of the night — and just as alarming. The last time I could remember receiving such a call was when Jamie was in middle school. That day the principal phoned to let me know that my son had been in a fight and needed medical attention. He was quick to say the fight wasn't Jamie's fault. In fact, as the crowd gathered around and the smaller boy began to taunt and jab at my overgrown son, Jamie had tried to defuse the situation by cracking jokes. In return for his peacemaking efforts, he'd ended up with a fat lip and three stitches on his chin.

This time when the phone rang, I was in the ladies' room, and the principal, Simon Murphy, had taken the call. His sharp rap on the door of the ladies' room, telling me that I had a phone call, only added to my sense of unease.

'Jeanne Cross speaking,' I said into the receiver in my most formal voice. I willed the caller to be someone impersonal, a dentist calling to remind me of a forgotten appointment, or perhaps Gavin calling to let me know he would be late for dinner. But the truth is, I never forget appointments, and if Gavin were going to be late, he would have left a message on the answering machine at home, apparently preferring the blankness of the machine to my voice.

'Jeanne,' said the caller. Just that. He spoke as if my name were so significant it deserved a sentence of its own. And then obviously attuned to the hint of panic in my voice, he quickly added, 'I shouldn't have called you at work. I'm sorry; it was a rather spontaneous idea.' The voice suggested warm butterscotch. It was at once utterly familiar, and yet not connected to any ready name.

'George Mather here.' Again there was a pause, and then he asked in that startlingly genuine way he had at the concert. 'How are you? Have you recovered from Saturday night?'

At once, I felt disoriented, remembering the last time I had seen George, feeling the reassuring warmth of his hand supporting my elbow the night of the concert. 'Yes, of course. I'm fine. Are you looking for Ali?'

'No, actually, I just wanted to make sure you were all right. You went down pretty hard, and to tell you the truth, I felt rather guilty. If I had only seen it coming, I might have broken your fall.'

Remembering the uncomfortable moment when I had seen the defaced sheet music — and Jamie's handwriting at the bottom — I once again felt hot blood suffusing my face. On the other side of the office, Simon Murphy watched me curiously. Obviously, the strange male voice asking for me, and my flushed cheeks intrigued him.

I turned away and spoke into the phone. 'As I said, I'm fine. Really. A little embarrassed, but beyond that, no lasting scars.'

'That's good,' George said, a trifle more

briskly, as if perhaps someone had entered his office. Or perhaps as if he were simply getting to the real point of his call. 'Actually, I was wondering if you were free for lunch. There's a little Italian place not far from the school, where Ali and I sometimes go. What's it called — Giovanna's?'

When I hesitated, George pressed. 'You do get a lunch hour, don't you?'

'It's only forty-five minutes. Not really enough time to leave the school,' I said, though I could easily have stretched it to an hour. The truth was that the idea of having lunch at Giovanna's sounded wonderful — but something in George's voice made me uncomfortable. Something I can only describe as lawyerly.

'They're very quick at Giovanna's; I promise I'll get you back on time,' he said confidently. 'Is twelve good?'

Again I hesitated.

'There's something I need to talk to you about, Jeanne,' George said, taking advantage of my awkward silence. 'I wouldn't call if it weren't important.' I pictured him in a somewhat cluttered office at the college, a cup of cold coffee in front of him. He would be consulting his watch, figuring out how much work he could get done before it was time to meet me. Obviously, it had not occurred to him that I might turn him down.

From the other side of the office, Simon glanced up every now and then, unable to restrain his curiosity, and I have to admit I somewhat enjoyed the mystery I was creating.

121

'I'll see you at twelve, then,' I said. But as soon as I hung up, I noticed my hands were trembling slightly. I promptly stuffed them in my pockets, chastising myself for my nervousness. It was George Mather, for goodness' sake. What did I have to fear from such an obviously kind man?

When I arrived at Giovanna's, there was no sign of George. Only after I entered the dimly lit restaurant did I see him heading toward me, looking like an overanxious date. Nervously, he ran his hand through the licorice black hair that was banded with thick streaks of gray. For one crazy moment, I was tempted to run out of the restaurant without explanation. What was I doing there anyway, furtively meeting my best friend's husband?

But as soon as I was close enough to look into his eyes, I was instantly reassured. They were large eyes, and so dark that at first you thought they were brown. Only on closer inspection did you see that they were a deep midnight blue. And though they were ringed with droopy lids and circles as dark as coal smudges, they were the kindest eyes I'd ever seen. As he had the night of the concert, George took me gently by the elbow. 'I'm so glad you could come,' he said. Despite his confident tone on the phone, he sounded like he doubted I would actually show.

'They have a wonderful antipasto here. When Ali and I come for lunch, we usually split one.' George smiled at the mention of his estranged wife's name. I couldn't figure out whether he was the world's most patient husband — or simply the biggest fool.

As soon as the waitress approached the table, George ordered a half carafe of merlot. And when I protested that I never drank at lunch, he filled my glass anyway. 'In my country, even children drink a little wine with their meal.' He smiled disarmingly as he raised his glass in a toast. 'To friendship,' he said.

And of course, I couldn't say no to that. As I lifted my glass, I felt I had entered the old world of George's Lebanese childhood, a world I found surprisingly warm and comforting.

At first, our talk was neutral and easy the way it had been the night of the concert. George told me about a law case he was helping his former partner with. A teenage boy had broken into a house in a nearby town, intending to burglarize an elderly woman. But when the woman had awoke and caught him in her jewelry case, the crime had turned more deadly. The boy had beaten her severely, breaking several fragile bones, and leaving her face dramatically bruised. As George described the incident, I could almost see the frail old woman being led from her house by the niece who found her. She was hiding her face as if she were the one who should be ashamed.

'How can you help defend someone like that?' I asked, surprised by the outrage in my voice. 'Try to get him out of it by any trick in the book — isn't that what you lawyers do? People like that boy, they — they deserve to be punished,' I fumed.

George took a leisurely sip of his wine, regarding me with those mysterious eyes of his.

Realizing I had gone too far, revealing the rage just beneath my polished surface, I put my wine down and dropped my hands primly in my lap. 'I'm sorry. I — I just get so angry when I hear things like that.'

George smiled. 'A perfectly normal reaction. In fact, I felt the same way when I first read about the case. However, when you see beyond the skeletal report you get in the papers or the one I just gave you, you realize things are a lot more complicated.'

The waitress appeared with our antipasto, and I wondered if George was thinking about Ali as he ordered the meal they usually shared. Though I had fleetingly worried that this invitation to lunch might indicate a romantic interest, I now saw clearly that for George Mather everything — including our lunch — recalled his obsession with his wife.

'Complicated? What do you mean?' I was just waiting for him to make an excuse for the boy so I could vent a little more of my unexpected rage.

'There are people whose whole life is a punishment. Kids who literally don't know the difference between right and wrong, people who 'know not what they do,' to quote the Master.' George speared a marinated mushroom and watched for my reaction.

'And you really think that's an excuse for the kind of crime that was committed against that poor old woman?' I said. I was already beginning to feel the wine I had sipped.

As George shrugged, I noticed his suit was baggy and ill-fitting. I wondered if he had lost weight recently, and quickly concluded that he had. Probably from all the trials of his relationship with Ali.

'No, not an excuse. Just the truth,' he replied. 'The complicated truth we try our best to simplify every day.' He dipped a piece of coarse bread into a fragrant white bean and garlic puree. 'This is excellent,' he said. 'Try some.'

My mouth was full of the chewy bread when he went back to our former topic. 'But, then, you know more than I do about adolescence. Didn't Ali mention you have a teenage son?'

I chewed my bread slowly, feeling the colour rising in my cheeks as I sensed George watching me intently. Too intently. 'A *normal* teenage son,' I said emphatically when I was able to speak. 'Living with Jamie hardly qualifies me to understand the kind of monster you described.'

Again George shrugged. 'Some people would say the term *normal teenager* is an oxymoron. Adolescence itself is an aberrational time.' He smiled, lifting the carafe of wine. 'A little more?'

I shook my head and held my hand over my glass to make sure he didn't pour any more. I was torn between the feeling that I should energetically defend my son from George's harsh generalizations, and an almost desperate desire to change the subject.

'As I said, you know far more about the subject than I do. What do you think?' George smiled with his lips, but his eyes, darkly hooded, remained fixed on mine.

'Frankly, I find it insulting to lump a normal teenager like Jamie — and yes, there is such a thing — into the same category as the boy you're helping to defend.' Without realizing it, I had raised my voice; two women at the nearest table turned to stare.

George, however, seemed so fascinated by my reaction that he didn't notice the embarrassing attention I had aroused. He sipped his wine quietly for a moment before he spoke. 'Is that what you think I was doing, Jeanne? Comparing your son to a disturbed young man? If so, I apologize for the misunderstanding. I'm afraid I was simply groping rather awkwardly at conversation. It's not often I find myself at lunch with an attractive woman other than my wife.'

Once again, I blushed, as if all this talk about adolescence had affected both of us more than we cared to admit. And when George signalled the waitress to order coffee, I quickly stopped him, having no desire to prolong the lunch. Obviously, my coming was a mistake. Contrary to George's promise, the service had been slow, and I was already five minutes late getting back. I only hoped that a few after-dinner mints would cover the wine on my breath, and that Simon wouldn't notice I was slightly tipsy. And then, there was Ali. Undoubtedly she had observed I wasn't around at lunchtime. What was I going to say to her on my ride home? Should I betray my implicit promise to George that I would keep our meeting a secret? Then, of course, I would have to explain why George had called me in the first place — and why I had accepted. Quite frankly, I didn't know the answer to either question. No, undoubtedly I would do what I did well and often. I would lie. Or not exactly lie. I would simply not tell.

Nearly upsetting my water glass, I clambered to my feet abruptly. 'I don't mean to rush out, but I really do need to get back to work.'

Graciously, George rose. 'I'm sorry I've kept you. There I was babbling on about my volunteer work while you listened politely. We egotistical men are all alike. Isn't that what you and Ali say in those long talks you have on Friday afternoons?' He signalled the waitress for the check, making a scribbling gesture in the air.

'There's no need for you to leave. You haven't even finished,' I said, avoiding his covert question about what Ali and I discussed. 'But thank you. The lunch was wonderful.'

Standing, his shoulders stooped in the light that fell through the cut glass windows in neat octagons, George looked like the defeated cuckold that he was. Obviously all this talk about abnormal adolescent psychology, which had made me feel so uncomfortable, was exactly what he'd said it was — nothing more than a man rambling on about his work. The mention of my son had been natural. Perhaps I had even imagined the probing look I thought I saw in George's eyes.

Of course, he insisted on walking me to my car. Hands jammed in his pocket, looking down at the freshly blacktopped lot, he fell oddly silent. Perhaps he was thinking about Ali and feeling disappointed he hadn't been able to steer the conversation to the subject of his wife. Like Brian Shagaury, he had probably invited me to lunch in the hopes of learning more about the secret life of the woman he loved. But in the end, George had been too much of a gentleman for the task. Now, walking through the parking lot, he seemed disappointed.

As I climbed into my car, he squeezed my hand, and once again, I felt the electric warmth that had so moved me at the concert. 'Thank you for coming, Jeanne,' he said with that rare sincerity of his. 'And I hope I haven't made you too late.' As he leaned forward to kiss my cheek, I noticed that beneath his white shirt, he was wearing a T-shirt bearing the logo of the Boston Red Sox, a detail that once again excited my sympathy. Was this obviously inappropriate choice for a professional man a sign of aging befuddlement? Or was it merely another tragic sign of a man who had been neglected and abandoned by his wife? In either case, I felt a rush of pity for George as he pressed his lips to my cheek.

I had already started the ignition, and George was walking toward his car, when he abruptly turned back, signalling me to wait. When he approached my car window, he seemed slightly out of breath, as if traversing even the short distance tired him. 'I was so busy talking about myself that I almost forgot the real reason I invited you to lunch.'

'The real reason?' I said, thrown by this belated admission that there had been an ulterior motive after all.

'Yes,' George said in the firm voice that had frightened me earlier. 'The other night at the concert just before you fainted, I caught a glimpse of your face, Jeanne. I don't think I've ever seen such sheer horror.'

I laughed nervously. 'My husband says I overreacted. It was probably nothing more than a prank.' I revved the engine of the car, reminding him that I had neither the time nor the inclination to discuss the night of the concert.

But George was leaning on my car by then, pinning me to the spot with his eyes. 'A student prank? I think we both know it was more than that, Jeanne.'

Instinctively, I put on my sunglasses, shielding my eyes from George's stare. 'Well, whatever it was, I don't suppose we'll ever find out who did it,' I said.

Standing up straight, releasing my car, George shook his head. 'Oh, I don't know about that. Frankly, Jeanne, this whole situation — the break-ins at Ali's house, the incident with her music — I think it's more serious than we first thought. The way you reacted, I thought you knew that, too.'

There were a lot of things I would later chide myself for not saying at that moment. First of all, I should have denied the implication that I knew anything about the matter. And certainly, I should have expressed my doubts that the incident with the sheet music had anything to do with the menacing occurrences at Ali's house. But not trusting the steadiness of my voice or the clearness of my eyes under George's unassailable gaze, I had merely gotten away as quickly as I could.

By the time I left the parking lot, I realized that nothing George had said at lunch was random or merely conversational, as he'd claimed. The talk about the troubled teenager he was helping to defend, his sly questions about Jamie — all of it had been planned. Even his last-minute question in the parking lot had been calculated to catch me off guard. As my hands clutched the wheel, I could feel the intensity of George's eyes fixed on my retreating car.

11

How long had it been since I'd been alone for any length of time? Really alone, alone in a silent house, with no one to shield me from the lies I told myself day after day? It must have been years. Though Gavin's absences had grown increasingly frequent, he always made sure I was never left idle long enough to ponder my life. Still, it seemed that he attended every orthopedic conference in the country. And when I questioned him about it, his voice had taken on the mildly threatening tone I knew so well. *Didn't I know that there were constant advances in the field, that he needed to keep up? Though he was only forty-six, he was in danger of becoming a dinosaur in the work to which he had dedicated his life. Did I know what it was like to compete with a growing army of bright-eyed young graduates, to constantly feel you could be replaced?*

Whenever he started his familiar diatribe, I quickly relented. Now I never questioned him when he said that an important conference was being held in Dallas. Or Cleveland. Or Cornfield, Iowa. Instead, I dutifully packed his clothes, dutifully took down the number of the hotel where he would be staying, in case of an emergency. Dutifully stood in the door and watched him leave, my hand poised in the same false cheery wave. Only when his car turned the

131

corner did I breathe deeply, basking in the freedom that Gavin's absence allowed me and Jamie.

But this particular weekend was different. For the first time since my son was born, Jamie and Gavin would be away at the same time. Since I knew Jamie had been planning the camping trip with Toby and his family for months, I tried hard to mask my dismay at the prospect of a long weekend in an empty house with nothing but my own thoughts. But when he found out his father had a conference scheduled, Jamie had quickly read the panic in my eyes. Obviously, he understood the fear of being alone with oneself.

'Don't worry, Mom. I'll stay home with you. I really don't like camping that much,' he quickly volunteered. Only his eyes revealed the disappointment that lay beneath his smiling surface. 'Besides, Toby says if it's warm enough they're going to go swimming in the lake. And you know how I hate swimming.'

Yes, I knew how he felt about swimming — and why. Though Jamie wouldn't admit it, he was terrified of taking off his shirt before another human being, terrified of revealing the freckled chest and back, the sprawling vulnerability of his midsection, which he tried his best to hide behind trendy loose clothing. Of course, Jamie never admitted his fears outright. Instead, he played the clown to his friends, and even to me; he joked that he couldn't swim, that he would sink like a great white whale if he tried, that one dive and he would empty the pool or the lake. It broke my heart to hear him laugh along with the other boys as he mocked himself, never revealing the truth: that he feared the sight of his own body the way I feared being alone in my own house.

Though in many ways I was tempted to let my son sacrifice his plans so that I wouldn't have to face the rhythmic truth of my own heart beating in these empty rooms, I knew how much the camping trip meant to him.

'No, you go, Jamie,' I said, remembering my promise. 'I mean it. I'll be fine. It'll give me a chance to catch up on my spring cleaning.'

But even when he was leaving, the entire Breen family waiting in the driveway, my son had hesitated. Putting down his heavy pack, he stooped to hug me, communicating our special understanding in the warmth that passed between us. 'I could still stay home, you know,' he said, his eyes brimming with sweetness. 'I could run out and tell Toby I'm coming down with something and I'll probably puke all over their new van; that would do it.'

And once again, for just an instant, I thought of taking him up on it. All the special conspiratorial weekends the two of us shared when Gavin was away came back to me, the fast-food meals we ate in front of rented videos, or just the way our easy laughter intertwined and flowed through the house in a way it never did when Gavin was home.

But putting those pleasurable memories out of my mind, I pushed my son gently toward the door. 'Get out there. They're waiting for you,' I said, smiling in a way that might have fooled anyone but my son. Or perhaps Ali, who had in only a few months of friendship learned to read me in a way that no one else had before. A way that sometimes frightened me. There was so much I didn't allow myself to think about, so much I buried in feverish flurries of redecorating, organizing — even baking, though I knew that the homemade eclairs I slaved over were the last things Jamie needed. I was afraid to think about what would happen if one day I just stopped.

Feeling slightly lost in my own rooms, I immediately thought of my friend. Despite an attentive husband and lover, Ali was alone much of the time. But unlike me, she loved solitude. 'In solitude, I find music,' she said, speaking in the mysterious language of the creative.

Thinking of those words, I poured myself a glass of wine and turned on the stereo. But before I had a chance to select a CD, I was startled by a blast of the last one that someone had been playing. It took me a moment before I realized it was a recording of Ali's quartet. As the restrained passion of the music rinsed over me, I recognized the *Paradise Suite*. She had played the piece for me at various stages of its composition, but I had never heard it in its final form. Nor did I know that the quartet had made a disc of it.

Feeling curiously betrayed, I got up and went to the stereo, turned off the music, and popped out the disc, which I studied as if I expected it to speak. But of course, the innocuous plastic case revealed nothing I didn't already know. The

134

label, which had been written in my friend's bold hand, simply listed the title of the work. Then, in smaller handwriting, she had proudly added 'by Ali Mather.' Looking at it, I felt a hint of the thrill and satisfaction she must have taken in its completion. I went back and reinserted it, then sat on the couch, waiting for the aching sound of Ali's violin to rinse over me.

As the music began to fill the room, to fill my mind and swell my heart, I wondered how this mysterious melody had gotten into the house. And why. Had Ali been here without my knowledge and left it in the CD player for me, thinking that she would surprise me? Somehow I couldn't imagine my friend prowling through the house without telling me — particularly after the strange incidents that had occurred in her own house. Was it possible that Ali had given it to Gavin?

Or most troubling of all, did this disc prove that Jamie truly was the one who'd been sneaking into her house all along — that he'd been there this very day? Had he, after stealing the disc, sat on this very couch listening to it furtively earlier that afternoon while I was innocently cruising the aisles of the grocery store? And if so, *why?* Was he fantasizing about the woman who had written it, the woman whose bow drew such a brilliant spectrum of emotion from her violin? Did he feel he had captured another piece of her soul when he took possession of her music?

'No, of course not,' I said vehemently in the eerily empty house. 'Jamie's not like that. He's a normal teenager. Not above a prank or two, of course. But certainly not capable of anything really sinister.' As I spoke, I pictured George Mather's eyes watching me. Sceptical eyes. Probing eyes.

Standing up abruptly, I upset my glass of wine, causing it to spill on the Persian carpet. But instead of rushing to act, as I would usually have done, I stood immobilized as the plum-coloured stain spread outward on my rug, forming a ragged heart shape. And then, as if I read something terrifying in the shape of that stain, in the sound of that remembered music on the stereo, I grabbed my jacket and purse from the hook near the door and ran out of the house, not even bothering to turn off the lights or to lock the door behind me.

When I looked back from the road, every room of the house was ablaze with light — as if my fear of being alone had been made visible for all to see. Of course, if anyone had asked me what I was running from, I couldn't have named it. A spilled glass of wine? Some violin music on the stereo? A house with too many lights on? But whatever it was, I sped away as if I were escaping with my life.

* * *

The only way I could muster up the courage to walk into Hannibal's, a trendy bar in the area of town where graduate students and the art crowd hung out, was to pretend I was Ali. Wearing a short leather jacket, jeans, and high-heeled

136

boots, I straightened my shoulders, flounced the hair that had grown almost to my shoulders, and sashayed inside. Looking toward the bar, I saw a blond man with wide shoulders who resembled Jack Butterfield from the back; knowing that he and Ali often came here together, I strode up and took the stool next to him. However, when he turned curiously in my direction, his face sported a thick mustache, and none of Jack Butterfield's roguish charm. But feeling reckless, I smiled at him anyway.

'What you drinking?' the man asked, sounding as if he were caught off guard by his good luck.

'Red wine,' I said. Then thinking of the spilled glass at home, the heart-shaped stain on my carpet, I quickly changed my mind. 'No, make it a margarita.' Though I never drank mixed drinks, Ali had ordered that when we stopped for a drink one Friday after school.

As the stranger paid for my drink, I guiltily twirled my wedding band around my finger. He stared at me vapidly, and nodded his head several times in a row, as if he were answering a question he had heard only in his head. 'So, what's up tonight?' he asked, staring conspicuously at the wedding band I fingered.

'Oh, not much. The usual,' I said, wondering if he had any idea how ironic those words were. As if anything could be less usual for me than being out alone in a bar, or accepting a drink from a stranger.

For an instant, I thought of repaying him and running out of there without taking a sip from the salt-rimmed glass. But then I thought of my house, a house with every window lit even though no one was home, and in the centre of it, the stereo where Ali's music was probably still playing. Clearly, I saw the dark stain on the rug that nothing would get out now. Eager to get that image out of my mind, I turned and smiled at the stranger. I remembered how Ali had spoken of her seduction of Brian Shagaury. She'd done it, she said, 'simply to see what it would be like.'

Fleetingly, I thought of how the night might progress, how I could make small talk with this bland but seemingly inoffensive stranger, and then perhaps follow him home to the small apartment or condo where he probably lived. But when I looked into his empty eyes, I remembered the warmth I had peered into just hours ago — Jamie's eyes; I remembered the sweetness I'd seen in them, and the comfort of his body leaning into mine just before he left.

'Actually, I just stopped in for a bite to eat,' I said, rising abruptly as I had done at home when I spilled my wine. 'Thank you for the drink, though.' The stranger, looking disappointed but not surprised, merely nodded.

Then taking my glass in my hand, I walked to a small table where I asked the waitress if I might see a menu. From the bar, the mustached man turned to watch me, as if wondering if he should join me. But this time, feeling as if I were an actress in a play without a script, I averted my eyes. When the waitress came, I ordered a Caesar salad. And another margarita.

I didn't look toward the bar again until my second drink was empty, and by then the stool where the stranger with the mustache had sat was empty, too. I felt grateful and sad at the same time. Grateful that I had avoided some tawdry experience I would surely regret later. And sad that there was no escaping my life after all. No escaping the empty eight-room colonial with a light burning in every window. The only room that remained in darkness was Gavin's study, the locked room he had implicitly forbidden Jamie and me to enter. The drinks I downed too quickly had already made me dizzy, but I fortified myself with a third before I had the courage to go home. The courage to do what I knew I had to do.

*   *   *

Walking through the first floor of my house, I turned the lights out one by one. Then I made my way through the hallway and up the staircase, generating darkness everywhere I went. I turned off the lights in the hallway, in the guest room, in the upstairs bathroom, in the room that Gavin and I shared meaninglessly. Until finally, the only room that remained lit was Jamie's room. Heading down the darkened hallway to my son's messy room, I steeled myself the way I had done when I entered the unfamiliar bar earlier. And when I reached the doorway, I thought of turning around, of retreating to the novel beside my bed, and if that didn't work, to the sleeping pills Gavin kept in the medicine chest, defense against the nocturnal demons he shared with no one. Though they hadn't been prescribed to me,

Gavin didn't seem to mind when I helped myself.

But this was not a night for hesitation. I pushed through the door and began pulling out Jamie's drawers one by one, riffling through the neat piles of socks and underwear, T-shirts with various sports logos and wiseass slogans, the oversize jeans he wore to hide his bulk. What exactly I was looking for I couldn't have said. *Nothing.* I suppose I was looking for confirmation that what I told George was true: my son was a perfectly normal teenager. I was hoping to find nothing that would prove otherwise. Except for the candy wrappers that proliferated everywhere, I was feeling increasingly reassured — exhilarated even — as I plundered every corner of the room: the desk where he kept his old homework sheets, the shelves littered with his baseball cards, comic books, alternative CDs, and soda cans.

Sifting through the litter under the bed and hidden in the closet, I felt beads of sweat beginning to accumulate on my forehead. 'See, there's nothing here,' I said, speaking aloud, not so much to myself as to George. Ali's nosy, prying husband, the man I could feel standing behind me. 'Nothing you wouldn't find in any teenager's room.'

I stood in the centre of the room with my hands on my hips, feeling satisfied that I had vindicated my son from an accusation that had been made only in my own mind. In fact, my hand was on the light switch, and I was ready to retreat to my usual nighttime rituals, a hot bath and a novel, when a shoe box that had been wedged behind the bookcase caught my eye. Probably loaded with more forbidden candy wrappers and chip bags, I told myself. Or perhaps it even contained an old pair of sneakers that had been jammed in there when he purchased his new ones. I flicked off the light and started down the hallway to the bathroom, where I began to fill my tub, adding a new lavender-scented bubble bath I'd bought at the mall a few days earlier.

However, some nagging question made me return to the room, the need to be sure I hadn't missed anything. Moving hurriedly, I once again flooded the messy room with light, reminding myself I would have to rearrange the drawers the next day so my son wouldn't know I had been going through his things.

The shoe box was wedged tightly in its spot, and I had to tug hard to get it out. Still expecting to find nothing unusual, I flipped off the cover and was immediately assaulted by the sight of the newspaper clipping on top. Ali's face smiled back at me. LOCAL MUSICIAN TO PLAY IN EMERGING ARTISTS SERIES, the familiar caption read. Of course, I had clipped the same news article only a week earlier. There was nothing so unusual about Jamie wanting to save a piece about a teacher from school, was there? But even as I sunk down onto the bed to examine the contents of the box more clearly, I felt something collapsing inside myself. The weight of our family's collective lies pressing in on me.

In a kind of trance, I pulled each item from

the box: small things I recognized as Ali's which Jamie had apparently filched from her house: the tortoiseshell clips she used to hold back her heavy hair, a pair of dolphin earrings, one of the trademark turquoise pens she always used to grade her papers. And there were papers, too. Pieces of sheet music and grocery lists, notes reminding herself of things she needed to do, and even an unfinished letter to Jack, which had been marked with red liquid and gouged childishly with a small knife in exactly the same way the score for the *Paradise Suite* had been defaced.

As the water from the tub ran over, spilling onto the bathroom floor and into the hallway, and the smell of lavender filled the house, I sat on the bed, fingering this evidence of my son's obsession. My first instinct was shock, but that quickly evolved into a need to protect Jamie. All I could think was that, thank God, I had found the box instead of one of Jamie's friends. I could picture their parents salaciously discussing Jamie's *problems*. The problems of the Cross family. And then, of course, they would have to go to the police. I could hear Brad's mother now. *I'm sorry, Jeanne, but it was the only responsible thing to do.* Slatternly bitch, I muttered to myself. She'd been jealous of my organized home, the themed birthday parties and group outings I had planned for years. Then I thought back on all the condemnation Ali had endured over her affair with Brian, the malicious lunchroom gossip that eddied around her. I could never endure that. Never. But what was worse was its potential effect on Jamie. It would destroy the one success Jamie did have: his popularity. I couldn't imagine who my son might become if he lost his friends; they were everything to him.

When I had finally regained enough presence of mind to turn off the bathwater and clean up my mess, I took the stuffed shoe box down to the fireplace, where I lit a fire. Then I sat there transfixed as I watched Ali's words, her music, and the small possessions that so reminded me of her, slowly turn to flame and ash.

★ ★ ★

The following day, I did something I had never done in my life. I slept till almost two in the afternoon. Aided by pills — how many times I had actually wandered into the bathroom and taken another, I'm not sure — I escaped my life for almost fourteen blissful hours. But apparently, even in sleep, I had carried my fears about my son because I awoke with Jamie's name on my lips and a feeling of panic in my chest. Only after I sat up in bed and sipped some water did I realize the phone was ringing.

I'm not sure why, but this time I realized it was no false alarm. This was *it* — the phone call I had been dreading since my brother's accident. Jumping out of bed, I reached for the phone and stumbled on the boot I had left in the middle of the floor the night before.

'Hello? Jamie?' I said into the phone, my heart hammering beneath my pyjamas, the panic in my

143

voice unmistakable. 'Is everything all right?'

I suppose if it had been a normal call — one of Jamie's evergrowing circle of friends who didn't know he was away for the weekend or one of Gavin's colleagues — they would have thought I was crazy to answer the phone like that. But as it turned out, it was not a normal call. Not a normal call at all.

At the sound of my voice, the caller took a deep breath before she spoke. 'Jeanne, I'm sorry to bother you. Obviously, you've already heard.'

Now it was my turn to hesitate. I took a seat on my bed. 'Heard what? And who *is* this?'

'It's Nora. Nora Bell,' the caller said, identifying herself with a certain impatience. But I was so disoriented and groggy that it took a moment for me to connect the name to the nosy cafeteria worker who lived across the street from Ali.

'I just thought that since you're such good friends with Ali Mather, you ought to hear it from someone you know before you catch it on the radio or something,' she babbled in an excited voice.

'Hear what?' I repeated, thinking of the image of my friend in the newspaper, which my son had defaced with his small knife. I had begun to tremble. 'Has something happened to Ali? What's this about?'

'No. Not Ali. So you *haven't* heard,' Nora said with obvious relish. 'It's her boyfriend, Jeanne. The CDT teacher. They found him in that motel last night. Like I say, I hate to be the one to tell

144

you this, but I thought maybe you could get in touch with Ali.'

I ran my hands through my hair, feeling a mixture of relief and dread. 'What are you saying, Nora? Exactly what happened to Brian?'

'That's what I'm trying to tell you,' Nora said, her voice once again bristling with impatience, and none of the compassion that might have softened the blow she was about to deliver: 'The man hanged himself, Jeanne.'

12

All I knew was that I had to get out of the house, the house where Brian's gruesome act would be forever entangled with the grim discovery I'd made in Jamie's room. I dressed quickly and climbed into the Jeep, not sure where I intended to go. I was desperate to talk to Ali, but her quartet was playing out of town that weekend, and I doubted she was home yet. But just as I was inserting the key in the ignition, I caught sight of a Snickers wrapper on the floor of the passenger seat and was flooded with nausea. I felt as if I'd eaten a dozen candy bars myself like Jamie often did. Was this the feeling he carried with him as he walked through the world, I wondered — simultaneously nauseous and ravenously hungry for more?

Suddenly claustrophobic, I fled the Jeep the way I had fled the house. But at least I had decided where I was going: I would walk to Ali's and wait for her. It was raining, but for once in my life, I had no desire to go back for an umbrella. What, after all, was I protecting? The image of Jeanne Cross, Dr Cross's wife, the perfect mother with her *elegant* home, and her *elegant* clothes, and her overeager bleached-out *elegant* smile? Jeanne Cross, who always wore heels, even for a trip to the grocery store? Again, I felt a surge of nausea.

It was nearly a mile to Ali's house, and with

every corner I turned, the rain grew fiercer. The lashing felt good, as if it were washing away every trace of the Jeanne who would never have considered anything so foolish as a walk in the rain. The Jeanne who lived a life of pretending, and who had taught her son to do the same. Taught him so well that nearly everyone in town saw Jamie as jovial and easygoing — gentle even — when beneath it all was a boy-man of hidden rages and insatiable hungers. I lifted my face to the rain and let it pummel me.

Every step I took toward Ali's house seemed to bring me closer to the son I didn't know. The son I had refused to see. I thought of all the evenings when Jamie went out after dinner, saying he was going to head over to Toby's to ask him some questions about his geometry. Toby was a stellar student, and always willing to help, so Gavin and I never protested when Jamie was out a little late. But now I wondered: was this where he came on those nights? While I pictured him bent over the kitchen table innocently working on parallelograms and trapezoids, was he entering Ali's house, rifling through her drawers, defacing her precious music? A car sped by and doused me with the water that had pooled on the street, but I just walked faster, as if it were possible to outrun my own thoughts.

The image of Brian as they found him in the motel was too horrible to contemplate, and yet my mind refused to stay away from it. But when I imagined the figure hanging from the ceiling in the depressing, impersonal room, I didn't see Brian. I saw the sad, hulking body of my son. I saw Jamie. I began to run, but each footstep on the sidewalk seemed to pound out the same word: *why?* Why had Brian allowed an affair to drive him to such a desperate act? And even more mysterious to me, why would Jamie risk arrest, risk his *future*, dammit, by breaking into Ali's house? Stalking her, for God's sake. He might have been overweight, but girls seemed to like him — and he was Dr Cross's son. Surely, he could find a girlfriend his own age. What did he want from the aging music teacher? By the time I reached her doorstep, I was out of breath, and hot tears streaked my face, mingling with the chill of rain.

The house, as I approached it, was clearly empty, but I knew that Ali always left the sunporch unlocked. Not sure what else to do, I stole around back, found a wicker armchair, sat down, and pulled my knees to my chest. I looked out into the bleak rain. I couldn't help wondering whether this was how Jamie had gained access to the house, if he had come in through the porch, and then jimmied the back door lock. The cottage was an antique building, and the door fixtures were charming but insecure. Or maybe by now, he had found a key inside and had it copied.

Once I sat down, I gave in to the trembling that resulted from a combination of cold and the chill wind of my thoughts. My clothes were so wet I could smell the sheep who'd contributed their wool to my sweater, and my jeans clung to me. I knew I should go home and get a hot shower before I got sick, but I couldn't leave. Ali had said she'd be home in the early afternoon, and it was already three. *Where could she be?*

I got up and paced, thinking of Jamie, who would soon be returning from his camping trip. I saw him plunking the gym bags stuffed with dirty clothes on the kitchen floor and calling for me in his innocent voice. *Mom, I'm back.* Later, Gavin would come home with his meticulously packed suitcases, and he would be equally mystified by my absence. *Jeanne?* he would say. *Jeanne, are you home?* Just thinking of his voice, the way he clearly enunciated every syllable, giving the words sharp corners, my trembling increased.

I don't know how long I sat there before I realized Ali was not coming home. Obviously, she'd already heard about Brian and was avoiding the place where they had spent the few impassioned hours that had meant little to her but which had showed him another life. A shadow life from which he could not escape. No, she would not come home that night. She would go somewhere she could hide from the images that crowded her mind as surely as they invaded mine. And unlike me, she had someone who would hold her and tell her it was not her fault as many times as it took to ease her guilt. Not sexy Jack Butterfield, who would only add to her grief with his own jealousy. But the man with the deep, empathetic eyes and the bearlike hands. As she always did when she was troubled, Ali would go home to her husband.

I got up and peered in the window at the warmth of her empty living room. Recently, she and George had painted the walls an apricot colour that was vibrant, or muted, depending on the lighting. It was not a shade I would have chosen, but it seemed perfect for Ali's house — as if she had captured a sunset. The cottage wasn't up to my standards of neatness, of course; and if Ali could be said to have a decorating style, it was probably shabby chic, but there was something magical about those rooms. Whether it was the cheery little breakfast nook where she took most of her meals, or the window seat laden with colourful pillows, a throw, and two or three books, every corner was an invitation to warmth, to creativity, to intimacy.

Shuddering with cold, I tried the door, suddenly desperate to get inside. It was locked, as I'd known it would be. If only I could warm up for a while, maybe slip into one of Ali's robes and fix myself a cup of tea while my wet clothes spun in the dryer, then I might gather the courage to face my life. I was certain Ali was gone for the night — and even if she did come home, surely she would understand. We were friends, weren't we? *Best friends*, as I whispered to myself when I was alone, though the term sounded too silly and childish to actually say it out loud. I looked around for something to jimmy the lock, and my gaze quickly drifted to a letter opener she had left on the wicker table — probably since the early fall. I pictured her out on the sunporch, watching the birds she attracted with her numerous feeders, and leisurely reading her mail. The peace of that moment seemed to belong to another lifetime.

The door opened easily. *Too* easily, I thought, once again feeling annoyed with Ali. She claimed to be terrified by her stalker, but never thought to replace her ancient locks. Then she left the perfect lock-jimmying tool just outside the door. I looked at the letter opener in my hand and wondered if this was what Jamie had used. Maybe he had been the one who left it behind — not Ali, as I'd first accused her in my mind. Hadn't I seen something similar in Gavin's office? Still shivering, I crept inside. I wrapped the letter opener in paper towels and buried it deep in Ali's wastebasket. *Like I was hiding a murder weapon, for goodness sake!* I said out loud, trying to reassure myself that I hadn't done anything wrong.

But now that I was inside Ali's rooms, I no longer felt so sure. What if George showed up with those prying eyes of his? The man would probably assume *I* was the one who'd been entering Ali's house illicitly. I was the sick person who found pleasure in rearranging her things, looking through her drawers, fingering her sheet music. After everything she'd been through, even Ali might misinterpret my presence. I had to get out of there, I quickly decided — and right away. I was heading toward the sunporch when I noticed the muddy footsteps my sneakers had left behind. Quickly, I unrolled some more paper towels and cleaned them up.

I was scanning the room to make sure that I'd left nothing out of place when an unwanted image of Jamie once again intruded. I imagined him standing where I stood, feeling his heart pound as I felt mine, creeping through the house, wreaking havoc with the cozy world of charm and security that Ali had created with every step he took. What had he been looking for? Impulsively, I removed my shoes, tiptoed into the living room, and opened the drawer to her desk.

The first thing I saw was the book covered in vibrant red silk. *Ali's diary*. It had been so long since I'd seen it that I had almost forgotten about it. If Ali harbored any idea that Jamie might be her stalker, this is where she would have confessed it. Before I had time to think about what I was doing, I opened the exotic-looking book and flipped through it.

It was immediately obvious that the entries were written hurriedly, impulsively, in what appeared to be fits of emotion. The penmanship hungrily slanted forward, as eager for life and insight as Ali herself was. There was an abundance of exclamation points and ellipses where her thoughts trailed off without answer. The names *George* and *Jack* peppered nearly every page. Obviously, this was the place where she worked out her tangled feelings for the two men in her life. I saw no mention of Brian Shagaury.

Assaulted by a surge of guilt, I was about to close the little book when I noticed my own name woven throughout a page scrawled in violet ink: *Jeanne, Jeanne, Jeanne*. Suddenly, my hands were trembling. My eyes blurred as I scanned what seemed to be an angry entry. Whatever it was, I refused to read it. If my closest friend had any secret grudge or hostile feelings toward me, I didn't want to know. Not now when everything else was falling apart around me. And yet, one question, all in caps, jumped out at me in spite of myself: *MY GOD, WHAT'S WRONG WITH HER?*

Did this refer to me? I thought of how she often tried to slip questions about my increasingly chilly relationship with Gavin into the conversation. Clearly, she disliked my husband as much as he disliked her. Was this what she was talking about? I was dizzy as I slammed the diary shut and replaced it in the desk drawer.

Still trembling, I passed through the French doors into the small room she regarded as her sacred space: her music room. There was a clutter of CDs and music books everywhere. And of course, her sheet music. Still not knowing what I was searching for, I riffled through dozens of pieces of sheet music before I found a new piece she was writing. Numerous cross-outs and indecipherable notes she'd written to herself in the same passionate hand I'd seen in the diary jumped out at me.

If Jamie were here, I thought, *this is what he would take*. It was the most personal thing in the house, more personal even than the diary with its violently slanted penmanship, its entries written in various coloured ink. No, this was the thing that contained more of Ali than anything else. Overwhelmed by Jamie's need to possess these little pieces of Ali, I crumpled the sheet into a ball.

Then, once again, I seemed to awaken from

my trance. At that moment, only one thing was clear: I had to get out of there. But before I did, I would need to throw that balled-up sheet music away, to bury it in the trash with the letter opener. Better for Ali to think she had misplaced it than to find it crushed on the floor, which would be a sure tip-off that someone had been here. She might even call the police and have the place fingerprinted, I thought, my mind skittering across the possibilities. What I needed to do was to calm down, think clearly. I reminded myself that the police had hardly taken her case seriously. What kind of burglar takes the trouble to break in and then takes nothing more valuable than hair combs or sheet music, for goodness' sake? Wasn't it more likely that she'd simply misplaced them?

I had just buried the innocuous sheet of paper when I heard the sound of someone coming up the walkway, and then the door opening. Trapped in the kitchen, I froze. It was Ali and she wasn't alone. Someone was helping her get her luggage and her instrument inside. The male voice sounded vaguely familiar and very young — not much older than Jamie. Probably Marcus, I quickly surmised, picturing the young college student who had recently replaced a member of the quartet who had left the area. According to Ali, the other musicians had protested that Marcus was too young, but she had argued vehemently for his talent, his passion for the music. His youthfulness was never more evident as he fumbled awkwardly for something to say to Ali at this difficult time. It was obvious that she'd

154

already heard about Brian.

'Are you sure you're going to be all right here alone?' he asked. 'I know this, uh, this thing hit you pretty hard.'

'I'll be fine,' Ali said to the boy's obvious relief. 'Really, I just need to get some rest. Maybe I'll call my friend, Jeanne.'

From the kitchen where I huddled in the creeping darkness, I was surprised that I was the one she would turn to in this crisis. Even before one of her men. However, as soon as Marcus left, she went to the phone, and it became apparent that she hadn't dialled my number.

'I know I have no right to call you, but there's no one else,' she said, crushing the brief fantasy about my importance in her life. Obviously, it was George on the other end of the line; and whatever he said, it opened the floodgates.

When she was able to speak again, she said, 'We weren't even that close — except in his mind. That's what makes me feel so guilty: even my grief is selfish. It just, you know, it brings that whole terrible incident back. Just when I think I've put it behind me, it comes back as vividly as the day it happened. How could Brian have done that to his family? *To his children?*'

For a moment, I was so engrossed in the conversation that I forgot the precariousness of my own situation. I had broken into the house! Broken in and gone through her things just like the person who had been terrifying her for months. And now I was standing there eavesdropping — just like Jamie. But as I stood there, planning my escape, I couldn't help

155

thinking how little I knew about Ali. I had no idea what the 'incident' that haunted her might be, for instance. But listening to the obvious pain in her voice, I began to get a glimmer of why she sometimes did the irrational things she did. And why George, who knew her so much better than any of us, remained so patient and forgiving in the face of her transgressions.

But this was no time to ponder Ali's life. I had to get out of the house before I lost the one friend I had in the world. When she began to sob quietly into the phone, I took advantage of her distracted state and quietly slipped out through the back porch. Then, like the criminal I had become, I crept through the adjoining backyard onto the street.

Walking home in my damp clothes, I never felt more lonely. Or more defeated. In the desolate light from the street lamps, the idea of telling Ali the truth about Jamie was revealed for what it was: dangerous and crazy. By now, Ali was not just scared; she was damn angry at the interloper who had turned her sweet little cottage into a hostile environment. Did I really think our friendship would stop her from going to the police? And even if she wanted to keep my secret, the men in her life would never allow it. No, I couldn't tell Ali, and I couldn't go to Gavin either. I was left to deal with Jamie's problem alone. For the first time, I understood how Brian must have felt steeping in his loneliness night after night in that dismal motel.

★　★　★

Jamie was in the kitchen, microwaving a frozen snack, when I came in. He jumped as I entered the room. 'Sorry, I thought it was Dad,' he explained, looking abashed. We both knew what he meant. If Gavin caught him eating the fat-laden snack, he would pull out one of his familiar lectures about diet and nutrition. Jamie pulled his meat-filled pocket from the microwave, poured himself a large glass of soda, and pulled up a stool at the island.

'Dad sent for takeout,' he said. '*Salads* from DiOrio's; I didn't even eat mine.' He rolled his eyes, hoping to pull me in. We both knew that Gavin often nagged him to eat more green vegetables, and that I always defended Jamie. 'Boys Jamie's age just don't like salad,' I'd say. 'They like burgers, tacos, pizza with extra cheese.'

Since I rarely missed dinner with the family — and never without calling — I expected my son to ask where I'd been. He at least might have noticed my wet clothes, or the hair that was plastered to my head. But when Jamie looked up from his greasy meat pocket, his fleshy face was florid with excitement. 'I guess you heard,' he said. And when I just stared at him, he added, 'About Mr Shagaury. Dad and I figured you went over to Mrs Mather's to talk about it.'

I continued to stare at him, this son I once thought I knew so well. This son who had been stalking my best friend, breaking into her house and threatening her. And who now seemed so elated over a teacher's violent death.

'Well, you did hear, didn't you, Mom? Mr

Shagaury offed himself over at — '

He had no time to get the words out before my hand was in the air. In almost sixteen years, I had never slapped Jamie. Not even when he was small and he ran into the street without looking. And I didn't hit him this time either. But we both knew I'd come closer than ever before. Immediately, the colour drained from Jamie's face. And from mine.

'We need to have a talk,' I said, slumping onto the stool opposite him.

'I'm sorry, Mom; I know you liked the guy,' he said, sounding chastened. 'I didn't mean — '

'It's not about Mr Shagaury. It's about us. It's about this family.' My voice had sunk to a whisper and yet, in some curious way, I had never spoken so loudly. I was so determined to get the words out, to say what I had been keeping inside for far too long, that I didn't even hear Gavin enter the room.

'Please, Jeanne, speak up; we're eager to hear what you have to say,' Gavin said, and his voice was as icy as the rain that had pelted me earlier. 'What exactly do you think this family needs to talk about?'

13

I kept my eyes on Jamie's face, which had run the gamut from flushed to pale to totally closed within the space of five minutes. I continued to stare at him as if Gavin hadn't entered the room. 'I just wanted you to know you can talk to me,' I said. 'Or if something was bothering you, and you didn't feel comfortable telling me about it, there are other people who could help. I could make an appointment with — '

'For God's sake, Jeanne, Jamie knows that,' Gavin interrupted, attempting lightness, but I still heard the tension in his voice. He crossed the kitchen and clapped his arm over Jamie's shoulder. 'Don't you, buddy?'

Jamie nodded self-consciously. 'Yeah. Sure,' he said, but he looked as nauseous as I had felt earlier in the day.

'And besides, it's not like there's any serious problems here,' Gavin continued. He punched Jamie playfully in the stomach while shooting me a dark glance. 'The boy might be a little too fond of his Häagen-Dazs, but aside from that, this is a pretty happy kid. Right, bud?'

Jamie attempted a smile. 'Sure. Actually, I was going to head over to Toby's. There's a geometry quiz tomorrow and — '

'No!' I blurted out a little too forcefully, but I still suspected that when he was supposedly studying geometry at Toby's, Jamie was actually stealing over to Ali's house. I pictured the darkened sunporch I had just left and wondered if Jamie was seeing the same image in his mind's eye. Imagining Ali alone in the house. As distraught as she was, she'd probably left the front door wide open.

For once, Gavin and Jamie were united as they turned toward me.

'The kid wants to study, not go out and smoke pot or hang out on street corners. What's wrong with you tonight, Jeanne?' Gavin looked me up and down, as if taking in my odd appearance, the still-damp clothes and limp hair, for the first time. He turned to Jamie. 'Be home by nine; you've got school tomorrow.'

Without even a glance in my direction, Jamie disappeared upstairs, where I heard him rustling around for his backpack. A few minutes later, the front door — an exit my son never used — slammed. I followed quickly behind.

Gavin called my name insistently as I ran out onto the driveway, but I hardly registered the sound. 'Jamie! Wait — please!' I cried after him.

Jamie stopped and lowered his backpack a little, but didn't turn around.

'This isn't the end of it, Jamie. We still have to talk.'

'Talk about *what*, Mom?' he said, spinning around. The hostility in his voice was unmistakable — and new. It was clear that Jamie felt that by my questions, particularly in front of his father, I had betrayed him. Betrayed our private alliance. But I couldn't stop now.

'About what I found in your room over the

weekend. And where you go at night when you say you're going to study.'

'I go to *Toby's*, Mom,' he said, turning away and starting up the driveway again. 'If you don't believe me, why don't you call Mrs Breen?'

'Maybe I will,' I called to his retreating form. *Maybe I will*, I repeated as I entered the house. Gavin was standing in the front hallway, which was so dark I nearly walked into him. He was standing so close to me that I could feel his breath on my face. 'What do you think you're doing?' he said, seizing my wrists. Each word contained so much suppressed anger that it seemed to explode in the air as he spoke it.

'I'm going upstairs to call Sharon Breen,' I said. 'I want to know how many times he lied when he said he was going to Toby's. And where he really went.'

'*Lied?* Where do you think he goes? Unfortunately, the boy's only vice involves nacho chips and Snickers bars.'

Did he really think that? I wondered. Could a man of his intelligence really be so clueless? Or was he just refusing to know, refusing to see, as I had been for so long?

I stared at Gavin, and was tempted to blurt out everything — my growing fears for our son and the way I kept reliving the moment when I found the shoe box, maybe even venture into discussing the marriage that felt more lifeless and oppressive every day.

But Gavin's stony demeanor silenced me before I got the first word out. I thought of the night of Ali's concert and how angry he'd been

161

when I suggested Jamie was involved, then how quickly he'd shifted the blame to Ali — and to me.

'A few times when he said he was at Toby's, they went out, that's all,' I said, instead of the truth. 'I want to know where he is.'

'What a wonderful idea,' Gavin said, sarcastically. 'Undermine him in the one area in which he has any success — his social life. You've sabotaged him every other way; why not?'

'I've *what*? Gavin, you know I'd do anything for Jamie. I'm the one who — '

But before I could get out the list of ways I'd tried to be a perfect mother, making sure he had the trendiest clothes, driving him and his friends all over town, providing snacks and DVDs that would make our home an attractive place to be, Gavin interrupted with his own list. A catalogue of my shortcomings.

'Every time he tries to lose a couple of pounds, you run out and buy him some more peanut butter cups and chips. And academically, you've destroyed his confidence. You've done his homework for him for so long, the kid has no idea how to complete a task for himself.'

It was a familiar litany, but to it he now added a new charge. 'And you've brought your unstable friends around at this vulnerable time in the boy's life. He might not show it, but Jamie was terribly upset about that teacher's suicide. Then there's your friend, Ali. Do you have any idea how her provocative behavior has affected him? He's an adolescent, Jeanne. He's curious about adult life. And *this* is what you're teaching him.'

162

I had no idea that a tiny word like *this* could hold so much disgust.

'Let. Me. Go,' I said, giving my words sharp corners like Gavin did. Apparently, he was so surprised by my assertiveness that he released me.

But not before his words had accomplished their dark mission. By the time I had locked myself in my bedroom with my cell phone in hand, I no longer had the will to dial Sharon Breen's number. What if Gavin was right? What if he lost his closest friend because of my questions?

I jumped when the phone I was clutching rang. But when I pressed the talk button, I seemed to have forgotten the appropriate greeting. On the other end of the line, Ali's words came out in a torrent. 'Jeanne, is that you? Jeanne, my God, please let that be you.'

Immediately, the drama that had been enacted in my house faded. 'Ali, you sound terrible. Are you all right?'

'I'm fine,' Ali attempted, then laughed at her own weak voice. '*Marvellous*. Can't you tell? Jeanne, I'm afraid if I spend another hour alone in this house, I might seriously go insane.'

'I'll be right over,' I said, even before she asked. Ali seemed startled by my out-of-character response. In the past, I would have worried how Gavin would react — and more significantly, what my son would think when he came home from Toby's and found me gone. But maybe Gavin was right. Maybe I *had* crippled my son with overprotection.

163

Impulsively, I pulled an overnight bag from the closet, and repeated my promise. 'Give me ten minutes.'

I was ready in five.

'When Jamie comes in, tell him I'll be back tomorrow,' I said when I passed Gavin in the living room. He, apparently, was too stunned to comment. In any case, I didn't give him the opportunity.

★   ★   ★

Just as I feared, the door to Ali's house was unlocked when I arrived. 'Come in,' she yelled in a muffled voice from the kitchen. I immediately locked the door and bolted the latch behind me. Then, before I even had time to say hello, she asked, 'Red or white?'

It took me a minute to realize that her question referred to wine, but no time at all to hear the slur in her voice that suggested she'd been drinking for a while.

Before I could answer, Ali appeared in the doorway, holding two stemmed glasses. It was obvious that she had been crying since I crept out of her kitchen. 'My god, Jeanne, look at you.'

'What?' I had forgotten the clothes that had been washed and dried as I wore them, the stringy hair and naked face I was presenting to the world.

'You look like shit. Absolute shit.' My dishevelled appearance seemed to have an uplifting effect on Ali's spirits.

'You've looked better yourself,' I pointed out,

flopping down on the couch and reaching for the glass she'd set on the table. 'I'll have a shower in a little while, but right now I need this wine.'

Perhaps it was the reference to a shower, but Ali's eyes darted toward my overnight bag. 'Are you staying?' she asked.

'You said you didn't want to be alone, didn't you?' I said, peering into my wineglass.

'Well, yes,' Ali said softly. 'But that's not the only reason you're here, is it, Jeanne?'

At any other time, I could have — and certainly would have — come up with an instant, tidy denial. But here in Ali's living room with my hair hanging in my eyes and my face unprotected by its usual flawless makeup, here in the shadow of Brian's suicide, I just wasn't up to it.

I was silent for a moment before I changed the subject. 'Your door was wide open. After everything that's happened, don't you think — '

Ali interrupted me with a brittle laugh. 'The only good news in this situation is that I don't have to be afraid anymore. And honestly, Jeanne, some of the things that he did here were pretty scary. I didn't tell you half of it.'

I took a long sip of wine, then composed my face. 'You really think it was Brian?'

'Apparently he had a history of depression. And after what he did in that motel — well, it's obvious he was in a desperate state. Who knows what would have happened if I had come home and surprised him in the house. I was *lucky*, very lucky,' Ali said. And then, almost in defiance of her words, she began to cry again.

'It's so horrible,' I said, looping my arm

around her shoulder. 'Unthinkable.'

'In spite of everything, he really was a sweet guy, Jeanne. Just very trapped and unhappy, and without the resources to know what to do about it — like a lot of people, I guess.' Ali got up and began to pace around the room.

Like a lot of people, I guess. Obviously, she was referring to me. I thought about the words I'd read in her diary, the angry slant of her handwriting, and my face burned. Was I really that pathetic? *Disturbed*, as she obviously believed Brian had been?

'Jesus, Jeanne, why do I feel so guilty?' Ali said, drawing me back to the here and now. 'I truly wanted to be something good in his life. And I was patient as hell with the man, even when he was stalking me, *threatening* me, for God's sake. Sometimes, I guess, a little kindness can be fatal.'

Suddenly, I was irritated. 'It was a little more than *kindness*. You slept with the guy, Ali.'

Ali shot me a look. 'You don't think sex can be an act of kindness?'

'No, I don't,' I said sharply. More sharply than I wanted to. 'I mean, if that's all it is, then it isn't kind at all. Brian was in love with you, Ali. Desperately in love. If you'd seen him that morning in the donut shop — '

But then, catching the despondent slope of her shoulders, I realized I had gone too far. 'I'm sorry; I didn't mean to sound judgmental. The truth is, Brian had problems; if you hadn't triggered this crisis, it would have been something else.'

But once again, Ali's face was streaked with tears. 'You were right the first time,' she said, sparing herself nothing. 'I slept with Brian on a whim — or maybe worse, to prove something to myself. To my almighty, insatiable ego. Meanwhile, Brian really thought we were going to be together. What I did was unforgivable.'

'How were you supposed to know the guy was so screwed up? You're not responsible for his mental health.' I went to my overnight bag and pulled out a prescription bottle.

'Here, take one,' I said, handing her one of my little blue escapes. 'It will help you sleep, and in the morning, nothing will feel quite so grim.'

Ali held the blue pill suspiciously between her thumb and forefinger. 'What is it?'

I refilled our wineglasses. 'Something to make you feel better. Like pinot grigio. You're not going to get moralistic on me, are you?'

'Who prescribed this? Are you seeing someone?' she asked, the hope in her voice obvious — and insulting.

'No, I'm not *seeing* anyone, Ali,' I interrupted. 'We've both had a nightmare day. I thought it would help you sleep, that's all. But if you don't want it — '

'I don't,' Ali said, but instead of returning it, she got up and threw it in the trash. 'For one thing, I don't want things to feel less grim. I want them to feel the way they really are.'

Now who's being judgmental? I thought to myself, but instead of saying it out loud, I got up and emptied my wine into the sink. 'I think I'll take my shower now. I got caught in the rain earlier, and I've been walking around in these damp clothes for hours.' My voice was deliberately neutral though I was seething inside.

'That's what you do, isn't it, Jeanne? Whenever things get uncomfortable, you leave the room. Find something that needs cleaning. Take a pill. Pummel your skin with hot water until you can't feel anything anymore. Talk to me!'

As she spoke, I envisioned the violently slanting handwriting I'd seen in the diary. But before she could say more, I was safe behind the bathroom door, out of the clothes that were starting to smell mildewy; the shower was on full blast, and yes, the water was hot. Hot enough to sting. Hot enough and loud enough that if Ali was still talking, I couldn't hear her. Couldn't feel the impact of her words.

*   *   *

When I emerged from the bathroom, Ali was still in the same spot, looking into the fire in her woodstove.

'You should get to bed. We have school tomorrow,' I said. I was moving around in my usual efficient way. Going about my evening routine. I had flossed and applied my night cream and my eye cream, and was about to lay out my clothes for the morning. Even as quickly as I'd packed, I'd thought to include a slim gray suit with black heels, suitable for a day of mourning.

Undoubtedly, the school would be providing grief counselling for the girls who would gather

168

outside the office, their faces streaked with mascara, and for the boys who tried to appear stoic but whose eyes would be cloudy with confusion. Probably the same students who had been laughing at Brian only weeks earlier, breathlessly repeating every detail of his and Ali's 'breakup,' I thought.

'I'm not going to work tomorrow, and neither are you,' Ali said, still looking into the fire.

I sunk down opposite her, my shoes still in my hand. 'Are you out of your mind? If you don't show up at that school tomorrow and walk past everyone — students and staff alike — with your head high, they'll interpret it as a sign of guilt.'

'Didn't you hear a word I said? I *am* guilty, Jeanne. Maybe not totally, but I played my part. At this point, the only way I can honor Brian's memory is to be honest about my mistakes. Not to hide from them or try to protect myself from blame.'

I shook my head. 'I'm sorry, Ali, but I don't see how allowing people to say vicious, ugly things about you is going to honor Brian's memory. Those people don't know a thing about your relationship.'

And then Ali did something that truly startled me. She *laughed*. 'You really don't get it, do you, Jeanne? I don't give a damn what people say about me. Never have. People who thrive on nasty gossip are going to wake up one morning and find their lives are as ugly as their words. No matter how good they look from the outside.'

Once again, I felt chagrined. *Was Ali talking about me?*

169

As if reading my mind, she reached out and seized my hand. 'I didn't mean you, Jeanne. You don't have a vicious bone in your body. Maybe a few scaredy-cat ones. A couple of cowardly bones, but not a single mean one.'

Was that her idea of a compliment? Feeling uncomfortable, I attempted to yank my hand away. 'Well, maybe you're not going to work tomorrow,' I muttered. 'But I have to be there. The kids will be devastated; they need to see familiar adults carrying on as usual.'

But Ali wouldn't release my hand. 'That's what you're good at, isn't it, Jeanne? Carrying on as usual, no matter what's going on around you. Making the beds and washing the dishes while the house burns. Pretending.'

I was already on my feet, my mind on the pills in my overnight bag, the little magicians who would make me forget Ali's words. Her judgments. The pills that would help me sleep soundly like I always did until it was time to get up and get lost in my routines. But one word stopped me: *pretending*. It was the same word Jamie had used to describe our family interactions.

'Is that really what you think my life is like?' I asked.

Once again, Ali reached for my hand. 'I'm sorry,' she said, but she refused to reclaim her words. Her accusation.

This time there was no escape. No busywork I needed to do right that minute. No opportunity to swallow a pill and lie back, waiting for oblivion's sweet rescue. When I succeeded in pulling my hand away, there was no place to run. I sat down on the couch beside Ali, put my face in my hands and wept.

Ali stroked my back. 'You know my worst regret?' she said. 'I knew Brian had serious problems, and I never did anything about it. That's one mistake I'm not going to make again.'

I felt myself bristling. 'What are you saying? That I'm like Brian?'

'I'm just saying sometimes I worry about you, Jeanne. And about your son. A few times Jamie has lingered outside my room like he wanted to talk. But when I called him, he ran away. Just like you tried to do a few minutes ago.'

Immediately, my mind flashed on the shoe box I had found in Jamie's room. I felt myself suffused with heat. Did Ali know? Earlier, she'd blamed Brian for the stalking, the items that were missing from her home, but did she really believe it?

'You're an attractive woman; lots of students are intrigued with you, Ali.'

'You know what I see when I look at Jamie?' Ali said, ignoring my attempt to make Jamie's fascination sound more benign. 'I see myself at that age.'

'Did you have a weight problem when you were a teenager?' I asked, startled by the comparison.

Ali shook her head. 'It has nothing to do with outward appearance. For people like Jamie and me, every mirror is a fun-house mirror. You look into it and you see a piece of shit no matter what's staring back at you. Jamie uses food to

171

run away from that mirror, and I — I, well, let's just say I had my own methods. But a couple of times, I've looked into his eyes and there's this sadness there. It's a sadness I'm well acquainted with.'

By then, I was totally baffled. Sure, Jamie had problems — more than Ali could imagine. But *sad* was one thing he was not. He'd been a happy child from birth. Even now his barking laughter could be heard throughout the school, reassuring me that nothing was really as bad as I thought. Ali's eyes were so empathetic they reminded me of the first time I'd seen her in the hallway, when her swinging violin case had triggered memories of my brother. For a moment I was tempted to tell her everything. About the eavesdropping. The shoe box. Jamie's stony expression when I confronted him in the driveway. An expression that was so blank and cold that there was no trace of the Jamie I knew in it.

Fortunately, the phone rang before I had the chance. From Ali's answers, I could tell it was our principal, Simon Murphy. And furthermore, he was apparently seconding Ali's decision to stay home from school the following day.

'Of course, you're right. My presence will only add to the chaos,' Ali said. She got my attention, then nodded in the direction of the wine. Compliantly, I got up and poured her another glass.

When I came back, Ali was obviously fielding a question about her own state of mind. 'Really, I'm fine,' she said. 'Jeanne is with me. She's going to spend the night.'

Simon's response was apparently a request to speak to me.

'It's good of you to go over there, Jeanne,' he said after Ali handed me the phone. 'A lot of people aren't feeling all that generous toward Ali right now.'

'It's — not a problem,' I said haltingly, hoping that Ali didn't pick up anything from my tone.

'I'm afraid that once the news breaks in school, she might even get a few nasty calls. Why don't you take the day off and man the phones. I'm sure this is difficult enough for her without listening to a lot of judgmental quacks.'

I hesitated. The last thing I wanted to do was stay in the house with Ali all day while she psychoanalyzed my family. 'The phones are likely to be pretty busy at school, too,' I countered lamely. 'Don't you think I need to be there?'

'We'll handle it, Jeanne. Besides, this has got to be rough on you. You were pretty close to Brian yourself.'

'Well, yes, I was, but I really want — '

However, before I could protest further, Simon said, 'I'll see you both on Tuesday morning.'

After I hung up, I thought briefly of calling home and letting my family know my plans for the next twenty-four hours. But then I remembered the look Jamie had shot me in the driveway. *Hateful* was the only word to describe it. Maybe Ali was right. Maybe I needed to spend a whole day thinking about my life. A whole day away from my routines. Away from the place that I had once thought of as a symbol of my good taste and success, my position as Dr Cross's wife. Now my home seemed more like a prison where the guilty returned to their cells each evening, each to their own secret life: me to my mind-numbing routines, Jamie to the bags of greasy, salty snacks that never satisfied his hungers, and Gavin to increasingly stiff drinks, and what he referred to as his 'medications.'

That life was over. To provide myself with visceral proof, I got up and tossed my pill bottles in the trash. Then, afraid I might be tempted to retrieve them, I went back and emptied the contents down the toilet. As I watched my little blue escapes disappear in the swirling water, I knew what I had to do. In the morning, I would call Erin Emory. I didn't know the psychiatrist personally, but I'd seen her name on many of the prescription bottles that were kept in the nurse's office, and I knew she was highly regarded. Maybe she could unravel the enigma that my son had become.

It was strange. I'd just spent one of the worst days of my life, but for the the first time in many years, I went to sleep without chemical assistance. And for the first time in even more years, I experienced a curious sensation expanding in my chest, forcing out the usual tightness behind my sternum. It was such an unfamiliar feeling that it took me a long time to recognize it was hope.

14

After I got up the courage to call Dr Emory's office, I spent the rest of the day rehearsing how I would break it to Jamie. I didn't have a lot of time. The normal wait for an appointment was two months, but Dr Emory reserved an hour on Wednesdays for patients who might be considered a danger to themselves or others. I was trembling when I said that, yes, my son fit that description. *Or might.*

'Wednesday, eleven A.M.,' I said, repeating back the secretary's words. On cue, Ali jumped up and rummaged through a drawer for a piece of paper. She wrote the date and time down in the violet ink she often used in her diary, then underlined them. *Wednesday, eleven a.m.* I had only two days to convince Jamie to get in the car with me and drive to Dr Emory's. All I could see was the way he had glared at me in the driveway when I confronted him. If he wouldn't talk to his own mother, how could I expect him to expose his demons to a total stranger?

Ali and I lounged around the house in our pyjamas half the day, not talking much but somehow comforted by each other's presence. In the afternoon, she went into the music room and took up her violin. I watched her through the French doors, amazed at how her face changed as soon as she began to play. The lines of tension and age that had been so apparent over the last twenty-four hours relaxed, and the luminous expression that had drawn both Jack and Brian to her returned. Watching her, I understood for the first time the secret of her agelessness. It was music, a private world of beauty and flight that she could enter any time she wanted to just by picking up her violin.

I left around three, hoping to catch Jamie before Gavin came home. If Gavin had any idea that I'd made an appointment for Jamie to talk to a professional, he would be furious.

Ali hugged me for a long minute before I left. 'He'll go,' she said, sensing my nervousness. 'Deep down, Jamie wants help. I know it. And you can't let Gavin stop you. This is too important, Jeanne.'

I was fortified by that hug and the lingering scent of Ali's perfume when I pulled into my driveway. The house that I had once seen as my sanctuary now seemed like a forbidding place. At least, Gavin's car was not in the driveway. He rarely came home before six, but after the events of the last twenty-four hours, I couldn't be certain he wouldn't show up at any minute.

I was barely out of the car, and was reaching for my overnight bag, when Jamie darted into the driveway, wearing his favorite pair of sweatpants and a T-shirt that he'd outgrown. Once again, I was grateful that he was home, but the look of consternation — almost panic — on his face alarmed me. Shoeless, he walked across the yard without seeming to feel the cold ground or the stones that assaulted his feet, and threw

176

himself into my arms like he hadn't done since he was a little boy.

Though he was clearly underdressed for the weather, his skin was sweaty and his face pinkened. 'Mom,' he said over and over as he clung to me. 'Mom. Mom. Mom.' Whether he was trying to comfort himself or simply to remind me of my role, I wasn't sure.

'Come on, honey; let's go inside,' I said, looking around to see who might be peering out their windows.

Jamie took a step backward, looking clearly chastened; the redness in his face deepened. Was this the boy Ali had seen when he lingered outside her classroom? I wondered. The boy she had described as *sad*? And how much would it take for that sadness to transform into anger? Even rage?

I slung my overnight bag over my shoulder and moved briskly up the walk. 'You better come in before you catch pneumonia. I'll make you some hot chocolate with real whipped cream.' It was one of Jamie's favorite treats, but as I offered it, I again heard Gavin's voice, accusing me of sabotaging my son's diet. Behind me, Jamie clambered awkwardly over the stone driveway, but he made no response.

Inside, I immediately noticed the kitchen was a mess. The counter was littered with the cereal bowls from breakfast, as well as signs of everything Jamie had eaten after school. I also noticed that Jamie had carelessly used my new stoneware bowls, not our everyday china.

'You could at least rinse your dishes and put

them in the sink. I know loading them in the dishwasher is too much to ask, but this cereal is so crusted on now, I'll — '

'I'm sorry, Mom,' Jamie interrupted, and this time, there was so much sadness in his voice that I couldn't ignore it.

I turned, the offending cereal bowl in my hand, and saw him standing in the doorway, his brown eyes lacquered with tears. It was obvious that he was apologizing for more than failing to put away the Rice Chex, or for leaving crumbs on the counter. Once again, my brain was invaded by an unwanted echo. This time it was Ali's voice: *That's what you do when you feel uncomfortable, isn't it, Jeanne? . . . You leave the room, take a pill, clean out a drawer, anything to prevent yourself from feeling . . . Isn't it, Jeanne? Isn't it? Isn't it?*

The heavy pottery bowl slipped from my hand and shattered noisily on the stone floor, but neither Jamie nor I noticed. 'Oh, Jamie,' I said, collapsing into his arms, or allowing him to collapse into mine; I wasn't sure which. 'You're not the one who should be apologizing here. *I'm* sorry. Sorrier than you'll ever know.'

By then, we were both sobbing. However, when the sound of a car crunched in the driveway, we tensed, and pulled away.

'It's just Brad,' Jamie announced, from beside the window where he was peering into the driveway from beneath the corner of the shade. 'Can you tell him I'm not home?' His apparent relief that it wasn't Gavin was matched by my own.

Once Brad had been dispatched, Jamie sat opposite me on a stool at the island and swiped at his wet face with the palm of his hand. 'Really, Mom, I need to say this,' he said.

I stared at him.

'I'm sorry for the way I talked to you yesterday, and for — for — ' He lowered his head uncomfortably, then picked up a napkin and twisted it in his fingers. 'For all that stuff with Mrs Mather.' When he looked up, his eyes were so plaintive that I could only wait for him to continue.

'I never meant her any harm, Mom. I swear I didn't.'

'But you broke into her house, Jamie. And not just once. You took things. Do you have any idea how serious that is?'

'I was just — curious,' Jamie said lamely.

'*Curious?* That's what you call it? Well, the state calls it a felony. A serious offense punishable with prison time.' I didn't mention that since Jamie was a minor, he would probably be handled more leniently. I wanted him to be as scared as I was. As scared as Ali had been. '*Why,* Jamie?'

He shrugged helplessly. 'The first time, I just wanted to talk to her. Her bike was there and the lights were on, but when I knocked, no one answered, so I tried the door. I thought she was home so I walked in. I don't know, Mom — the house looked so welcoming with the door open and the lights on — it didn't feel like I was doing anything wrong.'

'And after that? After Ali began to keep the

door locked, and you had to break in — how did you justify it then?'

'I guess it became a kind of game we were playing. Just her and me. It made me feel — I don't know — important.'

I got up and began to pace around the kitchen. 'You need to terrorize a woman to feel important, Jamie? Dear God!'

Again, my son choked back a sob. 'Jeez, Mom. I said I was sorry. And I promise, I'll never ever go near her house again. I'll do whatever you want. I'll go to Mrs Mather and apologize. I'll even go down to the police station and spill the whole thing. Just promise me one thing.' His face looked so childish, so downright *innocent* that I almost laughed out loud. Did he really think that this was like the time when he was five and he stole his best friend's Matchbox car? That all he had to do was say he was sorry and everything would be fine?

My next question should have been simple: *what did Jamie want me to promise him?* What could possibly be so important that he would risk facing Ali, going to the police, even risk the possibility of being sent to juvenile detention for it? But I was so focused on what would happen if those things occurred that I didn't ask.

At Ali's house, the idea of flaunting Gavin's unspoken edicts had seemed not only possible; it had seemed like the answer. But here, within the walls of my white, sprawling kitchen, it was the most terrifying prospect imaginable. Gavin might not be perfect, but he criticized Jamie only because he cared; and however stagnant our relationship might be, we rarely argued. What was my biggest complaint? That our sex life wasn't the stuff of novels and movies? Or maybe that he spent too much time in his study, reading research papers?

Digging deeper, I felt my deepest fear forming the real question: *who was I without him?* Plain Jeanne, whose brother had died tragically and whose parents had never recovered from the blow. Poor little Jeanne whose family could never get up the money — or the will — to make a down payment on even the most modest home, or to save for their surviving child's education. Now when I thought of them, it was the sound of their slippers scuffing through the house that I remembered. A symbol of their defeat in a home where the only voices to be heard were from the television set, a low-level buzz that filled their life, filled the rented house, snaked its way into my dreams. It was the sound of hopelessness, a hopelessness they escaped only when they listened to music, or at Christmas time when my mother dressed up elegantly for the annual Bach concert.

But no one in town had been fooled. I knew how people had *pitied* me when I came to school in holey tights and dresses that were too small. That pity had trailed me and driven me all my life. No, I would not be that girl again. Would never be that girl, no matter what it cost.

'Don't be ridiculous, Jamie,' I said — more harshly than I intended. 'If you tell Ali the truth, there's no telling how she might react. And the idea of going to the police is out of the question.'

Then realizing it was my perfect opportunity, I reached into my purse and pulled out the scrap of paper where Ali had scrawled the date and time of Jamie's visit with Dr Emory in dramatic violet swirls.

'I made an appointment for you to talk to someone,' I explained, passing it across the island.

'Dr Emory? Isn't she a — a *shrink*? What? You think I'm some kind of head case?'

'No, of course not,' I said, though the truth was, I had no idea what went on in Jamie's mind anymore. All I knew was that there was more to his obsession with Ali than he was telling me. 'You said you went to see Mrs Mather because you wanted to talk. Well, this is someone who gets paid to listen. Someone who can really help you, Jamie.'

Jamie stared at the piece of paper, then balled it in his fist. I expected his next move would be to toss it into the trash. However, something made him change his mind. He put the balled-up paper down on the island and ironed it out with the flat of his hand, then he looked up at me. All I could think of was how he looked at five when he struck out at T-ball while Gavin sat in the stands radiating silent disappointment.

'Okay, I'll go, Mom. But first you have to promise.'

'Promise *what*, Jamie?' I asked at last; and in spite of myself, I heard a hint of impatience in my voice.

'Promise me you'll never leave me alone again,' he said, his voice sounding small.

'For goodness' sake, Jamie,' I said. 'I was only gone for a day, and you weren't exactly alone.'

'Just promise, okay, Mom?' Jamie pressed. 'Otherwise, you can forget about me spilling my guts to any shrink.'

I was about to agree, albeit reluctantly, but was interrupted by the sound of the door opening. Both Jamie and I cringed as Gavin entered the house with his usual forced cheer. 'Well, well, nice to see the family all assembled to greet me.'

He walked over and kissed my cheek, but his lips were so icy they burned. 'Am I interrupting something here? You look like you've just been caught with your hand in the cookie jar.'

'Actually, we were talking about Jamie's algebra test. He thinks he did really well, don't you, sweetheart?' I said, seamlessly sliding into my usual role.

But when Gavin turned his back, I glanced at Jamie and mouthed the words, 'I promise.' Of course, at the time, I had no real idea how much that promise meant to my son. Or how much it would cost us both when I broke it.

15

At school the next day, things had calmed down considerably. Beth Shagaury had decided to bury Brian privately. No open viewing where the students would be forced to encounter the starkness of death in someone who was young enough to shake their adolescent sense of immortality. No memorial service where people who had ignored the CDT teacher — or worse, revelled in his daily downfall at school — could gush with emotion over his loss. Even the funeral notice in the paper had been stripped to the essence. *Brian Shagaury, age 32, father of . . . , son of . . . , brother of . . . , a teacher at Bridgeway High School.* As I read it, I imagined the hungry eyes of the town, the insatiable hearts, desperate for something to make their own miserable lives more palatable, scanning the words greedily. But there was nothing. Even the garish death in the motel with all its preceding despair and the terrible images it conjured was whitewashed into the familiar, bland description: *died suddenly.* The only thing that remained for the gossips to cut their teeth on was the conspicuous omission of Beth's name from the list of survivors.

I had stopped on the way to school and bought a dozen roses that I set up on a table outside the office with a small, tasteful placard: IN MEMORY OF BRIAN SHAGAURY: TEACHER,

COLLEAGUE, FRIEND. Nearly everyone who passed it stopped momentarily, the girls dipping their faces toward the sweet scent, and the boys fingering the placard as if to absorb the words through their fingertips. It seemed to provide the kind of restrained memoriam we all needed. In fact, everyone was so respectful that no one said an unkind word when Ali took one of the roses and put it in a bud vase in her classroom. At least not in my hearing.

When Simon Murphy came into my office to thank me for the gesture, I casually mentioned that Jamie had a dentist appointment the following day at eleven. Both he and I would be gone from the school for an hour or so. The principal immediately assented, not suspecting a thing. The rest of the day, I was too busy to think. There was a stack of correspondence from the day I'd missed that needed my attention, and it seemed that every teacher in the school was clamoring for my help. Forms needed to be copied, handouts typed onto the computer and printed. But as usual, I revelled in the activity. No matter how monotonous and 'unfulfilling' Gavin found my job, I knew otherwise.

It was three o'clock and time to go home before I knew it. However, Ali was working with a private violin student, and I still had some catching up to do in the office, so we remained at school for an extra hour. The day had flown by so quickly that I hadn't even smoked one cigarette. Maybe this would be the day I gave them up for good, I told Ali before I dropped her off.

I was so elated about the positive changes I was making in my own life that I'd hardly noticed how wistful she seemed on the ride home, or how she repeatedly sniffed at the rose she'd taken home with her. Only after she got out of the car did I realize I should have been more sensitive. I hadn't even asked if anyone had made any snide comments during the day. Or how she was managing her private grief. I was still thinking of Ali when I pulled onto my own street and was accosted by an unwelcome sight in my driveway: Gavin's white Mercedes.

'Shit,' I muttered as I pulled in behind it. 'What's *he* doing home at this hour?' Without thinking, I reached into my bag, pulled out my cigarettes and lit one up.

I was still in the driveway, smoking and leaning against my Jeep, when Jamie burst out of the house, his head down. He didn't even look in my direction as he stormed past me. At first, I thought he was so preoccupied with whatever had disturbed him that he didn't see me. But when I called his name, he kept going.

Only when he reached the end of the driveway did he spin around and face me. 'I knew it was a bad idea!' he yelled, his face splotchy with a fury I had never seen before.

'What are you talking about, Jamie?' I said, dropping my cigarette on the driveway and stamping it out.

'You've gone and made things about a hundred percent worse for me, that's all. I don't know why I ever *fucking* listened to you.'

For a full minute, I stood stunned in the

driveway as I watched the son I didn't know reveal his face for the second time. By the time I called for him to stop, he was already halfway down the street.

After the encounter in the driveway, I entered the house cautiously, as if I expected the shell that held our lives together to reflect the tumult I'd seen in Jamie. But I was quickly reassured by my gleaming kitchen, the sound of the jazz that Gavin sometimes listened to in his study. His coat was neatly hung in the closet, and when I traced my finger across the counter and put it to my nose, I was reassured by the scent of lime. Perhaps what had upset Jamie so much had nothing to do with Gavin. Nothing to do with me. Perhaps his hostility in the driveway was simply an unfocused adolescent explosion. I poured myself a glass of wine and reached in my pocket for the scrap of paper on which Ali had written Jamie's appointment. Feeling reassured, I kicked off my shoes, sunk onto a stool, and reached for the newspaper.

'Come here often?' Gavin said, startling me as he slid onto a stool beside me. He set his gin and tonic on the counter and smiled mirthlessly.

'Excuse me?' I said, so jolted by his sudden appearance that I spilled a little wine from my glass.

Gavin took a napkin from the holder and began to wipe it up. 'It was a joke, dear. A feeble attempt at humour. Something there's been far too little of in this house, feeble or otherwise.'

Recognizing the silly pick-up line at last, I attempted a smile. 'I'm sorry, I guess my mind was elsewhere. It was a pretty difficult day at school.'

'Oh, yes, I almost forgot about your ongoing drama,' Gavin drawled. 'How is poor Mrs Mather bearing up?'

I jumped up nervously, went to the sink for a sponge, and began to wipe the spot that Gavin had already cleaned. 'It's not a joke, Gavin; the man had a young family,' I said, trying to restrain my exasperation. Though I refused to look in his direction, I could feel him staring at me. The familiar knot behind my sternum returned so sharply it almost made me gasp.

'Please, Jeanne, save your lectures about the seriousness of life for people who need them,' he said, and this time his voice was frankly edgy. 'People like your friend who play with lives like pieces on a chessboard.'

'I — I didn't mean to lecture you, Gavin. I just — ' I stammered, but suddenly my mind was a blank. All I could think of was escaping the room. 'I was just about to go upstairs and get out of these clothes.'

But Gavin rose and blocked my path. 'I thought we were having a little drink together. Just like the old days. Remember the old days, Jeanne?' Once again he was smiling, but his eyes were steely. 'Those were good times, weren't they?'

I sat back down on my stool and took a gulp of my wine. 'Yes, good times,' I muttered, but I didn't sound very convincing, not even to myself.

'Did you ever wonder why I married you,

188

Jeanne?' Gavin said.

My head spun sharply in his direction as he prodded my greatest source of insecurity: my fear that I had never been good enough for my doctor husband. I was too stunned to speak.

Gavin patted my hand with mock kindness. 'I don't mean to bring up a sensitive point, dear, but we both knew what people said. That I married beneath me. An uneducated girl from a deprived background. A girl who tried so hard it was almost embarrassing, but still couldn't hide what she was.'

'I've — I've got to go upstairs,' I said, trying to flee his words, the truth I had been running from ever since I married Gavin.

But Gavin only seized my wrists as he had the night before I left for Ali's. 'And *why*? People wondered. Sure, little Jeannie was attractive enough, but hardly beautiful, and her attempts at fashion, though certainly earnest, were almost laughable — '

'Stop,' I said, my voice reduced to begging, as an image of plain Jeanne in stilettos at work rose up in my mind. I was sobbing by then, but still Gavin held my wrists like a vice.

'So don't you want to know the reason? The real reason I sought out little Jeannie at that concert. Took her to dinner in elegant restaurants where she had no idea which fork to use. Bought her the biggest, gaudiest diamond ring I could find.'

Against my will, I felt myself nodding. *Yes, I wanted to know. The question had haunted me. Why had Gavin chosen me, and how long would it take before he realized his mistake? How long before he sent me back to the desolation of my former life with my troubled, clumsy son in tow?*

'Because I thought I could trust you, that's why,' he said, interrupting the string of irrational fears that was coursing through my brain. 'And trust is very important to me, Jeanne. You might say it's *everything* to me.'

'But you could trust me,' I protested. 'You *can*, Gavin. For God's sake, let go of me.'

Gavin looked down at his hands and mine as if they were foreign objects, as if he weren't aware of what he was doing. He released my wrists as violently as he had seized them. He seemed startled by the white imprint his grasp left behind.

But he continued on as if he hadn't heard me speak. 'Of course, we've had our differences. You know I've never approved of the way you've handled the boy. The way you coddle him and feed his addictive behaviors. But I always believed you had the family's interests at heart. You were just misguided, like you were when you showed up for work at the hospital in some of those silly outfits. But how could I blame you? You were just acting out what you knew.'

'Everything I've done has been — ' I began, but I lost the heart to complete the sentence. I was no longer sure that Gavin was wrong. No longer sure that I wasn't the cause of Jamie's burgeoning problems.

But it didn't matter that I was unable to think straight or present any defense. Gavin was listening only to himself. 'I always thought you understood how important my reputation was in this town,' he continued. 'How important this family's reputation was. Really — what does a doctor have but his good name?'

'Gavin, I — ' I stammered before it all became clear to me. Jamie's scene in the driveway. Gavin's accusations. Suddenly, it all made sense. Almost forgetting my husband was in the room, I walked to the phone and pressed the play button on the answering machine. There were two messages from Jamie's friends that hadn't been erased from the day before, and one that had come in this morning. A message that Gavin had obviously heard before I had time to intercept it.

Before Dr Emory's secretary could finish her routine message, reminding us of Jamie's appointment the following day, I pressed ERASE. But it was a full minute before I gathered the courage to turn and face Gavin. Still, I could feel his eyes drilling me. Accusing me. Hating me.

'I was going to tell you,' I said when I finally turned to face him. 'I swear I was, Gavin. I was going to tell you tonight.'

But Gavin was already shaking his head. 'Don't insult me by lying, Jeanne. If a migraine hadn't sent me home from the office early, I wouldn't have known until it was too late.'

'Too late for what? God, Gavin, I was taking Jamie to talk to someone — not for a lobotomy.'

'Did you hear what I said about reputation? Dr Emory is a colleague of mine, Jeanne,' Gavin said with his usual self-important air. 'She might be a stranger to you, but I see her at the hospital nearly every day.'

'Jamie's visit would be confidential; you know that, Gavin. It's not like the woman would be whispering about him — or us — in the hospital hallways.'

'The only professional Jamie needs to talk to is a good nutritionist. And that's one thing you'd never allow, isn't it, Jeanne?'

'You're wrong, Gavin,' I blurted out, anger overcoming fear for once. 'Jamie has problems neither of us ever suspected. Serious problems.'

'Maybe you never suspected them, Jeanne. But I've been warning you about the potential consequences of your actions for years.' Gavin glared at me. 'Now it's gotten to the point the boy has committed some serious offences. Offences that could destroy his life, if anyone found out.'

My head spun. *He knew. Gavin knew everything.* 'Who told you?' I asked in a weak voice.

'Heard it from the horse's mouth, actually,' Gavin replied. He walked across the kitchen and began to fix another drink, cutting a lime in a precise way that suddenly infuriated me. 'Just before you came home, Jamie told me everything. And he promised me it was over. He'll never go near your friend again.'

'But what if he does? Or if it's someone else next time? Gavin, we can't just ignore — '

'I told you he *won't*,' Gavin bellowed. 'He made a mistake, Jeanne, and one that wasn't entirely unprovoked.'

'What are you saying — that it was Ali's fault that Jamie stalked her? Her fault that he broke into her house and stole her things?'

Gavin shrugged. 'I'm not absolving Jamie entirely, but obviously, the woman thrives on things like that. Recent events provide ample proof — '

'So now you're blaming Brian's death on Ali, too? That's not fair, Gavin, and you know it.'

'Brian's death doesn't concern me, Jeanne. *Ali* doesn't concern me. The only thing that concerns me here is my son, and as I said, he realizes his mistake. Now as long as you don't do anything foolish, this will be the end of it. If, on the other hand, you insist on involving outsiders, you never know where this might lead.'

'You cancelled the appointment,' I said defeatedly. There was no question in my voice.

'I told the secretary the problem has been taken care of. And it has.'

I nodded silently, not looking up at him.

'And please don't attempt to reschedule, Jeanne, because Jamie has already told me he'll refuse to go.'

Recalling my son's words as I stood in the driveway, I didn't attempt to respond. Clearly, Gavin was right. The only time I could remember feeling so hopeless was when I had peered at my brother's lifeless body in the casket. When I had furtively touched his cheek and felt not the warmth of the boy I knew but the hardness of wood. Metal. The rocky earth.

Gavin collected his drink and moved toward his study, but then he paused and turned around in the doorway. 'Oh, one more thing, Jeanne. When you first came home, you dropped a

193

cigarette butt in the driveway. You know how I feel about litter.'

Feeling numb, I merely stared at him. Then I put on my coat and went outside to search for the offending butt, grateful as always for a mindless task to anchor my churning mind.

16

After his confrontation with Gavin over the appointment, Jamie avoided me, spending more and more of his time with his friends. It was the first time I'd spent lengthy periods alone in the house; and I studied the contents of my own home like an archaeologist trying to make sense of a lost civilization. I stared hard into the framed photographs I'd hung by the stairway, the smiling faces of my family; I pored through the photograph albums and videos I'd diligently kept, recording every Christmas, every vacation, all the evidence I'd amassed to prove we were happy. Normal. A family not unlike the others on our street, in our town, the ones who smiled back at us from our TV set.

Exactly what I was looking for as I watched the old video-tapes of Jamie's birthday parties or the Christmas party we gave each year for Gavin's colleagues and their wives, I don't know. Maybe I was searching for the point where everything had gone wrong, something that would explain the aching loneliness I felt every evening when the three of us sat down to dinner, or the jolts of free-floating anxiety that often woke me in the middle of the night. Jarred from sleep, I often imagined I heard the phone ringing. But when I sat up in bed, drenched in sweat, my husband asleep beside me, there was nothing but silence. Silence broken only by the predictable tick of Gavin's alarm clock.

Routine had always been my ballast, routine that usually revolved around my husband and son. Now with both of them away nearly every weekend, I had no idea what to do with myself. I began to frequent bars on a regular basis. Well, not exactly bars — let's just say restaurants with darkened bar areas where a woman alone wouldn't look out of place. There I had my solitary dinner, usually a salad, or a half sandwich and soup, and a couple of exotic drinks with fun-sounding names. The kind that predictable Jeanne never ordered, but which Ali liked to try: frozen mudslides, mango margaritas, martinis in neon colours. I drank just enough to fortify myself for my real activity of the weekend: searching. Searching through a house with every light on for something I couldn't name, and probably didn't want to see. Searching with the same manic energy and fear with which I had first combed my son's room.

Of course, I didn't call it searching — not even to myself. I called it *cleaning*. Thus, when Gavin asked me what I had done with myself for the weekend, I could say with a certain sincerity, 'Oh, just a little spring cleaning. To tell you the truth, I'm exhausted.' The last part, at least, was true. Each Sunday night when Jamie returned from his weekend sleepovers, and Gavin came back from his conferences, they found me wilted on the couch, utterly depleted from a weekend of madly ferreting through closets and drawers. I sighed with relief when each thoroughly investigated corner of the house produced no

196

surprises, but was soon assailed by a fresh rush of fear when I thought of another drawer or closet I had yet to examine. Was it there? I wondered, though I couldn't have said exactly what *it* was.

I was hardly surprised when Jamie's room, which I inspected with the fever and thoroughness of an FBI agent closing in on a big case, yielded no further 'evidence.' If he possessed anything that might have alarmed me, Jamie was apparently careful not to leave it around. However, that didn't stop me from searching again and again. Nor did it prevent me from comforting myself with the ordinariness of what I found in the dark corners of the room — balled-up gym socks and empty packages of fruit pies and Hershey bars, crumpled algebra quizzes with failing grades and notes to *See me!* written in red at the top of the page. See! I told myself, surveying the room I'd plundered with satisfaction. Nothing to worry about here. Nothing you wouldn't find in any teenage boy's room. Each time I felt as if I had once again proven something to that prying George Mather.

Since I could hardly call my weekend search and seizures rational, I wasn't entirely sure I could trust my judgment anymore. Increasingly, I found myself agreeing with Gavin. Now when I thought of Ali's violet pens, her tortoiseshell combs, or her face smiling from the newspaper clipping that had been marked childishly with costume-store blood, most of my diffuse anger was directed toward her. I knew Ali was the victim, but did she have to be so — well, ostentatious? With her short skirts and boots, the hair coiled seductively over one shoulder, it was no wonder that a vulnerable adolescent boy had been captivated. It was almost as if she had unconsciously lured Jamie into her house, beckoning him with her pretty things, with the scent of lilies she exuded.

After satisfying myself that there was nothing suspicious among my son's things, I turned to the corners of the house that Gavin had claimed, poring through his meticulously organized drawers, the gym bag he kept packed and ready to go at all times, his closet, and the pockets of every suit and overcoat he owned. The only thing of interest I found was a small key tucked at the bottom of his sock drawer. For a few moments, I held the key in my hand, turning it over and over as if it could speak. Then imagining my husband's imperious scowl, I carefully put it back where I found it. Perhaps the next time Gavin announced he was going away, I would go back for it, I thought as I carefully covered it with socks.

That opportunity came only two weeks later. Coincidentally, it was the same week that school got out. It hadn't been the easiest week. As I'd feared, Jamie had failed two classes, and barely squeaked by with Ds and C-minuses in the rest of them. I was already worried how I would tell Gavin that our son would have to go to summer school if he hoped to graduate with his class. The report card remained hidden in the bottom of my purse, yet another secret Jamie and I were keeping from 'Dad.'

Since I had given my notice at school, I wasn't just off for the summer. I was finished. Of course, by then, I had convinced myself that Gavin was right: I was a doctor's wife with an ample family income. Why was I spending forty hours a week at a job I didn't need? Surely I could find something more fulfilling to do with my hours than organizing files or dealing with truculent adolescents. By then, I almost believed that quitting my job was my own idea.

Still, I felt shaky and almost light-headed as I left the school for the last time, carrying the contents of my desk and a big bouquet of roses that Simon Murphy had given me. When I got home, Gavin was packing. With a cursory glance at the roses, which were bleeding colour in my arms, Gavin announced that he was going to Burlington, Vermont, for the weekend. Apparently, he was meeting with another doctor to discuss a new surgical technique that was being used on athletes with serious knee injuries. However, when I expressed interest in the details, Gavin gave me the intimidating stare I knew well.

'It's not something that's easy to explain to a layperson,' he said dismissingly. As always, I backed down. No, I didn't really want to know, probably wouldn't understand it anyway. I was already thinking of the key I had held in my palm only two weeks earlier. Imagining how I would dig it out and use it this time, I felt a secret satisfaction.

★ ★ ★

That night, after I dropped my sullen son off at Brad's, I headed for Hannibal's. I tried not to think about how Jamie had lost himself in a radio tune in the car and gazed into the dark street as we drove toward Brad's — ignoring me the same way Ali had when we first met. I tried to forget how he had muttered a quick goodbye without even looking at me, or how he didn't even seem to care about his academic failure. Nor did I want to think about the contents of my desk at school, which I had carried home that afternoon. Fifteen years of my life stuffed into a cardboard box. As I had so many times, I wondered how I had let Gavin talk me into it. Almost make me believe that giving up my job — the one place where I felt needed and in control — was what *I* wanted.

After two cosmos, I paid my check and headed for home, but the alcohol hadn't erased Gavin's arrogant expression as he told me I wouldn't understand the new therapy he was learning. Or my son's fleshy face as he turned away from me in the car. I was tired of both of them. Them and their secrets.

The key was exactly where I had left it. For a minute, I congratulated myself on my superior sleuthing skills. Apparently, I had left the drawers and closets so neat that Gavin never suspected I had been sifting through his things while he was away. As my hand closed around the key, it felt clammy, but this time I would not back away from the truth. I walked downstairs and headed directly toward the locked door of the study.

Gavin had added the study on to the house

when we first bought the place, building his private sanctuary with his own hands. As I approached the door, I remembered the first time I had entered the room, excited that the job was finally complete. But as I crossed the threshold, Gavin had instantly jumped up from his desk where he was studying an anatomical illustration of the knee. 'Yes, Jeanne, what is it?' he'd said, his stance preventing me from coming farther. Later he had frankly asked me to stay out of the room, saying that he didn't want his important papers disrupted. Nor was I to touch the computer. Even if Gavin hadn't kept the door locked, Jamie and I would have stayed away, kept out by the dark scowl he assumed when he suspected we had been near the study.

Now I made my way toward the room with the same alcohol-fortified determination I'd marshaled when I picked through my son's possessions. I inserted the small key I had found in Gavin's sock drawer into the lock in the study door. Though I had never seen the key before, I was almost certain that it would fit. However, when it actually did, when the door to the room I hadn't entered more than three times in ten years yielded, something stopped me. No matter how careful I was, I knew Gavin would sense my intrusion. I could almost feel him watching me the way I sometimes imagined George Mather's midnight-blue eyes on me as I snooped around my own house like an intruder. But this time, the thought of Gavin's irritation gave me nothing but pleasure.

I flicked on the light switch, illuminating the

narrow room, and was immediately drawn into its quiet elegance. The walls had been painted a cool gray, and a Persian rug on the hardwood floors added to the warmth of the oak furniture. A strong whiff of Gavin's cologne and the look of his old textbooks lined up in the bookshelves, grouped obsessively in sizes from small to large, almost sent me scurrying from the room. But remembering Gavin's haughty glance as he said that I could never understand the advanced medical techniques he was going away to learn, I pulled out the chair and turned on the computer. However, a quick scan of the documents saved in Gavin's file revealed nothing but a highly detailed budget that was too boring to read (my husband was so cheap and meticulous, he kept track of every cup of coffee he bought in the hospital cafeteria), and several folders filled with notes on various patients. Feeling bored, I shut the computer down and stared at the blank screen.

I then turned to the desk and began to go through the drawers. That search was equally unrewarding, turning up nothing but more evidence of my husband's almost pathological orderliness. Even the paper clips were lined up in neat rows in their little cardboard box. The thought of Gavin taking the time to line up paper clips, or to make sure that each pencil stored in a mug was sharpened to a perfect point, filled me with revulsion.

Almost as an afterthought, I attempted to

open the final drawer of the desk and found that it, like the door to the room, had been locked with a key. Taking one of Gavin's neatly lined-up paper clips from the box, I attempted to pry it open. And when I still met with no luck, I searched the room more recklessly, trying to imagine where Gavin might have hidden the key. I was so deep in my search that I didn't notice that someone was knocking softly on the door. I didn't notice until the front door cracked, and a familiar voice called out, 'Hello? Jeanne, are you there?' It was Sharon Breen — Toby's mother.

That was when I caught sight of myself in a small mirror on the wall. Staring back at me was a woman I hardly recognized, her hair escaping in all directions from the clip I'd used to hold it back, the carefully made-up face I'd worn to the bar utterly erased by sweat. But most alarming of all were my eyes; they were so frenzied I quickly looked away. Maybe if I was absolutely still, Sharon would think I was asleep and go away.

But instead, she took a step deeper into the house, and called again, 'Jeanne, is everything all right?'

Why did people keep asking me that question? She sounded like George Mather. I stepped out and approached the foyer, so annoyed that I forgot how I looked.

'Well, of course, everything's all right,' I said, unable to keep the irritation from my voice. 'I was just doing a little cleaning, that's all.'

Apparently shocked by my appearance, as

well as by my uncharacteristic response, Sharon took a step backward. 'I'm sorry,' she said. 'I didn't mean to barge in. It's just that all your lights were on and your car was in the driveway and — '

For the first time, I noticed the silver-wrapped package in her hand. 'No, please, I'm the one who should apologize,' I said, feeling abashed. 'I just — I guess you startled me. Can I get you some tea, a soda maybe?'

'No, nothing, thanks. I just wanted to drop this off for you. You've been such a wonderful presence in the high school all these years. I have no idea how they'll ever replace you.' Sharon extended the prettily wrapped box in my direction. 'It's not much, really. Jamie told us you have a weakness for Belgian chocolate so — ' she began, and then reached out and touched my arm. 'My God, Jeanne, you're shaking. Are you sure you're all right? Because if you ever needed to talk — well, people say I'm a pretty good listener.'

There it was again, *that question*: is everything all right? Are *you* all right?

'I'm fine,' I said curtly, accepting the gift. But then I recovered, attempting a bit of graciousness as I ushered her toward the door. 'I guess leaving the job was harder than I thought it would be. It's been a rough day, Sharon. But I really do appreciate the chocolate.'

Sharon left quickly, saying all the right things, but nothing could mask the concern in her eyes. It was obvious that no matter how much I smiled and nodded, the truth couldn't be hidden any longer. Greedily, I opened the box and stuffed a chocolate in my mouth. Then I caught another glimpse of my image in one of the mirrors that were suddenly everywhere in the house. I looked like the madwoman who'd finally escaped from the attic.

17

It was Sunday afternoon and both Jamie and Gavin would be home from their weekend activities in a few hours. I had spent the day quietly and productively, determined to put an end to my crazy searches. With dinner simmering in the Crock-Pot, I decided to take a relaxing soak in the tub before it was time to face my life. I unplugged Jamie's portable CD player and carried it into the bathroom. Fortunately, this time I hadn't started my bath, thus there was no water to spill over and fill the bathroom with scented suds when I discovered *it*, the telltale item I had been looking for without knowing it. After all my feverish searching, it was right in the open — perhaps the way the truth had been all along, if only I had allowed myself to see it.

I had haphazardly gathered up the things I needed for my bath when the washcloth caught my eye. In the bright glare of the bathroom, its fluffy whiteness stood out. I picked it up and examined it closely, wondering how this foreign object had made its way into my house. It was then that I noticed the insignia at the corner: PARK PLAZA, it announced in its classy scroll. Though consciously I was still resisting the associations the words conjured, I immediately began to tremble.

Neither Gavin nor I had been to New York in years, and never to the Park Plaza — but I knew someone who had. Ali had been luxuriously ensconced at the Park Plaza when Brian Shagaury hung a rope from the ceiling fan in a depressing motel and ended his life. Was it possible that Jamie had been in the house since then, and taken the washcloth? Was he baiting me by leaving it in the linen closet instead of hidden in his room the way the shoe box had been? And if indeed he had been prowling around Ali's house again, what else might he have taken? Had I missed something in my exhaustive searches of his room?

I was about to go back to the messy room that was strewn with gym clothes, unfinished homework assignments, and the relentless litter of his junk-food addiction, when an image suddenly flashed before my eyes: I saw Gavin standing with Ali at the concert on the Cape. His eyes full of obvious appreciation, he was leaning toward her, a glass of wine in his hand. Almost against my will, the connections began to come. If Brian Shagaury hadn't committed suicide the weekend the quartet had played in New York, of course, I wouldn't have remembered it so clearly. But because it had been marked by tragedy, I remembered every detail of the weekend. I also knew I had been alone. It was the first of the many conferences and consultations that had taken my husband away in recent months. That weekend, he claimed to be attending a conference in Cleveland.

Looking feverishly through my appointment book, my hands trembling uncontrollably, I found the exact date. Penciled beneath it was the name of the hotel in Cleveland and the phone number that Gavin had left for me in case of an emergency — knowing that the chance I would call him was practically zero. My hands were still trembling as I picked up the phone in my bedroom and dialled the number Gavin had left for me those many weeks ago. The phone rang several times before someone answered it. By then it was late, and the person on the other end of the line sounded as if I had disrupted a nap. By the raspy sound of her voice, I guessed her to be in her eighties.

'Hello, is this the Sheraton?' I asked, though I already knew that it wasn't. Perhaps with my tremulous fingers, I had dialled the number wrong, I told myself.

'The what?' the woman repeated, apparently still waking up.

'The Sheraton. The Sheraton in Cleveland.'

'Cleveland?' the woman replied, her voice perking up. 'Honey, you're not even close. This is Boca Raton, Florida, here.' And then with more trepidation, 'What is this — some kind of practical joke?'

'No, and I'm sorry to have disturbed you,' I said quickly. But before she hung up, I read back the number that Gavin had written in his clear hand, just to make sure there was no mistake. There wasn't. In creating the false number, he hadn't even bothered to look up the area code for Cleveland.

After I let the poor old woman go back to sleep, I held the phone in my hand. I listened to the dial tone, allowing the digits of Ali's number to tumble around my mind. Though my first instinct was to call her and confront her, there was a nagging doubt. What if I was wrong? I reassessed the evidence I had collected. Fact #1: someone in my house had gotten hold of a washcloth from a hotel where Ali had stayed on a recent weekend. Fact #2: my husband had lied about his whereabouts on the same weekend. Though it was pretty incriminating, it proved nothing. But needing answers and needing them now, I no longer cared if I looked like a fool before Ali. I dialled the familiar number and was greeted by a message that had obviously been recorded recently. 'Sorry, but I'll be away this weekend. I'll get back to you on Sunday evening if you want to leave a message.' Her recorded voice had a teasing quality. It was almost as if she were taunting me with the information that she and my husband had left town on the same weekend. But once again, I remained too unsure to take action. It could still be a coincidence, couldn't it?

It was then that I thought of the locked drawer, the one place in the house Gavin had made damn sure I never got into. I could feel my hands steadying, my determination growing as I opened the phone book and scanned the yellow pages for a locksmith. *I was going to get into that drawer before Gavin came home. I didn't care how many locksmiths I had to call before I found one willing to come out on a Sunday.* The advertisement for Bob's Locksmith almost leaped out of the page at me: 24-HOUR EMERGENCY SERVICE it announced boldly.

'You called me out here to open a *desk?*' Bob said. He was standing on the threshold of the study, scratching the bald spot on the top of his head, surrounded by a monklike circle of bristly gray hair pointing in all directions. I must have pulled him away from his couch, where he was watching some sporting event; he hadn't even bothered to comb his hair. 'You know how much I charge to come out on a Sunday, lady? I thought you said this was an emergency.'

'It doesn't matter,' I said. I wanted to tell him it was my money, and I would define my own emergency. But instead I smiled my most polite smile, and said, 'I left my seizure medication in there, and apparently misplaced the key. I need that medicine right away or — '

However, before I could describe the medical emergency that might occur if he didn't get that drawer open fast, Bob produced a lock-jimmying tool, obviously satisfied. 'You got medicine in there? Well, what are we doing standing here talking?' he said, effortlessly unlocking the drawer that Gavin had obviously thought was so secure against me. After he had unlocked the drawer, Bob stood there a moment, as if waiting for me to open it and produce the prescription bottle I claimed to need. Instead, I pulled out the wallet I kept in my own desk drawer, the one where I stored my emergency cash. 'How much do I owe you?' I asked. I didn't even flinch when he named his exorbitant price. All I wanted was for him to get out of there so that I could investigate the contents of the drawer.

But after being dragged away from his Sunday

afternoon on the couch, and feeling like a hero for saving me from a seizure, he seemed to want to linger. 'Aren't you going to take your medication?' he asked. 'I thought you needed it right away.'

'I take it with milk,' I said, ushering him toward the door. I watched as his car pulled away,

The drawer, which I was certain contained proof of my husband's infidelity, remained closed though there was no longer a lock to keep me out. I yanked it open with such force that the — contents — all paperwork — spilled across the floor. To my surprise and momentary relief, I found nothing but bills among the loose papers. Gavin insisted on paying them himself, never letting me near the chequebook he used for our electric bill and mortgage payment. For my own personal expenses, forays to the mall, payment for Jamie's various activities, I had my own account. Still, after all my trouble, I figured I might as well look through the neatly filed envelopes.

The first few were the same ones that Gavin left for me to mail in an orderly stack at the beginning of each month: the insurance for car and house, cable TV, the mortgage. But then I came across a bill I had never seen before. Opening it, I realized it was for a Visa card I never knew Gavin had. My first thought was to wonder why he never left the bill with the rest of the stack when he asked me to mail them out. However, as soon as I read through the itemized charges, it all became clear. In fact, the whole miserable lie that was my marriage became clear.

The first things that caught my eye was the charge made at the Park Plaza on the weekend when Brian Shagaury had killed himself. Though I had wanted the truth, I felt nauseated with the sense of betrayal that rose up when I pondered the charges my husband and Ali had run up at the hotel that weekend. I pictured room service, long breakfasts in bed, bottles of Dom Pérignon at night. Later, of course, I would look through the bill more carefully, finding charges to hotels in every city where Ali's quartet had played. But that night all I could see was the two of them at the Park Plaza, Ali in the short black dress she sometimes wore, her hair streaming over her shoulders. How could she? I asked myself again and again, as I carried the bill up to my room. Oddly enough, it wasn't my husband's betrayal that drove me to the bathroom, where I threw up the gin I had gulped in the kitchen. It was Ali's. It was my best friend's.

By the time I made my way upstairs, the burning taste of the gin I'd thrown up in my mouth, I felt dizzy. I had reached the top landing when I heard it: the last movement of Ali's *Paradise Suite* snaking out the bathroom door and down the hallway, enveloping me in its seductive melody. Without caring what I broke or who saw it, I picked up the CD player and heaved it down the stairs, silencing Ali's music once and for all.

18

Before I left the house, I posted a note on the door of the fridge telling Jamie I would be out late; his dinner was in the Crock-Pot. I felt a certain satisfaction as I imagined Gavin's face when he read it. Why no note from the dutiful wife to *him*? he'd wonder. How long would it take before he noticed that the study door was open, and his locked desk had been tampered with? How soon before he realized that his carefully guarded secret was on the loose?

I picked up an extra large cup of coffee at Ryan's and began my stakeout, watching Ali's cottage from the corner. Several times I glanced in the direction of Nora Bell's house, hoping the nosy cafeteria lady hadn't spotted my car. But apparently Nora knew that Ali was away for the weekend; she wasn't likely to take up her spying until a light in Ali's window informed her that her fascinating neighbour had returned.

Unlike me, Ali left her house in total darkness without even a solitary light to welcome her — or to ward off the petty thief and vandal who had been stalking her. Taking that as another sign of her willingness to tempt harm, I felt my anger escalating. Still, I drank my coffee patiently, my radio turned to a medley of the trite songs that Ali and I sometimes listened to on our way to school. Silly girl dreams, we had called the fantasies those songs inspired. Silly girl dreams that my friend obviously continued to act out — no matter who she hurt. Like the darkened house, the songs drove my fury with their relentless beat, their sing-song taunts. *Love you, baby, love you forever.* How had I ever fallen for such crap?

It was nearly nine by the time a badly dented Subaru pulled up in front of Ali's house, and she got out. When the door opened, lighting the inside of the car, I recognized the viola player from her quartet, though I didn't know his name. Ali stood on the sidewalk for a moment, leaning forward into the car, probably giving him a good shot of her cleavage as they talked. I thought the Subaru would never leave, and when it did, Ali remained outside, watching it until it disappeared. Then, turning to face her house, she appeared to hesitate. She claimed she was no longer afraid now that Brian was gone, but I wondered if some fear lingered. Was she scared to go inside, afraid of what she might find there? Further evidence of another intrusion, more missing or misplaced items, or perhaps, this time, even the stalker himself, waiting for her in the dark? Little did she know that the real danger was on the street, listening to the Ronettes sing 'Be My Baby' in my cozy Jeep.

When I turned off the radio and opened the window, I was close enough to hear Ali's heels clicking down the walkway, and then a dull thud; apparently she had set down her travelling bag and instrument while she opened the door. In an instant the porch was flooded with light. A door slammed behind her. Knowing the ever fearless

214

Ali, I doubted she bothered to lock it. Headlights off, I drifted closer, then put the Jeep in park and got out. *She had to put on those front lights, didn't she?* I said to myself as I walked up the brightly illuminated path, hoping that Nora Bell wouldn't choose this exact moment to look out her window.

As soon as I got close enough to the house, the sound of Beethoven's *Moonlight Sonata* floated toward me. I tried the door: just as I suspected, it was unlocked. Inside, Ali was in the kitchen, humming along with the familiar piece as the refrigerator door opened and closed.

When I entered the kitchen, I caught her with her mouth wide open about to bite into a leftover piece of chicken. The chicken fell from her hand and onto the floor as she clutched her chest.

'Jeanne, don't do that to me; you almost gave me a heart attack,' she cried, breathless from her moment of fear but already smiling. After all, it was only me, good old Jeanne. There was nothing to fear from good old Jeanne, was there? She stooped down and began to pick up her piece of chicken. I smelled curry powder and the sweet fragrance of Ali's perfume.

'How long have you been here?' she asked, looking up, still faintly breathless. 'Is everything all right?' Perhaps she noticed that I hadn't yet uttered a word, because her smile had vanished and she was staring deeply into my face. Reading me the way her husband did. She took another deep breath.

'I needed to talk, and I figured you wouldn't

mind if I came by — us being such good friends and all,' I said, trying to keep the sarcasm out of my voice.

But Ali wasn't fooled. This time she was the one who was silent as she continued to stare at me. After she tossed the uneaten chicken in the trash, she turned and went to the stove, where she lit the kettle. 'I'll make us some tea,' she said. Her voice sounded tired.

'How about a drink?' I said. 'Isn't that our custom when we sit down for a good talk? Loosens the tongue, as you always say.'

'I'm tired, Jeanne,' Ali said, switching off the gas. 'Maybe tomorrow we could get together, have lunch and — '

'No, Ali. Now. And we won't be having lunch together — not tomorrow or ever.' She didn't look like she was about to offer me a drink, so I walked into the living room and pulled a bottle of brandy and two snifters from her armoire. I poured each of us a stiff shot.

From the couch, I looked around the room I had always loved, with new eyes — imagining Gavin here, basking in the warmth with which Ali surrounded herself, the improbable colour scheme that worked, the mixture of funky art and traditional New England. The result was at once disconcerting and fascinating — like Ali herself. I took a gulp of my drink and felt my throat burn.

'Aren't you going to join me?' I said, pointing at the snifter full of amber-coloured liquid.

'It doesn't look like I have a choice,' Ali said. She sat down opposite me, instead of sitting

216

beside me on the couch the way she usually did. For a long moment we stared at each other. After her long weekend, Ali looked worn, almost haggard. And her hair, uncoiled from its long braid, didn't look seductive or girlish as it usually did but rather foolish, the sign of a middle-aged woman desperately trying to pretend she was still young. The pale strands of hair that usually sparkled in the light were not silver that night; they were merely gray. For the briefest moment, I almost felt sorry for Ali.

Slowly, methodically, I pulled the evidence from my purse and spread it before her on the coffee table like a Tarot card reader: the facecloth from the Park Plaza, the Visa bills with all the charges from various hotels circled in red, and beside them, the quartet's itinerary for the last two months. In each case, the dates and cities on the bill corresponded perfectly with those of the quartet's concerts.

But Ali gave my carefully accumulated evidence only the most cursory glance. Obviously, she wasn't going to even try to deny it. The two of us glanced from the square coffee table to each other, studying each other like chess players.

It was Ali who spoke first, snapping me from various reveries of revenge with her steely voice, her bold stare. 'So you know,' she said flatly, taking charge of the situation the way she always did. She rose and went to the stereo, where she changed the CD, replacing the soothing sounds of Beethoven with Aretha Franklin.

As Aretha's powerful rendition of 'Respect'

filled the room, I wondered if Ali was taunting me. '*So you know* — that's all you have to say?' I desperately wanted to remain calm, the way Ali herself was, but my voice betrayed me.

However, when she turned from the stereo, chin up, coiling her hair nervously over her shoulder, I saw that her eyes were shimmering with tears. 'You never should have found out this way,' she said, starting toward me, then sinking down beside me on the couch. She even attempted to take my hand between the warmth of her two palms, but I jerked away.

'I'm so sorry, Jeannie — believe me, I tried to tell you many times in the last two weeks, but each time I was afraid — '

'You tried to tell me?' I said, feeling my eyes grow huge. What did that mean? Was Gavin planning to leave me? Were he and Ali planning to be together?

'At least a dozen times. But it was obvious you didn't want to know,' Ali said, almost angrily, as if she were the aggrieved party here. She was up again, walking up and down the room, with her drink in her hand. Though she'd said she didn't want it, she was gulping it now. Gulping it the way I had earlier.

'You're damned right I didn't want to know. But that's not the point, is it?'

'See, that's what I mean; that's why I couldn't tell you,' Ali said, pausing in the middle of the room, her soft voice mixing with Aretha's powerful one. 'God knows I wanted to, Jeanne. You've been so quiet lately. I knew you had an idea something was going on, but probably not

218

exactly what. But I kept reminding myself that you had spent your whole marriage refusing to look at the truth. Were you really ready to deal with it?'

I felt dizzy at Ali's audacity. My whole marriage? What was she talking about? Was she using the confidences I'd shared with her about Gavin's distance, my sense that he was keeping secrets against me now? Twisting my own words to justify her treachery? Perhaps even implying this was not his first infidelity, and thus it didn't really matter so much?

'What are you saying? That you weren't the first? That my husband has been involved with other women in the past, so why not you? Why not my best friend?' I hated the way my voice cracked at the end of the sentence. I hated the tears that were streaming down my cheeks in spite of myself. And most of all, I hated the fact that when Ali rushed toward me and wrapped her arms around me, I didn't have the strength to push her away. Or that when she took me by the shoulders and stared at me with her startling topaz-coloured eyes, I had no escape from her words.

'Me? Is that what you really think, Jeanne? That I'm the one Gavin's been sneaking off to see? I'm the one he's been running up bills for room service with? Do you really think I would do that to you?'

'You certainly had no hesitation about doing it to Beth Shagaury, did you? Not to mention your own husband.' Suddenly feeling light-headed and confused, the way I had at the concert just before I fainted, I pulled away.

'I didn't even know Beth Shagaury. And from what Brian told me about her, I didn't want to. Of course, I've done things that have hurt George, and you're right — there's no excuse for that. No excuse, but to say that we're separated. And he chooses to remain in my life, knowing what I'm like,' she said, sounding surprisingly hurt by my accusations. She, too, took a step backward, distancing herself from the truth of my words.

'I never claimed to be a saint, Jeanne,' she said, her voice sounding more tired than I'd ever heard it. She stood in a pool of light near the bar; the fine lines around her eyes and the deep crease between her nose and mouth had never been more evident. 'Believe me, what happened to Brian — it haunts me more than you'll ever know. But for God's sake, do you really think I'd do that to *you*? Do you really think I'm having an affair with your husband behind your back?'

I picked up the fluffy washcloth from the Park Plaza and held it up, but all the fire had gone out of me. 'Explain this, then,' I said, for the first time really hoping that she could. Really hoping that there was some innocent explanation for the whole thing. Something that would let me go on with my life as I had.

'You really don't know, do you?' Ali said, her voice full of sorrow. She finished her drink and poured herself another, then came toward me to refill my glass.

But I put my hand out stopping her. 'I don't want your cognac. And I certainly don't want

220

your pity. I've caught you red-handed, Ali. Both of you. Now you're trying to tell me that what I see here spelled out in black and white, dollars and cents, isn't true. That my husband hasn't been following the quartet around, lying to me, betraying me in every city where you played?'

'No, I'm not trying to tell you that. You're right, Jeanne. You've got the evidence in your hand. Your husband has been unfaithful to you. And I seriously doubt this was the first time. Gavin's probably been sleeping around since the first year of your marriage. But not with me, Jeanne. I only found out about this two weeks ago myself. And believe me, it's over now.'

In an unexpected fit of rage, I knocked over the bottle of cognac that Ali had left on the table, and watched it spill. The way my glass of wine had stained the rug on the night when I found the shoe box. Or spilled across the granite counter the day Gavin cancelled the appointment. 'I can't believe you're still trying to weasel out of this.' Suddenly, I felt like I couldn't breathe in her living room; I was choking on the scent of her cologne. The music from the stereo was pounding in my head. I started to gather up my things. 'I don't know why I came here in the first place.'

But Ali seized my arm, preventing me from leaving. 'You came here because you want the truth. The truth you know yourself, have probably known for years, but just didn't want to face. Think about it, Jeanne. Think about all the things you told me. How Gavin never seemed interested in you — even in the beginning. About how hard you tried to attract him — and he seemed almost angered by your efforts, about your sense that he was locked in himself, locked in by something he couldn't share with anyone.

'But as time has gone on, he's taken greater and greater risks until it came to this. He tried to be discreet, booking rooms on another floor, avoiding my concerts, keeping a low profile, but he must have known that eventually I'd find out.'

By then Ali was crying, but I continued to stare at her blankly, still not getting it, but waiting for her to whale me with the truth. She held my arms in place with her strong hands so I couldn't lash out at her. 'Oh, Jeanne, don't you see? It wasn't *me* Gavin came to see that weekend in New York. Or any of those other times either. Gavin doesn't want me any more than he wants you — or any other woman. It was the young cellist he visited in New York, Jeanne. It was Marcus.'

19

Ali tried to stop me from running out into the night the way I did, scattering the papers I had collected from Gavin's study as I ran. She even followed me into the street, calling so loudly that the lights at Nora Bell's house flashed on. I could almost feel the eyes of the old busybody on my back as I ran for the Jeep. My last vision of Ali was of her standing in a puddle of light on the sidewalk, calling my name.

As I careened onto my own street, I was disheartened to see that almost all the lights I'd left on had been switched off. The darkness served to emphasize the one room that was aggressively bright: Gavin's study. Just inside the kitchen door, he had left his luggage lined up with his usual military precision, and there were signs he'd recently fixed a gin and tonic. Every reminder of his presence made me shudder. Noiselessly, I slipped past the closed door of his study and headed for the stairs.

In my room, I quickly packed a bag and tried Jamie's cell phone. I was mystified when it went straight to voice mail. Jamie's phone was the lifeline that kept him connected to his sprawling social network, and he always answered it. With my bag in hand, I crept down the stairs as stealthily as I'd gone up. I intended to wait for my son in the kitchen so I could tell him my plans. But the sight of the band of yellow light from beneath the study door made me fear what would happen if Gavin emerged. No matter how much I wanted to talk to Jamie, I simply wasn't ready to face the man behind that door. I could already hear his bullying denials, could imagine the way he would somehow manage to portray his betrayals and lies as *my* fault. Imagining the man who sat rigidly behind the desk in that brightly lit room, I decided that as much as I hungered for the sight of my son, I would just have to call Jamie from the road.

I was almost out of the house when I was assailed by a blast of the violent-sounding music that Jamie liked — a cacophony that unfailingly set my nerves on edge. But strangely, it was emanating from the study. I crept closer, and rested my hand on the door-knob as the music continued to assault my fragile psyche. When curiosity got the better of me, and I pushed open the door, I'm not sure who was more startled — me or the boy who sat behind his father's desk.

'Jamie!' I said. 'My God, you scared me to death. What in the world are you doing in here? If your father comes home and — ' I began automatically, and then stopped myself as I noticed what looked like a gin and tonic in his hand. 'Are you *drinking*, Jamie?'

'He left it here when he took off so, yeah, I tried it.' He shrugged cavalierly, though a shamed blush travelled up his neck. 'Tastes like crap. I don't know how the dude can drink this stuff.'

'Before he took off?' I repeated, deciding that

sipping from his father's watery drink wasn't really all that significant in light of everything else.

Jamie switched off the computer without even bothering to shut it down. 'Yeah, first he went ballistic, accusing me of going through his stuff — I don't know, breaking into some secret drawer or something. Then right in the middle of his freak-out, he got a phone call. Some emergency at the hospital. He said he probably wouldn't be back till after midnight.'

Mocking Gavin's suave manner, Jamie took another sip of his father's gin and tonic, then mimed an exaggerated gagging reflex. 'Anyway, I figure if I'm being accused of sneaking around in his holy fucking study, I might as well do it,' he continued. This time he wasn't joking; his eyes burned with long-suppressed rage. It was a rage I'd seen only once before, when we'd discussed the home invasions at Ali's place.

'There's no need for obscenities,' I began nervously, but then found myself laughing out loud. *Be polite. Always say please.* Suddenly my whole life seemed like a cruel joke. 'Find anything interesting?' I asked. Knowing that Gavin wouldn't return any time soon, I felt myself relaxing.

'Nope. How about you?'

In response, I took the gin and tonic from him and flicked off the light in the study. 'Let's go have some hot chocolate in the kitchen. This room gives me the creeps.'

'I'm not five years old, Mom,' Jamie said with a disdain that cut through me. 'You can't make everything better with hot chocolate.'

Still, he followed me into the kitchen, and when I began to heat milk on the stove, and set out two cups, he took out the canister of whipped cream and sprayed a dollop into the palm of his hand. Then he promptly licked it off — just like he'd done when he was five.

'You planning to go someplace?' he said, glancing at my packed bag as he pulled up a seat at the counter. Once again, he attempted a look of suave indifference, but the little-boy vulnerability showed through.

'Just for a couple of days,' I said, still facing the stove. More than anything, I wished I could take Jamie with me. Tell him to pack a bag and forget about the summer school course that started the next day. *We were getting out of here.* But there was no way I could take him out of school now; his whole academic future was at stake.

When I turned to face him, he looked panicky. I knew how much Jamie hated to be alone, and how little solace he found in his father's frequently disdainful company, if that's what it could be called. Gavin was either absorbed in his workouts or locked away in his study. No wonder my son had grown so attached — perhaps overly so — to me.

'Jamie, I — ' I began, but didn't know how to explain my uncharacteristic behavior to my son. In all the years of my marriage, I'd never gone anywhere without Gavin and Jamie. *My family.* I'd clung to those words like a life raft for years after they ceased to mean anything. Suddenly, the scene, the words I'd heard at Ali's house began to replay in my mind, and I felt myself trembling.

'It's only for a couple of days,' I repeated firmly, skirting the whirling vortex that threatened to open up inside me. 'You'll be so busy with summer school and your friends, I'll be back before you know it.'

Jamie seemed to mull that over. 'Does *Dad* know?' he asked. The familiar and somehow comforting hush of co-conspiracy fell over the room. We had developed an implicit understanding of which secrets we could keep from *Dad*, and which we couldn't. A trip away was clearly not one of them. Not until now.

'I'll call him when I get there,' I said, stirring the hot milk. 'Jamie, there's some things I have to think about.'

I braced myself for the effect my words would have on my son.

But Jamie only exhaled deeply. 'Some things you should have thought about a long time ago,' he said. 'So you gonna tell me where you're going, or what?'

Where was I going? It was a question I hadn't even answered for myself — at least, not until that very moment in the kitchen as I spoke the words to my son. 'To New Hampshire,' I said, as if I'd been planning it for weeks. 'You know my parents' old cabin? The one I inherited after they died?' In all my married years, I'd only been there once. Gavin hadn't even gotten out of the car.

'You're going *there*? I thought that place was a

dump, Mom. Un — unin — what was the word Dad called it?'

'Uninhabitable,' I said, smiling, though my eyes were suddenly wet. 'That's one reason I'm going — so I can fix the place up. I was thinking you and I might spend the summer up there. When you finish your classes, of course.'

It was hard enough to keep Jamie away from his friends even for a weekend, so I braced for a flurry of protests. But he just looked down and picked a piece of lint off his pants. '*Without Dad?*'

'Just you and me,' I said as casually as I could. I poured our hot chocolate into cups and passed him one. 'You could visit him, of course, as often as you liked. I know you'd miss your friends, but they could come up there and spend some time, too.'

'And then in the fall, what? We stay up in the cabin and cut down trees to keep warm? Maybe hunt bears for food?'

'We've got the whole summer to figure that out. We have options, Jamie; we could even rent a place in town if you wanted to finish school here.' Without saying it, we both knew that staying in our beautiful home — even without Gavin — was a repellent idea.

Jamie looked at me directly for the first time. 'He'll never let us go, you know. When the lid comes off, he'll do whatever it takes to keep us here.'

When the lid comes off? Obviously, Jamie knew a lot more than I thought he did. Maybe he'd known about the affair with Marcus before

228

I did. Though I knew his relationship with his father had always been strained, I was surprised at Jamie's cavalier reaction when I implied I was leaving.

'And *I'll* do whatever it takes, too,' I said firmly. 'Whatever it takes to build a new life for you and me.'

After that, we drank our hot chocolate in comfortable silence — just as we'd drunk dozens, perhaps hundreds, of similarly steaming cups in the past. But we both knew that this hour, this moment, this cup of cocoa was nothing like the others.

After we'd finished, Jamie hoisted my bag onto his shoulder. 'You probably should get going,' he said, casting a furtive glance into the driveway. Though he didn't finish it, I knew the end of the sentence: *before Dad comes home.*

The perfect housewife to the end, I went to the sink and carefully rinsed our mugs, washed the pot and put it away. Then I wrote out the obscure directions to the remote cabin twice. I handed the first copy to Jamie and told him it was for his eyes only. I didn't have to say any more. Jamie folded the piece of paper into tiny squares and stuffed it into his pocket. The second copy I planned to drop in Ali's mailbox on the way out of town. For Gavin, I left only a quick note saying that I'd gone to New Hampshire, but not including the directions to the cabin. I was certain that he had forgotten them.

'I'll see you in a couple of days, then,' Jamie said as he loaded my bag into the backseat.

I desperately needed a hug, but Jamie promptly started back toward the house, probably trying to make the departure as unemotional as possible. But just before I pulled away, he turned back and watched me go. Looking vulnerable and pale, he stood in the driveway with his hands folded over his chest. It was the pose of a man, but his eyes recalled the little boy. Though the car windows were closed and I couldn't hear him, I could read the words on his lips. 'Bye, Mom,' he said. Just those two words. As I turned the corner of my street, tears blurred my view of the town, the marriage, the life I was leaving behind.

I was halfway to New Hampshire, blasting a pop station on the radio in a futile attempt to drown out my thoughts, when I suddenly recalled the promise I'd made to Jamie. I'd said I would never leave him alone. *I'd promised*. But really, I had no choice. If I took him out of summer school now, he wouldn't be promoted with his class. He might even be so demoralized that he'd never return to school at all.

Then I reminded myself I *hadn't* broken the promise; Jamie was hardly alone. It might do him good to spend some personal time with his father, maybe even prepare him for a time when I would no longer be a buffer between them. But I knew that whatever demons troubled my son and made him fear solitude, Gavin had never been able to keep them away. I couldn't think of that, though. Not now. Cranking the radio up a little higher, I reassured myself: it was only two days.

20

More than the house where I grew up or the playground where I skinned my knees the first day of school and lost myself in the rhythm of a thousand games of jump rope, the cabin held the secrets of my childhood. Several times Jamie had expressed interest in seeing the cabin, but remembering Gavin's warnings about the dangers of memory and the unsafe condition of the place, I always found a reason to put him off.

Still, I'd adamantly refused to sell it. The one time Gavin suggested that we clean it up and put it on the market, I had snapped at him. 'The cabin is mine,' I'd said, staking my rights in a way I almost never did. *I* would decide when it was time to sell — if ever. Startled by my uncharacteristic assertiveness, Gavin had dropped it.

I now found a particular satisfaction in the fact that I was going to an unreachable place, a place that no one who knew me could find except for Jamie and Ali, who both understood my need for privacy. Driving up the winding mountain road that was at times scarcely wider than a path, I wondered what would happen if the Jeep broke down and I was unable to find the cabin. In fact, it had been so long since anyone had visited the property, I couldn't even be sure the little structure was still standing. How easily I could be lost up here, I thought. I could die on one of these mountain roads, and no one would find me until it was too late. In my current state, the thought was almost comforting.

As soon as I made the familiar turn and the cabin came into view, I felt a rush of exhilaration. There was a broken window in the front, and a fallen tree had damaged the roof, but the tiny structure was much the same as I remembered it. Through the window I could even see the faded but still cheery yellow-and-white-checked curtains my mother had sewn for the combination kitchen/living room.

But as I unlocked the padlock that was supposed to keep out the world, I felt the dangerous rush of the past, the reminder that the real perils of life never come from the outside. I gasped when I pushed open the door. The ruin that had occurred after years of neglect was shocking enough, but it was the sharpness of memory that really derailed me.

One look at the black-and-white squares of linoleum on the kitchen floor or the pine cabinets erased time. In my mind, the empty cabin teemed with family life. I could smell the hot dogs my father barbecued on the grill, could hear the long-silenced voice of my brother telling me to find some clean jars: it was a good night to catch fireflies. *Come on, J.J., let's go!* And in the background there would be the music my mother played endlessly on her turntable: jazz, old folk songs, but mostly classical. During the summer when we left the relentless drone of our TV set behind, the impassioned music of Chopin and Mozart, which our mother hoped we would absorb into our bones, had been our only entertainment.

We came here only once after my brother's death; the memories were simply too painful. And somehow, it was here where we felt his absence most sharply. Once again, my parents turned to music for understanding, to the tragic operas and requiems that spoke to their grief in a way that nothing else could. By then, I had begun to rebel, and had retreated to my own little room with my own little radio, playing top forty as loud as I could. There I drowned out their music, their grief with the relentless drumbeats and cries of eternal love. But neither the music nor the grief from that time has ever really left me. Now, entering the cabin where I had encountered both, I couldn't help thinking that there really was a thing called fate. Destiny. In some way, everything in my life had led me to my friendship with Ali. Maybe I, who loved music, but had no talent of my own, had been groomed to be the sounding board of one who did. I had become the ideal listener.

But I didn't want to think of Ali now, didn't want to recall the vivid image of our last encounter in her living room, her words coming at me like a spray of bullets: *But surely you knew, Jeanne. It's not me Gavin wants, not any woman . . . the cellist . . . Marcus.* Despite my best efforts to drive them out, the words echoed in my head, the haunting revelation of what a fool I'd been, how naive, easily duped. *Surely you knew, Jeanne. Not you or me or any woman.*

233

I tried to form a clear image of the cellist in my mind. I wasn't sure what shocked me more — his sex or his youth. Slender and self-effacing, Marcus had been described as a prodigy. But how old was he? Nineteen or twenty? Perhaps even younger? I shuddered, refusing to imagine Gavin with this young man. Unable to imagine it.

Nor would I think of the mundane questions that usually occupied me, like what Jamie and Gavin would have for dinner that night. No, I wouldn't allow myself to remember the dread in my son's face as he watched me go. I might forgive myself for spending decades in such an unendurable situation; but how could I ever absolve myself for what Gavin's coldness had done to Jamie? No, I wouldn't think of that. Not now.

I put my things in my old bedroom, which reeked of mildew and pine. It was so small, barely the size of a walk-in closet, I wondered how it could possibly contain so many memories.

But after slamming the door on them, I quickly went back to the kitchen. My mother's old dustpan and broom were in their usual spot by the refrigerator, and beneath the sink was an array of cleaning supplies. Though they were decades old, they would have to do. Grateful for a problem that I could actually solve, I set about the task of making the cabin habitable with a rush of my usual energy.

By nightfall, my limbs and back ached, but the dirt and decay, the carcasses of dead insects, the pine resin and moldy residue that had accumulated over years of disuse had been partially vanquished. The tiny camp refrigerator and stove were restored to a shadow of their former whiteness, and the linoleum, though cracked and yellowed by time, shone from my strenuous waxing. After a day of airing and the help of a rusty can of Glade, the smell of decay that had assaulted my nostrils was gone, replaced by a false floral scent. However, the mattress from my cot, which had been airing out on the porch all day, still smelled musty. Well, it would have to do — just as the flashlight and candles I had brought would have to suffice for light, and the few items I had picked up at a convenience store would serve as supper.

That night, wrapped in my jacket, I slept curled up on the lounge chair that still seemed to hold the scent of my father's pipe smoke. I woke to the sound of birds. The stream was so close it sounded as if it had risen overnight and was flowing right past my door. Its rushing instantly reminded me where I was.

At first, I felt a surge of the old excitement and joy I always experienced when I woke up here. But then, I opened my eyes and looked around me. There were spiders in the kitchen sink, and an army of beetles and ants marching across the floor for the remains of last night's junk-food feast. And I was alone in a wild place. More alone than I had ever been. A thirty-seven-year-old woman who had lost her birth family, and whose attempt to create a new one for herself had failed abysmally. A woman who no longer had any home but this dilapidated shack in the middle of no place.

When I got up and washed my face in the bathroom, I saw a tiny mouse staring up at me from behind the toilet. Instinctively, I screamed. Then realizing that there was no one to hear me, and that a little mouse was the least of my problems, I laughed. I laughed so hard that when I glanced in the clouded mirror, there were tears streaming down my face.

21

The next day, I went into town to pick up a few supplies and read the HELP WANTED signs that hung on the wall at the general store. If Jamie and I were going to stay up here for the summer, we would need jobs.

'Where you staying?' the clerk asked as I paid for the few items I'd collected.

'Up on Mountain Road,' I said vaguely, eager to get back to the task of cleaning the cabin and getting it ready for Jamie.

'Mountain Road? Only thing up there's a couple a old cabins. Both deserted for years. What you plannin' to do up there? Bury a body?' he laughed, peering out the window at my out-of-state license plate.

Feeling edgy and turned off by his humour, I wanted to tell him to mind his own business. But if Jamie and I were to spend the summer here, it would pay to make friends with the locals. 'I'm renovating one of the cabins,' I explained. 'My parents' old place.'

'Renovatin', huh? You people love that stuff, don't you? Ask me, the only way to renovate those cabins is with a wrecking ball.' In his flannel shirt and well-worn overalls, his straggly hippie ponytail, the clerk appeared as outdated as the abraded sign over the general store, but he looked at me as if I were the time traveller.

'Thanks for the advice,' I said with as much

politeness as I could muster, though inwardly I cringed at the category he'd put me in. *You people*, as in well-heeled out-of-state vacationers who drove up prices, bought up the best real estate, cruised around like they owned the mountain all summer, then abandoned it at the first sight of winter's harshness.

When I got back to the Jeep, my cell phone was buzzing on the passenger seat. The innocuous sound that I heard a dozen times a day now caused my heart to lurch. It was quickly followed by the signal that a message had been left. Probably Gavin armed with a new campaign of manipulation, I thought, deciding I would wait till I got back to the cabin to listen to the message.

But when I finally poured myself a glass of the cheap chablis sold at the general store and played the message, it was neither my husband nor my son. Instead, the sound of Ali's anxious voice penetrated my mountain hideaway. 'Jeanne? I know you're there. Please, Jeanne. I'm worried about you. We're all worried. You have to come home.'

My hands folded protectively across my chest, I stood and listened to my friend's voice. In many ways I wanted desperately to talk to her, but I wasn't ready to relive the humiliation I had experienced in her living room. Wasn't ready to 'talk about it,' as Ali would surely want to do.

At first I found comfort in Ali's obviously caring voice. But by the third or fourth time I had played it back, some disturbing questions had arisen in my mind. *We're* worried about

238

you, she said. Who exactly was 'we'? Jamie knew what I was doing here, so she wasn't referring to my son. The only other possibility was Gavin.

Just picturing them — and maybe even the boyish Marcus as well — conferring about 'the problem with Jeanne' rekindled my festering sense of betrayal. But then I remembered the rage in Ali's eyes when she had told me about Gavin's infidelity. The rage on my behalf. No. No matter how concerned she was, Ali would not go to Gavin. Of all the people in the world, she was firmly and irrevocably in my corner. The one person I could trust. Just thinking of how she'd appeared the last time I saw her, I felt ashamed that I'd ever doubted her.

I was still thinking of her when the phone rang again; this time I picked up on the first ring. Not bothering with hello, the caller simply said my name. *Jeanne?* Gavin's voice sounded strained and tired. Stunned, I hung up. But before I could calm my ragged breathing, he called back, and I tentatively pressed the talk button — motivated by curiosity as much as anything else. How would Gavin handle this one? With more lies? The intimidating cold fury that worked so well in the past?

Apparently thrown off by my silence, Gavin cleared his throat. 'Jeanne, are you there?' he asked, sounding uncharacteristically contrite. 'Please, Jeanne, there's obviously been a horrible misunderstanding here.' He hesitated briefly waiting for me to respond. Then in a more firm voice, he continued, 'I can clear this up if you'll give me a chance, but you have to talk to me.'

I was startled by the sound of my own voice, resounding in the cabin, more resolved than it had ever been. 'As far as I'm concerned, there's nothing to talk about, Gavin. No more lies to be told. No more pretenses to be made. It's over.'

'You mean you're going to let some middle-aged slut ruin our marriage? Our family? Without even hearing me out? I can't believe you're taking *Ali's* word as Gospel.' Gavin spit out my friend's name like a curse.

'Yes, I do believe Ali. But not because I'm under her evil influence, as you seem to think. I believe her because she's telling the truth. The truth I've resisted for so long. Can't you admit it even now? We never had a chance, Gavin.'

'Don't be so melodramatic, Jeanne. Marriage isn't some kind of fairy tale. There are ups and downs, *misunderstandings*, as I said before. But people learn to readjust their expectations and deal with them.'

'Oh, and that's what you expect me to do now — *readjust my expectations?*' I snorted. 'Give up the quaint idea that my husband is supposed to love me, *want* me? Go back to a life of locked rooms, silent dinners, solitary weekends while you're off with Marcus or someone else? Is that what you expect me to do?'

Gavin paused for a long moment, obviously startled by my sudden fire. I could almost feel the tension bristling through the phone as he prepared his next assault. When he spoke again, his voice was dry and hard. 'I don't suppose you care how your actions are affecting your son. I heard him prowling around the house last night, going into the refrigerator to relieve his anxiety. You know the boy is troubled; you said so yourself.'

'When all else fails, try guilt. That's your tactic, isn't it, Gavin? Well, sorry; even guilt isn't going to work this time. But just to ease your mind, I haven't forgotten my son for a moment. As soon as the cabin is ready, I'll be bringing him up here for the rest of the summer.'

Gavin laughed drily. 'You're obviously very confused, Jeanne. Do you really think I'd let my son go off to an isolated cabin with you in this unstable condition? Besides, that place is so run-down, it's in danger of collapsing. If you intend to leave this marriage, I'm afraid there's nothing I can do to stop you. But please, don't think you have a chance of getting custody. Jamie stays with me.'

'Jamie hates you!' I blurted out. 'He'd never stay with you.'

'You really think the courts would allow a teenager with obvious emotional problems to decide that?' Gavin asked icily. 'Obviously, you don't know Judge Bryan.' With that subtle reminder of his powerful connections, he slammed the receiver in my ear, having the last word as always.

By then I was shaking so violently that I dropped my razorthin phone, allowing it to clatter onto the cabin floor. Clutching my midsection as if I'd been punched, I heard Gavin's threat resounding in my mind. It was the threat that had been at the heart of our marriage since Jamie's birth, the threat that had kept me from asking too many questions, from looking too deeply at our lives: *if you leave me, you'll lose Jamie.*

The worst part was that I knew Gavin was right. He was a doctor, a well-respected member of the community who could summon dozens of character witnesses at a moment's notice. Who would ever believe plain Jeanne, an unemployed school secretary with few close friends? And who would testify on my behalf; who in town would dare to contradict *wonderful* Dr Cross and his legion of supporters? No one but Ali, the town's most notorious adulteress. As I pictured her climbing into the witness box in one of her dramatic outfits, I shuddered. Unless Jamie was allowed to choose which parent he wanted to live with, I had no hope of gaining custody.

The circle I made as I paced the cabin shrunk in size until I found myself in the middle of the room, totally unable to see a way out. For the first time since Ali had forced me to face the truth, I pondered the idea of returning home and staying in the marriage until Jamie graduated from high school. After all, it was only two more years. Surely I could trudge through two more years, if the alternative was losing my son. And maybe now that Gavin had finally admitted our son had a problem, he would agree to make another appointment with Dr Emory.

Still I clung to the idea of bringing Jamie up to the cabin for the rest of the summer. I imagined myself bargaining with Gavin: if only he would give me this time alone with my son, then I would agree to come home in the fall. I would prepare his dinners and smile at charity functions; I would even pack his clothes when he left for the inevitable 'conferences' on weekends. I would go on doing what I had learned to do so well: I would pretend to be a wife. Pretend to be the perfect family.

★   ★   ★

I was pretty proud of the rapid progress I'd made at the cabin. Armed with nothing but my ancient collection of cleaning products, a few basic carpentry supplies purchased in town, and my own manic energy, I had managed to restore the place to a near livable condition in only two days. The only real obstacle to my plan was the roof. I'd discovered the numerous leaks the very first night when a thunderstorm pinpointed a particularly large one directly over my head. The newsboard at the general store again proved helpful as I located a roofer. He'd even agreed to check the cabin for structural safety — and document it, which would at least defray one of Gavin's objections. The only problem was the roofer couldn't make it out to the cabin till Friday afternoon — which meant I'd have to stay a couple of extra days.

I knew that the delay would probably frustrate Jamie, but when he saw what else I'd found on the newsboard, he'd quickly forget his disappointment. Staring straight at me from a flyer was the photograph of a little dog, his eyes reflecting heartbreak and pluck in equal measure. Immediately, I recognized a soul mate.

The words on the flyer were cryptic and to the point:

DOG FOUND NEAR SHOOTFLYING HILL
ABANDONED AND ABUSED
FREE TO GOOD HOME

How could I do anything but call the number? That night, late in the evening when Jamie prowled the house, I talked to him through the answering machine, forcing my voice to sound upbeat: 'Hey, Jamie. You won't believe what I brought home today. A dog. Skyler is the cutest little terrier mix you've ever seen. He's awfully skinny, and could use a good bath, but he seems to be pretty bright. And he's eating me out of house and home. *Jamie?* Jamie, are you there?'

I was disappointed no one picked up, but I smiled as I imagined my fastidious husband's reaction when he heard I was coming home with a flea-ridden mutt.

The next day was Thursday, and the first really hot day of the summer. Since I hadn't brought my bathing suit, I swam nude in the isolated stream for the first time ever. The cold water shocked my skin, but once I had acclimatized myself, it felt like a tangible symbol of my new freedom. While I floated on my back, Skyler stood on the shore and barked. I had brought a bar of soap, hoping to lure him into the water for a much-needed bath, but the dog was having no part of it.

I was thinking so hard of my son as I neared the cabin that when I heard the chimey ring of my cell phone, I began to run, my son's name ringing through the woods as if he could hear me. 'Jamie!' I cried. Sensing my excitement, Skyler barked and ran faster. I was just outside the screen door when it stopped. The voice on the message sounded so drained and frightened that at first I didn't recognize it as Ali's:

'Listen, Jeanne, I know you don't want to talk to me. And I can't say I blame you. The way I sprung that on you the other night was unforgivable. But that's not why I'm calling — ' She sighed deeply before she continued. 'Something has happened, Jeanne. Something serious. Please call right away; this isn't something I can talk about on voice mail.'

With the door still flung wide open and the little dog looking up at me expectantly, I stood absolutely still, frozen by the words that had infiltrated my private world, and by my own fears. Fears for Ali, of course, but more than that, fears for my son. Was it possible the break-ins had resumed? My God — was Jamie stalking her again? *And why?* Ali had never done or said anything to hurt him, at least as far as I knew. Once again, my husband's accusations swarmed through my mind like a deadly gas. I'd been so quick to blame Jamie for everything, but was it possible that Gavin was right? That Ali had lured my son into some deadly game for her own purposes? Maybe even to 'get attention,' as my husband suggested?

I called her back before even closing the door, but no one answered. Not even her machine. And when I redialled the number she'd called from, I reached only an unmanned pay phone. *Why would Ali be calling me from a phone booth?* I wondered. *Was she afraid to stay in her own house, or pretending to be? And why had she disconnected her machine?* I wondered if she'd received more threatening messages — messages she could no longer blame on Brian?

Banishing those thoughts, I dialled my own number, but there was no answer there either, and Jamie's cell phone went immediately to voice mail. My first impulse was to throw a few things back in my bag and drive home immediately. But if I did that, my whole trip would be a wasted effort. Without a thorough inspection and a patched roof, I had no hope of bringing my son here.

While the little dog tilted his head quizzically, I replayed Ali's message, analyzing each subtle nuance in her voice, listening hard for the things she didn't say. By the time I heard it for the third time, I convinced myself I'd simply been alone too long with my own crazy thoughts; I was overreacting. Why had I assumed the trepidation I heard in her voice had anything to do with Jamie? Ali's life was full of drama, for goodness sake. I thought of how volatile Jack Butterfield had looked the morning I saw him arguing with Ali outside her cottage; most likely it was a problem on that front which prompted my friend's distress call. And if I knew Ali, if she truly felt threatened, by now she was safely ensconced at George's house.

That night, I made pancakes from a box mix

for Skyler and me. It was a supper my mother sometimes made — but only at the cabin, where the rules of the real world didn't count. As I washed the chemical-tasting pancakes down with wine, I thought of how much my brother and I had enjoyed our casual suppers, and for the first time I allowed myself to get excited about the coming summer. I imagined myself showing Jamie all the special spots where we had built forts in the woods. In the days before my brother's car accident, we'd risen early, long before my parents, packed a lunch, and gone off to fish the stream. Then when we were tired of casting our lines, we dove into the water and swam with the fish we'd just been trying to hook. As I thought of sharing those forgotten pleasures with Jamie, it was almost like getting a piece of my childhood back. The sweetest piece.

With Skyler in my arms, I fell asleep in the old chaise longue where my mother had once read magazines in the sun. My slumber was blissfully dreamless for the first time in months. I might have even slept all night without stirring if my cell phone hadn't rung sometime around ten o'clock. First one call that went to voice mail. And then, a short time later, another one.

★ ★ ★

I had already packed and was bathing Skyler in an old corn pot I'd found beneath the sink when the phone rang the following morning. Since the pot had rusted and the water was seeping slowly through the small perforations in the tin, I worked quickly while the dog, compliant but miserable, stared up at me with pleading eyes. My hands were covered with soap and I was some distance from the ringing phone, but I lunged for it. As soon as I snatched it up, my husband's voice floated toward me. This time there was neither pleading nor anger in it, but something that sounded like the utter depletion I had experienced before I came to the cabin.

'Something terrible has happened, Jeanne,' he began. Allowing the dog to squirm from my hands and onto the floor where he promptly shook water and soap everywhere, I held the treacherous instrument so tightly my hands were white. If I could have smashed it in that moment, I would have. I would have done anything I could to prevent Gavin from continuing.

'Something terrible,' Gavin repeated, after taking a moment to compose himself while I stood in the middle of the floor, powerless to stop his words. 'I don't know how to tell you this but straight out. It's your friend, Ali, Jeanne. She's been murdered. They found the body this morning . . . Jeanne? Jeanne? Are you there?'

22

'We're going home,' I told Skyler as we careened onto my street. 'Home.' The little mutt tilted his head quizzically as I slowed down. But as I pronounced the word Skyler didn't know, I tried not to think of what I would encounter when I went there.

I had been unable to speak, hardly able to breathe, as Gavin had described the grisly scene they had found in Ali's music room: the fierce struggle that had left her beautiful Stradivarius smashed to bits, bloodstained music sheets scattered everywhere, and several pieces of furniture overturned. Ali's body was on the couch, as if she were merely resting amid all the chaos. But the abundance of blood that had radiated outward from her heart, soaking her shirt, her hair, the couch itself, belied her peaceful pose. Sparing me no details, Gavin said that Ali had apparently been tortured before she was killed. Though she had died from a gunshot wound, there were also knife marks on her throat, her chest. But despite the sadistic nature of the murder, the final expression on Ali's face was one of surprise, not terror. How characteristic that was of Ali, I thought. She would have believed to the end that the murderer would be dissuaded by her charm. Or simply that she would emerge from this fight unscathed, as she had from so many others.

It was George Mather who found the body. Apparently, Ali had been calling George all the previous day, leaving messages at his office and on his machine at home. Messages that initially tried to hide her fear, saying simply that she needed to see him. And then later, words filled with unabashed terror. On the phone, Ali told her husband that she knew who had been harassing her. And that the stalker was getting more desperate. She had a few errands to run in the afternoon, but she would be home by dinnertime. Would George please come by? She wanted advice on what she should do next. She would wait to hear from him before going to the police. Later messages, obviously made in the evening, sounded even more panicked.

Unfortunately, George had been out of town all day, and then had stopped for a leisurely dinner with a friend from the philosophy department. When he finally arrived home, it was late, and he was exhausted. He didn't even enter the study where the light on his answering machine was blinking with Ali's final, unheard cries for help. Thus he hadn't played back the nearly full tape until the following morning. Of course, he never heard much of it until later. After Ali's first admission of fear, George was dialling her number. Then, while his answering machine continued to broadcast her growing terror, he listened to the ringing in her empty house.

Before the tape had finished, George had dressed haphazardly and was out the door, his heart hammering wildly. Approaching his wife's cottage, he took in a cavalcade of increasingly alarming signs: an open door, a vase knocked over in the living room, the eerie silence that greeted him in place of the music that usually flooded the house. There was no response when he called his wife's name, though Ali's bike was in the driveway, and the lights that could not keep away the terror of the night were still blazing. But most disconcerting of all was the simple beauty of the day. George knew that Ali would never sleep through such a brilliant morning.

Still, nothing could have prepared George for what he found in the music room. And despite his professional knowledge, he had violated every commonsense rule in dealing with a crime scene. He picked up and handled the broken Stradivarius, the music stand; he fingered several sheets of the music that were scattered around the room. And worst of all, he was once again fatally drawn to the beauty that had ruined his life. Not concerned — or even aware — that he was immersing himself in the victim's blood, he went to the couch and took his dead wife in his arms, buried his face in her hair, and inhaled for one last time the scent of lilies that clung to her amidst the acrid odor of blood. Demonstrating the same recklessness that had inspired him to marry Ali in the first place and to remain loyal to her despite her faithlessness, George never thought about how he would explain the bloody fingerprints he was leaving behind. He never worried about the hairs and the fibers that would be found on Ali's body.

An hour later, covered in his wife's blood, George called the police from the same pay phone she'd used when she discovered that the phone lines were cut. He was calm by then — unnaturally calm, at least according to the officer who took the call. And in spite of the ways he had incriminated himself in the crime, George Mather was in possession of a new life-defining goal: he would find the person who had done this to her. No matter what it cost him in time or resources or grief, he would make sure that the person who had taken his beautiful Ali did not get away with it.

As Gavin poured the story through the crackling lines of my cell phone, tears streamed silently down my cheeks. Not only for Ali, but for the love that George had for his wife. It was an excessive and undeserved love — maybe even a fool's love — but no one could deny the depth or authenticity of it. It was there in George's eyes when he mentioned Ali's name, a bright light that nothing, not even death, could extinguish. It was the kind of love that Gavin and I could not even pretend to understand, the kind we had mocked with our empty marriage. Thus even our mourning for Ali and George was contaminated with the selfishness of our own regrets and loss.

Then, at the end of the conversation, his voice still weak from the horrific story he had just related, Gavin stopped me just before I hung up. 'Jeanne, I don't want you home just because of this crisis. I want you to come back to *me*. To give this marriage one more try. What Ali told you, what you found in my desk — I hope you know all that meant nothing.' He paused, apparently hoping for a response, but when I could think of nothing to say, he went on. 'In any case, I'm sorry. Sorry that it happened. And sorry that you found out the way you did. But once again, let me assure you it *meant nothing*.' Somehow Gavin managed to make even an apology sound like an order. I felt like I was being commanded to believe him, commanded to wipe this *meaningless* betrayal from my mind. This time there was no mention of his threat to keep Jamie from me if I even tried to leave him, but of course it was there. It had always been there.

In any case, I was too stunned and shaky to think about my marriage. 'We'll talk when I get there,' I mumbled. Then without even a polite goodbye, I hung up.

Less than ten minutes later, I left the cabin where I had briefly fooled myself into thinking I could begin a new life. Taking nothing but Skyler, my recklessly maxed-out credit card, and a couple of the candy bars I had been living on, I climbed into the Jeep. And there in the car where our friendship had begun to the driving beat of tunes from the radio, I felt Ali's presence as if she were still there beside me. Driving through a blur of tears, I would later remember nothing from that trip. Nothing but my sense that Ali was with me. Would always be with me.

* * *

The first thing I noticed when my house came into view was Gavin standing in the driveway. His eye trained on the street, he spotted the Jeep at about the same time I saw him. I wondered how long he had been out there waiting for me to make the two-hour trip from New Hampshire. At the sight of his familiar face with all its hardness and hidden fears, I felt something cringe inside me. Was I really ready to face Gavin, to deal with the truth of my marriage and Ali's murder all at once? I was so focused on the man in the driveway that at first I didn't even notice the car that was parked in front of the house. But as Gavin came toward me, his eyes revealing a new anxiety, I looked behind him and saw the blue and white of the police cruiser.

And thus Gavin's first words to me were not of the reconciliation he'd pushed on the phone, but of the business that would consume our lives in the coming months. 'Officer McCarty's inside with Jamie,' he said, his lip twitching the way it did when he was nervous or angry. 'Chuck Harrison helped me find a lawyer — a young woman named Courtney Rice.' Looking edgily at his watch, he added, 'She was supposed to be here half an hour ago.' So it was not me he was waiting for after all. It was a lawyer. Somehow, I was neither surprised nor disappointed.

By then Gavin and I were close enough to study every line and tiny freckle in each other's face for the first time since Ali had told me about Marcus. We stared honestly into each other's

254

eyes for the first time I could remember, and what I saw there was a dark reflection of our mutual fears for our son. Obviously, Gavin was no more surprised by the fact that Jamie was the prime suspect than I was.

23

The boy who sat at the table with Detective McCarty resembled Jamie, but he was not the same boy I had left behind only a couple of days earlier, the sweet, vulnerable son who had stood on a patch of grass in the yard and watched me go. No, something had hardened in Jamie, some new distrust that was visible in his eyes, in the stiffness with which he held himself, in the quickness with which he turned away from me when I entered. Even his impeccable grooming habits had given way; his normally shining hair fell over his eyes, lank and oily. When I kissed the top of his head, a smell that reminded me of old cooking grease drifted toward me.

'Aren't you going to say hello to your mother, Jamie?' Detective McCarty asked. But even in that simple question, I had the uneasy sense that he was studying us. From then on, it was obvious that our most minute family interactions would be amplified into 'clues.' The detective was drinking a cup of coffee at the table, as if he had simply dropped by for a social call. He even had the gall to smile up at me, revealing an uneven row of yellow teeth.

'Hi, Mom,' Jamie said passively, but he continued to avoid my gaze.

What I needed more than anything was time alone with my son, but it was obvious that McCarty wasn't going to give us that. If either of us were to make any incriminating remarks in this moment of crisis, he intended to hear them. 'Don't worry, honey,' I said in my strongest voice, giving Jamie's arm a reassuring squeeze. 'This will be cleared up soon. *Very* soon.'

But Jamie remained silent, his eyes intently downward.

The detective watched me avidly as I studied my son. 'You look like you need to sit down there, Mrs Cross. This can't be an easy situation for you,' he said. 'From what I understand, you and the victim were pretty good friends.'

By then I was feeling pretty annoyed with McCarty, who was shamelessly trying to glean information before our lawyer arrived. I cast him a steely glance, and made no response.

Sensing my annoyance, McCarty pushed back from the table, moving laboriously. A paunchy man in his mid-fifties, he had probably been made detective because he couldn't handle the beat anymore, I thought cynically. It certainly had nothing to do with his subtlety in asking questions. 'Well, don't let me disturb you, Mrs Cross. I know you want a little time with your family.' He glanced up at the wall clock, which said it was already nearly two. 'Mind if I use your phone?'

Actually, I *did* mind, but I had no choice but to point him toward the wall where the phone was mounted. It soon became obvious that he was calling the station.

'The lawyer's still not here. No, not anyone I know, some young kid from what I hear, fresh out of law school. *A girl*.' He glanced at his watch again, as if a lot of time had elapsed since the last time he checked.

Though Jamie pretended not to listen, I saw him stiffen as the officer spoke. But when I reached out to touch his shoulder, he didn't respond. In this passive state, how was Jamie going to defend himself against the likes of McCarty? Did he even intend to try? For an instant, I felt the sharp sting of tears in my eyes, but then my attention was pulled away by the policeman who was leaning his shoulder into the wall of my kitchen.

'Yeah, that's what I was thinking,' McCarty resumed. Nodding as he spoke, he caused his jowls to shake. 'So that's what I'll do. We'll give the kid another fifteen minutes and if she's still not here, I'll bring him in and she can meet us there. Okay, Jim.'

After he had hung up, he sauntered toward the window and pulled back the curtain to reveal the scene in the front yard. Gavin stood on the lawn, holding court with several of our neighbours. Obviously drawn by the sight of the police car in front of the house, and the news that must have made its way to their TV sets and radios, they formed a neat half circle. Coming over to get a glimpse of our misery, I thought bitterly. Fortunately all the years of pretending came in handy; my husband was playing Wonderful Gavin to the hilt. His features were arranged in just the right mix of concern and reassuring confidence. I could imagine him telling our nosy neighbours that the police had come to talk to me. After all, Ali and I had been close friends.

The police just wanted to know if Ali had mentioned anything that might be of help.

And come to think of it, why *hadn't* Detective McCarty asked me those logical questions instead of slyly poking around in my family life? If he wanted a list of people who disliked Ali — even people who had good reason to want to harm her — I could give him enough names to keep an army of detectives busy.

But the only thing Detective McCarty interrogated me about was Ali's diary.

'We hear Mrs Mather kept a journal; you ever see it, Mrs Cross?'

My mind travelled to the time I had entered the house when Ali wasn't home. To the slanted violet writing she crowded onto a page, and the passage that had mentioned my name several times. I shuddered inwardly as I remembered reading the words she'd written all in caps: *MY GOD, WHAT'S WRONG WITH HER?*

'A couple of times.' I shrugged, composing my face. 'She used to take it to school with her at the beginning of the year, but then she stopped. People were a little too curious about it, and — '

'Any idea what she wrote about in there?' McCarty interrupted impatiently.

'You probably know more about that than I do, Detective,' I snapped. 'I'm sure you've read it cover to cover by now.'

'I wish you were right, Mrs Cross, but unfortunately, the victim's diary is missing. Far as we know, it's the only thing the killer took from the house.'

I fought the trembling that threatened to

overcome me. I don't know what upset me more: the memory of a shoe box full of pilfered items, which flooded my mind, or the way he'd referred to Ali as *the victim*. 'How do you know that? Maybe she got rid of it herself. Maybe she burned the thing. Like I said, I haven't seen the diary in — '

But once again, McCarty interrupted me with a brisk shake of his head. 'Nope. One of Mrs Mather's neighbours stopped by the night before to give her some mail that had been wrongly delivered, and saw her writing in it at her desk. Whatever she was writing about, the neighbour said she looked pretty upset.'

Nora Bell, I thought with rising fury. She was probably on the phone reporting what she knew about Ali's life as soon as they found the body.

'Well, maybe you should ask the neighbour what Ali wrote about in her diary or who took it. *I* wouldn't know.' Thinking about that nosy Nora Bell made me so irate that my sanctimony must have been pretty convincing. The detective checked his watch, apparently finished with me.

When McCarty asked to use the bathroom, I reached for Jamie's hand. I had been waiting for the detective to leave so that I could have an unguarded minute with my son, but Jamie continued to stare downward. There was so much I wanted to say to him, so many questions I wanted to ask. But with Detective McCarty so close by, all I could do was lean close to him, squeeze his hand, and whisper, 'Just tell the truth, whatever he asks. Eventually, they'll realize they're on the wrong track.'

Jamie glanced at me, his eyes miserable, then pushed his greasy hair out of his face. 'You mean you don't think I did it? Even after that stuff you found in my room?'

I glanced nervously toward the bathroom. 'I *know* you didn't do it. You may have prowled around Ali's house a few times. Even taken a couple of her things, but that doesn't mean you could kill someone,' I said, my voice still a whisper.

'I just wanted to scare her,' Jamie said. 'But I swear I didn't kill her, Mom. Not that anyone's going to believe me.' He sank back into his chair, his eyes glazed over. It was as if the mask of the popular high school student had finally been stripped away, revealing the Jamie beneath the surface: a boy who stalked Ali for unknown reasons, and who trolled around her house when she wasn't home.

'No matter what McCarty says or even what happens today, just keep one thing in mind. The truth will come out — maybe not today or tomorrow, but it will. And the truth is that you're innocent.'

Jamie was about to say something, but just then I heard McCarty lumbering toward us, and I put a finger to my lips. He had been joined by his partner and they were deep in conversation. 'Did Dad tell you about the dog I got you up in New Hampshire?' I said in a louder voice, looking obliquely at McCarty. 'A little abandoned terrier who's been wandering around town and eating out of garbage cans for months. The guy who found him called him Hobo. But I thought he deserved a better name than that. Something with a little dignity.'

Almost in spite of himself, Jamie's eyes flickered with interest. 'Yeah, like what?' he asked.

'Skyler. You want to meet him?'

Sounding almost like his old self, Jamie said, 'You mean he's *here*?'

'I left him in my car. With the window open a crack, of course. I wanted to wait for the right time to bring him in — when all the confusion dies down. But if you want to see him — '

Whether he was thrown back into his former funk by the mention of the 'confusion,' or whether it was just the oppressive presence of the detectives, Jamie interrupted me, his momentary ebullience dissipated. 'Forget it. The last thing I need right now is some mangy dog,' he said.

Stunned by this reaction from a boy who had been begging for a dog ever since he could talk, I said, 'What am I going to do with him, then? I brought him home for *you*, Jamie.'

Apparently forgetting McCarty's presence, Jamie snapped, 'Take him to the pound. Or if he's so good at taking care of himself, let him go. It's gotta be better than living with this family.' After the outburst, he turned to the detective. 'Why do we have to wait for this stupid lawyer? I'm ready to talk right now.'

'Jamie!' I said, with more panic in my voice than I wanted McCarty to see.

His bloodshot eyes bright with his triumph, McCarty looked from Jamie to me and back again. But fortunately, before either my son or I could do our cause any more damage, Gavin burst in the door, followed closely behind by a young woman who, at first glance, appeared to be about fourteen. Scarcely five feet tall and slender enough to wear clothes from the children's department, she looked like a child beside Gavin. The long hair she had pulled back into a schoolgirl braid and the splattering of freckles across her nose added to the impression that we were dealing with Pippi Longstocking instead of the aggressive attorney I'd been expecting. Briefly, I felt my antagonism toward Gavin flare. With all his connections, couldn't he find a better lawyer?

But there was something in Courtney's assured manner that soon renewed my confidence — even if Detective McCarty didn't see it. When she extended her hand assertively toward him, saying, 'Detective McCarty? I'm Courtney Rice, Jamie's attorney,' I swear I could see the hint of a smile in his eyes.

'So pleased to meet you, Miss Rice,' he said, slyly glancing at me.

★   ★   ★

The rest of the afternoon was a continuation of the nightmarish blur that had begun with Gavin's phone call. For the first time since our courtship, Gavin and I held hands as we left the house, a phalanx of neighbours standing on their lawns to watch us go. His grip was so tight that I felt as if he would crush my hand in his, but I didn't ask him to let go. And for much of that afternoon and into the night, we clung to each other as we never had before, suddenly forced to admit that whether we wanted to be or not, we were in this together. We were inextricably a family.

As for Jamie, he resisted not only our comforting gestures but any efforts at conversation. And eventually Gavin and I stopped trying, feeling that each attempt only made his hostility more obvious — and more suspicious to the ever-watchful McCarty.

Despite a whispery voice that matched her small stature and the braid that had begun to remind me painfully of the way Ali sometimes wore her hair, Courtney Rice proved to be an aggressive advocate as McCarty and another officer grilled Jamie at the station for nearly three hours. Gavin and I, feeling more helpless than we'd ever been, watched our son's face, the face we had leaned over to kiss in the crib, the face that smiled out at us all over our house in a succession of school pictures that documented both his growth and his enormous weight gain. The face that contained all our hopes and dreams and indeed the only positive thing to come out of our marriage. We continued to hold hands, squeezing harder at tense moments as we stared at the taciturn young man before us. The son who had suddenly become a stranger. Still, strengthened by each other, we kept our expressions resolutely neutral.

The first questions were at once the easiest and the most treacherous. Did Jamie know the victim? How long had he known her? Could he remember the first time they met? What about the diary? Did he know she kept one? Had he ever seen it? Jamie answered mostly in grunts, shrugs, and monosyllables. Yes, he knew Mrs Mather. Well, sort of. Nope, he couldn't remember when or how they'd met or if they'd ever talked privately. He'd never had her as a teacher. These questions were asked mostly by the younger detective, Detective Anderson, a tall thin man with an open face. Several times, Courtney had to remind Jamie to speak up, to say yes or no, to address the officer directly.

Only the questions about the diary drew an impassioned response. When asked if he'd ever seen Ali's red-covered journal, Jamie mumbled a quick no. Then he promptly contradicted himself by adding, 'I don't know why you're so interested in the stupid thing. It's nothing but a book full of lies.'

Skillfully, Detective Anderson allowed Jamie's words to linger in the stunned silence that followed them. 'So you've read it?' he said at last.

'I told you I've never even seen the thing, didn't I?' Jamie replied, returning to his sullen manner.

'Then how would you know it wasn't truthful?'

'Because everything about that lady was a lie. *Everything*,' Jamie said angrily.

Detective Anderson merely nodded, giving everyone in the room time to register my son's outburst. Once again, Jamie hung his head and stared intensely at the floor. Clearly, whatever he knew about the missing journal, he wasn't about to say any more.

★ ★ ★

Was Ali a popular teacher? Detective McCarty wanted to know when it was his turn. He'd heard her classes were in much demand, that students waited for her after class, and that many even called her at home. But Jamie only shrugged. He wouldn't know . . .

'How about you, Jamie? What did you think of Mrs Mather — or Ali, isn't that what you called her? Did you think she was a nice teacher?'

'I didn't call her anything,' Jamie said, his voice rising in a way that made Gavin squeeze my hand almost involuntarily. 'And I didn't think anything about her either. I told you — I didn't even know the lady.'

'Come on, from what I heard, Mrs Mather stood out in the school. She was something of a celebrity. A real musician and composer. And pretty, too. I heard a number of students had crushes on her. Did you think Mrs Mather was pretty, Jamie?

Again, Jamie shrugged. 'She was old,' he said. 'Not that I ever really looked at her. I never even saw her that much. Like I said, I wasn't in her class.'

'Come on, Jamie, Mrs Mather wasn't only a teacher in your school. She lived only a few blocks from you, isn't that right? And from what I hear, she and your mom were pretty close friends. Of course, you knew her.'

The officer looked to me for confirmation, but my face remained stony.

Jamie shrugged again and sank lower in his seat.

'Well, now you've got me confused, Jamie,' the detective said with mock innocence. 'Were your mom and Mrs Mather friends or not?'

'I guess they were,' Jamie said, his voice surly. 'I don't know.'

'You don't know? Didn't Mrs Mather call your house a lot? Didn't they ride to school together? Didn't your parents occasionally socialize with Mr and Mrs Mather? Maybe attend some of her concerts?'

When Courtney interrupted, asking where the detectives were going with these questions, McCarty backed down. He got up and fixed himself a cup of coffee, offered Jamie a soda. He even smiled as he poured him a Coke. But when he spoke again, the detective's tone was more relentless than ever.

'You ever look at what we used to call girlie magazines, Jamie? You know, *Playboy*, *Penthouse*, stuff like that?'

Jamie glanced fleetingly at Gavin and me, his cheeks suffused with colour. 'I've seen them a couple of times. Kids from school had them. I wouldn't say I actually read them.'

McCarty chuckled like an old friend. A buddy. 'I don't think anybody actually *reads* those things,' he said.

Jamie smiled cautiously.

'Some hot girls in those pages, though, aren't there, Jamie?'

Again, Jamie shrugged. 'I guess so.'

'Come on, Jamie. You don't know a beautiful girl when you see one? First you tell me you don't know if Mrs Mather was pretty. And now you say you don't know if those *Playboy* models are good-looking? What do you like — boys?'

Jamie gazed up at him sharply. 'No!' he said vehemently, but McCarty was already pressing onward.

'From what I hear, the boys at school thought Mrs Mather looked pretty good in those tight jeans she used to wear, those short skirts. But not you, huh? You didn't even notice?'

'She was all right for her age, I guess. Yeah, I mean, she was pretty. But so what? What does that have to do with anything?' Jamie looked desperately in my direction.

'If you want to know the truth, it has everything to do with this murder, Jamie. Because from what we know about this crime, the killer had an obsession with Mrs Mather. You know what an obsession is, Jamie?'

'Not really,' Jamie muttered.

'It's kind of like a crush. You ever have a crush, Jamie? You know, one girl you just can't stop thinking about? One girl who keeps you up at night — a girl who seems so perfect, so special, that you can't get her out of your head?'

'Uh-uh,' Jamie said, glancing furtively at Gavin and me.

'You're what — sixteen years old — and you've never had a crush? Never seen one girl in that high school who really caught your eye?'

'I — I didn't say that — ' Jamie stammered. 'I

268

mean, yeah, I guess I did.'

'I thought so,' McCarty said with satisfaction. 'Well, then, maybe you can understand what an obsession is like. See, an obsession is just a crush that's out of control. You not only think about the person all the time, but you start to follow them around. Maybe even go into their house when they're not home. Take a few of their things home so you can look at them in the privacy of your own room. It sounds crazy, doesn't it, Jamie?'

'Yeah,' Jamie muttered unconvincingly while I glanced desperately at the silent Courtney Rice for help. Why didn't she do something? Surely there was some way she could stop McCarty. But she was watching Jamie as if she wanted to know the answer herself.

'You ever have that kind of crush on anyone, Jamie?' McCarty pressed. He had pushed his chair close to Jamie and was leaning almost into my son's face. 'Say, Mrs Mather, for instance? Weren't you a little bit obsessed with the music teacher?'

'I told you — Ali was old, old and ugly with long witchy hair!' Jamie blurted out. 'And she was mean, too. Oh, sure, she pretended to be nice, but she didn't care who she hurt. The only reason people liked her or fell in love with her was because she tricked them. She even tricked my mom!'

After Jamie's outburst, Detective McCarty skillfully allowed silence to fill the room, emphasizing the startling passion of my son's words. And I suppose he was also waiting for

Jamie to say more, or for Gavin and me to jump up with something incriminating on our lips. But when I tried to protest the unfairness of the questions, Gavin squeezed my hand warningly, and looked toward our lawyer.

Once again, Courtney spoke up calmly. 'So you've proved that Jamie, like most high school students, has some pretty definite opinions about his teachers. Where are we headed with these questions, Detective?'

'I'm trying to establish how young Mr Cross here felt about the victim. That's where I'm heading,' McCarty said.

He paused to sip his coffee before he turned back to Jamie, his voice sinuous, suddenly low and quiet. 'It sounds like you had some pretty strong feelings about Mrs Mather, Jamie. Or I guess I should call her Ali — isn't that what you just called her?'

Though the detective continued to prod him for several more minutes, Jamie had once again retreated to his previously impassive demeanor. And no matter how McCarty baited him, he got nothing but shrugs, grunts, and an occasional 'I guess so.' But it didn't matter. When Gavin and I glanced at each other in an unguarded moment, we both silently agreed that the damage had been done. Jamie had already revealed that he had inappropriately strong feelings about the murder victim.

When we thought the questioning was finished and we would have a chance to go home and regroup before the next phase of this nightmare, Detective Anderson took over, startling us with a new line of questioning. Gone was his former laid-back posture. This time, he, too, was in Jamie's face, bombarding him with a series of questions in rapid succession. Was Jamie interested in knives? Did he own one of his own? Again, Jamie shrugged. The detective hesitated, waiting for Jamie to say more. Well, he had one for Boy Scouts. But that was years ago. Hadn't seen it in a long time. What did the knife look like? Detective Anderson asked coldly. Did Jamie remember well enough to describe it? Jamie roughly estimated the size with his hands. What colour was it? the officer asked. And when Jamie shrugged, he pressed. 'Come on, a boy's scout knife is important. I'm sure you remember what it looked like. It must have had some distinguishing characteristics.'

'It had a red handle, I think,' Jamie added. 'But I'm not sure. Like I said, I haven't seen it in a long time.'

'Not since when — the camping trip you took with the Breen family a short time ago? Didn't you have the knife then?'

Jamie looked around the room like a trapped animal not sure where betrayal would come from next. 'Who told you that — Toby? Did Toby come in here and say that?'

'It doesn't matter who told us. We're asking you. Didn't you have the knife a month ago when you went camping with the Breens?' Detective Anderson's eyes were unnaturally bright as he turned and walked behind the desk.

'I took a knife camping, but I'm not sure it was the same one.'

271

Officer Anderson donned a pair of gloves, opened the drawer, and in one startling motion, produced a plastic bag which he carefully opened, revealing the familiar red-handled knife. An ordinary artifact from Jamie's childhood that I had seen dozens of times in his room. 'Well, let me refresh your memory a little bit, Jamie. Isn't this the knife you took on that camping trip? The same knife you took every time you went to the music teacher's house? The knife you used to cut Ali Mather last night?'

Of course, we all waited for Jamie to deny it. But he seemed almost mesmerized by the glinting knife that Detective Anderson held in his gloved hands. He stared at it a long moment. 'Where did you find that?' he said.

But even before the detective had time to respond, we all knew the answer. The familiar knife, which I had seen in Jamie's room so many times, had obviously been found at the murder scene. It was streaked with dried blood.

24

I dressed in dark slacks and flats the night of Ali's wake. No makeup. With my son in lockup and my best friend lying in Ruskin's Funeral Home, my rules about 'always looking my best' had dissolved into meaninglessness. I finished a stiff drink as I pulled my hair back in a clip. The plain-faced woman in the mirror looked more like a stranger than ever. In recent months, I had drunk more than in all my previous years combined, which might have been a cause for concern in other circumstances. But now the only thing that mattered was survival. I had no idea how the crowd who gathered for the wake would greet the mother of the boy who had been charged with Ali's murder. But by the time I had finished my drink down to the last ice cube, the only one I was afraid to face was Ali.

When I passed the family room where Gavin sat nursing his own liquid escape, he rose and came to the doorway. It was the first time we had really been alone in the two days since Jamie's arrest, the first time that Courtney or the numerous friends who filled our house to offer support or casseroles, or merely to catch a glimpse of our nightmare, had left us face-to-face.

His drink in hand, Gavin spoke tentatively, the way he had since I returned from the cabin. But nothing could hide the rising alarm in his tone.

'Jeanne, I hope you're not planning to go to Ali's wake. You know what Courtney said. Under the circumstances, it wouldn't look right for anyone in our family — '

I shot him a dark look. 'I'm going, Gavin. Maybe if this family had thought more about how things really were, and less how other people thought they were, we might not be in this situation.'

Gavin gulped his drink. 'Christ, Jeanne, it sounds like you think Jamie really *did* this horrible crime. And that we're to blame for trying to hold the family together.'

'Of course, Jamie didn't do it,' I snapped fiercely.

To my bewilderment, Gavin sank onto the couch and put his head in his hands. 'I wish I could share your certainty,' he said. 'But you saw how he reacted at the police station. He didn't even deny it. And the evidence — '

'The kid is sixteen years old and being accused of murder. Wouldn't you be confused? And as far as the evidence is concerned, it can be explained. It *will* be explained.'

I sounded confident, but even I had to admit the evidence was pretty staggering. They had found Jamie's old Boy Scout knife halfway between Ali's house and ours, still streaked with her blood. Then there was the physical evidence at the crime scene, the hairs and fingerprints that matched Jamie's. If that wasn't enough, the prosecution even had an eyewitness: the ever-vigilant Nora Bell was prepared to testify that she had seen a tall, heavy boy running from the house the night of the murder. Though it had been dark and she was near-sighted, she was almost sure that it was Jamie Cross.

Gavin shook his head. 'You expect anyone to buy that — even his own father? Come on, Jeanne, an innocent person accused of murder isn't just going to sit there like — like a zombie. Even when they produced the evidence, Jamie didn't say a word.'

'He *did* deny it. Later, when Courtney asked him. Surely, you haven't forgotten that,' I said. 'He told her he had gone to the house to ask Ali if she'd heard from me. Then, when he found the body, he ran out.'

'You have to admit that's pretty feeble,' Gavin said. 'Think about it from their perspective. I mean, if Jamie innocently stumbled on the scene as he says, why didn't he come to me? Why wouldn't he have called the police? And how *do* you explain the evidence? The knife, for instance. Jamie's fucking DNA!'

'He admitted he was there, but so was George Mather,' I said. 'That doesn't mean either of them killed her.' I felt sorry for Gavin in his obvious torment, but I was determined not to miss the wake. 'I know this is important, but we're going to have to to talk about it later.'

But to my surprise, Gavin suddenly got up and blocked the doorway. 'You're not going anywhere, Jeanne. I won't let you sabotage Jamie like this.'

Sabotage Jamie: it was one of his favorite phrases, one of the stock lines he used to silence me. Whether it was the alcohol or the gravity of

275

our situation, or just the eruption of years of accumulated silence and frustration, I exploded. 'It's not going to work anymore, Gavin. The guilt trips are over. *Be quiet for Jamie's sake. Play the perfect family for Jamie's sake. Pretend to be satisfied, fulfilled, happy for Jamie's sake.* It's over. I'm going to the wake no matter what you say. I have to see Ali.'

Standing on the bottom stair, I looked directly into my husband's eyes. I could feel the thickness of his chest against mine, and I was prepared to push him out of the way if I had to, confident that the adrenaline that was rushing through me would give me the strength I needed. But I didn't have to resort to that. Something — perhaps the desperation in my voice — made him step aside.

'You have to see Ali?' he said coldly. 'You make it sound like you were dropping over for a glass of wine and a chat.'

He couldn't have said anything that struck deeper. A glass of wine and a chat. There was nothing more ordinary than that. And nothing that more clearly defined the meaning of death: *never again.*

Despite the arrogant tilt of Gavin's head, I could see the vulnerability he tried so hard to hide. The fear. In that moment, I experienced a glimpse of what the years of lies and posing had cost him. I suppose if he hadn't ruined my life in the process and seriously maimed our son's, I might have actually pitied the man. But stronger than the impulse to stay with Gavin and talk was my need to see Ali one more time. I had to say goodbye to her and come to terms with the fact that she was really gone, that there would be no more wine and chats, not even a chance to apologize for all the ways I'd failed her. After staring at my husband for a brief moment, I turned and walked out the door.

★ ★ ★

Ali's wake was so crowded that the parking lot at Ruskin's Funeral Home was already overflowing when I got there. In the parking lot, groups of sobbing students inspired by genuine grief, but also by the drama of Ali's death, hugged each other or murmured words of comfort. When I reached the doorway, I found it, too, was clotted with people hoping to make their way inside. Though I expected to see the staff and students from school and the musicians I had met at her concerts, most of the mourners were strangers to me. Staring at the unfamiliar faces, I wondered what their connection to Ali was and how they dared block me from entering.

The crowd was so thick that for a moment I hoped no one would even notice me, one more mourner in the army of people who felt they had a claim to Ali Mather. The longer I waited in line, the more confident I became that the fears Gavin and Courtney had expressed were unfounded. I made my way slowly inside, my head lowered, allowing the hair I'd released from my clip to obscure my face. But just as I began to feel I might be able to slip through the line anonymously, I heard my name called out.

'Jeanne — Jeanne Cross!' Though it was uttered in greeting, nothing could keep the shock from Nora Bell's voice. At the sound of the name that I had always thought so ordinary, but which now sounded like an accusation, a hush fell over the room. Dozens of faces, both familiar and unfamiliar, followed Nora's gaze to the spot where I stood. But as the crowd shifted to get a better look at me, an opening was made. An opening through which I could see the coffin clearly — and resting inside her white satin bed, my friend Ali. The scent of lilies, so reminiscent of her perfume but now distilled to sickening sweetness, was overwhelming. Drawn to her as always, I made my way across the room, oblivious to everything and everyone around me.

Obviously thrown off guard by my boldness, the crowd moved aside to let me pass, their whispers growing louder as I approached Ali's body. I knelt before her, and stared at the carefully made-up mask of my old friend. Her face, smooth and peaceful, betrayed nothing of her tumultuous life, or the struggle that had led to her violent end. It was as serene as the music she coaxed from her violin, as serene as the final movement of the *Paradise Suite*, which I could hear in my head as I gazed at Ali's face. Her lips were slightly pursed, as if she were poised to whisper something to me, one final secret that she would share with no one else. I leaned my ear toward her and touched the marbled hand that had drawn such powerful music from her instrument. I kissed her cheek, noticing the trace of plum-coloured lipstick I had left there. I seemed to have forgotten the requisite prayers, or even what I had wanted to say to Ali when I saw her. The only thing that came to mind was her name, which I recited over and over. It was, I realized, my prayer . . . *Ali* . . . *Ali*. There was so much I wanted to tell her, but now that I knelt before her body, the words dissolved. But it didn't matter; Ali, who had listened so empathetically in the past to everyone who needed her, couldn't hear me.

I began to sob softly, almost forgetting where I was or the crowd of people behind me, when I felt a strong hand touch my shoulder. I turned and found myself staring into the deep, baleful eyes of George Mather. Though they were dry, I had never seen such great sorrow as I did in those eyes.

'Jeanne,' he said, embracing me. Just that. My name, spoken with such depth that its one syllable took on a healing power. Behind us, a low murmur arose, but all I heard was George's breathing in my ear; all I felt was the warmth of his presence, the first real comfort I'd had since Ali's murder. If I had any question about how Ali's husband would react to my presence at the funeral, I now had my answer.

After a long moment, George pulled away, and held me at arm's length. 'This must be doubly horrible for you, Jeanne. First to lose Ali, and then to be confronted with these accusations.' Tactfully, he avoided Jamie's name, avoided the cold words we were forced to read in the paper, hear on the news and in the courtroom: JUVENILE CHARGED WITH MURDER.

I closed my eyes and nodded silently.

Taking me by the elbow the way he had that afternoon in Giovanna's, George said, 'Come on, I want to introduce you to Ali's family.'

At first, I balked. But then remembering how Ali never backed down, I figured it was the least I could do for her. And perhaps the best thing I could do for Jamie was to walk through that curious crowd with my head up, projecting my absolute certainty of his innocence. I extended my hand to the two women who were standing near the coffin, greeting the lines of mourners.

'I'm Jeanne Cross,' I said before George had the opportunity to introduce us. 'Ali and I were close friends.'

Ali's mother and sister exchanged a brief questioning glance before the sister reached out and accepted my hand. 'George has told us a lot about you. Thank you for coming. I know Alice would appreciate it.'

Alice. It was the first time I had heard my late friend referred to by that name, and staring into her sister's eyes, I had a new sense of who Ali was. Where she had come from and what she was running from. Her sister, who introduced herself as Kathleen, was a dowdier version of Ali. Ali with wide hips and cropped gray hair. Ali without the benefit of contact lenses or the spark that quickly animated a room, a violin, a man's eye. Both women were dry-eyed, sensible, somewhat stern. However, their gaze softened measurably when they looked upon George. Kathleen even kissed him lightly on the cheek.

'She was a wonderful and unique person,' I

said, fumbling for the right words. 'It must have come as such a shock to you. I'm so sorry.'

'To tell you the truth, it wasn't such a shock,' Kathleen said drily. 'I've always expected my sister to die violently. Either in some fiery car crash, or even — well, like this. Ever since she was a girl, Alice has been a magnet for trouble.' I could hardly believe she was speaking so candidly. I looked briefly to George, wondering if Kathleen knew who I was.

Her mother, an older version of Kathleen dressed in a plain skirt and blouse, dabbed briefly at her eyes but did not contradict her daughter's harsh words.

Feeling stunned, I gazed around the room, 'There were so many people who loved her.' As soon as I'd said it, I realized how strange it must sound coming from the woman whose son had been accused of the murder. But I couldn't help it. I felt someone had to defend Ali from her sister's cruel judgment.

'And just as many who hated her,' Kathleen shot back unnervingly.

At that moment, her mother surprised me by taking my hand. 'If it makes you feel any better, Jeanne, we don't believe that boy of yours did it. As soon as we saw him on TV, we knew they had the wrong person. You can practically see the innocence in his eyes.'

I suddenly found myself choked with tears. 'I only wish more people could see as you and I do,' I said when I could manage it.

'We see as mothers, don't we, Jeanne?' the elderly woman said, her eyes drifting briefly toward Ali in the coffin before she turned back to me with a sad smile. 'And mothers see things that no one else can.'

Kathleen frowned. 'Why aren't they investigating her boyfriend? If you ask me, he's the obvious suspect.' She glanced apologetically at her brother-in-law, who shifted uncomfortably beside me. 'I'm sorry, George, but you know it as well as I do.'

Squeezing her brother-in-law's arm, she added, 'Imagine being married to a saint like George, and running around with the likes of that?' Her eyes, which were — coloured like Ali's but with none of their luster, peered from behind her glasses at Jack Butterfield, who was working the crowd like a politician.

With his thick blond hair gelled back, and his commanding physique, he looked like a screen actor making his way through a glut of fans, careful to give each one their due. Though I have never trusted men like Jack, I couldn't help admiring the fine cut of his suit, or the way his cheeks dimpled appealingly when he attempted a smile. However, as he approached the coffin where Ali lay, her hands folded piously on her lap as they never were in life, the colour drained from Jack Butterfield's handsome face. It almost looked like he had forgotten why he had come in the press of the crowd, and now, confronted with the inert body of his lover, he once again experienced the shock of her death.

While the crowd looked on as discreetly as they could manage, he walked toward the

282

kneeler. 'Oh, Ali,' he moaned, obviously fighting back tears.

Across from me, Kathleen rolled her eyes, while the crowd watched transfixed by this sudden explosion of manly grief.

For several minutes, Jack fought his emotions as he caressed Ali's hair and cheek; he didn't even pretend to pray. When someone laid a hand on his arm, Jack visibly straightened his shoulders, blew his nose into a handkerchief he had produced from the pocket of his elegant suit, and rose. He stood before Ali for a long moment, obviously aware of the eyes of the crowd. Then he pulled something from his pocket and placed it in the coffin. Only when he moved away did I see that it was a large diamond ring. It winked gaudily on Ali's finger.

After walking past the line of mourners, Jack seized on an acquaintance who had witnessed his dramatic gesture. 'Ali and I were hoping to be married as soon as her divorce went through,' he explained, choking back tears. Then, looking toward the coffin, he added, 'I was planning to give her the ring for her birthday.'

'What divorce was that?' Kathleen interjected, stepping between Jack and the woman he was addressing loudly enough for everyone in their vicinity to hear. 'My sister had no intention of divorcing George. From what I heard, it was you she had tired of.'

For the second time in a half hour, the colour drained from Jack's face. Then quickly regaining himself, he glanced briefly at George before meeting Kathleen's sharp eyes. 'I'm sure there are some people who would like you to believe that, but the truth was, Ali and I had never been closer. We — '

'Please, Mr Butterfield, spare us,' Kathleen said, her voice like a razor. 'My sister ended your relationship just days before she died. I know because I talked to Alice the night she was killed.' Her voice rose, demonstrating some of her sister's flair for drama, as she reeled in every observer in the crowd. 'Alice told me how scared she was that night, Mr Butterfield. And it wasn't some sixteen-year-old kid who had frightened her either. She told me that you couldn't accept it was over; you'd come by in the middle of the night several times, banging on her door, and then when she wouldn't answer, on the window of her room.'

While the crowd gasped in collective horror, Jack Butterfield abruptly pushed his way through the narrow path, and out the door.

Later, when I kneeled to gaze at Ali's face for one last time, I noticed that the ring was gone. I wasn't sure who I should tell — if anyone — but obviously in all the commotion that followed Jack's exit, someone had stolen the expensive piece of jewellery right off the dead woman's hand.

25

Sitting at a table in Giovanna's, I was uncomfortably transported back to the first lunch I had shared with George Mather. The permeating aroma of garlic, the darkness of the room which blocked the clear summer day with heavy curtains, and the dolorous old-world feel to the place recalled my uneasiness as George had plied me with wine — then taken the opportunity to ask pointed questions about Jamie. I glanced at my watch and saw that he was late: there was still time to change my mind and bolt before I blurted out anything that might be used against my son. I could only imagine how Courtney and Gavin would react if they knew I was having lunch with Ali's husband. The husband who had made it publicly known that he would not rest until he saw Ali's murderer incarcerated.

But despite my misgivings and the legal advice Gavin and I were paying dearly for, I just couldn't walk out the door. What neither Gavin nor Courtney — nor George himself, for that matter — knew was that I was no longer the gullible little pawn who had shared an antipasto with Ali's husband the first time. This time I would not be led into any uncomfortable discussions about adolescent psychology. This time *I* would do the leading.

I had ordered a cup of cappuccino and was

sipping it slowly when George appeared. He apologized for his lateness, explaining that he'd been held up at the college. Apparently, a student had come to him with personal problems. Though he obviously wished to elaborate, I quickly cut him off. I wasn't about to let him use another drama as a ploy to draw out my opinions as he had the last time.

'I don't care why you're late,' I said curtly. Though we were united in mourning at Ali's wake, I saw George as an adversary now. 'What I want to know is why you've been calling me, leaving messages on my machine. Sooner or later my husband's going to be the one who plays them back, you know.' A lady at the next table turned to stare.

George smiled, but sadness tainted the expression. 'You make it sound as though we're having a clandestine affair. I'm not trying to hide anything from Gavin. In fact, I made it clear he was welcome to join us for lunch.' He signalled to the waitress, pointing toward the bar. Apparently knowing what he wanted, she promptly returned with a carafe of Chianti and two glasses.

However, when she tried to set a glass before me, I waved her away. 'No wine for me, thank you. I'll stick with cappuccino this time.' This last was directed at George.

After the waitress had left us with our menus, I cleared my throat. 'You knew Gavin wouldn't come,' I said. 'My husband has the good sense to follow the advice of counsel.'

George took a leisurely sip of his wine. 'You

sound like you don't trust me, Jeanne,' he said, giving me that aching smile. 'I'm hurt.'

'Should I?'

'It depends what you want. If you want what I do — which is justice for Ali — then you can trust me implicitly. If, on the other hand, you're hoping to see the guilty go free, then consider me your worst enemy.' His eyes, so deep a blue that they looked brown in this dim light, focused on me intensely. Once again, I felt like I had entered the courtroom where George Mather's skills had once been legendary.

I pushed back my chair, which clattered so loudly that people turned to stare. 'I think my husband's right. Coming here was a mistake.'

As George rose to stop me, a hint of pleading entered his voice. 'Please, Jeanne. Don't go. You're the only one I can talk to — the only one who really loved her besides me.' His eyes suddenly filled.

Resignedly, I sank back into my seat. 'I saw a lot of people crying the night of the wake, George. Her students. People who admired her music. You and I weren't the only ones — '

'Yes, but how many of them really knew Ali, knew her as you and I did, and loved her anyway?'

I stared at him, silently, unable to come up with one name.

'My wife was a splendid woman,' George said, his eyes still glistening. 'And a royal pain in the ass. No one knows that better than me — or you, Jeanne. Perhaps you could say we loved her in spite of herself.'

'Sometimes she was so selfish, I almost hated her,' I admitted. 'But then she could be more understanding than anyone in the world — and she was always an original. There was no one in the world like Ali.' By then the waitress appeared and was poised to take our order.

Without consulting me, George ordered an antipasto for two. After the waitress walked away, he reached across the table and took my hand. 'That's really why I wanted you to come. Because no one else understands my grief, just as no one else understood Ali.' He momentarily closed his eyes, and when he opened them, they were surprisingly mirthful. 'Besides, I brought you a little gift. A small token of my esteem.'

He rooted around in his pocket. Then, still smiling, he retrieved a small object, which he enclosed in his hand, still keeping his secret. 'Well, do you want it or not?'

'I'm hardly in the mood for games,' I said, grateful for the appearance of the waitress, who babbled cheerily as she served our antipasto. Our eyes fixed on each other, I don't think either of us heard a word she said.

'Well, I'll leave you two alone. Enjoy your lunch,' the waitress said at last, obviously mistaking our locked eyes as a sign of romantic fascination.

George held out his closed fists like a child in the school yard. 'Go ahead, Jeanne. Choose one.'

Somewhat irritably, I tapped his right fist lightly. The item he was holding clattered onto the table before me. In the refracted light that was coming through a cut glass window behind me, it shone and glittered just as it had on Ali's lifeless finger only a week earlier.

'*You?* It was you who stole the ring that night?' I gasped. I picked up the oversize object and twisted it appreciatively in the light.

'Don't look so impressed, Jeanne. It's just a ring. But I have to admit, it was a stunning gesture on Mr Butterfield's part.'

I slipped the showy piece onto my finger and once again held it up to the light. Then I removed it and set it on the table between us, where it sat like an unanswered question. George served the antipasto, thoughtfully remembering that I loved artichokes but didn't much care for the fatty meats.

For the next fifteen minutes, we ate in companionable silence, only occasionally glancing at the meretricious object in the centre of the table. We had almost forgotten it when the waitress stopped by to see if we needed anything else. She was clearing George's empty carafe when she spotted the ring. 'Oh, my God, congratulations!' she gushed. 'I could tell you two were in love as soon as I saw you.' She winked, then stood back, discreetly glancing from George to me and back again. Behind her smile, I could see her shrewdly assessing the situation. A man clearly old enough to be my father . . . the oversize rock. Apparently hoping his foolish generosity would extend to her tip, she congratulated us again.

'Why, thank you,' George said graciously, then smiled in my direction. 'We're very happy.' Looking around the room, I was once again aware that we had attracted attention. Playing to the crowd as Jack Butterfield had been the night he presented the ring to a dead woman, George took my hand and stroked it affectionately.

Despite the fact that he was only acting, I felt a surge of warmth at George's touch. An almost electrical current that passed between us. Immediately, I retracted my hand. When we were alone again, I asked, 'Well, are you going to tell me why?'

'I'm not sure what you're asking. Why Jack gave the ring to my wife? Why I took it? Or perhaps you want to know why I've given it to you? Well, if you want to know if my intentions are honorable, I can only assure you — '

'Stop joking, George. This is serious. My kid's sitting in jail across town, charged with a murder he didn't commit. I don't have time to — '

His eyes were suddenly grave — and, for the first time since I'd known him, angry. 'Yes, Jeanne, your son is in a cell. And my wife is in the ground. Do you really think I called you over here for my own amusement, or that of our waitress?'

'Then why?' I asked, more softly this time.

'I told you before. Be precise. Why what?' he sounded like the kind of lawyer I wished Jamie had, instead of the diminutive Courtney, who in two weeks on the case hadn't yet gotten a coherent or convincing story from Jamie.

'Okay, why did you take the ring, for starters? Do you want to add a charge of grand larceny to your problems?' The waitress drifted toward us with the coffeepot but, sensing the tension at the table, backed away.

George shrugged. 'I hardly think Mr Butterfield would prosecute — not the way he turned tail and ran out of the funeral home. And even if he did, do you really think anything could hurt me now? Disbarment? Humiliation? Even imprisonment? In that sense, losing the only thing you really care about is the ultimate freedom. Nothing scares me now, Jeanne.'

His grief was a palpable thing; it was so close and overpowering I thought it might suffocate me. 'You still haven't told me why you took it,' I said softly. 'Or why you think that Jack gave it to her in the first place. After all, the man's a car dealer, not a millionaire. Why would he throw away that kind of money?'

George shrugged in a way that reminded me painfully of Jamie when he was being questioned by the detectives. 'I'll answer your first question first, and with one of my own. Did you really think I would let my wife go to her grave wearing that scoundrel's tacky ring? I can think of no greater travesty.'

'Are you saying you think Ali's sister was right — that Jack killed her?' I asked, embarrassed by the hopeful catch in my voice. 'You think he gave her the ring because he felt guilty?'

George shook his head thoughtfully as he sipped the last of the wine from his glass. 'You're thinking of the conversation Kathleen and Ali supposedly had the night of the murder,' he said, his voice coloured with an unmistakable sadness. 'Well, I'm afraid you can't put much stock in that. For one thing, my sister-in-law is extremely loyal to me. According to her and her mother, I was the best thing that ever happened to their wild little Alice. Mr Butterfield, on the other hand, is the embodiment of everything they loathed in Ali's life: he's far too sexual for their taste. Admit it, Jeanne. You think he's attractive, too. I saw you looking at him the night of the wake.'

Against my will, I felt my cheeks growing hot. 'Actually, he's not my type at all,' I mumbled.

'Well, maybe not. But he *was* Ali's type,' George said sadly, picking up the ring absentmindedly from the table.

'Ali and Jack had nothing in common,' I said. 'She told me that herself. She said she was planning to leave him, just as her sister said.'

Hardly comforted by my revelation, George nodded sadly. 'It always came to that in the end, the realization that it was good old George who shared her love of music and philosophy, of good wines and the theatre. But she was drawn to men like Butterfield again and again because she *did* have something in common with them, something she could never share with me. Call it a passion for life, a need to take risks — '

Call it an insatiable desire for attention. I thought, and instantly wondered where *that* had come from. Ali was my best friend — and she was dead, for goodness' sake. There was no point in analyzing her character now. I reached for one of the cannoli that George had discreetly ordered and changed the subject. 'Just tell me one thing. Do *you* think Jack did it?'

George lifted his coffee cup and stared into the dark brew as if it had answers, before he looked directly at me. 'Let me be brutally honest with you, Jeanne. The evidence against Jamie is pretty compelling. At this juncture, I'd have to say I'm inclined to agree with the DA. And if your son did kill Ali, then I will fight with everything in me to make sure he's adequately punished.'

I put down the cannoli and reached for my purse. 'So that's why you asked me here?' I said, feeling the anger rising in me. 'So you could hold my hand and pretend you understand what I'm going through, all the while hoping to trap me into incriminating my son?'

'You're not listening, Jeanne. I said I *think* your son did it; I didn't say I was convinced of it. And when they pronounce sentence on the person charged with Ali's murder, I need to be absolutely convinced.'

Still clutching my purse and prepared to flee, I tilted my head to one side. 'If you think the evidence is so compelling, then what's holding you back? Why aren't you down there with the DA, fighting to see Jamie tried in adult court, instead of sitting here eating cannoli with his mother?'

George took a leisurely bite of his pastry, then dabbed his lips with a napkin while I waited for his reply. 'There's the rather troubling issue of motive, for one thing. A boy with no history of violence walks out of the house one evening and murders his mother's closest friend, torturing her with the tip of a knife beforehand. Being a student of philosophy, my first question is *why*? And so far, I haven't heard any plausible answer.'

'Is that what you were hoping to get from me?' I said. 'An answer to your troubling questions so you can go after my son in peace?'

Once again, George shook his head with sadness. Then he grasped my hand in his own. 'Believe it or not, I wouldn't do that to you, Jeanne. Maybe before, when Ali first suspected that Jamie was sneaking into her house, I tried to get some information from you. But now that your son has been charged with murder, I wouldn't use you like that. I hope you know me well enough to believe me.'

I continued to stare into his heavily circled eyes as George continued, 'And what's more, Jeanne, I truly hope it's *not* Jamie. For one thing, I care far too much about you. And more selfishly, I want a real villain. Someone on whom I can vent all the rage I feel over Ali's loss. A troubled kid hardly fits the bill.'

I pulled my hand away. 'You still haven't told me why you asked me here. Give me — what did you call it? A plausible motive.'

George laughed. 'Please, Jeanne, don't turn into a lawyer on me. There are enough of them out there as it is. Isn't it enough that I enjoy your company? That I simply wanted to have lunch with a friend?'

I folded my arms across my chest. 'In a word? No. Not in this situation. It's far too complicated for that and you know it.'

Once again, George put his head back and laughed, momentarily dispelling his oppressive grief. But when he looked at me again, his eyes were serious. 'All right, Jeanne, if you really want to know, I asked you here because I think there were several other people who should have been investigated but were not. In fact, I've made a list of them.' He reached into the pocket of his sports jacket and pulled out a neatly folded sheet of paper. From the coffee stains and the abundant creases in it, it was obvious that it had been folded and unfolded many times.

'Shouldn't you be taking that list to the police?' I asked, though I was staring curiously at the still concealed names. 'What can I do about it?'

'Once the police are convinced they have their man, the investigation is over. They're hardly interested in the private suspicions of a grieving husband.' George and I were in such a deep huddle that the waitress, who had approached with our check, once again backed away.

'Once again I'm asking you, why come to me?'

'Who has a greater interest in seeing the real killer caught? That is, if indeed someone other than your son was involved?'

As George's intentions began to come into focus, I felt light-headed, almost the way I had the night of Ali's concert when I had fainted. 'So what do you want me to do? Play private eye? Do you really think I'd have the first idea how — '

'You're a mother trying to save her son. You can do anything you need to do,' George said, leaning closer to my face. 'And besides, you're shrewder than you let on, Jeanne. There's a whole side of your personality that few people have seen. Of course, Ali saw it, but besides her — '

'Give me the list,' I interrupted impatiently, driven more by curiosity than anything else. However, when I took the yellow legal paper in my hand, I found that I was trembling. I hesitated for a moment, afraid of what it might contain.

The four names were numbered and written out neatly like the answers to four questions on a grade school quiz, or like a reminder of things to be picked up at the store. There were only first names listed:

1. BETH
2. JACK
3. KATHLEEN
4. GAVIN

'*Kathleen?*' I said incredulously. 'The woman was in Minnesota. How could you suspect Ali's sister?'

'I have my reasons,' George said enigmatically. 'Reasons I will be happy to share with you once I've found out a little more.'

We were silent for a moment, and then he said, 'I have to admit I'm a bit surprised that you reacted so strongly to Kathleen's name. And not at all to the final name on my list.'

I folded up the paper and left it in the middle of the table with the ring. Then I met George's gaze evenly. And though I didn't speak immediately, I think George read my eyes accurately, read something that I was trying desperately to keep him from knowing. 'If you ask me, your suspect list is pretty obvious. Anyone could have come up with it.'

'This isn't a made-for-TV movie, Jeanne. In real life, the killer is found among the obvious.'

'In real life, it's usually the husband who did it. A lot of people would say that an abandoned husband who left prints all over the crime scene was a pretty obvious suspect himself.'

Once again, George laughed. 'See, you're catching on already. Unfortunately, this obvious suspect has an ironclad alibi. But that's the kind of thing I want you to find out. Where were they that night and with whom? When was the last time they saw Ali and what was the nature of that meeting? My plan is for you to tackle the two men on the list; I'll talk to Beth and Kathleen.'

'But I have no idea how to — '

'Of course, you do,' George interrupted forcefully. 'Pretend you're on their side, use your own anger at Ali, what you expressed to me earlier about her selfishness. Then when you have them where you want them, push a little. You saw how McCarty interrogated your son.'

'Yes, but unlike McCarty, I can't call them in for questioning. With Gavin, well, maybe I can get him to talk to me, though I haven't had much luck with communication over the past seventeen years. But Jack Butterfield — how in the world do you expect me to get to him? I don't even know the man.'

Reminding me he had a class in half an hour,

George consulted his watch and signalled for the check. 'I have faith in you, Jeanne,' he said, tapping me on the shoulder as he rose. 'You'll think of something.'

It served my purposes to agree, but I had no intention of talking to Jack. Why should I, when I already knew he wasn't the killer?

After paying the waitress and tipping her lavishly, George nodded briefly in my direction and started for the door. He was halfway across the room when, apparently having forgotten something, he returned to the table and snatched up his well-worn list of suspects. 'Don't forget your ring,' he said, winking at me before he walked out, moving at the rapid clip of a much younger man.

I picked up the ring that Jack had intended for Ali and stared at it for several long minutes; it was so bright it seemed to be giving off sparks of electricity in my palm. Then I shoved it into my pocket with the furtiveness of a born thief, and walked out.

26

In the days following my lunch with George, Ali was with me constantly. Until then, I had not realized the depth of her friendship. Somehow, she had known all along — or at least for some time — that Jamie was her stalker. But to protect me from further trauma, she had refused to go to the police. And ultimately, her loyalty had cost her her life. If Jack Butterfield was partially to blame for giving her the gun that was turned against her, then certainly I, too, had contributed to the dangerous mix with my years of denial.

Unable to sleep, I took perilous late-night walks, venturing through dark and rainy streets, and sometimes even to Paradise Park, where Ali and I had once picnicked. But in the dead of night, the friendly little park was transformed into a frightening place, a place owned by animals, by the wet moist smell of the earth, a place governed by the same mysterious forces that had abruptly closed around Ali. I thought morbidly and incessantly of her lying in the ground in her satin-lined box. Beneath the earth. Beneath our feet. Beneath the dark.

Driving back and forth to the Somers Detention Centre, where Jamie was being held, I played Ali's music in the car. Through her violin, she continued to speak to me. Her dexterous fingers and the inner fever that drove her to creativity and to folly filled the car. At times her music was angry and sorrowful; at other times serene, full of such perfect compassion that it made me weep. At times I felt her presence so vividly that I swore she *had* spoken, and each time her message was the same, a simple three-word communiqué from beyond the grave: *It's all right.* When I was filled with grief and sorrow at her loss, I felt that message resonate within me. And when I was almost crazy with fear at what was happening to my son, I again heard Ali's soft voice, more reassuring than it ever was in life: *it's all right, Jeanne. Everything's going to be all right.*

I wasn't sure which visits with Jamie were the worst, the ones when he virtually ignored me, when he peered out the window waiting for me to leave, or the ones when he looked at me hopefully, as if he believed I could make this nightmare go away, the way I had chased away the bogeymen of childhood with a night-light and a cup of hot cocoa. Though we desperately needed to talk about what had happened the night of the murder, we mostly sat together like strangers in a bus terminal. When I left, I always handed him a tin of homemade brownies or chocolate chip cookies.

I was tormented by *if onlys*. If only I had stood up to Gavin when he cancelled the appointment with Dr Emory. If only I had forced Jamie into counselling when I realized that he, like his father, was living a disturbing and mysterious secret life. If only I hadn't left Jamie to go off to the cabin. If only I hadn't been too blind and afraid to confront Gavin long ago

— then perhaps Jamie wouldn't have been raised on the deceptions that had poisoned him.

At times, I felt a new rage swirling through me, the kind of rage that my son had nursed silently in his room all these years. Rage at Jamie for shutting me out, rage at his silent, angry father and at myself for being too timid to face the truth. And sometimes, I felt a burst of my old rage against Ali, who represented all the freedom and honesty our family lacked.

However, if Jamie's fury was free-floating and likely to settle on an inappropriate target like Ali, mine was focused like a laser. In my mind, there was a clear culprit in the disaster that was our lives, and he lived in my house. Though Gavin was more considerate and communicative than he'd ever been in the years of our marriage, I rebuffed all of his efforts at reconciliation.

Following Courtney's advice that we give the appearance of a strong family, I had remained in the house, but I had moved all my things out of the bedroom I'd shared with Gavin for seventeen years. The first night I stayed in the guest room, and then I moved into Jamie's room. I took comfort from his basketball posters, and even from an old balled-up sock I refused to pick up from the floor. Somehow the sight of it made me feel that Jamie would be home anytime; soon I would hear the phone ringing as it did almost endlessly when he was around. Even Skyler seemed more comfortable, curled at my feet on Jamie's bed each night. And though I accepted the need to share a residence with Gavin, that didn't mean I had to speak to him. After our brief discussion on the night of Ali's wake, I avoided him whenever I could. Even when he suggested that we visit Jamie together, I recoiled.

'Why? So we can play the happy family again? Do you really think Jamie is fooled by that? That he's ever been fooled?' I was standing in the kitchen, eating a baked potato topped with melted cheese at the counter. It was the kind of on-the-run meal I had lived on since Jamie's arrest. As for Gavin, he subsisted on take-out from DiOrio's, but he never once complained that I had stopped cooking for him, stopped doing his laundry, stopped entering the room where we had slept, silent and separate for seventeen years.

But on this particular occasion, Gavin's patience splintered. When he spoke, his words slurred slightly. His drinking, like mine, had escalated steadily since the murder, but he clearly crossed some invisible line that night. 'Listen, Jeanne, whether we like it or not, we share a son. A son who needs us more than ever. And I, for one, am not going to put my personal feelings before the needs of my son.' In his drunkenness, the pompous posture he assumed in the doorway looked almost comical.

'That's right, play the self-righteous one to the end. That's a big help to Jamie,' I said, dumping my potato ceremoniously in the trash. 'I'm going out.'

Gavin snorted. 'And apparently you feel no need to tell your husband where?'

When I reached for my jacket, Skyler appeared at my feet, apparently hoping we were going for a walk. 'None whatsoever. But take heart — at least I have more respect for you than to lie. Not like you did all those years with your endless conferences and out-of-town consultations.'

Gavin scowled. 'Now who's playing the self-righteous one, Jeanne?'

I spun around so fast that I upset the plate I had left on the counter. It shattered on the floor. 'Don't you think I have a right to a little indignation? After seventeen years of betrayal?'

Gavin moved to clean up the plate, but I stepped between him and the shattered china on the floor. 'Leave it,' I commanded. 'I don't need you to clean up after me.'

Gavin sighed. 'Fine,' he said. 'Leave it. But don't blame me if you cut your foot the next time you come into the kitchen in bare feet.' He stood there holding the dustpan and broom in his hand.

'I *will* blame you,' I said defiantly. 'Just as I blame you for Jamie's problems, and for Ali's death, and for — '

Gavin put his fingers to his lips. 'For God's sake, Jeanne. The windows are open. You're practically admitting you think Jamie's guilty.'

'I said I blamed *you*, not Jamie. You with your locked rooms and locked doors.' In frustration and horror at the words I was about to speak, I reached for my purse. 'I don't know if I can stay here any longer, no matter what Courtney says.'

Gavin moved swiftly, taking me firmly by both arms. His eyes were darker than I'd ever seen them. 'You're not going anywhere, Jeanne,' he said. Though he was trying to sound normal, nothing could obscure the menace in his voice. 'Now take off your jacket, and go run your bath — just like you usually do.'

'I just realized why you hated Ali so much,' I said. 'You hated her because she told the truth, and truth is the one thing you could never deal with.'

As if suddenly exhausted, Gavin released my arms. He knew he no longer needed force to make me stay. There was no way I could get away from him, no way I could escape the tangle of lies and evasions that was our marriage, our family.

Gavin walked over and began to cut up a lime. He poured a strong drink from the bottle of gin he'd left on the counter, not even bothering to add the tonic. After he'd taken a sip, he turned to face me. 'Ali wouldn't have known the truth if she fell on it,' he said evenly. 'The woman walked around calling herself Mrs George Mather while she screwed every guy in town. That's your paragon of honesty?' Gavin shook his head in disgust.

'You're hardly the one to judge,' I said.

'I didn't,' Gavin shot back, his eyes emitting sparks. 'I wasn't the one who butted into someone else's life, forcing my high-minded 'truth' on a wife who obviously didn't want to know it.'

I followed him into the family room and sat across from him for the first time in years. 'Is that what you think? That I didn't want to know?'

He took a leisurely sip of his drink. 'Well, did

you?' he asked. He cocked his chin in the direction of his study, the room that was once again locked. 'Because if you had, I'm sure you could have conducted your little investigation years ago. Face it, Jeanne. In your own way, you've been as dishonest as I have.'

I was trembling as I got up to pour myself a shot of brandy, once again joining Gavin in the quest for oblivion. In his blunt way, he had voiced the thoughts that tormented me most: that somewhere in me I had known much more than I'd allowed myself to admit, that I'd seen things I refused to accept. Hadn't Ali said the same thing the last time we talked? I shuddered involuntarily at the thought of that conversation. The conversation I had all but completely blocked from my mind.

'Maybe you're right,' I said at last, setting down my brandy. 'Maybe I willingly played the fool. And my foolishness has cost this family — cost Jamie — dearly. But not anymore, Gavin. I'm not going to protect you anymore.'

Once again I started for the door. And once again Gavin rose to stop me. 'I'm afraid it's too late, Jeanne. You're in too deep; we both are. Now, why don't you do as I suggested? Go up and have your bath; take your sleeping pill just as you do every other night.' His voice was soft, but there was no escaping the thinly concealed threat.

For the first time I understood how much I had feared my husband. Feared him for years without ever admitting it to myself. But not anymore. What was it George Mather had said?

When you lose the thing you love most, you have the ultimate freedom. And in some way, I had lost the only one I truly loved: the son who sat silently and stoically in the state's home for juveniles, keeping his secret resolutely to himself.

I lowered my head and started up the stairs. To Gavin, I must have looked like the same gullible and easily intimidated wife he had learned to control so well. But this time, everything was different. This time I would not push back the dark truths that were welling up inside me, demanding light, air, an end. I couldn't. This time, what I had not wanted to hear on the night of the murder hit me with the force of a train cutting through the dark.

★ ★ ★

The following morning I rose before dawn, hoping to get out of the house before Gavin heard me. I knew I would have to be quick. Gavin was up and dressed in his jogging clothes every morning by six, predictable as sunrise. With only the glow of a small night-light, I pulled on a pair of shorts and a tank top. In the bathroom, I tugged my hair into a quick ponytail, brushed my teeth, and crept silently down the stairs. I paused briefly at the foot of the stairs, but there was no sound from Gavin's room.

It was still dark when I stopped at Ryan's to pick up a large coffee to go. I thought about the morning when I met Brian Shagaury there at a similarly early hour. Certainly, I had been another person back then. But this time, as I paid my check and crawled back into my car, even Brian's fate felt preferable to my own. Like Ali, he was safe beneath the earth, safe from the constant demands of truth.

The Somers Detention Centre was in near darkness when I arrived. Only one light shone from a small window: undoubtedly where the guard on duty watched television or dozed until the morning shift arrived. I sat outside for at least an hour, sipping the dregs of my cold coffee as the light slowly gathered around me. I watched the morning shift arrive. The night shift, looking tired and eager for sleep, headed blearily for their cars. I waited until I was reasonably certain that breakfast was over and that the forty boys who were housed there had begun their daily routines.

I was glad to see that Glenn was on duty in the office. A tall, thin black man, he was the only member of the staff I'd actually seen smiling, the only one who ever addressed me by name.

'Hi Glenn,' I said, doing my best to make my voice sound even. 'I know it's not visiting hours, but I really need to see Jamie. There's something I have to talk to him about.'

'Hey, Mrs Cross, I'd like to help you out, but visiting times are pretty much set in stone.' He looked up at me sympathetically. 'Unless there's some kind of emergency.'

'Actually, there is. A death in the family. My brother. Jamie's uncle,' I stammered. 'A car crash on route 2 last night. I don't know if you heard it on the radio.'

'No, ever since I got this new CD player in my car, I never hear the news anymore,' Glenn came out from behind the desk and embraced me clumsily. 'Gee, I'm sorry, Mrs Cross.'

I pulled away, feeling tears well in my eyes. 'Thank you,' I whispered. Whether I was crying for the ancient loss of my brother, or for my son, I wasn't sure. 'Do you think I could see Jamie — for just a few minutes. I don't want him to hear it on the radio.'

Glenn studied me for a moment, obviously moved by my tears. Then he picked up the phone and pressed an extension number. 'Hey, Sherman,' he said into the receiver, keeping his eyes on me all the while. 'What's Jamie Cross doing right about now?' There was a brief pause and then he nodded. 'Good. You think you could send him up here? There's something I need to talk to him about.' He nodded again. 'Yeah, right away. Great. Thanks, Sherman.'

After he hung up, Glenn explained, 'Only a few minutes, though. I know it's tough, breaking it to the kid and then walking out, but like I said, they're pretty strict about visiting hours. I'd probably be fired if they knew I made an exception.'

After I told him how much I appreciated his compassion, Glenn and I sat there awkwardly for a few moments before an almost imperceptible knock was heard on the door. Without waiting for an answer, Jamie pushed it open, and in an instant, his body filled the doorway.

A flicker of surprise crossed his face when he saw me, but then the impassive expression he had worn since the night of the murder returned.

Touching Jamie lightly on the arm, Glenn said, 'Your mom's got something to talk to you about, Jamie, so I'll leave the two of you alone.' On the way out the door he added, 'I'll be right outside. Just a few minutes, okay, Mrs Cross?'

I nodded, but when the door slammed, and I was alone with my son, I felt a sudden surge of panic. Exactly what did I intend to say to Jamie? Though I had lied easily to the guard, what emergency could I concoct for my son? Obviously, nothing but the truth would do.

Once again, Jamie's face registered a faint curiosity. 'What's up, Mom? Nothing happened to the dog, did it?'

I couldn't help but smile. His concern for the vagabond Skyler was so like my Jamie. The Jamie he had been before time and lies had turned him into the confused young man who stood before me. 'Skyler's fine.'

Jamie nodded watchfully.

'I've been sleeping in your room while you were away,' I said awkwardly. 'Somehow it makes me feel closer to you.'

At the mention of home, Jamie's face, which had been briefly open, closed down. He walked to the window and stared outside at the summer day that was happening beyond us. 'Is that what you came to tell me, Mom? That's the big emergency?'

'No . . . I — I just had to see you. I had to know you're all right,' I stammered.

Jamie turned to face me. 'Well, here I am,' he

said. 'Doing just great. So I guess you got what you came for.'

He started for the door, and though I wanted desperately to say something to stop him, I could think of nothing. Outside the door, I could hear Glenn clearing his throat, indicating our illegal visit was soon coming to an end.

In the end, Jamie and I both spoke each other's names at the same time. *Jamie? Mom?*

We laughed briefly at our intersecting voices, and then Jamie spoke up abruptly. 'Don't sleep in that room, Mom. I hate that room. I'd rather be locked up here for the rest of my life than go back there.'

There was no way I could back down now. '*Why, Jamie?*' My voice had become a whisper, but nothing could disguise the force of my question. 'What happened in that room?'

Once again, Jamie walked toward the window, where he stood looking outside. When he turned to face me, his face was streaked with tears. 'You know, Mom. Don't make me say it. *You know.*'

I closed my eyes and saw an image of Marcus. Marcus, glancing briefly in my direction at Ali's concert, his eyes huge and vulnerable. And for the first time I understood, *really* understood, what Gavin had wanted from him. It was that vulnerability. Not sex with another man, as I had first thought, but power over a boy. The same power he had once had over me, when I, too, had been naive and vulnerable. The same power he'd had over the winsome boy who stood before me.

And then I envisioned my cell phone in the

cabin, on the day I never wanted to think of again. The last day of Ali's life. After falling asleep on the porch early that evening, I had awakened and was stumbling toward the bathroom in the dark when I stopped and picked it up. Surrounded by the kind of pure darkness that you can experience only in the woods, I had pressed the playback button. Then, clinging to the little dog, I had listened to one of the final messages, the one that had brought all the hidden horror of my life tumbling around me.

Standing in Glenn's claustrophobic office, I could almost smell the pine scent of the cabin, could almost hear Skyler whining for food, and outside, the whispering river as I pressed the play button, and Jamie's voice filled the narrow space, breaking my heart with the fear I heard in it. It was probably the briefest message on the answering machine, a few short words not even preceded by hello. *Please, Mom, you've got to come home. You can't leave me here, with him.* Though the last two words were garbled, almost uttered against his will, they were the ones that pierced my heart.

Of course, I had called home immediately. But all I got on the other end of the line was the chill of Gavin's voice. My husband had answered the phone that night with all his usual formality, but when he realized it was me, he had begun to rant. Jamie wasn't home, he said. He had no idea where he was. If I was any kind of a mother, I would be at home; none of this would be happening. Realizing Gavin was drunk, I had hung up on him.

Now, as I had then, I felt myself beginning to tremble. At the time, I was unsure what Jamie meant. I wouldn't allow myself to know why he was so afraid of being alone with his father. In fact, I hadn't fully absorbed what he was trying to tell me that night until this very moment. But of course, Jamie was right: on some level I *had* known. And my knowing made me perhaps even guiltier than Gavin was.

'Oh, Jamie, I'm so sorry,' I said as I lurched toward my son. By then, we were both crying; and it was Jamie who comforted me, telling me over and over. 'It wasn't your fault, Mom. None of it was your fault.'

For perhaps the most honest moment my son had shared with me in years, Jamie and I gazed at each other. In that moment, I saw him as only a mother could, saw the bloated shell of his body, and the small boy who was concealed inside it. I saw the pent-up tenderness and rage that tangled in his chest every day, the years of pain he had tried to chase away with chocolate bars and an easy smile. For the first time, I understood how truly brave my son had been. There were a thousand questions I wanted and did not want to ask at that moment. *What exactly had Gavin done to Jamie in that room? And for how long had it gone on?* I closed my eyes, shutting out the horror.

Then abruptly Glenn was in the room. 'I'm sorry, Mrs Cross, but Jamie really needs to get back to the unit before I have some heavy explaining to do.'

My eyes riveted on my son, I nodded. But

when I closed them for an instant, Jamie was gone, and only Glenn and I were left in the room. 'You're looking kind of shaky there, Mrs Cross,' he said. His voice sounded like it came from far away. 'You want me to call someone for you?'

I wiped away the tears that were spilling down my cheeks. 'That's the trouble, Glenn. There's no one to call,' I said, amazed by the bluntness of my own words. 'There never has been. No one but Jamie and me.'

While the obviously mystified guard looked on, I walked out the door into the sunlight.

27

The next morning, the telephone rang early. I crept to the door of Jamie's bedroom, where I had been waiting for Gavin to leave for work, and listened through a crack, hoping to get a hint of who might be calling at this early hour. From the doorway, I heard Gavin speaking into the phone at the foot of the stairs. 'What do you need to speak to Jeanne about?' he asked the unknown caller. Despite the overwhelming curiosity — and yes, fear — that the words still elicited in me, my desire to avoid Gavin was stronger.

Ever since I'd faced the truth about what he had done to Jamie, I had remained in my son's room whenever Gavin was in the house. It felt like a prison — the frightening and solitary cell it had surely been for Jamie all of his life. Slowly, I watched the light ebb away each night, leaving me more and more alone, more and more afraid, as I forced myself to confront the nightmare that was Jamie's life in the most visceral way possible. And each morning, I awoke feeling more edgy, more isolated, more desperate. The sound of the ringing phone so early in the morning only added to my uneasiness.

'Listen, George, I think you know how sorry Jeanne and I are about Ali's death. But given the situation — ' Gavin said. He hesitated a long moment. 'Frankly, I find it odd that you would call here. We're on opposite sides of this thing, George — whether we like it or not. Jeanne has nothing to say to you; neither of us do.' After an abrasive goodbye, the phone clattered into its cradle.

I wanted to run down the stairs and ask Gavin how he dare speak for me, but my aversion to the sight of him was stronger than my outrage. And in some sense, perhaps, I was afraid to see him. Afraid of what I might do.

I waited until Gavin was gone before I crept down the stairs and made myself a strong pot of coffee. And though he couldn't have known why, Gavin was right — George Mather was the last person I wanted to talk to. His penetrating eyes were the last thing I wanted to see. However, in spite of that aversion, I dialled the number of his office. As I suspected, I was greeted only by a recorded message. Apparently, this time George had called me from home — away from the curious ears in his office, from the students who often waited there, hoping to probe his erudite and discerning mind — just as budding musicians had gathered around his wife. Imagining him in his bathrobe, a tired, aging man, wasted by grief, I felt a twinge of guilt as I began to speak into his answering machine. 'I'm sorry, George, but I won't be able to meet you for lunch today as we planned. I have to go up to New Hampshire. Nothing serious, but there's a speeding ticket I have to take care of. In any case, I've been feeling the need to get away for a couple of days, so I probably won't return until Friday for the hearing. If I have a chance, I'll call you when I get back.'

Then before George or Courtney or anyone else had a chance to tell me that leaving town wasn't a good idea, I hastily threw a few things into my overnight bag. His head tilted sweetly to the side, Skyler looked on alertly.

'We're going home, buddy,' I told the little dog as he followed me from room to room. 'Home to the cabin.' Was I imagining it or did the dog regard me sadly, his eyes seeming to remind me that there was no home for us. No home, no family, not even a close friend who would protect me from myself. After dressing hurriedly in shorts and a tank top, I poured myself a cup of coffee to go. From the doorway, I surveyed the kitchen. I had spilled coffee on the counter, and left out the cream — major transgressions in Gavin's code of neatness. But I didn't stop to clean up. Nor did I bother to leave a note as to where I'd gone or when I'd be back. What was Gavin going to do? Report me to the police?

Throughout most of the ride, Skyler slept beside me on the front seat of the car. But as the landscape changed, and the mountains emerged, he sat up vigilantly. And when I stopped in the centre where he had once played the town vagabond, he barked excitedly, obviously preferring the perils and uncertainty of his former life to the oppressive environment of my house. I tossed him a bone. 'Sorry, buddy, I know you want me to let you go, but I can't. You don't know him yet, but there's a boy who needs you badly. And you've got to go back to him.'

Realizing the same might be said for me, I

promptly paid my speeding ticket, then bought a couple of candy bars and a bottle of water at the general store. The clerk eyed me slyly. Obviously, the news of Ali's murder — and my son's connection to it — had spread even up here, where I had erroneously believed I might find the bliss of anonymity. Though I would have liked to avoid the house, the room that Jamie had called a bad place, for a few days, and though my son hardly seemed enthusiastic about my visits, I knew that more than one day away from the juvenile detention centre would be too long.

In the drive up the mountain road, Skyler began to whine excitedly. As for me, I felt a sense of peace I hadn't experienced since the murder, the safety of driving toward my childhood home, as if the lost innocence of that time could somehow be restored just by taking a certain road, by entering a certain house. But also on my mind was a secret motive for my visit here, a motive that justified leaving Jamie and taking the trip up here at this most difficult time. It was the memory of that ringing cell phone, and Jamie's message on it. 'Mom, please don't leave me alone — with him.' Just thinking of it, I almost swerved on the winding road. Sure, I was in a state of distress when I left the cabin, but how could I have left the cell phone behind? From his spot beside me, Skyler looked up at me, as if wondering if he could really trust this human who had taken control of his fate.

'I have to get that phone,' I said aloud, talking to myself though the little dog tilted his head quizzically, as if trying to understand. Ever since

I had remembered the words — and the tone — of Jamie's message, I had known that if it fell into the wrong hands, it might be used as evidence of his state of mind on the night of the murder. No, I had to erase the desperately veiled admission of his horrible secret before it had the power to do any more damage to my son.

I was still a good quarter mile from the cabin when I looked ahead and saw that the door was wide open. Though it was only an open door, the sight of it clenched my heart, recalling as it did Gavin's description of the murder scene. According to George, the first sign that something was desperately wrong was nothing more ominous than an open door. I struggled to regain composure. After all, what was I afraid of? There was surely no murder victim in the cabin. No, there had to be a logical explanation. Had I, in my panic on the day after the murder, left the door like that? I wondered. But no, I clearly remembered closing up the place the way my father always did at the end of the season, protecting the windows with closed shutters and finally locking the door with a padlock. An almost irrational panic seized me as I approached the place.

I tried to tell myself that it was probably kids — kids who had used the cabin for a drinking party, or perhaps a romantic tryst. Or maybe a group of teenagers had even pulled the door open out of nothing more than rebellious curiosity. But none of my rationalizations were convincing. I parked the car askew on the dirt road, and threw the door open. Skyler immediately leaped out of the car and took off into the deep woods after a squirrel. But I couldn't worry about the dog — not now. I raced toward the cabin. As soon as I entered the sweet little structure that listed slightly to one side, I gasped.

It had been totally ransacked. Books were thrown from the small bookcase my father had built, drawers pulled out and emptied, the bed overturned; even the moldy items I had left in the refrigerator had been pulled out and left to rot on the counter, filling the cabin with their stench.

But none of that mattered. Not the violation of my private world, or the further destruction of the cabin. Not anything the vandals might have stolen. The only thing that mattered was the phone. My eyes went immediately to the kitchen table where I had sat when I had heard the terrible news from Gavin. The table, like every other surface in the room, had been swept clean by someone's avid hand. A vase full of wild flowers I had picked, hoping to make the place homey for my son, was shattered and broken on the floor among the other detritus. Frantically, I searched through it for the little silver phone, not caring that I'd cut my hand on one of the shards of glass. But there was no sign of it. From what I could tell, my cell phone was the only thing that was missing from the cabin. Feeling unable to breathe, I went outside and raked my hand through my hair. Then I went back inside and began a calmer, more systematic search. I forgot hunger, forgot the little dog I

319

had left outside and probably lost for good this time, forgot everything but my single-minded desire to find that phone.

Within an hour I had pulled apart every corner of the cabin, leaving some areas more chaotic than they'd been after the vandals had done their work. By the time I finished, it was clear that the object that had brought me back to New Hampshire was gone. Had the thief taken it randomly, simply because he wanted a cell phone? It was, after all, the only thing in the cabin of any value. Or had he, like me, come in search of the evidence that was stored inside the little silver device? But who else was aware that the voice mail held the secret of my son's fate? And what exactly did they plan to do with it?

Outside, there was no sign of Skyler. I stood there and called his name for at least half an hour before I was forced to give up. The hopeless echo resounding through the mountains seemed to reflect my mental state. The little name tag I'd linked to his collar would be useless out here. Who would ever find him? But I had no time to search for the dog — not now with the phone missing and my son's future on the line.

That night, from a motel room halfway between home and the cabin, I dialled Courtney Rice's number. I was so caught up in my own drama that I didn't realize it was after midnight until I heard the lawyer's sleepy voice on the other end of the line. For a brief moment, I considered hanging up before she knew who had disturbed her sleep. But just before she slammed down the receiver, the exigency of my question forced me to speak. 'Wait, Courtney, I need to talk to you. There's something I have to ask you.'

There was silence on the other end of the line where I imagined Courtney running her fingers through her long red hair, trying to rouse herself from sleep. 'Jeanne? Is that you?' she asked, at last. 'Is everything all right? Nothing has happened to Jamie, has it?'

'Jamie's fine,' I said. 'Or at least as fine as any kid who's been messed up by his parents for sixteen years and is now facing capital murder charges can be.'

'It's late, Jeanne,' Courtney said, bringing me to the point in lawyerly fashion. 'What is it?'

I took a deep breath. 'What would happen if Jamie were actually convicted of this thing, but the court decided there were mitigating factors? Say he had some serious emotional issues; would he get the help he needs?' Then before Courtney had a chance to respond to my questions, I blurted out another. 'Even in the worst-case scenario, they wouldn't hold him past his twenty-first birthday, right?'

'We've already been over this,' Courtney sighed. 'As long as we keep it in juvenile court, Jamie will probably end up in a therapeutic setting until he turns twenty-one. But I still don't know why you're calling. Jeanne, is there something I need to know? Some new information about Jamie perhaps?'

'No, no, of course not,' I said. 'You know

we've told you everything.' Then I cleared my throat, apologized to Courtney for having bothered her, and placed the receiver in its cradle so delicately you would have thought it was made of glass.

28

On the morning of the hearing, I dressed as Courtney instructed me to do. In a dark dress that skirted the knee, expensive shoes, and my hair elegantly styled, I reenacted the role I had played for years: Dr Cross's proper wife. Looking at myself in the mirror, I almost laughed at how far I had travelled from that benign image.

When I visited Jamie early that morning before we left for the courthouse, he was oddly buoyant, more cheerful than he'd been since his arrest. In his chinos and a navy blue polo shirt, his hair freshly cut, he looked almost like his old self.

'Look at us,' he said. 'We look like we used to when we all went to church on Sunday. The perfect family does court.' He looked from Gavin to me. It was the first time we had visited him together since the day he'd been arrested, and he had fallen into his old role, expertly pretending nothing was wrong, pretending I didn't know what I knew. But in his glance, Jamie seemed to measure the distance between his father and me.

'Sarcasm is hardly going to help your cause, son,' Gavin said drily.

'I'm not worried about my *cause*, Dad. I talked to Courtney earlier. She says there's no chance they'll take this to adult court. And even less chance of a conviction. Besides, say by some long shot, they do convict me as a juvenile, the most I'll get is five years in a place like this. No real jail time. I mean, how bad can it be?'

In his false cheeriness, I saw for the first time how scared Jamie really was. I reached out and took his right hand while Gavin put his hand on Jamie's left shoulder. When Jamie recoiled from his father's touch, Gavin quickly pulled away, and I shivered inside. How many times had I witnessed similar scenes between father and son, but had been unable — or unwilling — to understand what I saw? Only the need to make it through this court appearance as a family prevented me from physically attacking Gavin when he tried to touch our son.

'How's Skyler doing, Mom? Is he still sleeping on my bed?' Jamie asked, pulling his hand away. Weeks ago I had told Jamie that Skyler spent every night sleeping at the foot of his bed, and every day sitting by the window, as if waiting for his new master to come home.

'He's fine. A little lonesome, but fine,' I lied, unwilling to tell Jamie that I had lost the little dog in New Hampshire. Like so many other things, I would just have to find a way to make it up to my son once he was free. Before they led him away, I squeezed Jamie's hand. And he squeezed back. For hours, I would feel the sweaty pudginess of that hand in mine, the tentativeness of his grasp, the fear.

* * *

Despite Jamie's outward optimism, the hearing was more of an ordeal than we could have imagined. On entering the courtroom, we were buoyed by the large number of Jamie's friends and supporters who had chosen to attend. Courtney put up an impressive string of character witnesses: Jamie's old scout leader, our pastor, two former teachers, including Tom Boyle from the high school, who glanced obliquely at me as he stepped off the stand, his eyes full of such pity that I immediately turned my face away.

All of them said the same thing, that Jamie was a normal teenager in every way, respectful, diligent in school despite his learning disabilities, responsible, popular. When questions were asked about our family, the witnesses were quick to swear to our exemplary character; mention was made of Dr Cross's fine reputation in the community, of our regular church attendance, my involvement with the PTO and Cub Scouts when Jamie was small. We had presented the front so long and so convincingly that every witness appeared ready to stake their life on its veracity. In fact, before I met Ali and she began to force me to see the truth, I would probably have staked mine on it, too. It was horrifying to think, but I wondered if I would have even believed Jamie's oblique accusations against Gavin if I hadn't been transformed by Ali's friendship. Or would I have brushed them aside as something I had misinterpreted, something I would think about later?

When the adults were finished, three of Jamie's friends attested to his well-known sense of humour, his frequent role as peacemaker among their group of friends, and above all, his normality.

'Did Jamie ever express an excessive interest in Mrs Mather?' they were asked one by one. Their faces looking scrubbed and open, Matt Dauber and Brad Simmons quickly said no. They'd never heard Jamie speak of Mrs Mather at all, except perhaps to mention that she was a friend of his mother's.

The tension in the courtroom was temporarily broken when Brad testified that the only thing Jamie was obsessed with was Reese's Peanut Butter Cups.

By the time Toby Breen took the stand, Courtney looked almost bored by her own questions. Like the others, Toby testified that Jamie was in all ways a normal teenager, exceptional only in his popularity. But when she asked whether Jamie had ever shown a particular interest in Ali, Toby fidgeted with his tie and looked nervously at Jamie before he responded.

'I wouldn't exactly say he was *interested* in her, but he did stay after school to talk to her a couple of times at the beginning of the school year,' Toby said, looking down as he spoke. 'I waited for him, but he was in there so long, I gave up.'

'What did he go to see her about?' Courtney said, obviously caught off guard by this unexpected testimony. 'Maybe a problem he was having in class. Or perhaps he had some interest in music?'

The prosecutor jumped up to protest that Courtney was leading the witness. But not about to be led anywhere, Toby was already shaking his head. 'Jamie wasn't in her class. And he hated music — at least the kind Mrs Mather played.'

'Then what did they talk about?' Courtney asked. Later she would tell me that she had committed a lawyer's most deadly mistake — asking a question to which she didn't already know the answer. But once again, it didn't matter. Toby only shrugged. 'I asked him,' he said, looking puzzled. 'But Jamie wouldn't tell me.'

In the end, Toby's testimony had hardly proved damaging. After all, it wasn't unusual for a student to stay after school to talk with a teacher, particularly a popular staff member like Ali Mather. But for me, the news that Jamie had met privately with Ali to discuss some unknown matter hit like a lightning bolt. Unlike the judge, who didn't seem particularly impressed by this casual piece of information, I knew Jamie. He wasn't the kind of kid who went in for long heart-to-hearts with anyone — least of all a teacher. I wondered why he hadn't told me about his meetings with Ali. And why, after we became friends, Ali had never mentioned them.

Then as I sat there on that hard bench, the past began to rearrange itself in my mind: I recalled how Ali had called me out of the blue and asked me for a ride to school. At the time, I had wondered why she selected me. But now I realized her unexpected call had probably come right after those visits from Jamie. Were the two incidents connected? Was that why she had asked such probing questions about our family?

I snapped to attention as Courtney's final witness, Elise Winchester, a fourteen-year-old girl who lived across the street, finished telling the judge how, just hours before the murder, she had been Rollerblading on the sidewalk in front of our house. And when she'd fallen and scraped her knee, Jamie had rushed out to help her up. 'He got me a Band-Aid and a cold drink and everything,' Elise said, smiling shyly in Jamie's direction.

'Was this unusual behavior on Jamie Cross's part?' Courtney asked.

'No,' the carefully rehearsed but obviously sincere Elise replied emphatically. 'Jamie's always doing nice stuff for people. He's just like that.' With Elise's testimony, Courtney rested.

Of course, the prosecutor had countered with the extreme cruelty of the crime, bringing on a string of detectives and medical people to say that Ali wasn't just murdered, she was methodically tortured. The furious battle between victim and assailant that preceded the murder was imagined in detail. The smashed Stradivarius was introduced. But of course, the greatest emphasis was put on the surface cut that had been made across her throat.

'Using the tip of the knife, the murderer barely broke the surface of the skin,' the medical examiner testified.

'And what would you say the intention of such a precise cut would be?' the prosecutor asked.

'The assailant was obviously terrorizing Mrs Mather. Perhaps making her beg for her life,' the aging doctor answered evenly.

Unable to help myself, I turned to look at Ali's family who had gathered in the back. Ali's mother clung to George's hand and wept silently as the details of the crime were discussed. But Kathleen's face revealed a stern fascination — and something else. Was it, perhaps, a hint of triumph at the abasement of her lifelong rival? When he realized that I had turned to look at the family, thus attracting the ever-present attention of the curious, Gavin nudged me with his elbow.

Immediately I readjusted my attention to the proceedings in the front of the courtroom. But it was too late. I had already been seared by the pain I read in George's eyes, a sorrow that was a clear reflection of my own. *We were the only two who really loved her*, he had said, and in that moment, I felt the truth of those words acutely. The only difference between us was that while George wanted justice for Ali, I wanted only what was best for Jamie: therapy, a chance to deal with the rage that had built up inside him for all those years, a reason for the persistent hope I read in his eyes.

When a psychiatrist for the prosecution testified that given the nature of the crime and Jamie's lack of remorse, my son could never be rehabilitated, I wanted to stand up and scream. What did he, after three hours of interviews, know about Jamie? If he was so brilliant, why hadn't he uncovered the secret shame that motivated so much of what Jamie did? But as Courtney had instructed me, I sat in my seat, my face a study in blankness. In the most difficult part of the testimony, when Detective McCarty had testified, saying that Jamie had been 'surly' and 'emotionally absent' after the arrest, I felt myself beginning to tremble. As Courtney had feared, McCarty described Jamie's outburst at the station as a semi-confession.

'Under pressure,' McCarty said, staring Jamie straight in the eyes, 'the defendant admitted that he hated Mrs Mather. 'A witch,' he called her. 'A witch who deserved everything she got.' If you ask me, he was within an inch of a full confession when his lawyer stopped him.'

Of course, Courtney had instantly objected. But it didn't matter. Not only had the judge heard it, but the person in the courtroom whose verdict I feared even more than the man on the bench had also absorbed those damning words.

As we left the courtroom to await the judge's decision — a decision that meant the difference between Jamie getting the help he needed or facing the possibility of spending the rest of his life in the unendurable world of an adult prison — Gavin tried to take my hand, but I pulled away as if I had been singed by his touch, and began to move through the crowd, searching for George. However, by the time I reached the area where Ali's family had been sitting, he was gone.

Instead of his discerning, dark blue eyes, I found myself face-to-face with the strained face of the woman I had so often encountered under ordinary circumstances. It seemed another lifetime when Beth Shagaury and I had innocently chatted about soccer or the high price of children's cereal in the aisles of the Shop n' Save. Lost inside the bland, dark clothing that had become too large for her months ago, her skin stretched taut across prominent cheekbones, she bore little resemblance to the distracted young mother I had known back then. She looked as stunned by my face as I was by hers. However, before I had a chance to get a word out, Beth lowered her head, turned abruptly, and lost herself in the crowd.

When I went back to find Gavin and Courtney, I saw my husband leaning toward one of Jamie's friends in deep conversation. Just the sight of Gavin's proximity to that vulnerable boy — *that child* — sent a deep shudder through me. Veering through the crowd, I had never felt more alone in my life. Or stronger. While heads turned or reporters pushed in close, hoping to pry a comment from the mother of the defendant, I lifted my head and pressed for the street, no longer concerned how my separation from Gavin looked to the public. No longer concerned about anything but that elusive thing Ali had insisted I face: the truth.

29

The next time we assembled in the courtroom, I was trembling so much that I was afraid I might create a scene by fainting the way I had at Ali's concert. As they led Jamie inside, he flashed a brief, wan smile, his eyes drifting from his father to me. The judge entered the courtroom a minute later, but I kept my eyes on Jamie's straight shoulders, his valiantly lifted head.

While the judge shifted some papers and poured himself a glass of water, I felt, once again, an almost overwhelming impulse to turn around and search for George Mather's face. Several weeks had passed since the strange lunch we had shared at Giovanna's. And though we had promised to get together again to discuss the results of our amateur sleuthing, we had not done so. In fact, after George's one call the morning before I left for New Hampshire, I had not heard from him again. Nor had he responded to several messages I left in his office and on his answering machine at home. As I listened to the slow, measured voice on his tape when I called the number late the night before, I felt almost certain George was home. It was obvious that he was avoiding me. The only question was why. Had he simply decided that I was too close to be objective about anything I might learn? Or had he discovered something that he didn't want me to know? Had his personal snooping led him to the belief that he and I were on opposite sides after all? My eyes veered protectively toward Jamie as the judge cleared his throat, about to pronounce on my son's future.

By then, my heart was hammering so insistently that I could hardly make sense of his lengthy statement. As he went on for several moments about the seriousness of the crime, I felt almost certain that he was about to transfer Jamie to adult court. And if that happened, I was utterly prepared to stand up in the courtroom and tell him exactly why that should never happen. However, just as I felt myself lurching forward, poised to rise in the most dramatic act of my life, his tone changed. Though Ali had been cruelly taunted with the point of Jamie's knife before the actual murder, he didn't believe the assailant had intended to kill. If he had, wouldn't he have used his own weapon? No, the shooting itself appeared to be a rash act; there was no evidence of premeditation. Given that rashness, Jamie's strong family background, and ties to the community, the judge felt he was an excellent candidate for rehabilitation if he were convicted of this crime: the court had decided that Jamie would be tried as a juvenile.

While Jamie's friends let out an unceremonious whoop, getting themselves ejected from the courtroom, I felt the muscles in my body that had been poised for action go limp. The spectacle of Toby and Brad being escorted from the courtroom gave me the opportunity to turn and stare. I looked to the spot where Ali's family had sat throughout the hearings, hoping for a glimpse at George's reaction. But to my astonishment, the seat Ali's husband had occupied during the hearing was empty. In the row where her three closest relations had gathered, Kathleen and her mother now clustered together alone. Reading the dismay on their faces, I quickly turned away.

As the judge left the courtroom, and Jamie was led away by the guards, I felt myself assailed by the press of emotions in the room. I was embraced several times — with genuine feeling by Courtney, who stood at my right, and then more guardedly by Gavin, who seemed to recall our estrangement now that the moment of tension had passed. And then by other people, the strong community that the judge had cited as he reached his decision. Our pastor's wife pressed close, exuding a cologne that reminded me painfully of Ali's. Toby's parents, Sharon and Walt Breen, both with tears in their eyes, pushed their faces close to mine, saying that they were a hundred percent behind Jamie; they always had been. There were others, too, a queue of them: teachers who worked with me at the school; Gavin's friends and colleagues as well as his parents, who'd flown in the day before; neighbours; people I had sat beside at church for years but never known well.

Even though I knew that their support was for the false family we had only pretended to be, I was incredibly touched by their presence. While I wiped away tears from my cheeks, I wondered how many would be there if they knew who we really were. Still, I was grateful for the protective wall they formed around us, separating us from the anger of the other side: the prosecutors, who were already vowing to appeal; Ali's musician friends; and looking isolated and aggrieved, her mother and sister, whose tearstained faces indicated they felt they had been victimized again.

Once again, I scanned the crowd for George, but there was no sign of him. Nor was Jack Butterfield present to demand justice for the woman he still referred to as his 'fiancée.' Was it possible that Ali had been abandoned by her men now that she could no longer dazzle them with the charms of her physical presence?

However, as I was searching for some sign that the lovers on whom she had lavished so much of her time and attention had not yet forgotten her, I saw once again the solitary figure of Beth Shagaury, making her way toward the exit. Again, her head was down, so I had no opportunity to read her face. Of all the people who had put aside their responsibilities for an hour because they felt a need to stand up for someone they cared about, either for Jamie or for Ali, Beth's presence was the most mysterious. What, I wondered, would cause the young widow with four children and scant resources to hire a babysitter and show up for the proceedings time after time? What stake did she have in them? I knew she hated Ali, but she despised me as well. In a courtroom that was sharply divided into two sides, Beth Shagaury was probably the only person present who had not tipped her hand. Had she come for Jamie and me, perhaps believing in his guilt, and seeing him as the avenger of her own personal score? Or had she changed her mind about Ali, as so many people had since the violinist had joined the sainted dead? I thought of the wake, where colleagues from school who had never mentioned the music teacher's name without adding a catty piece of gossip had tearfully reminisced about what good friends they'd been. Had Beth experienced a similar change of heart? Instead of blaming her for Brian's death, did she identify with Ali in her victimhood? Or was she, unlike the rest of the sharply divided crowd, pursuing her own agenda?

While those questions reeled in my mind, Beth Shagaury disappeared from sight. But as I craned my neck to follow her with my eyes, my mother-in-law tugged at my sleeve. 'Come on, Jeanne,' she said. 'Once we escape these reporters, Gavin is taking us all out for lunch.'

'I can't go,' I said, responding before I had time to think about the words. 'There's something I've got to do right away.'

Pulling away, I grabbed my purse and jostled through the crowd, leaving Courtney, my in-laws, and Gavin clearly dazed.

30

George Mather opened the door to his apartment even before I had time to knock. From the aureole of hair around his head and his rumpled clothing, I suspected he had been roused from a nap. When he saw me on his doorstep, he smoothed his hair with the palm of his hand and cleared his throat. 'Come in, Jeanne,' he said, standing aside. 'You look like you need to sit down.'

He took me solicitously by the arm and led me into the small studio apartment he had rented after Ali and he split up. As I stepped inside, I blinked. All the shades were down, and it took me several moments to adjust to the darkness of the place. I wondered if this was George's normal way of living or merely a reflection of a deep depression that had taken hold of him since Ali's death. Immediately, he began to clear surfaces, uncovering a place for me to sit.

'Ah, the sorry truth about the male of the species comes out at last, doesn't it, Jeanne? Underneath all our bravado, we are done in by the simplest tasks,' he said, watching me as he always did. He removed a coffee cup that looked like it had been there for weeks. Then he switched on a small window fan, filling the stale room with a refreshing coolness, and began to open shades. While dust eddied around in the sunlight, George disappeared into the kitchen. In a moment he returned with a snifter of brandy.

Vaguely insulted by this acknowledgment of how much I had come to depend on alcohol, I held up my hand in protest. 'It's eleven in the morning, George. No brandy for me.'

'A cup of tea, then? Isn't that what you and Ali sometimes shared?' He smiled warmly, as if enjoying the memory of the two of us curled like bookends on the couch while we sipped tea and shared secrets. But as always when he mentioned his wife's name, a shadow of sorrow darkened his face. I noticed that when he went into the kitchenette to make the tea, he left the brandy on the table — just in case I changed my mind.

While George clattered about the kitchen like a man lost in his own home, I looked around the apartment unimpeded. It was a confining, small place, and he had made no effort to embellish it. Besides the overstuffed bookcases, which lined every wall, there was almost no furniture to diminish the severe effect of the room. Nothing but the shabby couch on which I found myself, and a battered coffee table. Judging by the litter on the small rectangular table, it functioned as both the table where George took his lonely meals and a desk.

I thought of George traversing the lonely trajectory between his office and this dark untidy apartment, and for a moment I felt a surge of anger toward Ali. How could she have left a man like George to such a fate? Why hadn't she realized how lucky she was? If only she'd had the sense to stay with George, she would be alive today. Yes, in so many ways, her sister, Kathleen, was right: Ali had been courting death and peril for years, perhaps all her life.

Feeling unsteadied by my own thoughts as well as the upheaval of emotions in the courthouse, I took a brief sip of the brandy George had left for me. It burned going down, but immediately filled me with a soothing warmth. By the time George had time to return with our tea, I had finished it.

Smiling, George glanced at my empty snifter. 'Your colour looks much better,' he said approvingly. 'Do you still want tea?'

'It's not tea I've come for,' I said, emboldened by the liquor. 'It's information. Why haven't you returned my calls? Why didn't you show up in court this morning?' My voice sounded accusatory, almost angry.

'I wanted to call you, Jeanne. In fact, I've dialled your number more times than I can count.' He paused briefly. 'But each time I hung up before the call went through. I thought it better to wait until I had more to tell you.' He was obviously referring to his own private inquiry into Ali's murder. For a moment, George scowled, lost in his own preoccupations. Then shaking himself from the loneliness that had encompassed him since Ali's death, he seemed to remember I was in the room once again. He smiled sadly, then poured tea for both of us.

'I was sure you'd want to hear the judge's decision today,' I said. 'Kathleen and her mother looked like they could have used the support.'

'Yes, I'm sure they could have. But I don't

think I'm the one to give it to them.' He frowned mysteriously, thinking of his troublesome in-laws. 'Tell me, how did the judge decide?'

'You mean you didn't even bother to put the radio on?'

'Obviously not.' George ran his hand through his dishevelled hair. 'Do you want me to wait for the morning paper?'

'The judge decided that Jamie is an excellent candidate for rehabilitation,' I said, suddenly choked with the emotion I had not yet had time to feel. 'He's going to be tried as a juvenile.'

George immediately reached out and squeezed my hand, his eyes filled with the sincerity that always made me feel like I was about to weep. 'You must be very relieved, Jeanne,' he said. 'I'm happy for you.' Though he had vowed that whoever had killed Ali would pay for the rest of his life, he seemed particularly sympathetic toward the person charged with her murder. Maybe he was onto something.

I rose abruptly, almost upsetting the tea I had placed precariously near the edge of the table. Distractedly, I began to pace up and down the room, filled with conflicting emotions. 'If you want to know the truth, I'm *not* relieved. I won't be relieved until this is all over. When my son and I are far away from here, far from anyone who knows anything about this ugly story. And when Jamie gets the help he needs,' I blurted out.

'You almost sound as if you believe he's guilty,' George said. His eyes turned a deeper blue the way they did when he was listening intently.

'Of course, I don't,' I snapped. 'But that doesn't mean Jamie won't need some counselling — especially after all of this.'

Abruptly, George got up and went back into the kitchen. When he returned, he brought the bottle of brandy and another snifter for himself. 'To tell you the truth, I've never been much of a tea drinker.' After filling the glasses, he went to his stereo and put on a CD. 'I found this the other day among her things. It's something I'd never heard before,' he explained.

At first, I was startled by the intrusion of Ali and her music. But as the hypnotic sound of her violin filled the room, I closed my eyes and gave in to it. It was almost as though a door had opened and she had entered, as though she were sitting on the couch beside me, stroking my hair.

George was silent for several moments and when I looked over at him, I saw his face was streaked with tears. Though he had remained stoic throughout the funeral and wake, the sound of Ali's music apparently drew on feelings that even the sight of her inert body could not.

'I'm sorry,' he said when he caught me staring at him, but he made no attempt to wipe the tears away.

'I've wanted to listen to some of her pieces so many times, but I was afraid to turn them on,' I admitted, leaning back on the couch, my snifter in hand. I took a slow sip of the alcohol.

'It's a part of Ali that even the killer couldn't take from us,' George said. 'A part of her that will be with us always. And there's more than I ever imagined. I've been going through some of her CDs recently, hoping to make some copies for her friends.'

'And what about the family? Have you made copies for her mother and Kathleen?' I said. Remembering George's earlier, almost hostile remark about his in-laws, I hoped to steer the subject back to that provocative subject.

George snorted. 'The family's only interest in Ali's music concerns the money involved. You know what Kathleen said to me a few days ago? "I suppose the royalties will go to you." Can you believe that? As if I want Ali's money.' George stared at the stereo, a rare bitterness on his face.

'I get the feeling Ali and her family weren't very close,' I said. 'In fact, she only mentioned her mother to me once. And I never even knew Kathleen existed.'

'Like a lot of people, they misunderstood Ali,' George said, seeming to concentrate more on the music than on my presence. 'She was so unlike them.'

'Is that why Kathleen hated her? Because she was different? Or was it simply a mundane case of envy?'

George looked somewhat shocked by the mention of the word *hate*, but he did not deny it. 'Obviously, Ali got all the talent and beauty in the family. But there was more to it than that.'

As Ali's music streamed over me, I forgot my own problems once again and got lost in the deeper mystery of my dead friend's life. Just a month earlier, I believed I knew everything about my best friend, but now I was beginning to wonder if I had known Ali at all. Since her death,

I'd already learned she had been meeting mysteriously with my son. And now I was finding out that the woman who allowed others no secrets had plenty of her own.

'Ali was a person who simply couldn't lie. As you know, she tortured me with her honesty about Butterfield — and the others. Nor did she allow those around her their little deceptions.' As he paused to sip his drink, George looked genuinely pained by his recollections of Ali's relentless veracity.

But I didn't much notice. I was thinking of the way Ali had forced me to face the truth about my marriage — and even about Jamie. I wasn't sure I was entirely grateful for her intervention. Even now. 'Sometimes the truth can be pretty cruel,' I said.

'It certainly was in Ali's family,' George said. It was as though the spirit of Ali unleashed through her music had infected him, and he was revealing things he might have otherwise kept to himself.

When I looked up at him curiously, George smiled sadly. 'You said that Ali rarely spoke of her mother, and never of Kathleen. But what about her father, Alvin? The man who played violin concerts all over the world. The one who taught her to play — I don't suppose Ali ever told you about him.'

'Actually, she did,' I said. 'She told me he was a brilliant musician. And that he died when she was very young. Too young to remember much about him.'

George shook his head sadly. 'Even our Ali

343

had her secrets, didn't she? Even for her, there were subjects that were more easily glossed over, covered with semi-fabrications.'

'But you yourself just said that he was a talented violinist,' I said, feeling increasingly confused. 'Where's the lie? Are you saying he isn't dead?'

'Oh, the bastard died, all right. But not before he left his daughters with enough memories to last a lifetime. Ali was sixteen the night her father went up into his music room and put a pistol in his mouth.' George looked up at me. 'You know, I never made the connection before, but it's ironic that both father and daughter died violently in their own music rooms.'

However, at that moment, I wasn't thinking about the coincidental manner of their deaths. Nor was I even focusing on the revelation that Ali's father had committed suicide when she was at such a sensitive age — sixteen, Jamie's age exactly. No, what bored into me with the force of a brand was the darkness contained in the earlier part of his statement. *He left his daughters with enough memories to last a lifetime.*

'What are you saying, George?' I blurted out.

'Alvin was a selfish, selfish man. A man who tyrannized his wife, and mercilessly berated poor Kathleen for her shortcomings, cruelly and constantly comparing her to her more talented and beautiful sister. The two of them suffered so many years of unmitigated abuse they believed his insults were true.'

'And Ali?' I repeated. 'You said she was the favorite.'

For a moment, George looked away. Then he turned to face me. 'You know the story,' he said enigmatically. 'Ali was the favorite. And thus the repository of all her father's hopes and dreams. The one he almost destroyed in the name of love.'

I had begun to tremble so forcefully that I could no longer hold my drink.

'I always thought that was why Ali always ran from those who loved her,' George continued. 'Because her earliest experiences were with a monster. It — 'the abuse,' as people call it now — went on for years. But it wasn't till her sixteenth birthday that Ali went to her mother. And that night, while Kathleen was frosting the birthday cake with pink icing, Alvin went into his music room with his pistol, leaving them all, but especially Ali, with a legacy of guilt and rage she would never live down.'

I thought of how bitterly Ali had wept after Brian's suicide, and how I'd heard her on the phone, tearfully telling George that the incident had 'brought it all back.' Finally, I understood. As George stared into my eyes, I realized the music had ended and an engulfing silence had entered the room.

For the first time, I felt the connection between Ali and Jamie as strongly as I had felt her presence in the room when her unfinished concerto began to play. They understood each other in the way that only fellow victims can. In some way I could not describe or understand, I

345

felt sure that they recognized the dark place within each other.

Abruptly, I got up and reached for my purse. 'I have to see my son,' I said, surprising even myself with the urgency of my words. Though I knew that I was probably adding to George's suspicions about Jamie, I couldn't control myself. My only focus was on getting out of George's stuffy apartment, away from the dark knowledge in his eyes.

'You're going to see Jamie *now*?' George asked, appearing stunned.

'If they'll let me in,' I said. 'There's something I need to ask him.'

George walked me to the door and watched me go. I was halfway up the walkway when he called my name. 'While you're there, Jeanne, tell the boy something from me.'

I turned, blinking back the sun of an astonishingly clear day.

'Tell him not to worry,' he said. 'This thing's never going to go to trial.'

I took a step toward him, unsure what to ask first. What did he mean it would never go to trial? Was he expecting Jamie to confess? Or did he know the identity of the real killer? 'What — '

But George had already begun to close the door. 'I wish I could tell you more, Jeanne. But I can't. Not yet.' And then, before I could stop him, he pushed the door closed between us. If that weren't a clear enough message, I heard the click of a lock. I considered continuing to knock, refusing to leave until he told me how he could possibly know such a thing. But I could already see that it was futile. It was obvious that George, like Ali and even Jamie, was determined to keep his secret until he decided it was the right moment to speak, and no amount of coercion on my part would change his mind.

31

Once again, I was pleased to find that Glenn was on duty at Somers. Of all the guards, he seemed to be the most compassionate, perhaps because as he once told me, he had spent some time in a place like this when he was about Jamie's age. 'It doesn't have to be the end of the world,' he told me once when he caught me crying as they led Jamie away. 'Some kids really put this behind them.' But though his words were meant to be comforting, they were not. All I heard was the qualifying *some* kids. Yes, *some* kids like Glenn were able to change and recover from their time in lockup, but what happened to the rest of them?

However, when Glenn led Jamie in, I quickly put aside my fears. For the first time since his arrest and — if the truth were to be told — probably months before that, Jamie smiled when he saw me.

'You're alone,' he said, the relief on his face evident. His face was noticeably thinner than it had been a month ago. And his institutional khaki pants were baggier than they had ever been.

'It's just you and me, kid,' I said, trying hard not to burst into tears at the sight of the boy who had been thrust into adult-size torment long before his time. *Just like Ali.*

I turned to Glenn, who had settled into a chair

in the corner of the room. 'Do you think Jamie and I could be alone for a little while?' I asked. 'I promise I don't have any hacksaws in my purse.'

For a moment, Glenn hesitated, but then looking from Jamie's face to mine, he relented. 'It's against the rules, you know, but to tell you the truth, I can't see the harm. And I could use a smoke break.' He opened the door to leave, then turned around and added, 'I'll be right outside if there's something you need.' Though he didn't say it, it was obvious that he was also warning us not to try anything.

'What's that all about?' Jamie said, sinking uneasily into his chair. 'Glenn's cool. Why'd you make him leave?' The happy look he had worn when he first saw me had dissipated. He almost looked like he was afraid of me. Or perhaps he was just afraid of being alone with any adult.

I shrugged. 'You've lost weight,' I said, hoping to begin with a neutral subject. 'I guess I was so fixated on the hearing, this is the first time I really noticed.'

'The food's pretty horrible here,' Jamie said, smiling. 'And there's no peanut butter cups.'

'Well, I can't say it's done you any harm; you look good,' I said. It was true. Though I *hadn't* noticed the gradual weight loss in the past, a handsome young man had begun to emerge from beneath the layers of flesh, a young man with my eyes and Gavin's strong bone structure. It pained me to think that even if I banished Gavin from seeing Jamie forever, he would still be there. There in the very lines of our son's face. Though I had brought Jamie a package of peanut butter cups in my purse, I didn't pull them out. The last thing my son needed was to stuff himself with more false sweetness.

We gaped awkwardly for a couple of minutes, as if seeing each other for the first time, and then abruptly Jamie rose, his metal chair clattering noisy on the linoleum floor. 'Don't you think we should call Glenn back in? He probably thinks we're planning some kind of prison break in here.'

But I only shook my head. 'In a little while. There's a couple things I want to ask you, Jamie. And I don't want Glenn — or anyone else — listening in.'

'Don't you think you've asked me enough already?' Jamie asked nervously. He walked over to the one small window in the room and looked out on the street, obviously desperate for escape.

I sympathized with his fear, but I pressed on. 'Why did you go to see Ali after school those times, Jamie? Just tell me that, and then we can call Glenn.'

Jamie inhaled sharply, nervously. Then, abruptly, his fist slammed the wall. 'What do you want from me, Mom? I mean, what good does it do to talk about all this stuff? It's not going to change anything that happened.' His teeth were clenched and as he spoke, his voice grew increasingly loud. I was afraid that Glenn would hear him from the hallway and come back in before I could get my answers.

'You're right. It won't change the past. It won't undo what your father did to you, or bring Ali back, but it just might change the future.

350

Please, Jamie, just tell me why you went to Ali, a stranger who wasn't even your teacher. Then we can drop it.'

Slowly, Jamie returned to his seat. He shook his head as if he were arguing with himself, and ran his hands through his hair several times before he spoke. 'You really want to know?' he asked, looking like a little boy when he gazed up at me.

'No, I'm not sure I do,' I said. 'But I'm your mother, Jamie. I *need* to know.'

'Okay, then,' Jamie said. Once again he was on his feet. He turned the small visitors' room into a cage as he paced up and down, mentally returning to that school building when Ali first entered it, changing everything, both for Jamie and for herself.

'It was like the second week of school,' he said, beginning slowly. 'And Mrs Mather — Ali — she came into our health class to give a lecture. It was a lecture about . . . about abuse.' He looked away as he said those words. 'Anyway, it wasn't just one of those dry lectures like we usually got. It was about real stuff that happened to her. Stuff her father did. To be honest, it was pretty gross. Anyway, I sat and listened to about as much as I could stand and then I got up and ran out of the room. I didn't even know what I was doing, Mom. I just bolted. I think I said something lame like 'Excuse me, Mrs Mather, but I think I'm going to be sick.' I wasn't lying either; I really thought I was going to hurl.'

'And did you?' I asked, thinking that Jamie

was looking pretty pale at that moment. 'Did you get sick?'

'I barely made it to the men's room before I shot my lunch. So there I am, heaving in the toilet, smelling that disinfectant the janitor uses, when all of a sudden I realize someone's in the bathroom with me. And they're not using the urinals or anything. They're just standing there watching me puke my guts out. Well, you'll never guess who it was.'

'Ali,' I said, closing my eyes as I envisioned the friend who wouldn't have let a men's room sign or even the prospect of surprising a boy at the urinal keep her away from a kid in trouble.

'She was standing there holding some wet paper towels. 'Feel better?' she asked. As soon as I looked up at her, I realized she knew . . . she knew everything. If I could have, I swear I would have run out of that school and never gone back, but she was blocking my way out. I already knew she was going to make my life hell from then on.'

'It wasn't Ali who made your life hell, Jamie. It was — '

But Jamie interrupted with surprising ferocity. 'She should have stayed out of it, Mom! What business was it of hers? I mean, if she wanted to go around telling the whole world her sick little story, fine. But what right did that give her to butt into my life?'

'Ali just wanted to help you, Jamie,' I said.

'Well, you can see where it got the two of us. She's six feet under. And I'm locked up until I'm twenty-one — if I even get out then.' Jamie's voice was laced with a bitterness I had never

352

heard from him before.

'So that's when she asked you to see her after school . . . ' I surmised.

'It's not like I wanted to go, Mom. But I didn't have a lot of choice. I was afraid that if I didn't show, she'd go to my guidance counsellor about it. Or worse, tell you. Already, that day, I was starting to feel like all my teachers were looking at me weird. Like they knew. Like everyone knew. I know they didn't, but that's how I felt. Like this whole sick thing was something you could see as clear as a giant pimple on my nose or something. I didn't plan to tell her anything. I planned to lie my brains out like I always did. But somehow — I think it was her eyes more than anything — it was like she already knew — anyway, she got it out of me.'

'That was the first time you went to see her . . . ' I said, beginning to put things together, remembering how strangely Jamie had been acting those early weeks of school. Gavin and I had even discussed it, deciding it must be a problem with another student or one of his classes. 'But as uncomfortable as it was for you, you returned a second time.'

'Once again, it wasn't like I had a choice. I was at the door, just trying to get out of that room without breaking down and blubbering like a little kid, and she clobbers me again. You know what she said to me?' His voice still sounded incredulous.

I shook my head.

'She says, 'Well, now that we know the truth, we'll have to decide what we're going to do about it.' *What we're going to do about it?*' Jamie repeated, once again running his hands frantically through his hair. 'As if you could. I mean, what are you going to do, press rewind, go back in time and make the past different? Because aside from that, all you're gonna do is make it worse . . . '

'So you went to see her again,' I said, pressing him to continue, as Glenn cleared his throat impatiently outside the door.

'Yeah. And this time it was even worse,' Jamie said, sitting down across from me, his voice a whisper. 'This time she tells me that what Dad did was a crime, and that he deserves to be punished for it. Get this — she wants me to call the police on my own dad! And worse, she wants me to tell *you*. Well, that was where I drew the line. I walked out of there, telling her where to go and what she could do when she got there. Let her tell the guidance counsellor, I thought. It can't be any worse . . . '

'And that was the end of it?' I asked. Unconsciously, I had begun to whisper, too.

But at that question, Jamie leaped up again. 'Of course, that wasn't the end of it, Mom! It wasn't the end of it until Ali was laying there dead on the couch.'

Instinctively, I put my finger to my lips, thinking that if Glenn — or anyone else — heard what Jamie had just said, they might take it as a confession.

But Jamie wasn't listening. He was back into his grievances against Ali; they propelled him

354

around the room where he walked, unconsciously pummelling one hand with his other fist. 'The next thing I know, she's calling you, asking you for a ride to school. The way I saw it, the woman was trying to torture me, making me worry day and night just what she was telling you in the car every day.'

'So you decided to torture her back,' I said, suddenly finding a new meaning in the objects Jamie had taken from Ali's house, in the defaced sheet music, the subtle threats. Even the times I'd caught him eavesdropping on the phone now made sense.

'Exactly,' Jamie said, smiling slightly at the memory of his own campaign of terror. 'But unfortunately, she didn't scare easily. Whenever I saw her in school, she'd look right at me — the same way she had that day in the bathroom. And then when everything hit the fan, and you left for New Hampshire, she actually started calling me . . . I mean, can you believe it?'

'What did she want?' I asked, reliving the guilty feelings I had whenever I thought of the time I had spent in the cabin while my son was left at home with his tormentor.

'She said I shouldn't be alone in the house with Dad. She even offered me to come and stay at her house. As if I'd go there in a million years. And when I told her to leave me alone, to just stay out of it, she said that if I didn't deal with the situation, she would.'

'But how?' I asked.

'She said she'd go to the police herself. You should have heard her, Mom. She said it was her responsibility as a teacher. What bullshit.' Jamie's face was suffused with blotchy anger. 'That's when I decided to kill her,' he said in a low voice. 'I didn't want to, but she left me no choice. It might sound crazy, but I saw it as self-defense. I mean, can you imagine Dad opening the door and seeing a couple of cops standing there with a warrant for his arrest?'

'Jamie, don't say any more,' I said, looking around the room suspiciously, suddenly wondering if it was bugged. What had I led my son into this time?

But finally released from his prison of silence, Jamie wasn't about to be stopped. 'But I *didn't*, Mom,' he said. 'I didn't kill her. That's the amazing thing. Sure, I went to her house intending to do it. I had my stupid knife, and my adrenaline was pumping; I swore I was ready. And Ali was so stupid, she made it easy. Even after everything I'd done to her, she left the door unlocked. I didn't even have to break into the place. Then, get this — I walk in there with a knife in my hand, looking like a madman. And she just lays on that couch. Like she wasn't afraid of me at all. Not until I went over and put that knife to her throat did she realize I was serious. And not only serious, but *strong*. I think that up until that moment she thought of me as some little kid in a big man's body. But at that moment she realized that I was no kid . . . '

I closed my eyes, tears streaming down my cheeks in sharp rivulets. 'But you couldn't do it. You don't have it in you, Jamie. Even then, pressed to your limit, you couldn't do it.'

Jamie lowered his head and shook it as if disappointed with himself. 'I could have, I think I could have. When I smashed that violin, it felt so good, I thought I could bust up the whole world. But when I cut her, I looked in her eyes and she was so scared. I knew what it was like to be scared like that . . . and it was like waking up out of some nightmare and saying, my God, what am I doing here? I jumped up and ran out of there, leaving her on the couch. Terrified and cut up a little bit, yes, but alive. Ali was alive when I left her that night, Mom. I swear to you, she was.'

It was the first time Jamie had told the whole story of what had happened that night, the first time he had risked exposing the shame that he had nearly committed murder to conceal.

'I know she was, Jamie. And I can promise you this. You're not going to be punished for a crime you didn't commit. Not for one day.'

'But how can you be so sure, Mom? You heard Dad — the evidence they have against me is pretty overwhelming. Even he believes I did it. And even if I do just get stuck in juvey for five years, I'll be branded a murderer for the rest of my life.'

I took his hands and passed on George's mysterious promise just as the door opened and Glenn entered. My eyes focused unblinkingly on Jamie's, I spoke in a strong voice, adding a reckless codicil to the assurance that Ali's husband had given me. 'Promise me you won't worry,' I said, gripping Jamie's hands for dear life. 'Because this

357

thing's never going to go to trial.'

'But how do you *know* that?' Jamie asked, oblivious to Glenn's presence in the room, as was I. 'How could you possibly know that?'

'Because the person who really did it is about to be exposed,' I said with a self-assurance that could only be described as crazy.

★ ★ ★

That night when I got home, I was relieved to find the house empty. Apparently, Gavin had taken his parents out to dinner. But then, I didn't think I was likely to see much of the elder Crosses before they were scheduled to go back home. Now that he was aware of what I knew, Gavin would make sure I didn't get the opportunity to tell them.

When I entered the family room, I saw the light on the answering machine blinking. With some trepidation, I pressed the button, and heard an unfamiliar voice identify himself as an animal control officer in Towers, New Hampshire. 'This is a message for Jeanne Cross,' he said. 'I just wanted to let you know we found your little dog. He's hungry and dirty, but it looks like he's going to be all right.'

I don't know why, but as I heard those words, I let loose all the tears I had held back in the visiting room. Somehow the image of the battered little survivor filled me with so much hope I found myself weeping and laughing at the same time.

32

When Katie Breen opened the door, she stifled a gasp. Only then did I realize how I must have appeared to Toby's thirteen-year-old sister as she stood in the brightly lit doorway in her flannel pants and T-shirt, her long hair slanting over her eyes.

'Hi, Katie,' I managed to say. As if my appearance at the door in a rainstorm with a soggy malnourished dog in my arms was normal. As if anything about my life in recent months had been normal. After I left Jamie the night before, I had driven straight to New Hampshire, where I'd picked up Skyler and headed for home. As I stood in the doorway, I realized that I hadn't eaten anything but a couple of donuts in the past twenty-four hours. My hair plastered down by rain, a poorly hidden desperation on my face, and holding a bedraggled little dog, it was no wonder that the teenager hardly recognized her neighbour. In a flash of self-consciousness, I stood up straighter, pushed back my hopelessly wet hair, even attempted a smile.

'Oh, Mrs Cross,' Katie said, standing aside. 'Come in.' She was obviously embarrassed that she hadn't recognize me.

Gingerly, I stepped onto the welcome mat, but refused to follow her more deeply into the house. 'I don't want to get your floor wet,' I said, extending my arms to reveal how thoroughly the rain had penetrated my windbreaker. 'Look at me! I'm drenched,' I said, trying a laugh. After parking the Jeep in my own driveway, I had walked the two blocks to the Breens impulsively, impervious to the rainstorm that buffeted me. Similarly, the stoic little dog, who was not surprised by nature's fickleness, had not protested at being carried through such punishing weather. However, once inside the Breens' cozy walls, Skyler was squirming in my arms, anxious to get free. The inside of houses, as we both had learned the hard way, can be dangerous. A trap of the worst kind.

But by that point, Katie had stopped looking at me and was focused on the little dog. 'Oh, my God, it's *so* cute. What's its name?' she said, approaching the dog eagerly.

But at that moment Skyler leaped out of my arms and began to yip at the door, causing a chain reaction in the house. First Sharon called from the kitchen, 'Who's out there, Katie?' And then Toby appeared at the top of the stairs. Oblivious to my drenched appearance, he stared at the dog, which had already given up the idea of escape and was beginning to lick Katie's hand.

Toby's first words were for the dog. 'Skyler! Come here, boy.' Then he turned to his sister. 'That's Jamie's dog,' he explained. 'He's written to me about him from, uh — from that place he's in.'

The teenager's open face darkened briefly at the mention of *that place*, and then he turned self-consciously to me. 'Hi, Mrs Cross.' His eyes quickly looked away in typical adolescent fashion, veering back to the little dog that was now wriggling in his sister's arms.

Just then, Sharon Breen pushed through the door from the kitchen, wiping her hands on a dishcloth. 'Jeanne, what are you doing there in the doorway? Come in. My goodness, look at you! You're soaking wet. Let me fix you something hot to drink.' Her eyes drifted toward the paw prints scattered like dark snowflakes across her gleaming wood floors. But then she politely looked away and smiled at me. 'You better get that jacket off before you catch pneumonia.' She was at my side by then, tugging at my windbreaker.

But I resisted her solicitations. 'I can't stay, Sharon,' I said. I tried to keep my tone light, to pretend I was simply a neighbour who had unexpectedly gotten caught in a downpour while walking her dog, but I couldn't pull it off.

Sharon read the desperation in my voice. Turning to her children, she said. 'Why don't you guys take Skyler into the kitchen and clean up his paws. There are rags under the sink. You may even find a box of Sam's old dog biscuits in the cupboards.' Sam was the aging golden retriever they had put to sleep only weeks earlier. For the first time, the younger Breens were not sent back into the dark memory of that day at the mention of Sam's name. All their attention was focused on the bedraggled and obviously needy Skyler.

'Come on, boy, you want a biscuit?' Katie said in her lovely lilting voice while Toby coaxed the dog across the floor.

When we were alone, Sharon said, 'Are you sure you don't want something to drink? I could brew some coffee. Maybe some hot chocolate?' Her eyes were the same steadfast blue they had been when she attended every one of Jamie's hearings. Staring into them, I almost wanted to weep in gratitude. Surely, I had never done anything to deserve such loyalty.

I shook my head, scattering moisture from my hair. 'As I said, I need to ask you a favor. A fairly monumental one, so please don't feel like you have to answer right away. Take a couple of days and think about it.'

'Anything, Jeanne,' Sharon said, standing before me in her unpretentious uniform of jeans and a T-shirt. In all the years I'd known her, I rarely saw her in anything else. 'I've told you that before. Whatever I can do . . . '

'It's the dog,' I said, looking toward the kitchen, where Katie's cooing sounds mixed with Toby's whoops and Skyler's occasional yips as the teenagers attempted to clean him up. 'He means so much to Jamie. Just the idea of getting out and knowing that something is waiting for him, something joyous and innocent and oblivious to all the chaos we humans create for ourselves . . . ' I paused, shivering slightly as the chill from the rain penetrated my skin.

'I think it's wonderful that you bought Jamie the dog. The perfect thing at a time like this,' Sharon said, tilting her head in bewilderment. 'But what do you need from us?'

'I can't keep him, Sharon,' I said, bluntly. I opened my mouth to say more, to offer an explanation for the huge favor I was asking of her, but then fell quiet.

Sharon's eyes asked the obvious question: *why not?* But she said nothing. For a moment, we were silent as she assimilated all that I was saying and, more important, all that I was not saying.

'You want us to take Skyler?' Sharon said, posing the question I had not asked.

I nodded.

'But when? And for how long?' Once ahead, Sharon's head was tilted quizzically, reminding me of an expression I had often seen on Toby's face when he and Jamie were playing video games in our family room. Such innocent times seemed to have happened centuries ago, to another family, not my own.

'Well, as soon as you decide. I'm going to board Skyler at the Rider Kennels until I find someone to take him.'

'You're putting him in a kennel — *today?* But why, Jeanne? Is it Gavin? Is he allergic to the dog?'

But I only lowered my head, allowing the rain to drip from my hair onto Sharon's shining wood floors. It was clear to both of us that I would not — or could not — say more. There was a long silence in which I stared steadfastly at the floor, feeling the weight of Sharon's gaze on me, testing once more the loyalty of neighbours who thought they knew our family.

'How long will you need us to keep him?' she asked at last.

'I'm afraid I don't know that either, Sharon,' I said, looking up at her. 'At least until Jamie gets out. Maybe longer.'

Sharon stared straight into my eyes with her own, which were pale as water and just as clear. She knew that I was asking far more of her than to simply take care of a little dog. We eyed each other with a frankness that needed no words.

And then with all the generosity that she was known for in the neighbourhood, Sharon stepped forward and embraced me, allowing the rainwater that clung to my coat to seep onto her. 'Of course, we'll take him, Jeanne. And please, there's no need to kennel the little guy. We'll take him tonight — *now* if that's what you want. And for as long as you need.'

Having no words to thank Sharon, I hugged her harder. 'I should go . . . ' I said.

'Are you sure?' she asked, stepping back to look into my face. 'I just made a huge pot of marinara sauce. Dinner's nothing fancy — a little pasta and a salad, maybe some garlic bread, but Walt will be home in a half hour, and we'd love to have you.'

Even before she had gotten the invitation out, I was shaking my head. 'Thanks, Sharon — for everything. But Gavin is expecting me.' As I spoke my husband's name, I felt something harden within myself. Something apparently visible because a fleeting expression of alarm crossed Sharon's face. She looked at me as if she sensed that I had become a dangerous woman.

'Jeanne, is there anything you need to talk about? I know we've never been as close as you were to your friend, Ali, but I hope you know that anything you say to me would stay with me.'

I reached for the glib answer to smooth over the moment. It was just the strain of the trial, my concern for Jamie. There were a number of things I might have said, but nothing came out. Instead, I just shook my head, and turned to go.

As I left the house, I heard Skyler in the background, yipping in protest. Though I had proved a royal failure as a master, he still wanted to stay with me. Trudging toward home, I felt his absence in my arms, the soft warmth that told me I was not totally alone. I was grateful that it was still storming; the salt of tears mixed with rain on my face as I turned onto my own street.

33

The house, as I approached it on foot, was almost alive with lights. A mockery of welcome and warmth, I thought as I slowly climbed the hill. Despite the wild rain, I walked leisurely, in no hurry to face my in-laws. Or Gavin. I removed my sodden boots and jacket in the mudroom, then moved through the house as furtively as a burglar. I had lived here for seventeen years, but it no longer felt like home. Perhaps it never really had. However, as soon as I entered the kitchen door, a rush of quiet told me something had changed.

Gavin's car was in the driveway, but there was no sign of him. Or of his parents, who had left little trails throughout the house in the days that they'd been there. The bottles of red wine my father-in-law enjoyed with dinner, saying it was good for the heart as he refilled his glass, were gone from the counter. And my mother-in-law's magazines, the kind that were filled with a contradictory mix of fattening recipes and weight-loss strategies aimed at Jamie, were no longer scattered across the kitchen table where she usually left them — probably as a hint for me. When I looked in the front hall closet, there was no trace of their coats. Apparently, my loose-cannon behavior had convinced Gavin that he no longer needed his parents' support as much as he had previously claimed. I could only imagine what he had told them in order to get them to change their flight schedule and leave three weeks earlier than planned. For a brief moment, I wondered if he might have gone with them. But of course, he would not desert Jamie before the trial was over. If for no other reason, he would be concerned with how it would look to the legion of friends and acquaintances who still regarded him as Wonderful Dr Cross.

However, the telltale scent of lime, an aroma that caused me to shiver in my wet clothes, informed me that my husband had recently been in the kitchen. I turned and saw his shoes lined up beside the door. Just the sight of their aggressive neatness made me feel a chill that even the cold rain had not produced.

'Gavin?' I called as I moved through one bright empty room to another. He was not in the family room, as he usually lingered at that hour. Nor was he in the dining room, where he ate his take-out dinners by himself when we were alone in the house.

However, when I looked down the hallway, I noticed that the door to his study was ajar; the room I had not entered since the night of my ruthless searching was flooded with light. In most houses, a light on created a sense of security, but in our house the bright lights that shone on our empty rooms were eerie. I moved toward the study cautiously, calling Gavin's name. But once again, I was met with silence.

Just outside the study door, I hesitated, held back by something I could not name. Perhaps the memory of the first, last, and only time I had entered my husband's sanctuary held me back. If you thought about it, everything that had happened to us had flowed from the hour when I had called the locksmith and begun exhuming Gavin's secrets. My flight to New Hampshire. Ali's murder. Jamie's arrest. If only I could go back to the study and put back the Visa bill that had ultimately led me to the deadly truth about my husband, my son, myself, could I have stopped all those things from happening? But of course, I knew I could not. The roots of our tragedy were far deeper than the simple events of any one night.

I shook off my useless thoughts and backed away from the door. There was no sound at all in the study, no movement, no rustling of papers. If Gavin was in there — which I suspected he was — he had probably passed out. Gavin passing out in the study or in the family room had become a fairly common occurrence in our house. But my husband's drinking, which predated my own use of alcohol as the great healer by several years, was another thing I had tactfully failed to acknowledge in my marriage.

This might be easier than I anticipated, I thought as I backed away from the door. Perhaps my few harsh words earlier, the threat that I would tell his parents the truth, and the larger implication that I would no longer keep his secrets, had been enough to keep Gavin away from me. But then I remembered what I had to do. I had to see him, if only this last time.

I moved purposefully up the stairs, stopping occasionally to call my husband's name as I went. But the brightly lit house was shining with emptiness. He wasn't in Jamie's room when I poked my head in and took one last look at the room that my son had warned me not to enter, saying it was a bad place. Shuddering slightly, I flicked off the lights. Then I moved to the guest room that Gavin's parents had recently vacated, and darkened it.

Before I entered the master bedroom, I inhaled deeply. 'Gavin?' I called one more time, but my voice was weak, attenuated by fatigue. Like all the other rooms in our house, it was relentlessly neat — and utterly empty. Somehow, now that I knew I was leaving, I looked around at the room I had shared with my husband for all those years, and wondered how I had endured it. On my side of the bed, there was the nightstand where I kept the novels I read obsessively, desperate to enter lives other than my own. And on Gavin's side of the bed were the things I never looked at, the appointment book he pored over, rigorously planning his days, the alarm clock that marked the number of hours he would have to spend in the room that was a prison for him as much as it was for me. For seventeen years, the two of us had been held hostage to lies. To each other. But most of all to our own fears. For a brief moment, I almost felt sorry for him. Then I thought of Jamie, and a wave of nausea came over me; I went to the closet and got a suitcase. However, after I had opened it and stared into its gaping emptiness, I realized I did not need such a large bag. An overnight bag would suffice.

But when I pulled out the overnight bag and began to contemplate what to bring: a change of underwear and a nightshirt? My toothbrush? The latest novel I was reading? All the accouterments of my old life, everything that had once seemed essential, no longer mattered. I looked at my bureau, where a few framed photographs of my family formed a semicircle. There were my parents posing outside the cabin, my brother showing off a smallish trout he had caught in the stream earlier that day. And there was a shot of Gavin, Jamie, and me on Cape Cod; it had once been one of my favorite photographs. With the wind at our faces and the sea providing a background for our family drama, we crouched together on the beach, smiling mindlessly into the camera. Jamie must have been about four. Staring at the picture, I could almost feel the last vestiges of his baby softness; I could almost smell the ocean. After looking into it for a long moment, I took it from the spot it had occupied on the bureau for at least a decade and dashed it against the wall.

Then I picked up the most recent addition to my collection from the bureau. It was a shot I'd taken of Ali one afternoon at Paradise Pond. She was walking, head down, eyes closed; and her hair, like that of the false family by the sea, had been lifted by the wind. But what I loved most about it was her secret smile. She was smiling about something she had obviously just shared with me. After taking the small bottle of sleeping pills I kept under my pillow, I turned off the light and left the room, leaving the pictures of my beloved few on the dresser. What need did I have for photographs when their faces had been burned forever on my mind? Then, impulsively, standing in the hallway, I realized I wouldn't even need the sleeping pills. I took the bottle and tossed it onto Gavin's side of the bed. 'Maybe you can use them,' I said to the empty space that he had filled with his lies.

As I prepared to return to the study for one final confrontation, I continued to turn off lights as I went. I switched off the light in the upstairs hall, darkened the dining room, the downstairs hall, the living room, the downstairs bathroom. Though I knew I would have to find my way through darkness on the way out, I shut off the lights in the kitchen, the mudroom. I had my hand on the switch in the family room when I was startled by the sound of movement from the study. I jumped, but then steadied myself and switched off the light. The only source of illumination that remained in the house emanated from Gavin's sanctuary.

I was standing utterly still when my husband came into view. 'Going someplace, Jeanne?' he said, slouching in the doorway. From the mottled look of his skin, his bleary eyes, it was obvious that he had drunk even more than usual. It also appeared that he had been crying.

I took a step backward, deeper into the darkness I had created in the house. Though I knew I should say something to defuse the moment, I froze. Mutely, I remained in place, feeling intensely alert but unable to move.

Gavin chuckled softly. 'You're leaving me,

aren't you? And without even the courtesy of a proper goodbye. Really, Jeanne, I thought you had better manners.'

I knew that I should get out of the house immediately while I still could. But I had to play this out. 'You can see where all our fine manners have gotten us.'

I turned to go, but with surprising agility for a drunk, Gavin reached out and seized my arm. He stood over me, tall and as heartbreakingly handsome as ever. 'Do you have any idea what I've gone through to make this marriage work?' he said through clenched teeth.

He was holding my arm so tightly that I thought it might snap. I knew the wisest thing to do was to say nothing. To simply be still until he had finished what he had to say. But once again, I could not will myself into silence. Not anymore. 'And what about me? What about what I've gone through? What about *Jamie*?' My voice betrayed me when I spoke my son's name. *Jamie. What about Jamie?* I repeated in my mind, but I could no longer speak.

However, to my even greater surprise, Gavin, too, seemed deflated by the mention of our son's name. He let go of me and stepped backward into the study. The fluorescent lamp that was the only illumination in the house emphasized the darkness of his face, the caverns that had appeared overnight. He closed his eyes, and for a minute, I thought the invincible Dr Cross was about to break down before my eyes.

Inexorably drawn to the end of the drama, I follow him into his little room of secrets. But as soon as I stepped inside, he slammed the door, then locked it with the bolt that he had once used to keep me out. While I tried to hide my mounting fear, he leaned against the desk, staring at me from a pair of the most tortured eyes I have ever seen. 'So now you know, Jeanne,' he said. 'What do you intend to do about it?'

Though I was still wet and cold, I felt a rush of hot electricity shoot through my body as I realized he was not only talking about what he had done to Jamie. There was something else that Gavin assumed I knew.

34

'I have to go,' I said, slinging my bag over my shoulder. I was torn between desperately wanting to hear what Gavin had to say — and the fear that once I knew, there was no way he could let me walk away with his secret. I deftly unlocked the door of the study, trying to keep my tone casual, my actions free from panic.

'What do you mean, 'you have to go'? You're home, Jeanne. For better or worse, this is what you've chosen. There's no place to *go*. Not for either one of us. Don't you know that by now?' Gavin's voice was laced with familiar, sharp derision. And suddenly he was standing over me, the implied threat that had always been there, that was in fact the governing principle of our marriage, in the open at last. Roughly, he pulled my bag off my shoulder; I stood and watched helplessly as the contents spilled into the centre of the room, where my blusher broke in half. Though it was an awkward, drunken gesture, the shattered blusher, the clatter of spilled coins, gave it an air of violence.

'I'm — I'm meeting someone,' I said. 'If I'm late, they'll come looking for me.' Spotting my keys in the middle of the detritus on the floor, I reached for them. The bag with my license and credit cards, the makeup and grocery coupons I had once deemed essential could be left behind. All I wanted now was my means of escape: the small clutch of keys.

But just before I grasped them, Gavin again seized my arm. 'And who might *they* be?' he said mockingly. 'We both know Ali was your only friend.'

I stared at him evenly, assessing exactly how drunk he was. Taking in his reddened eyes, slightly feverish speech, I calculated what it would take to knock him off balance for just an instant — long enough to grab the keys and run.

Gavin pulled me closer. 'The least you could do is have one little drink with me. One drink and a nice talk. Isn't that what you always wanted to do, Jeannie? *Talk?* In fact, I bet that's what the brilliant Ali recommended as the solution to all our marital problems, isn't it? 'You two need to talk more' ' he said in a syrupy imitation of Ali's voice.

Feeling a surge of my dead friend's courage, I yanked away from him. 'Ali told me to leave you,' I said fiercely. 'If only I had listened in time.'

Gavin smiled. 'My, we are feisty this evening,' he said as he reached for the keys and slipped them into his pocket. He eased past me into the kitchen, where he began to fix two gin and tonics. Though he was trying to appear relaxed, I could read the tension in his shoulders, the effort it was taking to mask his drunkenness. One more drink, and he would be lurching toward oblivion. Then, perhaps I could sneak the keys out of his pocket.

Feigning resignation, I removed my jacket, accepted the drink, and drifted into the family room. I took a spot on the white love seat I had chosen despite its impracticality. Since I rarely sat in that room — and never when Gavin was there — I felt like a guest. I looked around, taking in the tasteful decoration, the oriental rugs, fine cherry furniture, original artwork on the walls. All I could see was the pain that was masked by these trappings of comfort. 'What is it you want to talk about?'

Gavin stirred his drink as he watched me. 'I told you. I want to hear what you're planning to do now that you know.'

Genuinely confused, I took a quick gulp of my drink. 'Now that I *know*?' I said, my voice raspy from the rush of gin. I stared into Gavin's eyes and for the first time, I read not only cruelty but also pain. And yes, *fear*. We stared at each other for what seemed like an endless moment. I made a move to stand, but suddenly feeling dizzy, remained in place. 'Exactly what are you saying here, Gavin?' I said, trying to keep my voice as normal, reasoned as possible. 'You know who killed Ali?'

'Of course, I know who killed the bitch; so do you,' he snapped with his old impatience. 'Don't you think it's time to get it into the open?'

Gavin took a long swig of his drink, then reached for the bottle of gin, and added another shot. 'All right, Jeanne, if you don't have the guts to say it, then I will. Jamie killed Ali. *Our son*. You know it and I know it, but that doesn't mean he was entirely responsible. I probably should have listened when you said Jamie had some serious problems.'

I shook my head as if to clear it. Stunned, all I could say was, 'Or maybe we should tell the court about the years of emotional and sexual abuse Jamie suffered. The *incest*. Maybe that would be considered a mitigating factor,' I said, a rush of emotion in my voice.

I was prepared for an irate denial, but after the initial shock, Gavin put his face in his hands and began to sob. When he looked up, he said, 'I swear to you, Jeanne, I was drunk that night. Drunk out of my mind. And it was only one night, only one insane drunken mistake. If you don't believe me, ask Jamie.'

'As a matter of fact, I *don't* believe you,' I said, my voice rising with every word. 'Not that it matters. Whether it was one time or a thousand times, you inflicted a lifetime of pain on Jamie. And no, I'm not going to ask him about it. It almost killed him to talk about it the first time. I wouldn't put him through that again.' Suddenly our roles were reversed and I was standing over him, watching him sob helplessly. 'Turn yourself in if you really want to help Jamie,' I added. 'Go to the police and confess what you've done to your son.'

'And give up everything I worked for? Don't be absurd, Jeanne. That would only hurt us all.'

I closed my eyes and shook my head. 'You still don't get it, do you? There is no *us*, Gavin; there never was.' And somehow, just speaking those words, I felt cleansed, released, as if all the false bogeymen I had created in my own mind had been suddenly shrunk down to size. Standing in front of Gavin, I extended my hand. 'Give me my keys.'

For a moment, Gavin hesitated, but then he sighed deeply and reached into his pocket. 'That's all you have to say to me — 'give me the keys'?'

After I had the key ring firmly in my grasp, I turned toward the door. But from the doorway, I said, 'No, that's not all. There's one more thing.'

Gavin cocked his chin with a hint of the old arrogance that told me he would survive. 'I'm listening.'

'You've never known Jamie. All these years criticizing him, berating him for not being the son you wanted, you never got to know the son you had. And you know what, Gavin? It's your loss — because my son Jamie is one helluva kid. The sad thing is that everyone in town knows that but you.'

'Of course, I know the boy. Just because I wanted him to try a little harder at school, maybe lose a little — '

That was where I interrupted him. I wasn't about to listen as Gavin pulled out his familiar list of Jamie's inadequacies. Not this time, and not ever again. 'If you knew him at all, you'd know he didn't kill Ali. That he *couldn't* have.'

'Come on, Jeanne. We're all capable of it — if pressed far enough. You can deny it all you want, but Jamie's like the rest of us. He's human.'

I shrugged. 'Maybe you're right. Maybe Jamie *is* capable of murder. Maybe, as you say, we all are. But how could you look in your son's eyes and not know he was telling the truth?'

Gavin stared at me as I answered my own question. 'Because you don't know Jamie. You don't see him. If you really saw him, you never could have done what you did to him all these years. And if you really knew him, you'd know he was telling the truth.'

My hand was on the front door, an exit I almost never used, when I caught sight of a padded mailer on the end table. The handwriting, in the heavy black ink of a felt pen, was oversize and sloppy; my name appeared to have been scrawled hurriedly — perhaps before the writer could change his mind.

'This is for me,' I said, picking up the envelope curiously. There was no return address in the corner.

'I was going to give it to you,' Gavin said defensively.

'Of course. But only after you examined it yourself first.' Though my words were caustic, there was little more than weariness in my voice.

But Gavin reacted only to the bitterness. 'I thought that the end of our marriage was more important than the mail. Sorry I didn't have my priorities straight.'

I fingered the envelope gingerly, noting the size and shape of the object inside it; I already knew exactly what it was. And furthermore, who sent it. How could I tell Gavin that the contents of the package were more earth-shattering than the dissolution of our family? That the lie I had told earlier had suddenly become true? There *was* someone I had to meet — and soon. I looked at the VCR clock: it was almost seven, the hour when he would surely drift to a predictable spot. 'I have to go,' I said, unable to expunge the exhaustion from my voice.

'Now?' Gavin said. 'So there *is* someone you're going to?'

For a moment, I stood in the doorway, staring into his familiar face. A face I had alternately loved and feared, depended upon and loathed. There should have been something profound to say, some summation of our seventeen years together. But peering into his eyes, I realized I owed Gavin nothing. In the end, I only repeated the same phrase: *I have to go.* It was the same message you might give to a pesky caller on the phone, or a casual acquaintance encountered in the store.

Sensing that all the weapons in his arsenal had been exhausted and that he could no longer hold me in front of him like a shield against the world, Gavin stood shakily. 'At least, answer one question before you go, Jeanne.'

I continued to stare at him.

'Tell me what I should do,' he said.

We probably stood there for less than a minute, but it felt longer. The question hung between us in our tastefully decorated room filled with all the things that had failed to make us happy.

'I don't know,' I said at last. 'And to tell you the truth, I don't care.' And with those words, I turned and let the dark house swallow him up.

35

I stepped outside, glad to note that the rain had diminished to a gentle mist. I had walked out of my life, taking nothing but my car keys and the manila envelope from the end table. I had no idea where I would sleep that night or what turn the rest of my life would take. But I was not afraid. I would never be afraid again. I walked purposefully, like someone out for a little exercise after the long rain. Wistfully, I thought Ali would be proud of me.

It wasn't far to her house. It had never been nearly so far as I had believed to that other world in which she lived, a world of music and travel, adventure and fearless honesty. That was one thing I had learned from my friend: that the things you believe you can never have usually lie behind a barricade in your own mind. As soon as I turned the corner of the street, I saw her snug little cottage outlined in shadow. In contrast to my own rambling colonial when I'd approached it earlier, Ali's house was in total darkness. Even from a distance, you could feel its emptiness. Its silence. Inside, there would be no more music from Ali's violin, no warmth, no fragrant pots of tea; through the window, you would never again catch a glimpse of her brushing her hair or moving gracefully through her rooms.

When I heard the sound of George's heavy footsteps on the pavement, I could feel the desolation he exuded; it travelled through the mist, seeped through my damp clothes. Though he had never told me he still went to her house every night at seven, still kept their ritual date, as if expecting her to dash from the porch and take his arm for a stroll, I knew he would be there. Faithful to the end.

George's face when it finally emerged from the darkness was somber and sad, but it registered no surprise. Wordlessly, he took my arm like the gallant old-world gentleman that he was. When he closed his eyes and squeezed me subtly, I had the distinct feeling I had become a ghost to him. I had become Ali, back to take one final turn around the block. We walked to the end of the road in silence, and then without needing to say a word, turned and walked back. But this time, George withdrew his arm and stuffed his hands conspicuously in his pocket.

'Why do you do it to yourself?' I asked. 'Why come here like this? Isn't it too painful?'

George shrugged. 'Some things are worse than pain,' he said. 'Forgetting, for one. Or numbness. To me, those things are far worse than grief.' We walked a few more feet and then he added, 'And I suppose it's a form of penance, too.'

'Penance? For what?'

George sighed. 'For not loving her well enough, not being able to make her happy. If I had been there that night — well, I suppose such regrets are foolish, aren't they?'

Though I knew that no one could have loved Ali more than George had, and further knew that no one could have quelled her demons, I gave no response. Instead, I reached into my pocket and pulled out the padded mailer, which I opened, without breaking step with George.

From the envelope, I extracted the thin cell phone that had been stolen from my cabin in New Hampshire. Stolen by George Mather who, in a rare fit of desperation and rage, had ransacked the place. Except for that one small item, the envelope was empty. There was no explanatory note, no threat, no demand. Just the phone. When I held it up, it glittered beneath the street lamp. George watched me without curiosity.

'Feel like a cup of coffee?' he said suddenly, without looking at my face. I realized he hadn't looked at me once since we met on the street. Was he still fantasizing that he was with Ali? I remembered her saying that they often capped off their night walks with a cup of coffee from Starbucks.

'As long as you're buying,' I said. 'Because I'm pretty low on cash right now. And can we go to Ryan's?' I said, hoping the bright lights in the donut shop would remind him exactly who he was with.

Without answering, George once again took my arm and we walked in silent agreement toward Ryan's. I was still clutching the phone in my hand.

Through the shimmering plate glass windows, you could see the donut shop was empty, and that a lone employee was already mopping the floor. 'It looks like they're closing up,' I said.

Under the street lamp, George consulted his

watch. 'It's only seven-thirty,' he announced. 'We've got half an hour.'

Half an hour. Could everything that needed to be spoken be said in a half hour? Apparently, George thought that it could. He pushed open the door, causing a cheery bell to ring. The teenager manning the mop looked distinctly annoyed by our intrusion. 'We're closing up,' he said, irritably. Though he was probably a couple of years older than Jamie, his face was vaguely familiar. I was almost sure that I had seen him playing basketball in our driveway. And now that he had gotten a better look at me, he seemed to recognize me, too. The deepening colour of his eyes announced that he realized I was Jamie's mother. The mother of an accused murderer. 'Mrs Cross?' he blurted out. 'I'm Roger Stewart, remember me? I — I just wanted to tell you that I believe in Jamie. All of us guys do.'

'If you really mean that,' I said, looking him squarely in the eyes, 'you will soon be proved right.'

George cleared his throat. 'All we want is some coffee, young man. And maybe a couple of those famous lemon donuts if you have any left.' He pulled a twenty-dollar bill from his pocket. 'You just go about your business and we'll clean up after ourselves.'

When George told him to keep the change, the lanky boy smiled, stuffed the money in his pocket, and disappeared into the kitchen. 'You two make yourself at home out there, okay? I've got some cleanup to do back here.'

'Thank you,' George called after him. He

carried the small tray to a table in the corner.

As soon as we sat down, I realized that stopping at Ryan's was a mistake. The lights were too bright, for one thing. In this sharply illuminated room, there was no getting away from George's piercing glance. No escape from the pain in those hooded eyes.

After we had fixed our coffee, I once again pulled the phone from my pocket and laid it on the table between us. 'I suppose you made a recording of the message,' I said, as casually as I could.

But to my surprise, George shook his head. 'I trust you to do the right thing, Jeanne. Just as Ali did.'

I closed my eyes and swallowed hard. If he could have said anything more devastating, I could not imagine what it was. When I opened my eyes and stared at George, I found his face to be amazingly unchanged. It still reflected the same astounding patience he had always had — with his faithless wife and with me. Amazingly, there was no anger or judgment in that face.

'How did you know?' I asked, my voice suddenly raspy.

George stared at me for a moment, letting my words hang in the air of the donut shop where I had once shared so many innocent treats with my parents, and later with my own family. *How did you know?* How much guilt was contained in those four innocuous words?

George shrugged. 'The same way Ali knew things,' he said. 'By intuition.'

Again there was a strained silence, in which we both sipped coffee and allowed the unforgiving light to probe our faces. 'But don't give me too much credit. At first, I was like everyone else. Quick to blame the obvious suspect. More than anything, I started to dig into things because I wanted to convict Jamie in my own mind. I wanted to be absolutely sure.'

'Remember that day in Giovanna's when you gave me your list of possible culprits? Did you suspect me then?'

'I wouldn't have toyed with you like that, Jeanne. No, I sincerely believed it might have been one of the people on my list. But after I spoke to each of them, I became convinced that all those trails were cold. That's when I requested permission to visit your son.'

'You visited Jamie? But when? He never told me — '

'About a month ago. Just before I stopped calling you. It was painful for him to talk about the night of the murder, but I guess he felt he owed me that much,' George said. He took a bite of his donut and then wiped sugar from his mouth with a napkin.

Suddenly a terrifying thought occurred to me — that Jamie had known what I'd done all along, that he had been protecting me. 'Did Jamie tell you that I — '

'No!' George said quickly. 'I'm convinced he doesn't know. And even if he did, I don't think he would have incriminated you. That's a very fine son you've got there, Jeanne.'

Unexpectedly, tears rose to my eyes. 'Go

ahead and say it . . . Unlike the mother who let her own child take the blame for her crime.'

'No one's taken the blame yet. Not till there's a conviction. And that's one thing I knew you would never allow to happen. I knew that even before you did, Jeanne.' He reached over and handed me a napkin.

'So what did Jamie say that changed your mind?' I dabbed at my eyes.

'He said he didn't do it. Same as every other defendant. The only difference was that I believed him. I guess that's an old lawyer's greatest skill, learning to read people. You've got to know who's Hollywood material and who's not.'

'And you decided Jamie was not?'

'The kid probably couldn't tell a convincing lie about a missed homework assignment — never mind a murder. I left that detention centre absolutely convinced that Jamie was innocent.'

'But if Jamie didn't know, and I didn't even make your list of suspects, what led you to me?'

George gulped the coffee that had begun to grow cold. 'Ali did,' he said. 'After I left Jamie that afternoon, I went straight to the cottage. Just as you did today. I paced up and down for probably an hour, reliving the events that Jamie had described. That nosy neighbour of hers — I forget her name — moved from window to window as I walked, following me with her eyes. I must have given her a stiff neck by the time I was done.'

'Nora Bell,' I said, filling in the name for him.

387

'So that was when you figured it out?'

'Not exactly. At the time, I wasn't even thinking of the murder. I was thinking about what happened after Jamie left her that night. I thought of Ali, whose throat had been cut by the tip of Jamie's knife — not enough to do any real damage, but certainly enough to scare her. I was sure that her next step would be to reach for the phone . . . '

'But Jamie had severed the lines and taken her cell phone,' I reminded him.

'Yes, so Ali would have no choice but to drive to the all-night convenience store a couple blocks away and make a call. I could picture her discreetly wrapping a scarf around her neck, not wanting to arouse questions. Not wanting to incriminate the boy she was trying to help. At least not yet . . . The only question was, who would she call? Anyone else would have thought of her safety first and called the police. Or at least called me. Even Butterfield, for God's sake. But this was Ali we're talking about here . . . '

By then the tears were streaming openly down my face. Several times, George stopped and wiped them for me with all the tenderness he would have shown to Ali that night if only she had dialled the right number. If only she had reached him instead of me. By then, Roger had emerged from the kitchen and was standing near the donut counter, openly eavesdropping on our conversation. 'Do you want to leave?' George asked. 'We could go someplace else . . . '

But I shook my head. 'It doesn't matter. Let Roger here be the first to know that his belief in

Jamie is vindicated.' Hearing his name, Roger blushed furiously and began to wipe the already clean counter.

'So that was when you knew?' I asked when George and I were alone.

'I knew that Ali would call you before doing anything else. She wouldn't want you to be hit with this out of the blue. But that was all I knew. I still wouldn't let myself think that you might have been the one.'

'Then you remembered my cell phone.' By then, we were both staring at the incriminating silver phone that still held Ali's voice on that night. Though I had heard the rambling message only once, it had been seared onto my mind — just as it had been on George's. As we looked at it in the centre of the table, we were both hearing Ali's final message again. Every desperate word. She hadn't said much, hadn't even let on what had happened, but the unfamiliar pleading in her voice had told me that it was serious. *For God's sake, Jeanne, I have to talk to you! It's Jamie, he's done something. If you don't call me back right away, I'm going to have to go to the police . . . Please, Jeanne!*

George shook his head, as if trying to forget the voice that haunted him. 'Of course, my next question was: when had you heard her message? Was it that night — in time to get in your car and drive to her house? Of course, I was still hoping you had slept through it. That you heard it the next morning when it was too late to do anything about it.'

I stared at him quizzically, waiting for him to

explain how he had figured out that it had been the former.

'Then I remembered that you had mentioned something about a speeding ticket you had gotten up in New Hampshire. Since I knew you had spent most of your time alone in the cabin, and none on the highway, I wondered when you could have been stopped for speeding.'

'So my poor driving record got me in the end?'

'You were just a few miles from the Massachusetts border when you were stopped by the state police that night.' George sighed, the inevitable conclusion hanging in the air.

In the silence that followed, we could hear Roger bustling around the tiny kitchen, trying to pretend that he wasn't listening. George looked at his watch. 'It's quarter of eight,' he announced.

Though it felt as if we had been sitting in the glare of the fluorescent lights for hours, we had been there for only fifteen minutes. And fifteen more remained of our allotted time. A quarter of an hour in which to tell my story, and try to make George understand how, in one rash moment, I had devastated nearly everyone I loved.

36

'You may not believe this, but I haven't thought about that night or what happened in Ali's house since it occurred. It wasn't just the murder, it was everything between Ali and me, the words as deadly as gunfire that we exchanged — I almost succeeded in blocking all of it out of my mind. In fact, by the time Gavin called in the morning to tell me Ali was dead, I was genuinely shocked. And the more I pretended I knew nothing about it, the more unreal it all became. During the rare times when my mind drifted back to that night in the cottage, I immediately turned it off — like a bad B movie that I didn't have to watch. And when you told me your list of suspects that day in Giovanna's, I sincerely wondered if you might be right. Could Jack have done it? Or what about Beth Shagaury? She certainly had the motive. Of course, there were times when I flashed on the truth, but I quickly told myself that I had dreamed that horrible night. Surely, I hadn't been the one who killed Ali. Not me, her best friend. You said it yourself: we were the only ones who truly loved her. How could I have murdered her? I suppose such self-deception sounds incredible to you, the desperate excuse of a mother who let her own son sit in detention for a crime she committed. The only one who really understood it was Ali. Ali, who knew the extent of the lies I had told myself for all these years.

The lies which were, in fact, my whole life.

'In any case, I had fallen into a troubled sleep early that night. It had been a bad day, one that had persistently challenged my thin veneer of sanity. First there had been a number of disturbing calls from home. And as I listened to Gavin's tense voice, I felt my anxiety grow almost to the breaking point. And then, of course, Jamie called and I knew it was all over. I had to go home and face the truth about my marriage. The truth about my life, a truth even darker than what Ali had revealed to me when she told me about Marcus.

'It must have been after midnight when the phone rang. Since I was sleeping on the porch, I didn't hear it right away, but when I did, I jumped up to answer it. I was through hiding from my family and friends. But as I said, I was in a pretty deep sleep and the ringing phone didn't penetrate my consciousness until Ali was already speaking into my voice mail. Recording her final message. And if her words weren't alarming enough, when I called back, I found out her phone was out of service.

'I knew right away that Jamie must have cut the lines. Well, you can imagine the state I was in that night, driving toward Massachusetts. And it was raining, too. Raining bullets as if God were punishing the earth — just the way it was earlier today. I had no idea how fast I was going. That was the last thing on my mind. If I could have made the car fly, I would have. And when I was stopped, I had nothing with me; I hadn't even grabbed my wallet, so I had no license, nothing.

To make matters worse, the cop was one of those macho types. 'I ought to take you in,' he said when he found I had no identification. Do you know how many times I've said to myself: *if only he had*. But then, that is only one of many regrets I have about that night.

'By the time I got to Ali's, I felt like every nerve ending in my body was frayed. When Ali didn't answer right away, I banged at the door frantically; I was so loud that I'm surprised old Nora Bell didn't get up and turn on her light. But then I guess even your friendly local neighbourhood snoop has to sleep sometime. I don't know how long I stood there in that lashing rain, but I was drenched by the time Ali came to the door. 'Who is it?' she asked from behind the still-closed door. Once again, I could hear the dread that laced her voice on my phone.

'But when she finally opened the door, I saw that terror had only magnified her beauty. Her hair was down and flowing, and all the excitement of the evening had lent her eyes, her skin, a kind of glow. And yes, you were right, she was wearing a scarf around her neck, hiding what Jamie had done to her. When she saw it was me, she threw her arms around me, and I felt the fearless Ali trembling beneath her thin clothes.

' 'Jeanne! I knew you would come,' she said, as if I had vindicated her faith in me. 'Thank God you're here.'

'But right in the middle of her warm words, I felt something sharp in my ribs. When I stepped backward and touched the spot, Ali laughed nervously. Then she pulled out the little silver pistol that Jack Butterfield had given her when the stalking first began.

' 'Please, take this foolish thing away from me,' she said. 'I've never fired a gun before in my life. I'm probably putting myself in danger by carrying it around.'

'As it turned out, the words were prophetic, but neither of us could have known it at the time. Since I had no more experience with guns than Ali did, I took the little silver pistol and laid it on the coffee table between us. It was so small and toylike that I had trouble taking it seriously as a real weapon.

' 'Tell me what happened,' I said. It was the first time I had spoken. 'In your message, you said . . . ' But then my voice trailed off. I simply could not repeat the words she had said about Jamie. But just then, the scarf slipped; and when I caught sight of the fresh wound on her throat, I gasped. Suddenly, the room was spinning around me, and for the second time in a matter of months, I thought I was going to faint.

'But Ali was so intent on what she wanted to say, she didn't seem to notice. 'Do you remember the first time I called you for a ride to school?' she asked, unconsciously pulling her scarf closer, as if it had the power to protect her from further harm. 'I told you I had injured my knee.'

'Though it seemed like an odd time to reminisce, I nodded as I sank onto the couch, eager to return to what seemed like a more innocent time. 'You *did* hurt your knee. I saw — '

'But Ali was already shaking her head in denial. 'I put on a bandage to make it look good, but the truth was, my call to you was hardly random. And it had nothing to do with any injury. I called you because there was something I needed to tell you.'

'Utterly mystified, I got up and helped myself to Ali's brandy, which I downed quickly. 'I don't remember you saying much at all when you first started riding with me,' I said. Still facing the liquor cabinet, I replenished my glass. 'In fact, as I recall, it was damned uncomfortable in that car the first week or so.'

' 'That's because I knew you wouldn't believe me. I could see it the way you held yourself, your tight smile. Even if I told you in the plainest language possible, you would have found a way to deny it. To discredit me — and in the process, Jamie.'

'At the mention of my son's name, I felt twitchy, uncomfortable; I would have done anything to escape that room. To escape the truth she was trying to force on me and had been since I'd known her. But since there was no getting away from Ali, I finished my drink, and rose to pour myself another. 'So you're saying that our whole friendship has been a fraud? I don't understand.'

'At that, Ali reached out and placed her hand on my arm. 'Jeanne, you know that's not true. Maybe in the beginning I had an ulterior motive for befriending you. But in all these months — you became the best girlfriend I never had. I was always so busy with my music, I never had time when I was young. And then — well, I guess I just didn't trust women.' At that her eyes darkened. She still held my arm, and through the thin fabric of my shirt, I thought I felt her shudder almost imperceptibly.

'Once again, I gulped the alcohol that was my only escape from the almost unbearable tension coursing through my body. 'So did you ever get around to telling me whatever it was?' I asked, trying to keep my voice light. 'Or did it turn out to be so unimportant, you forgot about it?'

' 'As I said, I wanted to be sure you were ready. Sure you would act. Because if you didn't, if you still tried to deny it, then it would have been worse than never knowing at all. But now — after what's happened, I can't wait anymore.'

'*Still*. There was that word again. That word she used when she told me about Marcus, implying that there was something I knew, had always known on some level, but would not allow myself to face.

'I closed my eyes and felt the effect of the three drinks I had consumed in rapid succession. My skull felt like it was expanding dangerously. 'Please, Ali, whatever it is, I think we should talk about it tomorrow. I'm going to go home, see Jamie. Maybe even try to get some sleep.'

'At that, Ali's voice rose with anger. 'Don't you understand a word I'm saying to you, Jeanne? I've waited too long already; we both have,' she said, whipping off the scarf dramatically. She stretched her long neck to reveal the skin-deep incision Jamie had made with his knife. Then, apparently seeing the terror in my face, she once again forgot herself. 'I'm sorry — I should have prepared you. Really, it's not as serious as it looks.' Then, staring at my blanched face, she said, 'My God, Jeanne. You look like you did that night on the Cape. Are you okay?'

'While Ali went into the kitchen to get me a glass of water, I started for the door. Though I had driven eighty miles an hour straight from New Hampshire, desperate to hear what Ali had to say, I was now willing to do nearly anything to avoid it. Somewhere in my alcohol-clouded mind, I was beginning to understand that I had sacrificed the best years of my life — even sacrificed Jamie — all to avoid the truth. The truth that lay in the centre of my marriage.

'I actually got up and headed for the door, hoping to get away before Ali could do or say another thing that might shatter my life. It sounds crazy, but I felt as though I were escaping from a burning building. And I almost got away, too. My hand was on the doorknob. But then I thought of the gun — the gun that Ali had taken out to protect herself against Jamie. Of course, the inevitable question arose: what if Jamie came back? Even if she didn't intend to shoot him, she might, in her inexperience, panic and fire. Obviously, I couldn't leave the little silver gun on the table where it might be used against my son. I decided to take it — just for the night of course. When everything cooled down, when this whole nightmare was behind us, I would return it to Jack Butterfield.

'But just after I had slipped the little pistol into my pocket, Ali appeared in the doorway.

From the slightly alarmed expression she wore, I thought she had witnessed my little theft. But the gun wasn't what was on her mind. 'There's no point in trying to run away, Jeanne,' she said wearily. 'I'll only come after you.'

'When she placed the glass of water on the table, I again thought she might notice the gun was missing. But she trusted me so completely that she had obviously forgotten the lethal weapon that had been lying there moments earlier. I kept my hand in my pocket, touching the metal, just in case she mentioned it. Of course, if she did, I planned to explain exactly why I had taken it. But since she didn't notice, I continued to hold on to it.

'In any case, Ali had other things on her mind. With her two hands, she took my free one in hers and looked intently into my eyes. Oddly, Ali's startlingly topaz-coloured eyes were bright with tears. 'Before we say another word to each other, I want you to promise me something,' she said.

'I stared at her blankly.

'But my lack of response didn't stop her. 'Promise me you'll never leave Jamie alone with Gavin again.'

'I jerked away, and in an instant, I was on my feet. It was the same promise Jamie had asked me to make back when I scheduled the appointment with Dr Emory. He, however, had simply said, 'Don't leave me alone.' But now for the first time, I understood that being alone with his father was what he truly feared. For the first time, I realized how completely and tragically I had broken my promise.

'"That's ridiculous, Ali. Gavin is Jamie's father,' I said, arguing back with my own intrusive suspicions, as well as with Ali. Then as the panic rose in my voice, I glanced at the door.

'"Your son came here with the intention of killing me tonight, Jeanne. This is not some little problem that we can talk about at a later date. You're going to face this thing, and you're going to face it now.'

'I took a step backward, feeling as if Ali had physically assaulted me. 'One trauma at a time,' I pleaded. 'First you tell me that the man I've been married to for seventeen years is gay. Now you apparently have some new revelation.'

'"Gay? Is that what you've told yourself — that Gavin is gay?'

'I took a step backward toward the door, my hand instinctively on the pocket where I'd stuffed the gun — almost as if I thought it could protect me from what Ali was trying to tell me. 'Isn't that what you said — that Gavin was in love with Marcus?'

'"No, I certainly never used the word *love*. Nor does what happened between Gavin and Marcus make your husband gay. Gay men go after other *men*, Jeanne, not boys. For God's sake, Marcus is barely eighteen, and confused about his sexuality. What Gavin did to that kid was abuse — not love.'

'When I put my head in my hands, I felt the room reeling around me; all of its bright colours blurred into a vivid red. 'Please, Ali, let's talk about this tomorrow. What do you want from me?'

'But all of Ali's concern was for Jamie now. 'I just told you what I want. I want to be sure you never leave Jamie and Gavin alone together again. Promise me you'll never walk out on that boy like you did the other day. Or I swear, I'll pick up that phone and call the police. I won't stop until they've taken him away from both of you.'

'Feeling cornered, I turned on her. 'No one will believe you,' I shouted. 'And I don't either. Everyone in this town knows you'd do anything to get attention. For all I know, you did that to yourself and now you're trying to blame it on Jamie.'

' 'Not on Jamie, Jeanne. He may have been the one who took a knife to my throat tonight. But he's not the dangerous one. Gavin is the dangerous one here. And you, too! My God, Jeanne, people like you — *like my mother* — you're the most dangerous people on earth. You're the good women. The self-sacrificing women. The ones who build a nest for evil, and then silently do whatever you can to protect it.' I had never seen her so angry. It was as if her anger were a physical force that had entered the room, pushing me backward. It was the kind of anger, the kind of confrontation that I had always avoided at all cost.

' 'I . . . I have no idea what you're talking about,' I stammered. 'But I don't have to listen to this. And I'm not going to — '

'But then Ali stepped forward and took my shoulders with surprising violence. 'You are going to listen, Jeanne. This time, you have no

400

choice. And then you're going to act. You can't take the coward's way out any longer. Not hearing. Not seeing. Not knowing. God, Jeanne, do you have any idea how much I despise you?'

'Ali was so close to me then that there was no escape from her eyes. Eyes that were afraid and angry. And incredibly brave. For the first time, I understood that she was not only forcing me to confront my demons — she was also confronting her own. Though she was speaking up for Jamie's sake, she was also fighting an ancient battle of her own, saying things to me that she had obviously wanted to say to her mother for many, many years.

'I swear, looking in her eyes at that moment, I never admired anyone more. Or feared them. I could see that Ali had the power to destroy everything — all the illusions and lies I had spent years protecting. And she was not afraid to use it. In fact, she would not rest until she did. I swear, I didn't want to kill her. I never wanted to kill her, George. But I had to stop her. I had to make her be quiet. I couldn't let her tell everyone how I had failed my son. And most of all, I couldn't bear to hear it myself . . . I had to *stop* her, don't you see?'

★ ★ ★

At that moment in my confession, I woke, as if from a long dream, and looked around me. In the half hour in which I had been speaking, I had lost track of time, forgotten where I was, even forgotten my audience. I was so fully adrift in

401

that terrible night that I didn't realize I had risen to my feet and begun to pace up and down the brightly lit donut shop. Now I stopped and looked around me like a sleepwalker, taking in the familiar yellow-checked curtains, the black-and-white tiles of linoleum, the scrubbed white walls. Of all the places to confess to murder, this scene of my most innocent childhood pleasures seemed the most unlikely.

Realizing that my face was wet with tears, I reached for a napkin from the counter, then turned to face my audience of two: a bereaved husband who had just relived the death of his wife, and a gangly teenage friend of Jamie's who was staring at me with a mixture of terror and fascination in his eyes. I turned to face George.

'It happened in an instant,' I said. 'I was deaf and blind with panic when I pulled out that gun. And by the time I realized what I was doing, it was too late.'

'I need to know one thing, Jeanne. Did she suffer?' George asked. His face, which had been a catalogue of human emotion as I told my story, was now bright with tears.

I shook my head. 'She looked startled more than anything else. There was no sign of pain. Then she reached out for my hand, as if the gunshot had brought us away from the terrible play we were enacting and reminded us of our friendship. Of how much we cared about each other. At first, I thought I had missed. That we would go back to the couch and have the drinks she had poured; we would stop this horrible talk, and be the way we used to be together. But then she fell back onto the couch, and I saw the blood. I saw her eyes. I sat there and watched as everything that was Ali left those eyes.' I paused for an instant, then went on. 'But then she refocused, and squeezed my hand. She even whispered something to me, George.'

He stared at me, perhaps hoping to hear that her final words had been a message to him. But Ali had not died thinking of herself, or any of the men she loved — at times faithlessly and badly, at other times with a passion and self-giving that made her unforgettable. No, Ali's last words were spoken in concern for the young boy in whom she saw so much of herself.

'Promise me, Jeanne,' she rasped. Just that. 'Promise me.' And of course, I did; I promised her — though I'm not sure if Ali ever heard me.

Again the donut shop was eerily silent, with only the sound of the dishwasher in the back room whirring quietly. And then George said, 'So that's why you couldn't tell the truth. Because you had to keep your promise. You couldn't turn yourself in and go to prison because that would mean Jamie would be alone with Gavin for good.'

I nodded. 'Believe me, it would have been easier to go to jail than to see my son in that place day after day, to see what it was doing to him. But before I was sent away, I had to make sure Jamie would be safe. The trouble was that I didn't know exactly what I was protecting Jamie from. It was obvious of course, but I refused to connect the dots. I'd refused for years. And even after I found out, I wasn't sure how I could use the information to keep him away from Jamie. Of course, I could have called the police, but then Jamie would have to testify against his father — something he would never do. And the only other person who could have testified for Jamie convincingly was Ali. With her gone, I had to find a way for Gavin to incriminate himself. And I had to find a new home for Jamie.'

'Before you came to me tonight, you must have figured out a solution,' George said.

Once again, I took a seat opposite him, and nodded. I reached in the pocket of my raincoat and pulled out a small tape recorder. After rewinding the tape I had made in the study with Gavin earlier that evening, I nervously pressed the play button. It was just an old tape recorder of Jamie's. Had it really gotten the drunken confession Gavin had made as I followed him through the house? Had I recorded his noble-sounding promise to turn himself in, a promise I already knew he would never keep?

At first the voices that filled the donut shop — Gavin's and mine, two ugly voices caught in a battle that was nearly two decades old — were muffled and unclear. But then, apparently, I had moved close enough to him, and our sharp words ripped through the room. Every accumulated bitterness. Every reproach. Every terrible admission. Everything I needed to keep Gavin away from Jamie for good. When I finished playing the tape, I handed it to George for safekeeping. The clock overhead revealed it was almost nine — nearly an hour after the donut shop should have closed. I turned to Roger and apologized for keeping him so late. 'You'd better lock up; your parents will be worried about you,' I said calmly, ever the solicitous parent.

George stared at me with eyes that were so deep they were nearly black. 'Are you ready to go?' he asked. Just that. The most ordinary of words. But in them my fate was contained. Mine and my family's.

Wordlessly, I took his arm.

Epilogue

I'd been in prison almost a year when I was sent to see a young prison psychologist named Kerry. A pathetic attempt at suicide with one of the only implements available to a prisoner — a plastic butter knife — had landed me in her office on the first anniversary of Ali's death. With such a blunt implement, it had taken an intense combination of patience, rage, and self-loathing to draw a few drops of blood from the vein. But as soon as I saw the vivid red colour of my own life seeping onto my sleeve, I knew I wanted to live. The only thing I didn't know was why.

I didn't expect much from the prison psychologist. Like everyone else in the system, most of the professional helpers I met there were jaded by all they'd seen and heard. But with a freshly minted B.A. and her idealism still untrammelled, Kerry was different.

At first, she barraged me with what I had come to know as the routine psychiatric questions, but I answered only one: *did I plan to try again?*

'Just keep me away from the plastic silverware,' I said, rising from my chair. Increasingly, I found myself playing the surly inmate that people expected me to be.

'Those restrictions are already in place,' Kerry said stonily, brushing a flap of shiny blond hair off her cheek. 'Now if you'd please take your seat; we're not finished here.'

It reminded me of the way some teachers had talked to troublesome students back in my old life. I bristled and continued to stand. 'Maybe you're not, but — '

'Jeanne, I've looked through your files, and your case is very — *complex*,' the psychologist interrupted. 'I think you should begin a journal.'

She opened her desk and pulled out what looked like one of the blue books they used for essay tests in school. 'Your assignment is to fill one of these each week.'

'With what?' I asked. 'My suicidal impulses?'

Kerry shrugged. 'If that's what you feel like writing. Or maybe you could just tell your story. A chapter at a time.'

'The last thing I want to think about is what happened,' I said.

'The day you killed Alice Mather,' Kerry corrected, her eyes refusing to turn away. 'It's not *what happened*. It's what you did.'

'No one ever called her Alice,' I said softly, feeling something inside me beginning to crack. 'At least, no one I knew.'

'Then begin with what they did call her. Or just begin with the day you met.'

And that night, alone in my cell, I had. Of course, I could never pick up my pen without imagining Ali's diary. The beautiful red-silk-covered book I'd first seen in the teachers' lounge, and last seen when I threw it into the river near the cabin in New Hampshire on the night of her murder. I imagined it becoming bloated with water, and the ink, the passion of

Ali's words and life, being slowly blurred, until it was eventually washed from the page. Her story and mine dissolved by time and nature.

Within six months, I had filled a stack of blue books, and the therapy sessions I'd begun to look forward to were finished. Kerry was so proud of me that she dropped her professional demeanor and hugged me. She smelled so clean and young, it almost made me cry. But when my cheek brushed hers, I realized I wasn't the only one who'd been moved by the hours we'd shared. And the progress I'd made. Then she cleared her throat and returned to her chair. She had sat in the same chair every week when we met in the visitors' room.

At first, I watched her expectantly, expecting praise for my overachieving efforts like I'd always received from my teachers. But Kerry wasn't focused on my grammar, my vocabulary or style. Like Ali, she harped on my evasions, the truths I refused to face — even in my own diary. The first time I wrote about the day of Ali's murder, Kerry had angrily thumped the notebook on the table between us.

'I just read several pages about washing the dog, eating candy bars, listening to messages on your cell phone. This is the night you killed your closest friend, Jeanne. Wasn't that significant enough to make the cut?'

'I know what happened,' I snapped, rising from my chair, looking for an escape like I always did. 'But that doesn't mean I want to go back and relive it. You're my therapist, for Christ's sake; I thought it was your job to make me feel better.'

'Actually, my job is to help you become a healthier person. Not a sick one who *feels* better about herself.'

'Well, if being healthy means wallowing in the worst moment of my life, no, thanks,' I said, pressing the button that would summon the guard. 'These meetings are over.'

'If that's what you want, Jeanne,' Kerry said, coolly gathering up her things. Neither one of us reached for the journal. In fact, I was out of the room, and my most recent blue book was in danger of being tossed in the trash and lost forever, when I was seized with the kind of panic I once felt as a young mother when I couldn't find Jamie in the mall. 'Wait, I forgot something!' I told the guard.

Fortunately, it was one of the more benevolent guards, or the tattered notebook I clung to like a life raft would have certainly been lost. I almost wept when I saw it still on the table where I'd stubbornly abandoned it. I vowed to try harder, but that week, I remained unready to write about Ali. To write about that night.

Neither Kerry nor I was surprised when we both showed up at the same time the following week as if our little scene had never occurred. My fellow inmates suspected I stuck with my therapy because I was hoping Kerry would testify at my parole hearing. But in truth, I was afraid of being released. Afraid of interacting with my son in the outside world. And since it was clear that I probably would be free eventually, I really did want to become the healthy Jeanne that Kerry envisioned. No matter how I might protest to the contrary.

And so, once again, the day came that I couldn't avoid. The day when I no longer had any place to run from the truth. After she read the chapter that detailed my confession to George, Kerry pushed the notebook across the table. 'Read it out aloud,' she said.

Of course, I balked, but I already knew that Kerry wasn't going to relent until I did as she asked. My hands shaking, I opened the notebook to the final pages. And then, Kerry added the final codicil: 'Read it as if you were talking to Ali.'

And somehow to my infinite amazement and heartbreak, I did.

★ ★ ★

In prison, where your whole world is defined by walls, you identify yourself by the way you fill the empty space beside your bed. Many prisoners, in the throes of newly embraced religion, hang crucifixes or other religious symbols; others prefer to fall asleep with the poster-size image of a sexy celebrity over their heads. But in the women's unit, the most prominent places are almost always given to children. Thus snapshots of the children left behind grin at you from nearly every cell. There are polished school photographs with neatly combed hair and grainy snapshots of toddlers celebrating the endless birthdays and holidays that pass without the presence of their mothers to light the candles or decorate the living room.

My wall is no different. Five years' worth of photographs chronicle the years of my son's life that I have missed. There are snapshots taken in the juvenile detention centre where he spent almost a year after he was sentenced for assaulting Ali on the night of the murder. Fortunately, the weeks he spent there before my confession were deducted as time served. Though he is smiling valiantly in all the pictures (usually shots that captured him in some rehabilitative activity like wood carving or CDT), I feel a palpable loneliness rising off the glossy photographic paper. And the shame. Not only shame for his own crime. But the additional burden he carries for Gavin's crimes. And for mine. At times, I've thought of putting those early photos away, just stuffing them in a drawer, but something always stops me — perhaps because even in those sad, shamed snapshots, I see Jamie's growing strength. I see signs of the man he is becoming. The courageous, honest man who Ali recognized long before anyone else did.

But it is the more recent photographs that I turn to first thing in the morning, just before sleep at night, and in the hours when I think I can't endure one more moment of my life. There are snapshots taken by Sharon Breen during the year Jamie spent in their home: one showing a trimmed-down Jamie in a swimsuit by the Breens' pool, another of the boys in graduation gowns leaning together like brothers, the sorrows

411

of his past almost obliterated by a blinding smile. How often I have held that photograph in my hand and wondered if it is really over for Jamie. If he has really been able to put it all behind him. The evidence says that in many significant ways, he has done exactly that. His high school grades, while never stellar like Toby's, were good enough to get him into a small college in California, where he has managed to maintain a C average and win a coterie of new friends.

Though we've never discussed it, I'm sure that his decision to attend a college so far away was based on a desire to be defined by more than the sensational day when his mother and his father were arrested for separate crimes. Of course, I miss the regular visits we used to have, but knowing that Jamie is thriving in a place where there is nothing to remind him of his past gives me even more pleasure than the joy of his company.

My most recent photograph shows Jamie with his girlfriend, Julianne, on his twenty-first birthday. It is my favorite picture of all, the picture of a tall, handsome young man peering boldly into the lens of a camera, into a future he no longer has to fear. He still does not fit society's definition of thin — nor is it likely he ever will — but, removed from Gavin's incessant criticism, he is finally comfortable in his own skin. And without me around to feed his addictive eating, he's a lot less compulsive about it.

Of course, I save his letters, reading and rereading them until the pages are ragged and smudged with longing. Since I entered prison, I've received little else in the way of mail. I have no family but Jamie, and the secretiveness of my former life prevented me from developing many friendships. I receive few of the birthday cards and holiday greetings that my cell mate displays for months after the occasion. Only Sharon Breen never fails to remember my special days. Her cards, too, have been saved. Though they are the usual drugstore sentiments, I pull them out when I find myself losing faith. This neighbour, who has given more to me than I ever deserved, reminds me of the essential goodness and generosity that lies in all of us.

Occasionally, Sharon encloses a newspaper clipping she thinks I might find interesting. A brief item in the *Gazette*, for instance, informed the residents of Bridgeway that George Mather had reopened his law office. Why he went back to the profession he abandoned years earlier, I can only speculate. But I suspect that after Ali's death and my subsequent trial, he decided that the quest for wisdom and truth was sometimes more effectively enacted in the gritty and frequently unfair world of an ordinary court-room than in an airless office of the philosophy department.

And George wasn't the only man whose life's path was altered by Ali's death. A few months after George returned to the work at which he was so gifted, Jack Butterfield's business was foreclosed upon, and he left Bridgeway. I could only wonder what he had done with the engagement ring he'd bought for Ali, which I had slipped into an envelope and left in his mailbox shortly after George gave it to me. The newspaper article Sharon sent provided only the sparest details of his ruin, but I knew the story anyway. I had read it in his eyes the night of the wake, had seen the grief that circled back on itself, taking a little more of his soul with every loop.

Sometimes I wondered what Ali would think if she could see how much her death had changed the good-looking businessman who was once known for his swaggering self-confidence and easy smile. Intellectually, Ali knew she was loved by the men in her life, but the great tragedy of her life was that deep down, she never truly believed it.

But the news I hunger for most are the banal notices of life's passages: former friends of Jamie's, or students I knew at school who've gone on to win scholarships, to complete basic training in the marines, to marry or to become the parent of a baby with a new optimistic-sounding name. Scanning the weddings section, I was stunned to find a familiar face staring back at me. Though I had thought of the bride in the picture often, she looked so frankly happy that it took me a moment to recognize Beth Shagaury. I suppose there is nothing extraordinary in the story: a widow puts a painful past behind her and remarries. But I return to that clipping often, as if it had something to tell me. As if some promise, deeper even than a wedding vow, was conferred in Beth Shagaury's shining moment of happiness.

414

There was hate mail at first, too, mostly in the form of nasty, rambling letters from the many students who idolized my victim. Since there was no way to make them understand that I missed Ali as much as they did — or more — I did not respond to any of them. I also got a particularly stinging missive from Gavin's mother, predictably blaming me for everything — not only Ali's murder but Gavin's penchant for adolescent boys as well. After reading her letter with more sadness than anger, I ripped it into tiny confetti-like shreds.

And yes, every now and then I hear from Gavin. At first, the letters were filled with the same cold fury that had made me fear him for years. He was angry about the recorded confession that resulted in a rape conviction. And furthermore, he blamed me when other boys came forward, boys who Wonderful Gavin had befriended and then abused when he coached their baseball team or taught them in Sunday school. According to Gavin's early letters, all those accusations were my fault. I had made him a target of every boy in town who wanted attention, or who wanted to pin their own unacceptable fantasies on someone else.

Fortunately, a jury saw things differently. For his crimes, Gavin received a long sentence; he won't be eligible for parole until just before his fiftieth birthday. In recent months, he has begun the difficult but essentially healing process of facing the truth. Not only has he admitted that the charges were true, but he has stopped blaming the emptiness of our marriage for his

415

pedophilia; his therapists claim that he is making real progress.

Last Christmas, Gavin joyfully reported that he had received a card from Jamie, the first communication between them in nearly five years. And though such a gesture would have filled me with terror in the past, I now accepted it as a necessary part of Jamie's healing. Gavin and Jamie will never have a normal father-son relationship, but I am pleased that Jamie is strong enough to begin to forgive. It was the one thing Ali never had the opportunity to do with her own dead father, and somehow I think that cost her more than she ever admitted.

However, the one letter I long for most (besides Jamie's of course) I have never received. I began to write to George Mather after I had been here about a year. Realizing that in the long, rambling confession I made to him in the donut shop, I had never once apologized for what I had done, I took pen in hand. It was, I felt, the least I could do after all I had taken from him. I suppose I have no right to expect anything in return, but every day since I wrote that first letter, I have watched the mail for a reply that never comes.

Why George has not written back, only he knows for certain. All I can say is that his silence does not spring from a failure to forgive. I read forgiveness in his eyes that night in the harsh light of Ryan's donut shop, even as he struggled to cope with the details of Ali's final moments. His face was also washed with forgiveness at my trial, which he attended every day. And on the day of my sentencing, when he got up to read a victim's impact statement, making the court feel the presence of the talented musician, the inspiring teacher, and the fascinating woman I had taken when I impulsively shot Ali Mather, he startled everyone — especially me — when he ended with a plea for leniency. Of course, I tried to thank him when he passed by me, but George had only one thing to say: he had done it for Ali.

In any case, due largely to George's magnanimous remarks, I was convicted of manslaughter, not murder. That means I will be given the possibility of parole in only five more years. Sometimes, I tremble as I imagine building an entirely new life at forty-seven. And yes, when I'm released, I will be exactly Ali's age. As the date looms closer, and I wonder where I will go or what I will do with the freedom I really never had before, I take out the little photograph I keep inside my drawer. It is the snapshot I took that day in Paradise Park: Ali with her hair blown back, her eyes mysteriously closed. Despite the torments of her own past, or the harsh wind that came up off the pond that day, she was smiling. It is that smile which sustains me.

Acknowledgments

Every writer should have an agent like Alice Tasman. She brought faith, tenacity, and an amazing attention to detail to the entire process. Her complete engagement with my characters and my work has been pivotal — both in this novel and in my life.

I am also grateful to Mollie Glick and Jennifer Weltz at the Jean V. Naggar Literary Agency, who read my manuscript at key points and offered suggestions and support.

My editor, Laurie Chittenden, had an almost uncanny ability to make me rethink an entire character by crossing out a few adjectives or asking a key question. Every time she put her pen to my manuscript, the novel grew stronger, deeper, truer. I have been truly fortunate to work with her.

My luck held when Julie Doughty took the reins. Her enthusiasm and care have made her a terrific champion of the book, and have done much to quell a new author's anxieties.

Thanks are owed to Nellie Lukac and Stacy Francis for reading early versions of this story, for their thoughtful and incisive criticism and loving support.

Three communities in cyberspace introduced this solitary scribbler to real writers and amazing friends: I am thankful to Readerville, to the writers of the Publisher's Marketplace community, and the friends of my blogs, *I'm Really Not a Waitress* and *Simply Wait*, for advice, camaraderie, and much more.

Closer at hand, the friends I've met though waitressing have supported my work in many ways. They read manuscripts and offered suggestions, helped with research, made tea on bad days, and popped corks on good ones, covered shifts when I needed to write, and bought lunch when I was broke. They always believed. Thanks to Gina Cacciapaglia, Aileen Duarte, Patricia Howe, Rona Laban, Janet Linehan, Laura Mysliewiec, and to all my friends at New Seabury and the Sheraton.

Thanks to my *cugina*, Alison Larkin Koushki, for a lifetime of insights, inspiration, and shared adventures.

Gabe, Josh, Nellie, Jake, Lexi, and Emma: you are at the heart of everything I write and everything I do. I thank you and I love you.

Twenty-five years ago, a young man named Ted Lukac took a seat at one of my tables and changed my life. Despite the scant evidence, he believed me when I told him I was a writer, and never stopped believing it. He was the first reader of this manuscript, and saw it through countless drafts. His suggestions were invaluable; his love and support — everything.

We do hope that you have enjoyed reading
this large print book.

Did you know that all of our titles
are available for purchase?

We publish a wide range of high quality
large print books including:
Romances, Mysteries, Classics
General Fiction
Non Fiction and Westerns

Special interest titles available in
large print are:
The Little Oxford Dictionary
Music Book
Song Book
Hymn Book
Service Book

Also available from us courtesy of Oxford
University Press:
Young Readers' Dictionary
(large print edition)
Young Readers' Thesaurus
(large print edition)

For further information or a free
brochure, please contact us at:
Ulverscroft Large Print Books Ltd.,
The Green, Bradgate Road, Anstey,
Leicester, LE7 7FU, England.
Tel: (00 44) 0116 236 4325
Fax: (00 44) 0116 234 0205

Other titles published by
The House of Ulverscroft:

DARK ECHO

F. G. Cottam

She is a seductive ship: a magnificent sailing yacht built for an American playboy. Yet her history is full of fatal accidents and three of *Dark Echo*'s owners met tragic, violent deaths. Now she has been rebuilt, crossing the Atlantic with new owners, and only the truth about Harry Spalding, the man who built her, can save them from the same fate. . . . And this is the story of an evil man, an incredibly brave woman and a secret more powerful than any of them . . .

TWILIGHT HOUR

Carol Smith

Alone on Dartmoor, campaigning journalist Erin O'Leary is in hiding from Russian assassins. In a gated community, built on the ruins of an ancient manor house, she shares her exile with a disparate group of new neighbours. They are Gerald and Sylvia, early retired with social pretensions above their means; Ned and Lisa, newlyweds who know each other through work, though not very well; and beautiful embittered Auriol, left with the dog her husband no longer wants. None is exactly what they seem. And when the killing begins, they all have motives. Winter approaches; the nights draw in. The mists roll down and eclipse the moor, and shadowy figures among the trees appear to be watching the houses. Out there, a terrible evil exists.

THE ANATOMY OF DECEPTION

Lawrence Goldstone

Philadelphia, 1889. In the morgue of the city hospital, physicians uncover the corpse of a beautiful young woman. What they see takes their breath away. Within days, one of the doctors, Ephraim Carroll, strongly suspects that he knows the woman's identity. His investigation takes him from the bloody and brutal medical world in which he practises and into the drawing rooms of Philadelphia's high society, where he soon learns that nothing — and no one — is what it seems. Plunged into a maze of deception and deadly secrets, Carroll is forced to choose between exposing a killer, undoing a terrible wrong and, quite possibly, protecting the future of medicine itself.

CITY OF THE SUN

David Levien

Twelve-year-old Jamie gets on his bike before dawn to deliver newspapers in his neighbourhood. Somewhere en route, he vanishes without a trace. Fourteen months later, still with no sign of Jamie and having lost all faith in the police, his parents make one last desperate plea for help. Enter private investigator Frank Behr — a tough, reclusive ex-cop, abandoned by his former colleagues, separated from his wife and haunted by his own terrible past . . .